A DESPERATE MANEUVER

Mike deployed the air brakes and brought the Harrier to a hover. He rotated the craft, and, as he had expected, the Foxbat was screaming down on him, behind a missile. Mike couldn't see the missile itself, but he could see its bright exhaust plume. Mike didn't know whether it was possible to shoot down an air-to-air missile with a gun, but he was going to try. The Harrier's engine, running at full power to maintain the hover, produced a hot plume that made a giant target for what Mike guessed would be an IR-guided missile. It would head straight into his gunfire. If he ██████ed the missile, he'd get a good shot at the Foxbat as it

██████ed the Harrier's nose and fought to keep it stable; ████████ slide back on its tail.

████████own the firing button.

SILENT DOOMSDAY

ROBERT PAYTON MOORE

LEISURE BOOKS   NEW YORK CITY

This book is dedicated to my wife, friend and lover of forty-four years, and to my sons, Duane, Bobby, Alan, and Tim, the treasures of my life.

A LEISURE BOOK®

June 1998

Published by

Dorchester Publishing Co., Inc.
276 Fifth Avenue
New York, NY 10001

ISBN 0-8439-4395-5

ACKNOWLEDGMENTS

I would like to thank Captain G. E. "Mitt" Mitterdorff for his technical review and advice. His patient explanations made it possible to write realistic descriptions of air combat. Most of all I would like to thank my wife, Lorna, for tedious copy editing and unfailing patience and support.

SILENT
DOOMSDAY

Prologue

Alexandria, Virginia

The blade's point pressed into his neck beneath his jaw. He'd thought she intended to kiss him, and he'd been lying on his back as her lips descended toward his.

She sat straddling him, her short skirt revealing long, firm thighs. After the kiss, he'd expected that they would undress and make love.

At first he hadn't been able to believe that it was cold steel penetrating his flesh, but the lance of pain made him believe.

Horrified him.

Terrified him beyond reason.

He gathered his strength.

"No! Don't!" she hissed.

He froze.

Her eyes were alert. There was a hard glint in their depths that he wished he'd noticed before. "Don't move. You'll make me really hurt you. You're already bleeding." She wound her free hand in his hair, immobilizing him.

He felt a trickle of blood and started to moan. Her eyes and slight movement of the knife silenced him.

"You want to scream, don't you?" she commented.

Terror halted his breath.

"It's amazing how differently men react to pain," she observed. "Particularly when they know it's killing them. Have you ever heard a man scream while dying in agony? Like you'd scream if I did something horrible with this knife?" She smiled and waited for his answer.

He couldn't answer. Panic had paralyzed his vocal cords.

"No, I guess you haven't," she answered herself, a hint of contempt in her voice.

"It's interesting," she continued in a clinical tone, her eyes bright. "Some men squeal, like a pig being butchered. It's amazing. You would never expect a man with a deep voice to squeal like a soprano."

He felt very cold.

"Others scream hoarsely—like they have a frog stuck in their throats." Her laugh made Omar shiver.

Her face sobered. "Some men shout. Shout all sorts of things. Their mother's name mostly. Americans, French, Chinese—it doesn't matter—most of them call for their mothers."

Her face grew puzzled, and a little angry. "It's so strange . . . these men . . . who have defiled and tortured women . . . even their own mothers—" Her face turned vicious. The knife went a little deeper. He would have soiled himself, but terror had squeezed his sphincter shut. "In their final agony, they shout for a woman's help," she said angrily.

"You *do* think that's strange, don't you?" Her smile was back, her voice gentle once more. But it was not comforting.

"What will you do?" she wondered.

The "will" horrified him.

"You're afraid I am going to hurt you, aren't you? Were you going to hurt me, or just do nasty things to me? Make me have oral sex? Anal sex? You do that to American girls, don't you? Force them to perform perverted sex acts. Humiliate them. Make them feel so ashamed they won't tell anyone—even if you've raped them."

His vision blurred. He felt faint.

"Maybe I won't have to hurt you. I don't really enjoy mutilating a nice body, and I like your body— except for your ass. I don't like your ass. It's an arrogant ass. Men with arrogant asses like to hurt women with sex—make them scream."

The knife probed deeper.

He gasped, and his gut tried to crawl through his backbone. He grew dizzy from holding his breath.

"Do you try to make women scream?" She searched his face with terrible eyes. "Of course you do," she answered for him. It was a pronouncement of doom. Omar's heart thundered in his chest.

"Don't worry. I'm not going to ruin your nice body. When they find you, you'll look perfect, except perhaps for some misplaced parts.

"I actually have three choices from this position. I could kill you quickly—sever your jugular vein. Or I could just push. The blade will go up through your neck. That would be a hard death. You'd slowly drown in your own blood. Have a long time to think about dying. Flop around a lot. Try to pull the knife out. Maybe you could. But that wouldn't save you."

She sighed. "All that blood, though. You have such a nice apartment. Be a shame to splatter blood all over it.

"Maybe I should just shove hard. The blade's long enough to reach your brain. You'd die instantly. There

11

wouldn't be much blood.'' Her lips thinned. Her eyes
seared his. "But do you deserve such a merciful death?
I don't think so."

He drowned in terror. Urinated. Defecated. The
stench filled the room.

"Of course, I might not have to do any of those bad
things to you." She eased the pressure on the blade.

He dared breathe again, but was afraid to hope.

"I'll let you live if you answer some questions cor-
rectly, but I don't think you can. I'm going to ask anyway. Give you the opportunity to save your life.

"They are simple questions. Not hard at all. But if
the answers aren't correct . . . if I think you're not sincere . . . if you lie . . . I will have to kill you."

He tried to speak.

"No!" She punctuated the command with a twist of
the knife. "Don't speak unless I ask you something. I
only want to hear answers to my questions. Nothing
more."

His stomach clenched into a painful knot.

"Do you like it here in America?" Her eyes challenged him to lie. Her knife arm tensed.

Suddenly he knew! Knew who and what she was!
He knew who'd sent her. They'd been watching him.
It seemed as if they'd read his mind.

Denial died in his throat; if he lied . . . "Yes," he
choked. "I like it here."

"Very much?"

He let go of hope and croaked, "Yes."

"Too much?"

He grasped for the lie, but fear snatched it away.
"Yes, but—" The knife silenced him. He knew he was
going to die, and he begged Allah for a quicker death
than she had promised.

"That's very good. You didn't lie." She withdrew
the knife slightly. "I don't have to kill you. Not yet.
Now, tell me the name of your homeland."

"Chad."

Her eyes grew fierce. Like a hawk's. A hawk with a bloody beak. She didn't say anything. She waited. Poised.

"That's what I tell the Americans," he gasped.

Still she waited. Watchful.

"Libya. My homeland is Libya. I'm Libyan," he admitted hoarsely.

"Your country has spent a great deal of money on you, hasn't it?"

"Yes," he gasped.

"What has it gotten for its money?"

He struggled desperately for an answer that would save his life. There was none.

"Say it!" she demanded viciously.

"Nothing," he rasped.

"I didn't hear you very well."

"Nothing!"

"Well, as Americans say, it's payback time. It's time for you to return home with all you've learned and serve your country."

"But I don't understand. The work I do here—it only concerns waste disposal."

"Perhaps we have a trash problem."

"But—" A jab of the knife cut off his question.

"Don't ask questions. Just be happy to return to your homeland alive. You *are* happy to return, aren't you?"

"Yes," he choked out.

"Good." She smiled. "I don't think I will have to kill you after all."

He dared to hope, despite the terror that still held him in its icy grip.

"Poor boy, I've frightened you, haven't I? Made you soil yourself." Her sympathetic words intensified his humiliation, as he knew they were meant to do.

She lowered her mouth to his, the knife still at his throat. He knew her lips had to be warm and soft, not as icy and stiff as they felt. She forced her tongue between his lips and raped his mouth. For a long time. Then she sat up with a satisfied smile. She took the knife from his throat, but held it in a grip that threatened instant death.

"You are quite beautiful, but I don't suppose I need to tell you that." Contempt colored her smile. "Too bad you aren't as strong as you are beautiful. What's the American term? Pretty boy?" She laughed, a hard-edged, insulting laugh. "You are a very pretty boy." She seemed intent on deepening his humiliation, and she succeeded.

She suddenly left the bed and stood looking down at him, as if he were a disgusting insect. "You stink. You need a shower. Your bed needs changing, too. You probably need a new mattress."

He would have been enraged if he dared.

"Get up!" she ordered harshly.

He stood, acutely aware of the filth leaking from his underwear and creeping down his legs. He felt castrated. Reduced to a naughty child who'd failed potty training. He dropped his eyes, fearing her response to the hate in them.

She went to the door, turned and fixed him with a hard glare. "You are to be ready in six weeks—with cultures, samples, the codes, everything. Reservations will be made for you. A name for the reservations will be given to you just before it's time for you to leave. I don't think I have to tell you what will happen if you can't duplicate what you've done here, or decide you'd rather not go." She raked him with cruel eyes, then was gone.

He sat in the middle of his bed the rest of the night, soaked in cold sweat. He didn't think he would ever want to have sex with a woman again. He didn't know if he ever dared sleep again. The nightmares would be too awful.

Chapter One

The Pentagon

Navy Captain Mike "Crash" Boen knew that in the next sixty minutes a few words on a briefing chart could end his Navy career. Not even the Iraqi missiles that had dumped him out of two F/A-18 Hornets had been able to do that. But what mattered a great deal more to him was the fate of his development program. It made him sick to think of how many people might die because of a game of ambition and politics played out in a conference room buried in the bowels of the Pentagon.

In order to continue the Non-Explosive Strike Warhead (NESW) development program, which he managed, Mike needed approval of the Chief of Naval Operations, the Navy's top officer. He also needed concurrence of the Assistant Secretary of the Navy for Research, Development and Acquisition. The ASN(RDA) was the civilian executive who controlled the Navy's

RDA budget. The CNO and his organization defined operational requirements, but the ASN(RDA) decided which programs would be funded to meet those requirements and who would manage them.

The CNO and the ASN(RDA) were both seated at the head of a long conference table. Most of the admirals seated around the table were members of Resources and Requirements Review Board. The R3B advised the CNO on RDA matters. He seldom ignored the R3B's advice. Without R3B approval, the NESW program's prospects were dim. So were Mike's. If the program was canceled, his Navy career would likely be canceled along with it. The manager of a program personally killed by the CNO did not have a bright future.

Mike resented the Washington bureaucracy's often illogical decision-making process. He was a combat pilot, not a bureaucrat, but the Navy didn't let you fly forever. At forty-four, he'd completed his quota of tours as squadron leader and air group commander (CAG). His air-combat days were over.

Giving up flying had been a lot like dying, but Mike had been assigned to manage a program that he believed could revolutionize warfare. Leading such a revolutionary development didn't equal the thrill of flying, but he did find it exciting.

The CNO ended a private discussion with the ASN(RDA) and fixed Mike with piercing, black eyes. The CNO's round face made him look too young to be the Navy's top officer, despite his gray hair. He examined Mike for any flaw in his appearance.

Mike's uniform fit his muscular, five-eleven frame perfectly. Every strand of his black hair was in place. His dark-brown eyes betrayed no nervousness. The CNO liked the determined set of Mike's square jaw. He knew he wouldn't hear any bullshit from this officer.

"Let's get on with it, Captain," the CNO ordered.

Mike got control of the flutter in his stomach and began. He established program requirements with a shower of statistics and titles of formal requirements documents. He paused, and took a deep breath before plunging into the heart of his briefing. "Studies have shown that the NESW can reduce the amount of ordnance and sorties required to destroy targets by a factor of ten. We are talking effectiveness on the scale of a small nuclear weapon, but without the collateral damage. NESW also avoids risking escalation to a nuclear holocaust, since the NESW is a nonlethal weapon. It kills machines, not people."

Mike's matter-of-fact tone belied the importance of the nonlethal aspect to him. After each strike, he'd wondered how many innocent noncombatants he'd killed. A dedicated strike pilot couldn't afford a conscience like his. Though cross-trained as a strike pilot, Mike had spent most of his career as a fighter pilot. Fighter pilots rarely had conscience problems. They fought other skilled killers, who were either attempting to kill them, or on their way to kill someone else. Downing a fighter saved lives. The Gulf War had plunged Mike into the strike world.

"As I'm sure you're all aware, Congress has increased funding for nonlethal weapons development and directed DoD to plan a joint-service program. The President has issued a National Security Decision Directive defining program objectives that expand the country's strategic options as well as limit noncombatant casualties. Tentative planning assigns the Marine Corps the lead. However, nonlethal-weapons development has been under way by the Navy and other services for years. At least one such weapon was used in the Gulf War to disable power plants, and others were deployed to Somalia."

Mike summarized the current "nonlethal" warfare

research. Being investigated were directed-energy weapons, such as lasers and high-power microwave transmitters; the use of infrasound—an extremely low-frequency sound wave that creates debilitating, yet temporary nausea and bowel spasms; electromagnetic-pulse (EMP) generators, capable of destroying electronics over a wide area; and chemical agents that would change the molecular structure of base metals or alloys of critical parts of aircraft, ships and trucks. Mike emphasized that such weapons could serve only as adjuncts to current weapons and could not produce adequate reduction in ship ordnance requirements. He concluded that the NESW program offered a more effective Navy alternative.

Mike then explained that the NESW program was based on revolutionary new thin-film technology. Instead of exploding, the warhead would disperse an agent that would rapidly cover objects over a wide area with a film a few molecules thick. The film would destroy the surface characteristics of a wide variety of materials: Low-friction-bearing surfaces would become high-friction, freezing engines and other machinery; the refractive index of lens surfaces would change, disabling gun sights and electro-optical missile guidance; and conductors would turn into insulators and insulators would turn into conductors, disabling critical electronic systems. Aircraft would fall out of the sky, tanks stall, guns jam and supply trucks and ships stop.

Mike presented results of system-effectiveness studies that indicated that one carrier armed with NESWs would be able to halt the entire industry of a small country, destroying both its economy and its ability to wage war. Assured disruption would replace assured destruction as a deterrent. An aggressor would be faced with immediate and total economic ruin.

Mike pointed out that it would take only a few molecules to obtain the same results as pounds of explosives. That was the good news. Then Mike presented the bad news.

The thin-film warhead problems were much the same as chemical-warhead problems: limiting spread of the agent, obtaining uniform dispersal, fratricide, and neutralization of the agents before friendly troops advanced. Also, each class of materials required a different film agent. A multi-agent warhead had to be developed; otherwise a prohibitive number of different warheads would be required to disable the large variety of systems found on the battlefield—each composed of many different types of materials. So far only a few of the agents had proved compatible enough to be incorporated in a single warhead.

Mike outlined program management: work-breakdown structure, costs and schedule. "This is a high-risk program, but it could have an impact on warfare similar to the invention of nuclear weapons," Mike concluded. He anxiously studied the faces around the table, attempting to determine whether the program and his career had been trashed.

"Thank you, Captain," said the CNO. "That was an excellent presentation." Mike breathed easier. At the very least, he hadn't blown the brief, and the CNO's compliment would discourage personal attacks.

"I apologize for the short fuse, Admiral Stallings," the CNO told the R3B chairman. "I realize your board hasn't had time to review this program, but the Hill and the White House are demanding immediate decisions on nonlethal-weapons development, and this has become a high-profile program. I'd like board input before I respond."

"I think the best way to proceed is to have board members and the other flags concerned comment and see if we have some kind of consensus," Vice Admiral Stallings suggested.

"Good idea. Time is pressing, gentlemen, so keep

your comments brief,'' the CNO instructed brusquely. ''We'll start with Eighty-six.''

Mike tensed. Rear Admiral William Kruger, N86, was Director of the Surface Warfare Branch in the Deputy Chief of Naval Operations office. His branch set requirements for surface ships and their weapons systems. Mike knew the admiral wanted to kill the NESW program. Kruger considered NESW an aircraft program that diverted funds from his ship programs.

Kruger glanced down at a point paper, which had been prepared by his staff and technical experts. ''Captain Boen, your brief indicated that the multi-agent warhead problem is a showstopper. Unless you develop compatible film agents, you will be unable to produce an effective warhead. Nothing in your brief indicates you have a handle on this problem. Until we solve this fundamental problem, I don't see how we can justify spending any more development money on this program. This should be a basic research program, not a weapons-development program.''

Mike's stomach turned over. The admiral had pinpointed the technological barrier that threatened to kill the program. Mike hesitated, fighting a battle with his conscience. He didn't want to lie or exaggerate, even though he believed the problem could be solved. ''We do have a handle on the problem, sir,'' Mike argued. He felt uncomfortably close to lying. ''We have identified a number of compatible agents, and we are looking into a National Science Foundation program which has developed technology that appears to have solved the problem.''

''National Science Foundation!'' Kruger exploded. ''They do unclassified research, not weapons development. How do you—''

''Admiral Kruger, why don't you have your people discuss the technical details with the program office later,'' the CNO interrupted. Irritation ruffled his voice.

The CNO's harsh reaction to Kruger's criticism dampened further comment. The CNO obviously supported the program, and no one had good arguments against it. Mike knew that didn't mean the program was safe; it never would be safe with powerful admirals waiting to ambush it. And the ASN(RDA) was yet to be heard from. He could end the program, despite the CNO's support.

The service secretaries—the Secretaries of Army, Navy and Air Force—existed to ensure civilian control of the military, a basic tenet of U.S. democracy. The ASN(RDA) didn't often ignore CNO requirements, but could and sometimes did, particularly when requirements conflicted with political and foreign-policy objectives.

The ASN(RDA), Dr. Kieran Welcome, was a large blond man who looked more like a football player than a man with a Ph.D. in electronic engineering. He'd been vice president for engineering of a large aerospace company before being appointed ASN(RDA). His intense blue eyes bored into Mike.

"I'm worried about the treaty implications of this program," Welcome said, his brows furrowed. "This sounds an awful lot like chemical warfare. The treaties are very clear on CW; they prohibit all offensive uses of chemical and biological warfare, and we are definitely talking offense when we talk strike."

"I'd like to comment on that, Dr. Welcome," said Scott Corbett, Mike's GS-15, Deputy Program Manager. He rose from his seat against the wall. Scott stood over six feet and had the body of a marathon runner—which he was. His intelligent hazel eyes looked from rugged features tamed by a bit of boyishness. His curly black hair stopped just short of his collar.

"We wrestled with the treaty implications, and had an army of lawyers advise us," Scott informed the ASN. "Everyone who looked at it has concluded that

NESW falls in the same realm as explosives. If the definition of chemical weapons was stretched far enough, explosives would be included—they are, after all, chemicals.''

''Well, I still have a concern,'' Welcome persisted with a frown, ''but that doesn't mean I don't support the program. The potential payoff justifies the risk. And the program will definitely help us with the nonlethal-warfare supporters on the Hill.''

Exhilaration surged through Mike. His intestines unwound, and he could breathe freely again. With both the CNO and the ASN(RDA) behind it, the program would be difficult to kill.

The program had survived. He'd survived.

''Captain, thanks again for an excellent briefing . . . and for finishing on time,'' the CNO said, getting to his feet, signaling the end of the meeting. ''We have a lot of potential here.''

Everyone stood at attention as the CNO exited.

Rear Admiral Jake Kittering, Director of Naval Intelligence, approached Mike. ''Great brief, Captain,'' he said, smiling and shaking Mike's hand. ''We need to talk. It's urgent. I want to see you in my vault tomorrow at 0900. Something I want to show you, and someone I want you to meet. And I wouldn't make any plans for the next few weeks, Captain. If you have any, cancel them. I need to borrow you for a while. I'll speak to your bosses.''

''Yes, sir. I'll see you in the morning.''

The admiral's words were ominous—as if he wanted to pull Mike off his program and bury him in some deep hole in spook country. Mike wanted to say the program needed him too much to help, but captains didn't refuse a flag officer's request without a better excuse than that.

''I'll be happy to help you any way I can, Admiral,'' Mike offered.

"Hey, why the glum look?" Scott asked, after Kittering departed. "You won today, won big."

"Kittering says he has something he wants me to do for him. And when a spook admiral wants me to do something, I get nervous. But you're right. I should be happy to be leaving here with my balls. Look, it's 1700. Why don't we have Lieutenant Blodgett secure the viewgraphs and toast our survival with a few glasses of bad draft."

"Sounds like a winner."

A Navy car delivered them to their office building, Crystal Plaza One. It was located at the north end of Crystal City, whose high-rise buildings sprawled along Jefferson Davis Highway between the Potomac River and Alexandria, Virginia. Mike and Scott left Lieutenant Blodgett at the elevators and descended a ramp to the Crystal Underground, a complex of shops, restaurants and theaters lining tunnels that connected the Crystal City buildings. They found their way through the crowded passageways to a small bar they favored for its cool, dim interior and good draft beer.

Civil servants and uniformed military crammed the bar. Mike and Scott found a table in a dark corner and ordered two drafts from a pale, blond waitress in a frilly micro-skirt. They emptied the first glasses without a word. It felt almost as good as sex to sit silently in the soft breeze of the air conditioner and let the stress drain away.

"How you making out with NSF and Lesatec?" Scott asked after the waitress had replaced their empty glasses.

"With NSF okay. With Lesatec and our good Dr. Julie Barns, not okay." Worry squirmed in Mike's gut. They needed the NSF program results more than the brief had implied. The computer modeling programs Lesatec had developed for NSF could solve their multi-agent problem. The programs could rapidly formulate the combinations of the compatible thin-film agents that they needed.

NSF had agreed to cooperate, despite its reluctance to become associated with a classified weapons-development program. But the research was being performed by a contractor, Lesatec Inc., and the Lesatec program manager, Dr. Julie Barns, vigorously opposed cooperation with the Navy. She argued that supporting military programs would be misuse of her research and fall outside the scope of Lesatec's contracts. Lesatec's management supported her position, claiming their software was proprietary—not developed with contract funds—and did not belong to the government.

Several large aerospace companies had created Lesatec as a joint venture to demonstrate their concern for health and the environment. Lesatec's objective was to use recent advances in genetic engineering to develop products for waste disposal and pollution control. Use of Lesatec R&D for military applications would risk a fatal public-relations disaster: Lesatec could be accused of using government funds intended for environmental protection to develop weapons technology.

"Have you found anybody else working the problem?" Mike inquired hopefully.

"No, and I don't think we will. It's a new field. The Lesatec program is the only program we've found that can help us any time soon."

"Well, I'm meeting Julie Barns tomorrow—drinks, then dinner."

"Sounds like the old Boen charm is working."

"Not a chance. Strictly business. Our Dr. Barns is a dedicated peace and save-the-world person, and she wants nothing to do with the military—either its programs or its people. We're meeting here for dinner because it's convenient. She has an apartment in Crystal City, rides the Metro home from work and refuses to set foot in our office."

"Well, our people have been working with Naval Research Laboratory experts and have come up with a plan to accelerate things. We can get it done without Lesatec, but it might take a year."

"I don't think we have a year," Mike objected. "A year delay will give N86 and other program opponents the time and ammunition they need to kill the program."

"Right now, I've got everything on hold, waiting to see what happens with NSF, but we need to get going on *something*."

"Don't wait any longer," Mike ordered. "Get the lab people moving. I'll keep working on Lesatec and NSF, but probably all I'll get is more pissed off."

Chapter Two

Tripoli

Colonel Muhammad Aziz was terrified. As always. He'd lived his entire life on the edge of panic. Muhammad didn't fear death as much as he feared the manner of dying. The hoarse screams of the dying men he had tortured haunted him. Muhammad Aziz, colonel of the Libyan Air Force, didn't sleep well.

It was like that when you planned an assassination. An assassination so many others had failed at. Assassination of the Great Leader—who'd survived so much.

Colonel Gadhafi.

Was the dictator crazy? Maybe the dictator was very crazy. The insane seemed capable of premonition. Seemed able to read the minds of their enemies.

Was he awaiting Muhammad Aziz with a horrible surprise? Muhammad shivered. The night air was warm, but fear chilled him.

In the hour after midnight, the streets in this remote section of Tripoli were silent, except for the scattered barking of dogs. The air hung heavy with scent: flowers, incense, excrement. Dark, threatening shadows crawled across the moonlit streets like tentacles of a malevolent beast. Muhammad shuddered at the thought of what nightmares might lurk in their depths.

He felt naked. He never walked the streets. He always traveled in an armored Mercedes with guards in cars fore and aft. But he had walked this night. He had walked a long way. He couldn't let anyone know of his absence, let alone his destination.

Muhammad felt clammy under the robes he wore to cloak his identity, and the kaffiayh made his head itch. He normally wore a uniform or a business suit.

The robes didn't cloak Muhammad's bulk. He was a broad bear of a man, six feet of astonishing strength. His skin was dark—not brown, not black, not dusky . . . dark. It absorbed light. Darker still were his eyes—obsidian, a cruel glint in their depths. His hair was black, thick, lying close to his large head. A hawkish nose broke the heavy planes of his face. A thin mustache slashed above full lips.

Muhammad studied the shadows. He couldn't quite make himself believe that he hadn't been followed. He gathered his courage and strode quickly across the street to the massive door of an ancient palace. It had been the abode of some minor sheik in the distant past. It was a crumbling ruin now, no vestige of past opulence left.

The hinges screamed in protest when the colonel forced the doors open enough to slip through. There was a flash of panic when he couldn't close the doors after him. The rusty hinges finally yielded, and he felt his way along the wall for a few feet, then stood for a long time in the smothering darkness, worrying about the noise the door had made, alert for sounds of movement.

Muhammad's eyes detected a dim flickering in the distance. He moved toward it, feeling his way carefully around mounds of ruined furniture and trash. He reached stairs that wound down through the stone floor. Yellow light wavered up the dusty passageway.

Muhammad took the Steyer tactical machine pistol from the holster beneath his robes and started down the stairs, scarcely daring to breathe. The stairs widened into a large hall, lit by torches burning some foul-smelling substance. In the center of the cavernous space was a massive wooden table. Its heavily scarred top sat on intricately carved legs. The table was surrounded by a dozen heavy chairs with rotted cushions.

Muhammad had planned to arrive early, but he hadn't planned on being the first. He searched the ominous darkness beyond arches hovering over entrances to subterranean passages.

"We have been betrayed." The words knifed the air behind him.

Muhammad's breath caught. His finger tightened on the TMP's trigger.

An apparition floated from the darkness. A black robe covered the figure from head to foot. Only the black eyes were visible, eyes that glittered like diamonds in the shifting torch light. As always, the arrogance in those eyes angered him. "Do you understand?" It was a woman's voice, hard-edged and cruel. Muhammad knew the voice could be melodious and seductive. He'd heard it hoarse with passion. He also knew the strong, lithe body under the dark robe well, very well indeed.

"No. I do not understand," he replied harshly. He didn't want to believe it, not when they were so close.

"The traitor intends to capture or kill the rest of you tonight. He will reveal everything, and hand the ones captured alive over to their governments.''

"Who?" he asked. Her delay in naming the traitor made him suspicious.

"Sudan. Abdul Bandar."

"Why?"

"This has proved too secular for him, and he fears you will fail. He seeks to save himself."

"How do you know all of this?"

"You know I will not answer such questions."

"And I am suppose to believe—"

"Colonel! Has not my information always proved correct? Otherwise both of us would be dead."

It was true, but wagering his life on the word of one woman made him feel as vulnerable as a young virgin in a soldiers' barracks. How could she know so much? Could her band of spies and assassins be that pervasive, or was there another level to this plot he didn't know about? Were the seven of them just pawns, waiting in ignorance to be sacrificed in some gambit they'd never know about?

"We must leave at once," Muhammad said tightly.

"No."

"No?"

"It is already too late."

"What do you mean?" he asked, filling with dread.

"His people are already outside. They know who you are. They can't be allowed to leave here alive."

Muhammad's fear didn't increase, but his anger did. He'd come so far, survived so much, only to die because of an owlish runt whose brain was besotted with religious nonsense.

"Colonel, if your people are forced to flee, they will lose the courage to continue. It will be the end. Someone will talk. All will die."

"How can you be so sure that Abdul has told no one in his government, or in ours?"

"We are still alive."

Muhammad knew she was right.

"Abdul has informed only those he needed for tonight," she went on.

"How many?"

"Not enough. That is his mistake."

"How many?" Muhammad insisted.

"Nine."

"Nine! And that is not enough! They are probably all trained killers, and what we have, besides ourselves, are six frightened politicians. I doubt that any know how to properly aim those weapons they are so fond of carrying."

"The two of us will be enough. It is dark. They suspect nothing."

"The two of us?"

"It will be better without the others. We can't depend on them, and the whole world would hear them blundering about, firing their weapons at shadows. Abdul's people would slaughter us."

Muhammad did not share her confidence, but there was no alternative.

He filled with rage and frustration. A large chunk of the world was almost in his grasp, and it was about to be snatched away by a religious fanatic—a fool who probably hadn't read the Koran in ten years and had never understood it. Muhammad hated the thought of dying in the dirt of an old ruin; it was not the way for an air warrior to die. It would have been better to have died in Iraq.

Muhammad had been training with Russian pilots in Iraq when the war started. He could have fled, but the lure of flying advanced MiGs in combat had been too great. He'd fled only when the allies launched their ground offensive.

"Abdul is already in the passageway, waiting," the black-robed woman informed him. "He wants to be the last to arrive. One man is with him. Most likely that one will stay in the tunnel until Abdul thinks the time is right. Abdul will signal, and the man will fetch the others.''

"You speak as if you can read Abdul's mind.''

"No. I read my own. I have much experience at such things. I will dispose of Abdul's man, and then Abdul.''

"No! Abdul is mine!''

"It is not practical.''

"*I* will kill him,'' Muhammad insisted.

"How? Shoot him? Shots will bring those outside. It must be silent and swift. Done before those around the table have time to react. They must believe that you hold their lives in your hands, that you have people everywhere that can strike them dead in an instant.''

Muhammad pictured the scene: The seven of them would be seated around the table with him at its head. It would be impossible for him to reach Abdul in time with a knife. If Muhammad drew his weapon, it might precipitate a gunfight. "All right,'' he said with a bitter sigh.

"It must be done swiftly and with no mistakes.''

"I know!'' he spat back angrily. The bitch was insufferably arrogant, but she held the key to the enormous power that was almost in his grasp. He would wrest that key from her someday, and he would enjoy killing her . . . very slowly. It would be better than sex with her. The prospect gave him a slight erection.

Fatima Sundari was a tentacle of one of the Libyan dictator's most fiendish terrorist creations: a cadre of merciless women who enjoyed bringing death and agony to men who'd so often abused them. The dictator had tapped the hidden rage of Arab women, who were eager for the chance to wreak retribution for ages of abuse by men who'd used the Koran as justification for their cruelty.

This Sisterhood was an insidious nightmare, a tribute

to the dictator's twisted creativity. Whether robed and veiled, or sensual in Western dress, they remained free from suspicion. No one suspected that an obedient Arab woman or an empty-headed Western slut could be a skilled assassin. They were particularly useful in eliminating political rivals. The Sisterhood included wives and mistresses of powerful men throughout the Arab world; these men didn't know they slept with death.

The dictator's ego had caused him to make the very mistake he'd counted on others to make when he had created his band of killers. He'd never worried that pliant Arab women turned into killers might develop ambitions of their own and turn on him.

It had astounded and frightened Muhammad to discover that the dictator maintained a cadre of assassins hidden from even his most trusted henchmen. This band of invisible killers was the perfect weapon for elimination of people like Muhammad.

Fatima had come to him in Monaco, like a bad dream.

Monaco, One year earlier

Muhammad lay beside her on the bed, drained. It had been more like combat than sex. He was left sated but unsatisfied. Even in the midst of the act, she had maintained the cool elegance that had attracted him when she'd taken the seat beside him at the baccarat table. It was an elegance he found hard to associate with her American English. It was an elegance that didn't belong in bed. It isolated her. He'd been able to touch her flesh, but not her.

She'd used her body with the cool purpose and skill of a race driver who knew every curve and bump in the track. And like a race driver, she obviously enjoyed using those skills to win. She steered her lover's passion as precisely as a race car, and he had the feeling she would have enjoyed it even with someone she hated.

As she lay on her back, eyes fixed on the ceiling, Muhammad studied her. She was dusky, with long, thick midnight hair and hollow black eyes. Her face had high cheekbones and a narrow nose that was a little too long and pointed. Her tall body was slim, with just enough flesh to soften the outlines of sinewy muscles. She had small breasts with large, dark nipples. A thick bush jutted from her pelvis. Even naked, with a sheen of sweat covering her body, she was one of the most elegant women Muhammad had ever been to bed with.

"Would you like to make love again?" she asked—in perfect Arabic.

It took a moment for Muhammad to realize she'd spoken in Arabic . . . to accept it . . . to grasp the implications.

Muhammad stiffened. He hardly breathed.

She smiled disarmingly. "You thought I was American, didn't you?"

He was too shocked to answer.

"We do the bidding of the same Great Leader."

Muhammad's heart thudded in his chest. "Who are you speaking of?" he asked, knowing the answer and dreading it.

"Our supreme commander, the Colonel."

"What do you do for him?"

"Kill people like you."

Muhammad's heart paused. There was nowhere for a nude woman to hide a weapon. There had to be others outside.

"I know your ambitions," she stated flatly. "I know about Mauritania, Sudan, Chad, all of them. I know who they are. Who they've killed. Who they intend to kill."

She fixed him with chilling eyes.

33

Muhammad's heart hammered. He didn't doubt her. But shouldn't he be dead? Or begging for death?

Maybe he soon would be. But he'd kill her first.

She saw it in his eyes. "I came to save you, not destroy you."

He hesitated.

"We've known since the meeting in Atar, and you are still alive," she pointed out. His life had been in her hands for over a year. She wanted something. What was worth his life? Worth her risking the dictator's wrath?

He could kill her and flee. Maybe there was no one on the fire escape, and there was the bank account in Costa Rica. But she was a professional. She wouldn't be so careless. And the dictator's pursuit would be relentless. Costa Rica? The moon wouldn't be far enough.

"What is it you want?"

"Something from your revolution. A small thing, really. And in return I—and my sisters—will give you victory beyond your wildest dreams. You aspire to control a few poor North African nations. We can give you the whole continent and the Middle East. Europe will do your bidding, and America will fear you too much to attack."

She didn't continue, just stared blankly at the ceiling.

Muhammad shivered. A madwoman held his life in her hands. "What is it you want?" he finally asked, unable to stand the suspense, which he knew she was using to make him vulnerable. She wanted him to think about death, and the horrible manner in which he would die, if Gadhafi's people caught him. He'd often used that particular cruelty.

"We want a new order for Arab women," she answered emotionally. "We want rules and laws to protect women. We want punishment for men who violate

34

them.'' Her voice was harsh, filled with violence and brimming with anger.

She took a deep breath before she continued, seeming to regain control of the emotions that had shaken her composure. ''All we ask is that Arab women be treated like human beings, not like slaves, not like dogs. We want Arab women to be free. We want you to proclaim it. Write it. Make it so.''

Small thing! By Allah! This was no small thing! Libya maybe, but the others . . . Abdul Bandar of Sudan, who would have been a cleric except for his greed, would never accept such a secular thing.

''Do you know what you're asking?''

''Yes.''

''Then why do you ask? I do not have it to give.''

''But you will. We will provide it.''

''What will you provide?''

''Fear.''

''Fear?''

''Terror.''

Muhammad sighed and lost hope.

Bombs, fires, assassinations. Hopeless. Tiresome. They never learned.

She knew what he was thinking. ''Not bombs. Not murder. That's what we do for our leader. It never is enough. Never will be enough. We have the means to terrify whole nations . . . even Bandar's Sudan. They have little, but they don't want to lose it. They don't want to be savages again. It terrifies the greedy to know they will have less rather than more. They will reinterpret the Koran if they have to. Their new ayatollahs will do it.'' She paused. Her eyes burned. ''We kill clerics, too. We believe the *shahadah*: 'There is no God but God and Muhammad is his prophet,' but we aren't religious. Bandar would say we aren't Muslim. True. Our goals will not permit it. But we *are* Arab. We must

35

leave being Muslim to others. We are willing to sacrifice our souls."

Muhammad shuddered. How many of these women were there! But it didn't matter how many. Not even sacrificing their souls would get them what they wanted.

"Are you going to give me the hydrogen bomb?" he asked sarcastically. "And please, don't tell me about chemical and biological weapons. Saddam had those."

"None of those. But we have the technology to paralyze whole nations. Destroy their economies, make their armies helpless, leave their people starving in the street. We can send a nation back to the Stone Age.

"But we won't have to," she continued. "One demonstration on a small nation with few friends will be enough. The world will tremble before you and seek to appease you."

"The threat of mass death and destruction brings death and destruction," he objected. "The whole world turned on Iraq, and the Americans have been waiting for years for an excuse to bomb our country into oblivion. No weapon is enough to defeat the whole world."

"We will not threaten death and destruction, only disruption. Only machines will die. No civilized country can survive without its machines—not even a miserable nation like Sudan."

"What is this doomsday machine?" Muhammad was sure his fate was sealed. His life was in the hands of an insane bitch whose mind was enmeshed in ridiculous fantasies.

"Do you read the American military journals?"

"Of course."

"Then you've read about nonlethal warfare."

"The pipedream of some institute."

"We have the technology."

Muhammad was startled. It had to be a fantasy, but

if somehow . . . "Even the Americans don't have it yet," he pointed out.

"They don't *know* they have it."

"Where did you obtain it?"

"From the Americans. The world obtains its technology from the Americans, and applies it while the Americans continue to debate its value."

"You are spies as well as assassins?"

"Yes. Also, there are Libyan students, scientists and computer analysts working in the United States. They provide us technology when we need it. Sometimes they must be reminded of their loyalties, but we are very good at reminding."

Muhammad knew how much Libya had invested in infiltrating student-exchange programs, unclassified laboratory staffs and assembly lines. There were also Libyan refugees who could be coerced. But the return on investment had been just a fuzzy dream up until now. It was a rarely used resource. Had this woman and her fellow killers found a way to tap that resource?

"Do you expect me to believe these people, who will not return to Libya unless exposed, have provided you with such technology?"

"Not yet. I only ask that you allow us time to make you believe. In return for your life."

Muhammad wondered what kind of scheme she had devised to ensure he'd keep his promise. She was too clever to trust promises.

"The others will never go along with this . . . this declaration of women's rights. The coalition will be destroyed before it's born."

"They need know nothing of our arrangement yet, or of the weapon. Once the coalition is established and you demonstrate the technology, you can proclaim anything you wish. We are patient."

Muhammad thought about it. Suppose she wasn't insane. The possibilities were dizzying. She was offering him the military equalizer the Third World had sought for so long, and she was right. A nonlethal weapon might not provoke the unified response that nuclear or chemical threats would. If they were prudent, and did not go immediately rampaging into other countries, they might seize control of a quarter of the world without suffering the destruction visited upon Iraq. The intimidation would be more powerful than an army. And the power would be his.

Worsening economic conditions had fueled a rise in Muslim fundamentalism that threatened governments throughout Arab world. Support for the Israeli-Palestinian peace agreement had Muslim fundamentalists seeking the blood of leaders who they believed had betrayed the Arab world. The extremists had the sympathy and tacit support of many secular Arabs who'd lost confidence in their governments and leaders. Arab nations were ripe for coups. Even Moammar Gadhafi had had to dispatch troops to eliminate unrest that threatened his iron control of Libya. Muhammad and his counterparts intended to exploit the discontent to seize control of most of North Africa and form a new Arab coalition.

Muhammad had hoped to emerge as the most influential leader of the coalition by virtue of Libya's military strength. In North Africa, only Egypt's military capability exceeded Libya's. Like Saddam Hussein, Gadhafi had used his oil money to procure the technology and weapons to make Libya an impressive military power.

If this woman proved sane, Muhammad would be more than a leader; he would be a ruler—the most powerful ruler in the Arab world.

Chapter Three

Tripoli

The future leaders of North Africa quietly slipped into the room during the next half hour. The cavernous hall was the terminus of a maze of underground passages whose remote entrances were hidden in gardens and cellars scattered about the city. Each of the conspirators had a map of the maze, and to guard against treachery, each chose his own route in and out.

There was little trust here. Eyes were full of suspicion. Greetings were more grunts than words. What they were about was suicidal. Only lust for power and greed kept them together, that and the realization that Colonel Muhammad Aziz had enmeshed them too far to turn back. They'd already done the unforgivable. If discovered, they would die in a most unpleasant manner. There was no way to leave this endeavor alive. But Abdul Bandar, Foreign Minister of Sudan, believed he'd found a way out that would make him a hero instead of a traitor.

These men, particularly the arrogant Libyan, offended Allah with their secular ways, and that offended Abdul, offended him greatly. He'd come to the conclusion that Allah would never let them succeed. He had decided he wasn't going to perish with them.

Abdul Bandar was the last to enter the hall, as Fatima had predicted. He was an academic figure: a small man whose face was owlish behind thick glasses. The glasses mirrored the flickering torchlight, hiding his eyes, but Muhammad knew there was treachery in those eyes, and he fought to restrain his rage. He cursed all of the insane hypocrites who called themselves fundamentalists. He doubted any of them understood the Koran, or wanted to. They only used it to justify oppression and sadism.

"Brothers, we should be about our business," Muhammad urged. "It is not good to linger together too long." Muhammad slipped off the long cylindrical case that hung across his back from a shoulder strap. He opened one end, pulled forth a large map and unrolled it on the table's surface. The others helped him position stones to keep it flat. It was a large map of the African continent and its Middle East and European environs. There was a band of countries, colored red and yellow, that stretched across North Africa from the Red Sea to the Atlantic. Colored red were Mauritania, Mali, Niger, Libya, Chad and Sudan. Morocco, Algeria, Tunisia and Egypt were colored yellow. It was an area three times that of Western Europe. This was to be the new Arab coalition. It would be an empire, if Muhammad had his way, and he'd be the emperor.

North Africa was separated from Europe by the Mediterranean and by an even larger gulf in political, economic and military power. This small, furtive band of men believed they could narrow that gulf and at the same time acquire great personal wealth and power.

"It is time to set a date," Muhammad announced. He waited for objections. There were none.

"Twenty-one days from now," Muhammad declared. "It must be done swiftly and on that date by all. Whoever delays will face those warned by what has happened in other countries. He will fail. Mauritania?" Muhammad asked, pointing to the map.

"All is ready," the large dark man replied. He was the Minister of Commerce.

Muhammad thought he heard a muffled cry from somewhere in the darkness. "Mali?" he asked quickly, hoping to cover any more sounds of struggle.

"It shall be done," answered Mali's Finance Minister.

Muhammad called on each in turn, leaving Sudan until the last. "And you, Abdul, are you ready?"

Abdul took a long time answering. Muhammad couldn't see his eyes, but Muhammad knew Abdul was searching the darkness for his people. He had been doing something with his scarf for the last ten minutes, undoubtedly wondering why his signal hadn't been answered.

"Of course. Everything is ready," Bandar answered without conviction. "But what about them?" he asked, pointing to the countries colored yellow. "What will they do?" The countries tinted yellow on the map had not been enmeshed in the plot. Only the weaker, unstable countries had been subverted. Algeria and Egypt alone had a combined population of almost seventy million people, and Egypt had a powerful military machine backed by the U.S. They represented a serious threat if they decided to intervene.

"We have discussed this many times, Abdul," Muhammad replied angrily. He knew Bandar was attempting to delay the meeting and give his tardy thugs time to act. "Nothing has changed. It is a risk, but a small one. None of those countries have stomach for warfare so soon after Iraq, and they are too busy dealing with their own dissidents to interfere in other countries' affairs. When they see the strength of our union, they will join. Their dissidents will give them no choice. We must act swiftly while we enjoy such fortunate circumstances.

"All are agreed?" Muhammad asked. There was no dissent, only Abdul Bandar's hostile face. "Then we have only one last detail to take care of," Muhammad continued. The faces were puzzled—except for Abdul's. It filled with apprehension. "We must eliminate a traitor, and agree on his replacement." There was a collective gasp.

Abdul brought the compact Berreta 12S machine gun from under his robes, but Death slid out of the shadows and stung him at the base of his skull.

He stiffened.

He tried to scream.

He couldn't pull the trigger.

There was a finger in the guard with his.

The slender blade slipped between his vertebrae.

Bandar's mouth stretched wide in a silent scream.

He sprawled across the table, still trying to scream.

The others around the table scrambled to their feet, drawing their weapons. They were undecided as to where to point the formidable array of high-tech automatics, but most were trained on Muhammad.

Muhammad's blood roared in his ears. He knew he teetered on the edge of death.

Eyes searched the shadows, but Fatima had disappeared back into the darkness before Abdul's body had ceased its final shudder.

"Muhammad! What is this!" shouted the Interior Minister of Niger.

"Abdul was ready to betray us." The eyes were questioning, incredulous. "He was never accused,"

Muhammad reminded them. "His guilt made him draw his weapon."

"All is lost," someone choked.

"No! I said he *meant* to betray us. He hadn't yet had the opportunity."

"But surely he didn't expect to do it alone. There must be others."

"True."

"Here?"

"Outside. But not many. Abdul believed the glory of acting alone would save his life and make him a hero." Muhammad fought to keep his voice calm as he lied. Would they believe such a ragged tale? Or would they kill him and take their chances? If Abdul's men grew impatient, or anyone encountered them on the way out, there would be disaster.

"What are you going to do about his people?"

"They are being taken care of," he lied again.

"I don't like this," complained the Defense Minister of Chad. "You have deceived us." Fingers tightened on triggers. "Only we were to know. Only we were to meet here."

"I have brought only those needed to dispose of the traitors." Muhammad declared. "My people know nothing of this. Only who to kill. None of you are acting alone, Suad," Muhammad reminded him. "You must trust someone. We have to trust your people. You have to trust ours. There is no other way."

Weapons lowered. Muhammad had survived the crisis with his life. Now he had to get them out before Abdul's killers became impatient.

"Youssef al-Amir is my choice," Muhammad announced, as if nothing had occurred. "He had no part in the treachery, but he has been one of us from the beginning."

The men looked at one another, but there were no objections. "You will take care of it?" asked Suad.

"Yes." They stared at him, realizing for the first time how far and deep Muhammad's tentacles were spread. This night had convinced them that Muhammad had assassins everywhere. And he did. There was the Sisterhood.

"When next we meet, we shall all be rulers," Muhammad trumpeted. "Nothing can stand before our union. When we cry 'God is great,' the world will tremble."

"Yes!" they shouted so loudly that Muhammad feared Abdul's men would hear.

Muhammad knew they shouted a lie. Necessity would keep the coalition together until the coups were accomplished. Then the bickering would start; the centuries-old rivalries and feuds that had kept the Arab world from its destiny for thousands of years would shatter the coalition. But Muhammad wouldn't let that happen. He had the tool of mass terror needed to weld the coalition together permanently. It would also bring Egypt, Algeria and the rest of North Africa into the coalition . . . or destroy them.

"You should leave quickly," Muhammad urged. "Use the furthermost entrances."

"But you said Abdul's people had been—"

"My people don't know you. They have orders to kill those outside this place. They might think you one of them."

They left the room as swiftly as dignity would allow. Muhammad nervously watched them depart. He expected a hail of bullets from the guns of Bandar's thugs at any moment.

Fatima emerged from the shadows. "Those outside undoubtedly grow impatient," she said. "We must hurry. If they enter, it will be difficult. There will be shooting."

"The one inside?"

"Dead, of course." Muhammad shivered. She'd already murdered two men this night.

"We can't use guns," she said. There was a wolfish gleam in her eyes. He half expected her lips to drip blood.

"I know that."

"There are four in front—two just inside the door, one behind a car at the curb and one across the street. The others are hiding in the garden behind. We can leave by the passages and surprise them from behind. I will take the ones in the garden. You take the ones in front," she instructed.

Muhammad again felt a flash of rage, and wondered how long he would have to wait to kill this arrogant woman. How dare she give him orders!

"The lion fountain in the wall—do you know it?" she asked.

"Yes."

"I will wait nearby. Walk by in two hours. If all is not well, drink from the fountain, then go across the street to the entrance of the garden. I will follow and do the same. If neither drinks, we will part. Otherwise we will enter the garden, and speak of what is to be done. There should be nobody about at this time of night, and if there is they will think we are going to an assignation."

"That would be considerably more pleasant than what we are about to do."

"Really? I thought you enjoyed killing, my colonel."

"I am a warrior of the air. Skulking through the dark to murder unsuspecting dogs is not worthy of a soldier. It is the work of assassins," he finished meaningfully.

She stared at him a moment, then said, "Tonight you will become one of us."

He wanted to say that he'd never be one of them, but there was no time to further indulge his irritation.

* * *

Muhammad slipped silently through the shadows. The man was very careless. A lighted cigarette dangled from his lips, betraying his presence to all but the blind. Muhammad seized him from behind, crushing his windpipe and sealing off his scream. Muhammad thought his feeble thrashing too noisy. He slipped the blade of his knife through the man's back into his heart.

Muhammad carefully lowered the limp form to the dusty street. The cigarette lay on the ground, still glowing. Muhammad crushed it under his boot.

Muhammad moved down the street and crossed it in the concealment of a long shadow. He flitted between parked vehicles, pausing frequently to ensure he hadn't been seen. It took him a long time to work his way back to the man crouched by the car.

This man was alert. No cigarette. He held a short, ugly Hechler and Koch MP5KA1 with his finger on the trigger. He could probably get off a burst before Muhammad could kill him.

Patience: Muhammad didn't have time for it, but there was no help for it. Sooner or later the man would take his finger away from the trigger to shift position, relax his tense muscles, something. Muhammad squatted by the rear wheel, barely concealed by the car's shadow. It happened sooner than Muhammad had a right to expect. It was *more* than he had a right to expect. The man had to urinate.

The killer's eyes searched the street. Satisfied, he leaned his weapon against the car. His hand went under his robes, seeking his member. He never found it. Muhammad cut his throat. He made a small gurgling sound and thrashed longer than Muhammad had anticipated. Muhammad cursed silently to himself when an arm thumped loudly against the car door before the man collapsed into the dust.

Muhammad crouched behind the car. He put away

the knife and took the TMP from beneath his robes, silently cursing when the sight snagged. If those inside had heard, the knife would not be enough.

As he waited, Muhammad could feel the man's blood soaking through his robes and causing the cloth to cling to his flesh. He shouldn't have cut the man's throat. The geyser of blood had soaked him. Now he couldn't afford to be seen by anyone. Messy. But he'd never claimed to be an assassin. He was a soldier, and soldiers killed with a great deal of noise and rending of bodies.

Muhammad waited until he thought it was safe, and then waited some more. There was only silence. Those inside either hadn't heard anything, or didn't think the noise worth investigation, or . . . they were waiting for him.

Muhammad abandoned stealth and strode quickly to the entrance. Those inside had no reason to believe anyone other than their companions would be entering. Muhammad slipped through the partially open doors, knife in hand. He sensed rather than saw the man on his right and struck.

It wasn't a good blow. The knife struck a rib and skittered across the man's belly, slicing deep but not fatally. The man screamed. Muhammad knew that for a moment, the killer would be occupied with the shock of his wound. He whirled, seeking the man's companion. Guided by a gasp of alarm, Muhammad was on the other killer like a ravening beast, slashing and stabbing.

The man was brave. He fought back with furious determination. A hot lance of agony ran along Muhammad's ribs and an arm locked him in a deadly embrace. The pain left his ribs, and Muhammad knew it would find his throat next. He managed to get the point of his knife against something substantial and shoved with all his strength. His adversary stiffened, then collapsed, pulling Muhammad to the floor with him.

Muhammad struggled to untangle himself from the body, and scrambled to his feet, expecting an attack from the wounded man. Then he heard it, the sound of racing footsteps outside in the street. The killer was escaping.

Muhammad cursed and rushed out the door. The man was a hundred meters away. He was running as if Muhammad's knife had never touched him. From the garden came a burst of gunfire. Rage swept through Muhammad. The arrogant bitch had failed!

Muhammad sprinted after the assassin. He didn't know the significance of the shots. Didn't *know* that she had failed. But all would be lost for certain if this one escaped.

It seemed that they had run miles, and Muhammad had not gained a step. He was near collapse, each breath a burning agony. His heart threatened to burst from his chest. Hope began to fade, but Muhammad snatched it back and forced more from his failing legs.

The man stumbled and fell to the street. He struggled to his feet and fell again. He started to crawl.

Muhammad slowed his pace. Allah had smiled on him once more. The man's strength had drained out through his wound along with his blood.

The man sensed Muhammad behind him and screamed weakly for help. Muhammad smashed him to the street with a knee to the back, choking off his feeble cries.

Muhammad gripped his knife firmly, grasped the man's hair and yanked his head back. The man's windpipe was surprisingly tough. He gurgled noisily before the knife all but decapitated him.

Muhammad rose from the body, and stood swaying with fatigue. His robes were filthy and soaked with blood. Too much of the blood was his own. He was exhausted, but he had to go back. He had to know whether Fatima had disposed of the others, or whether they had disposed of her. He cursed her again and stumbled off.

Brackish water dribbled noisily from the crumbling lion's mouth into the cracked bowl at the base of the fountain. Muhammad was too exhausted for caution. He approached and put his face under the halting stream. He didn't have to pretend to drink. He needed the water. It mixed with his ragged breath and almost choked him. He hoped he wouldn't contract a disease from the foul-tasting liquid.

Muhammad straightened slowly, and crossed the street to stand beside the garden gate. The garden was protected from the street by a high stone wall. The rusty gate hung from broken hinges beneath an arch whose intricate design had long ago crumbled before the assault of wind and sun.

He was beginning to lose hope when the black-robed figure came down the street, picking its way from shadow to shadow. Fatima paused at the fountain, and stared across the street at him. He stepped through the gate and waited. She passed him without a word and walked into the garden depths.

The garden was poorly tended. The vegetation grew high and ragged. Dead palm fronds and trash littered the stone pathways. The smell of excrement overpowered the fragrance of the few scattered, wilted flowers. Muhammad was barely able to follow Fatima through the tangled shadows. She stopped deep in the garden at an elaborate fountain, which was dry and crumbling. She turned to him.

"What is it?" she asked coldly.

"I heard gunfire."

"It couldn't be helped. One died too slowly. But he was the last. No one heard."

"I heard."

She didn't answer.

"I said I heard."

"Has anyone come?" she snapped. "What about you? All four?"

"Yes. All," Muhammad snarled.

"Then it is finished." She turned and disappeared into the night. He looked after her in anger and disgust. The blood soaking his robes had dried, making the cloth stiff and uncomfortable. Interrogations were sometimes messy, but Muhammad could torture a man to death without getting a spot of blood on his suit. Now he felt like a dog who'd rolled in the filth of a rotting carcass.

Muhammad started for the gate.

Chapter Four

Alexandria, Virginia

Captain Mike Boen groaned awake and tangled himself in the sheet, reaching for the alarm, which was two minutes from filling the room with its grating buzz. He stretched his muscles carefully, alert for the charley horses that sometimes galloped through forty-three-year-old bodies early in the morning. He could hear his mother-in-law bustling about in the kitchen downstairs. Carrie Polaski insisted on rising at six every morning to prepare breakfast for Mike and Susan. She didn't enjoy eating breakfast alone, and her husband, Tim, hadn't risen early enough for breakfast since the day he'd retired.

"Dad, you decent?" Susan called from the hallway, knocking on his door.

Mike pulled the sheet around him. "Your father is always decent."

Susan burst into the room, combing her mass of unruly brown curls into place with one hand and stuffing her blouse into her skirt with the other. There was a lot of her mother in Susan, but Susan was her own unique person. Ellen's eyes had never looked out on the world with such brashness. Ellen had calmed you. Susan stirred you. Susan's body was a compact, full-breasted five feet. Her mother had been tall and slim. Her mother's face had been calm and elegant. Susan's bright, round face constantly churned with emotion.

"Dad, I've got to run," Susan informed him, still struggling with hair and blouse. "Got to prepare for a chem exam this morning. I won't have time for breakfast, and I wanted to let you know I'll be working late at the Patriot Center tonight."

"I'll be late, too. Going to dinner in Old Town. Probably be after ten before I get home."

"Oh? With a girl?"

"No. With a *woman*," Mike answered, smiling.

"Who?"

"Dr. Julie Barns."

"A doctor?"

"Ph.D. Genetic engineering."

"Heavy! Nice?"

"Don't know her well enough to say."

"Think you will after tonight?"

"It's not a date. Just a business meeting."

"Is she young? Pretty?"

"Thirties and . . ." Mike searched his images of Julie. Pretty? Beautiful? Plain? He realized he hadn't thought of Julie Barns as a woman, just an obstacle. ". . . she's attractive," he waffled.

"Think you'll go out again?"

"Depends on whether she gives me what I need."

"On the first date!"

"Susan Boen, you have a dirty mind for one so young. And a low opinion of your father's morals. She has data we need. *That's all.*"

Susan's expression said she didn't believe him.

"Well, have a nice time anyway, and Dad . . . women don't like to be rushed."

"Susan. I *told* you. This is strictly business."

"I know, but you never know what can lead to a beautiful relationship. Shouldn't pass up *any* opportunity for a beautiful relationship."

"Ann Landers, will you get out of here!"

Susan started for the door, then stopped. She turned, her face grave. "Dad . . . sorry . . . for prying. It's just . . . that I love you and want you happy."

"I am happy."

"Then why are your eyes always so sad? You smile. You laugh. But your eyes never do. I want a father with happy eyes . . . like before . . . fun eyes."

"But why wouldn't I be happy?" Mike protested, startled and confused.

"I think maybe . . . because you don't have anyone to love . . . to be in love with. I think you're lonely."

"But I have you. I have Carrie and Tim. I have all of the love I need."

"Love is not being in love . . . like you were in love with Mom."

A sudden ache assailed Mike's heart. For a moment he couldn't speak. She had scraped the scab off a wound that would never heal. "That was enough being in love for a lifetime," he told her. "I don't need to be in love again."

"But you do! Don't you see? A big piece of your life was being in love. That piece is gone. It left a big hole in your life. The only way you can fill that hole is to be in love again."

"I have memories to fill that space."

"It's wrong to use Mom's memories that way—to keep from falling in love. It would make Mom *so* sad if she knew. Memories are treasures, but we should use life to make more memories . . . add to the treasure.

"I gotta go," she said abruptly, as if suddenly embarrassed, and hurried out.

Mike stared after her, his insides twisted. He had never been able to come to terms with Ellen's death. *He* was the fighter pilot whose life expectancy was none too good, but *she* had been the one to die in an aircraft. He'd known he was torturing himself, but he couldn't help it: Over and over again, he'd watched TV images of the big airliner cartwheeling down the runway and exploding in flames.

Mike had lived his Navy career with death peering over his shoulder. He'd lost good friends, and viewed some horribly mangled remains. But none of it had hardened him for the trauma of his wife's death. He'd had to fly to the crash scene to identify her body— before the cosmetics. Luckily his insanity had been the mind-numbing kind. Those around him had mistaken his near-catatonic state for courage. He'd been the pillar of strength that had gotten the family through it. Only he had known how hollow that pillar had been— how full of tears and pain it was. The pain was still there—would always be there.

Mike had decided to retire from the Navy. His daughter needed at least one full-time parent, not one at sea for years. Giving up the Navy would have been almost as painful as losing Ellen, but Susan needed him. The Navy would survive without him; his daughter might not. But the Gulf War had canceled everyone's retirement plans.

When Mike returned from the Gulf, he'd been assigned management of the NESW development program. Navy personnel policy dictated that his next career move to be promotion to admiral or retirement: up or out. NESW management was the first of a series of increasingly responsible assignments he'd be given before being promoted or retired.

Mike had abandoned the idea of retiring to care for

Susan. The years Mike had been enmeshed in the Gulf War and its aftermath had transformed Susan into an independent young lady, and shore duty meant the end of long separations.

Mike got to his feet. He smiled. A good woman. Sailors' time-honored solution for the doldrums. Suggested by his own daughter? He shook his head in disbelief. Every day she surprised him with her maturity. His little girl had been replaced by a perceptive young woman. He felt a sense of loss. Who needed him now?

His mother-in-law's plump face twisted with disappointed when Mike told her that he'd have to skip breakfast. He had scheduled an early-morning meeting with Scott to review program plans.

Mike left his in-laws' large, rambling colonial house and began his hike to the King Street Metro Station. The house stood under stately trees at the end of a narrow lane, which twisted up a steep grade to King Street. Some of the neighboring mansions had been the homes of George Washington's cronies.

Mike's in-laws had insisted he and Susan live with them after Ellen's death. "Having Susan here . . . well . . . it'll be like having Ellen home again," Carrie had told him, her eyes moist. "Taking care of you two will keep us from missing Ellen so much."

Despite his in-laws' protests, Mike insisted on paying the same rent he'd paid for the Crystal City apartment he'd moved out of, and he paid half the utility and living expenses. He knew his in-laws needed the help. Real-estate taxes had skyrocketed, and Tim's pension wasn't indexed to inflation.

At the station Mike plunged into a river of people, sent his card through the automatic turnstile and reached the escalator just as a train arrived at the platform. He dashed up the escalator and pushed into a packed car just as the doors hissed shut.

*   *   *

Crystal City, Virginia

"It's hard to believe that Lesatec is the only organization working on this," Mike said. He and Scott were sitting at the small conference table crowded into Mike's office, along with a large wooden desk, three file safes, a wheeled cabinet with a VCR, TV and slide projector, and a computer workstation. A large window gave a panoramic view of the Potomac and the National Airport runways.

"It's unlikely anyone else has the same requirements," Scott replied. "Both battlefields and landfills contain a large variety of materials. Whether you want to destroy weapon systems or make trash biodegradable, you need a mixture of compatible agents. Ours are produced chemically; theirs are produced by genetically engineered microbes. Their microbes convert surface atoms into film molecules that are chemically identical to ours. The films spread far faster than the microbes themselves, and just like ours, make surfaces highly reactive to atmospheric constituents. They corrode instantly." Scott shook his head in wonder. "I still can't believe how fast the reactions take place. Seems to violate the laws of physics.

"Landfills are filling up with waste that's not biodegradable—plastics, metals, stuff like that. Lesatec claims that its thin-film combinations can make everything biodegradable, and even large masses can be transformed into ash. Volume can be reduced fantastically—extending landfill life by hundreds of years.

"Lesatec's developed supercomputer modeling and simulation programs that produce genetic codes for the microbes and also identify compatible film combinations. That computer software is what we need."

"But they claim to have developed the software with

their own money," Mike pointed out. "NSF contracted for development of waste-disposal techniques, not computer programs."

"But without NSF money Lesatec will go under before they can produce a salable product," Scott countered. "If NSF was to turn the screws hard enough, Lesatec would have to cooperate."

"But NSF is not chartered to do defense research, and its management doesn't want to pressure one of its contractors into supporting a classified weapons program," Mike explained. "NSF has promised full support, but only if I can work something out with Lesatec."

Mike's secretary, Lila Jones, hurried into the office. She was a slim black woman, with hair cut very short and large brass earrings hanging from her ears. "Your car is downstairs, Captain."

The Pentagon

The car delivered Mike to the Pentagon's Mall Entrance, which overlooks the Potomac. After stopping to let the guards scrutinize his badge, he walked along E-Ring to the winding staircase leading to the fourth floor. The wide stairs were flanked by massive wooden banisters. DoD reserved E-Ring for its top officials.

Mike climbed to the fourth floor and followed E-Ring to the sixth corridor. He walked through the corridor to B-Ring. Twenty yards into the B-Ring, a massive steel door blocked his way. It protected one of the many high-security areas buried in the bowels of the Pentagon.

Mike searched out Rear Admiral Kittering's office number on the directory posted beside a wall phone and dialed. He was informed an escort would meet him at the door. When the door clanked opened, a woman yeoman first class stepped into the hall. "Captain Boen?"

"Yes."

"Please, this way, sir." She ushered him through the door to a rigid-faced Marine guard. The guard carefully studied Mike's badge and face before allowing Mike and his escort to sign a logbook and proceed.

"Admiral Kittering will be right out, sir," the yeomen informed Mike as she ushered him into an empty conference room. "He would like to have a word with you before the others arrive." Mike took a seat at a long conference table, on which sat a chrome decanter of coffee, cream, sugar and foam cups. "Coffee, sir?"

"Black." The yeoman filled a foam cup with coffee, set it front of him and departed, passing Rear Admiral Kittering on the way in.

Mike rose swiftly to attention. "Please, sit down," said Kittering. He set a large coffee mug on the table and lowered himself into the chair at its head. He was a gruff, chunky man with white hair. His full face was weary, and the years showed in the deep wrinkles radiating from his flinty, black eyes. There appeared to be a thunderstorm lurking behind those eyes, a storm poised to descend on subordinates who displeased him.

"Captain, I want you to be clear on what I want you to get involved in before the others get here. I've talked to Mill and Brian; they are willing to loan you to me for a few weeks. But I want to give you a chance to say no."

Chance to say no! Mike rankled at the statement. The admiral knew he wasn't going to say no under any circumstances. If you wanted to stay in the Navy, you didn't say no to a flag, especially when that flag already had the concurrence of your bosses, who were also flags. Besides, the admiral wouldn't have asked him here without thoroughly checking him out, being sure Mike matched whatever job he had in mind. He would know Mike had lived on the edge of disaster his whole career and liked it.

"What I want you to do, Captain, is unofficial—not illegal or prohibited—but not authorized. It's way out there politically. If we blow it, it will raise an international stink. I'll be hung and so will you. You understand what I'm saying?"

"Yes, sir." Mike understood. Such operations were common in the Washington bureaucracy. What needed to be done would be made clear, but no one would ask that it be done or take responsibility for doing it. However, there was always an ambitious subordinate who would take it upon himself to get the job done. If the operation was a success, the subordinate would be rewarded with advancement. If the operation turned sour, the subordinate's bosses could truthfully deny authorizing the operation or having any prior knowledge of it. The subordinate was expected to take heat. Sometimes things got out of hand, rules of the game were broken and even bosses were fired or sent to jail.

Worry furrowed the admiral's forehead. "We won't go down alone either. I don't give a shit myself. Another year and I'll be retired—whether I like it or not. Trouble is I've called in a lot of markers on this one. Got a lot of people involved. This thing turns to shit, or the wrong people find out about it, everyone involved will be in trouble—big-time trouble. Because they trusted me. Because they're my friends. But I have a real bad feeling about this one, and your briefing yesterday made it worse.

"Getting involved in this could get you bounced out of the Navy, Captain. Maybe get you killed. I want you to be clear on that."

Mike didn't like what he was hearing. It sounded like Kittering wanted to involve him in a renegade operation. Kittering had a reputation as a cowboy. He had embarrassed the Navy enough times to prevent him from getting another star, despite a career of outstanding accomplishments.

The admiral waited for Mike's response with a stony face.

"I understand, sir. When are the others coming?"

"They're due now. Pour yourself another cup of coffee. This may take a while." A self-satisfied smile filled the admiral's face. He was sure he had his man. Mike wasn't so sure. If Kittering wanted him to do something illegal or something that would embarrass the Navy, Mike intended to refuse, no matter what the consequences.

The yeoman ushered two civilians into the room. "Good morning, Admiral," the older of the two said. He was a craggy-faced man with bright blue eyes under bushy brows. He had acne-scarred skin and a thicket of unruly, white hair. His nondescript brown suit was rumpled, and his tie clashed with everything he wore.

"Glad you could come on such short notice, Andy," replied the admiral, shaking his hand warmly. It was obvious that they were old friends.

"Glad to."

The admiral shook the other man's hand. "Sorry to make you come back, Mr. Desault. Understand I made you miss your plane."

"No problem, Admiral. I'm enjoying Washington, and anything that can help us clear this up will be greatly appreciated by my government." Desault spoke with a heavy French accent. He was a dark, slender man. His dark eyes matched his black hair and were set deeply in a long narrow face. He wore an expensive three-piece black suit.

"Gentlemen, I would like you to meet Captain Mike Boen," the admiral said. "He is going to help us with our problem. Mike, this is Andy Staples, CIA—better we don't discuss what he does there." Mike shook Staples's hand. Staples had the grip of a grizzly bear. "And this is Mr. Pierre Desault, representing the French government. Can't say what he does either."

Mike suppressed a flash of anger. The admiral was asking him to put his ass in a wringer and refusing to tell him who was turning the crank.

"Let's get started, gentlemen," said Kittering. "We don't want Mr. Desault to miss another flight." Staples took a seat next to Mike. The Frenchman sat across the table from them.

"Mr. Desault, would you please show Captain Boen the pictures?"

Desault lifted a slim briefcase to the tabletop and spun its twin combination locks. He removed a sealed envelope, tore it open, extracted a stack of photographs and spread them in front of Mike. They were aerial photographs of three helicopters resting on desert terrain. North Africa, Mike guessed. He suspected Chad. The French had been involved in repelling Libyans from Chad and extracting French and other foreign nationals when insurgents had overrun the country.

Two helicopters were large cargo craft, AS 332L Super Pumas. The third was a gunship, an AS 550C Ecureuil. There was little remarkable about the scene. The helicopters rested in a sandy area between two rocky ridges and appeared undamaged.

"Let me explain, Captain Boen," Staples began. "Correct me if I get anything wrong, Pierre. This is what's left of a quite potent force—superior to anything we know to exist in the area. They were on a . . . rescue mission. As you can see, they didn't come back."

"What happened?" Mike asked.

"That is what we'd like to know. None of the craft appear to be damaged—no reason they couldn't have used them to escape."

"Any survivors?"

"None," answered Desault. "We have high-resolution photos—which I could not get permission to take outside the country—which show the bodies. The commander radioed they had been attacked, and he was concerned about an airburst. He suspected a chemical weapon had been used.''

"Wouldn't that explain everything?" Mike asked.

"No," replied Desault. "They were prepared for such an eventuality, and there is nothing we know of that could act so quickly. Their transmissions stopped five minutes after they reported the burst."

"Did you send anyone in to investigate?"

"At the time we couldn't . . . for reasons I can't talk about. Now the range is beyond any resources we have in the region. And I must be truthful; my bureaucracy doesn't want to risk sending good after bad, as you Americans say. The original mission failed, and there is nothing left for us in this area—no reason to take more risks.

"I'm here pretty much on my own. I was given permission to talk with your analysts to ascertain if they can help determine what happened—if there is some chemical or biological threat we should be aware of."

"Is there anything more we need from Mr. Desault, Andy?" the admiral asked.

"No. I think that covers it."

"Well, let's let him go catch his airplane," said the admiral, rising and shaking Desault's hand. "Mr. Desault, we will do what we can and keep you informed." The admiral dialed for the yeoman, who escorted the Frenchman from the room.

"There is more data that we can't discuss with you, Captain," the admiral said after Desault's departure, "but I can tell you that your briefing yesterday could have been taken from what we know. We haven't let on to the French that we think it could be anything other than a new CW threat, but the people in that force didn't die from chemicals. They were overrun and shot. They had time to get those helicopters off the ground. They didn't do it. The people were in good working order, but their machines and weapons weren't.

"There is a Libyan chemical plant nearby—just across the border. The Libyans claim it's a fertilizer plant, but who the hell needs fertilizer in the middle of the desert? We believe it's a chemical-and-biological-warfare development facility. When we pressured them—threatened a strike—they closed it. That's when they started building the thing under the mountain. Recently they've reactivated some of the desert facilities—not enough for manufacturing, but enough for a test program. If the Libyans have developed and tested the technology that you briefed, we're in deep shit. Be the biggest terrorist threat we've ever faced."

Mike picked up a photo and studied it. A chill crawled up his spine. Could the Libyans have solved the weaponization problems? The chemicals required were available to everyone, and even a single-agent weapon might disable a helicopter. They would need a sophisticated laboratory to turn raw chemicals into a film agent, but it would be a lot easier than making a nuclear bomb. Libya was as capable as Iraq, and if the Gulf War hadn't intervened, Iraq would have joined the nuclear club. Advanced technology was no longer the exclusive province of the big guys.

The admiral and Staples watched Mike expectantly. He laid the photo back on the table. "It's possible," Mike mused. "Awful hard to believe, but possible."

"We need samples from the site," said Staples.

"And we need your experts to analyze them," Kittering added. "You've got the only organization in the country—maybe in the world—with the expertise we need."

"We'll put our best people on it, Admiral," Mike promised. "You just get us those samples."

"That's what we want you to do," replied Kittering.

A cold fist seized Mike's stomach. "I don't understand, sir."

"We need someone to fly to the site and collect samples, Captain. That someone must know what he's looking at. That someone needs to be qualified to fly the aircraft we have to use. That someone is you."

It *was* a renegade operation, just as Mike suspected. And Kittering had picked him to be the chief renegade. For the first time in his career, Mike considered refusing a mission. There was no way they could get official approval to fly into Chad with such flimsy evidence.

"What aircraft are you planning to use, Admiral?" Mike asked, his mind reeling with the implications.

"An AV-8B Harrier jump jet," Kittering said. "It has more speed and range than a helicopter, but can land vertically. Can't land a conventional fixed-wing aircraft anywhere near there. We've arranged for Air Force fighter escorts. We've put together quite an operation. Code name is Illogic."

Mike was aghast. He hadn't flown an AV-8 in seven years. And he didn't have enough hours to qualify him to fly a Harrier into North Africa on a secret mission.

"We've got to do this right away, Captain," the admiral said urgently. "The Libyans, Chadians, whoever is involved—and I wouldn't put it past the Russians or Chinese to be testing funny things out there—aren't going to let that stuff sit around very long."

Mike knew he could still refuse the mission, probably should, but they had to know if Libya had the NESW technology. And he had the best chance of finding out.

"I'll need some time in the Harrier, sir. It's been seven years." Mike had done a short exchange tour with the Marines, and had taken advantage of the opportunity for cross-training in support of a joint Navy-Marine avionics test-and-evaluation program. He had never expected to fly a Harrier again—certainly not on a real mission.

"I know how long it's been," Kittering said impatiently. "There's a Harrier for you at Pax." Pax was the Patuxent River Naval Air Station, located on the shores of Chesapeake Bay. It was a major aircraft-systems test facility and home of the Navy's test-pilot school. "The aircraft is configured the same as the mission bird. I want you down there by close of business tomorrow. You have a week to get yourself current."

"A week, sir?" Mike choked.

"One week. All you have to do is get the thing off the deck of an LHD and onto the ground and off again—once. If you can't get it back onto the boat, you can ditch it—as long as you save the samples. This mission is worth an aircraft.

"I suggest you get a move on, Captain," Kittering said, rising. As far as the admiral was concerned, everything was settled. "Hand off to your deputy—seems like a good man—and do whatever you have to do at home. A Navy car will take you down in the morning. I'll authorize pickup at your residence. Good luck, Captain, but I hope you don't need it." Kittering walked out of the door.

Chapter Five

Crystal City, Virginia

As she rode the elevator to her apartment, Dr. Julie Barns was almost too tired to stand. Julie was a lot of almosts. She was almost beautiful; her body was almost too tall and lean; her breasts were almost small; her almost long hair was almost black; her eyes were dark brown, almost black; and her face was almost too angular, its smooth planes sharply defining high cheekbones and jaw. The frustration and creeping fear weren't almosts. They made her question her decision to leave the cloistered security of the university for Lesatec.

Julie had been teaching genetic engineering and heading a small research project when Lesatec had offered her an obscene salary, the position of chief scientist and the opportunity to perform research in an area that excited her: pollution control. Julie believed that genetic engineering could be a potent new weapon in the fight against the pollution that threatened to overwhelm the world. The money didn't matter as much as the work. She couldn't resist the opportunity to improve the quality of life for hundreds of millions of people. The research excited her enormously and made her feel good about her work and herself. She would have worked for free.

The small technology company needed the prestige that Julie had brought with her. The papers she'd published in scientific journals made her a widely recognized expert in the genetic-engineering applications that the company was established to develop.

The program had exceeded Julie's wildest expectations. Her small group of young, enthusiastic investigators had succeeded where world-class experts with unlimited money and huge staffs had failed. No one else had developed simulation and modeling software that reduced the generation of genetic codes to a routine, computer-aided-design (CAD) process. They had also developed a biosystem model for waste-disposal sites, and had reduced microbe culture to a simple, automated process that could be performed with portable equipment. The digital tapes produced by a supercomputer could be used by a desktop personal computer along with the automated processor to select and produce the right mix of compatible microbes needed to manage varying waste loads and environmental conditions. But they had a major barrier to overcome before the system could be safely tested and used outside a sealed laboratory. No practical method for limiting the multiplication and life of the microbes had been developed. If not contained, the organisms would spread beyond disposal sites and run amok. Julie didn't want to think about the widespread devastation that might result. It made her sick to realize that she might have created a monster that could do more damage to civilization than all pollutants put together.

Thus far the team had only succeeded in containing the microbes by chemical means that were impractical outside the laboratory. Julie worried endlessly about the adequacy of the safeguards designed to prevent the microbes' escape.

Their efforts were now concentrated on genetic engineering of neutralizing microbes. These would feed only on the destructive microbes. The neutralizing microbes would die when all of the destructive microbes had been consumed, and the process would halt.

The effort had been handicapped by the loss of a key staff member. Omar Salim had been a foreign student who'd been hired after obtaining his Ph.D. Adept at both theory and practical engineering, he had designed the equipment that transformed digital data into living organisms. His genius was irreplaceable.

Omar had called in sick, and Julie had been shocked by his appearance when he returned to work two days later. He'd changed from a bright, energetic, handsome young man into a haggard bundle of raw nerves. A few weeks later he had vanished. Julie had concluded that he had returned to Chad because of a family crisis. It hadn't worried her that Omar had taken his notes with him, but it had worried company management a great deal. They'd suspected industrial espionage, and had hired private detectives to find Omar. The detectives had tracked him to the Baltimore Washington International Airport, and had concluded that Omar had returned to Chad, as Julie had suspected. Because the company didn't consider Chad a business threat, Julie had been able to convince them not to call in the FBI. She'd wanted Omar to be able to return without harassment.

Julie did worry that Omar might have taken dangerous cultures, which he might not be able to contain properly. She had no way of knowing whether he had taken copies of computer tapes with genetic codes, but she didn't consider that likely. They would be useless without computers and a genetic-engineering laboratory; Chad couldn't afford food for its children, let alone high-tech research facilities.

Julie now spent most of her time with her computer-software engineer, Saba Saunders. Lesatech had contracted with George Mason University for access to their supercomputer facilities, and Saba had a terminal connected to the GMU machine in her office. They were attempting to modify the supercomputer software in order to give it the capability to generate genetic codes for neutralizing microbes. The software had to be made to produce genetic codes for species entirely different from those for which it was originally designed: microbes that attacked other microbes, instead of materials. The modifications would make the software flexible enough to generate genetic codes for an endless variety of microbes and generate them thousands of times faster than the old software.

A computer-program bug had frustrated them for two months. The computer would grind away, produce a few bits of code, then spew out streams of nonsense. As weeks stretched into months, Julie's feeling of impending disaster grew. Somehow, some way, the microbes would escape from the laboratory and there'd be a holocaust.

Julie stepped off the elevator and forced her weary body down the hall to her apartment. When she unlocked and pushed open the door, hot, stuffy air rushed out. Julie berated herself for not having left the air conditioner running. She switched it on and stripped off her clothes in the living room under one of the air outlets. Despite the wash of cold air, she felt sticky and smelly. She made her way to the shower. The tingling spray revived her body, but didn't wash away the anxiety slithering around inside her. All it did was clear part of her mind for another worry: Captain Mike Boen and the Navy.

If NSF insisted, Julie feared her management might cave in and give the Navy what it wanted. Lesatec desperately needed additional NSF funding to complete development, and would do almost anything to keep NSF management happy. Julie had considered just giving up and letting the Navy have what it wanted. But she had never been able to just give up on anything she believed in without a fight, and she believed her research should not be used to kill people. The technology had been developed to save lives and improve the quality of life. Using it to kill and destroy was a perversion that she couldn't accept.

Julie shut off the shower and leaned against the wet wall. She was *so* tired. She considered calling Boen and pleading illness, but immediately dismissed the idea. She had this thing about commitments. She'd do almost anything to keep a promise.

Julie emerged from the shower wondering what the evening would be like. Mike Boen mystified her. She understood he was a "Top Gun," or something like that, and had fought in the Gulf War. But he didn't fit her image of a "Top Gun" person. His decisive, no-nonsense manner made it obvious he was used to being in command, but she couldn't picture him as a womanizing macho-maniac. Even more disconcerting was his talk of saving people, instead of killing them. He seemed sincere and honest and to truly care about people. Was it a slick facade that Navy aviators used to get women into their beds? Julie wondered. But it wasn't her pants Captain Mike Boen wanted to get into; it was her technology.

Julie examined herself in the mirror. She didn't like the tired, worried face that stared back. Stress? Yes. Age? But she was only thirty-two. The reflection depressed her.

She decided to wear something frothy and provocative. Wearing exciting clothes always lifted her spirits. She chose a long-sleeved, black dress that fit like a glove to the waist before exploding into a profusion of ruffles. She slipped her feet into matching high-heels, which she knew enhanced her firm calves. When she examined herself in the mirror she did feel better. Seemed years had dropped away. She smiled. Maybe the "Top Gun" would come on to her—reveal his true self and make it easier to resist his seductive pleas. The man sounded so reasonable and sincere. He made her wonder if *she* was the unreasonable one. If she could work up a healthy disgust for him, he'd no more get into her technology than into her pants.

At 1745, Scott finally stemmed the flood of Mike's detailed instructions. "I really won't screw things up that bad while you're gone," he protested. "Now get out of here! You're supposed to meet our good Dr. Barns at 1800. You got fifteen minutes."

"Damn! Forgot about that! I should have called it off. I have to pack, write checks for bills and do all of the stuff I haven't remembered yet."

"Well, it's a little late to call it off. She's probably waiting wherever you're supposed to meet her."

"I'm supposed to meet her in the Underground, have a drink, then go to Old Town for dinner. I'll have to cancel dinner. She's going to be pissed, and that won't help our cause a bit. Damn, Kittering could have given me a few days!"

Mike stuffed papers in his briefcase and rushed out of the office. He gave up on the interminably slow elevators and ran down the stairs. He hustled down the ramp to the Underground, and pushed his way through the rush-hour crowd to a restaurant bar adjacent to the food court. Julie had secured a corner booth, and a waiter was placing a large fruit-and-rum concoction in front of her when Mike arrived. Her appearance startled him. At their company meetings she'd always worn the standard businesswoman's uniform: dark-blue suit with straight skirt, low pumps and white blouse with red kerchief tied at the throat. She'd been a professional adversary, and he'd hardly noticed her femininity. He noticed it now.

"Sorry I'm late," he apologized as he slid into the seat across from her and pushed his briefcase under the table. He watched apprehensively for an angry reaction.

Instead she smiled. "It's all right."

"What's not all right is that I got shanghaied by an admiral today, and—"

"You don't have to explain, Captain Boen. You're only a half hour late, and I just got here myself."

"No, I need to explain, because I'm not going to be able to go to dinner tonight."

"Oh?" She looked more relieved than irritated.

"I've been ordered to report to Patuxent River tomorrow morning. A Navy car is picking me up at the crack of dawn, and I've got to pack, get my daughter squared away, write checks—and stuff I probably haven't even thought of yet. Look, I'll make it up to you when I get back," he offered. "You pick the place. Don't worry about prices."

"My dear captain, at your age you should know better than to make offers like that to women you don't know—even to ones you do."

"I throw myself on your mercy."

"You'll regret it," she warned, eyes twinkling. "Have time for a drink?" she asked.

"Yes. I need it." Mike ordered a rum and Coke from the waiter hovering near the table.

"Have you decided what you might be willing to give us?" Mike asked.

"I wasn't aware I'd been deciding to give you anything," she said brusquely.

72

"Look, maybe if I explain—"

"Captain—"

"Mike. It's Mike."

She stared at him a moment, reluctant to become that familiar with him. "Mike," she said uncomfortably, "I don't need any more explanations. Besides, you don't have the time tonight."

"You're right," he said heavily. "I don't have time, but if you change your mind, call my deputy, Scott Corbett. I have one of his cards."

"I won't be needing his number," she snapped.

"All right, but when I get back—"

"Captain—Mike, I'm not going to change my mind."

"Okay, but let me tell you about the program anyway," he persisted. He managed to keep the irritation she fueled out of his voice. The woman was as stubborn and unreasonable as a mule. "It's your field, and we may have something that interests you. I take it you want to save lives, and this really is about saving lives."

"All right," she agreed reluctantly. "I'll listen, but I warn you—"

"I know, you won't change your mind. I want to explain anyway, maybe get your opinion on some things."

"You already have my opinion."

"Peace! Like you say, no time to discuss it now, just time enough to piss each other off."

"I think we had better go," she suggested coldly. "You need to get home, pack and do whatever."

Julie took a long drink from her half-empty glass and got to her feet. Mike retrieved his briefcase and walked with her to her apartment-building elevator. "Sorry about tonight," he apologized. "Tell you what, we won't talk business over dinner and ruin our appetite. We'll set another time for that. I'll come out to your office, meet you at NSF, wherever.''

She regarded him suspiciously. "I guess that'll work—the no-business dinner," she finally said. "As for the visit—"

"Just think about it."

"I told you, I already have."

The elevator arrived and the doors slid open. "Good luck," she said as she entered. Her image remained embedded in his mind after the doors closed, affecting him in a way he couldn't understand.

Chapter Six

Red Sea

It was exhilarating to be at the controls of an aircraft sitting on a flight deck again, but it seemed unreal, like a dream. Ten days ago Captain Mike Boen had been sitting behind a desk piloting a pencil. He had believed his flying days to be over, but in a few minutes he would pilot the Harrier off the deck of an amphibious assault ship (LHD) cruising through the predawn darkness of the Red Sea. He kept wondering when he was going to wake up, but the roar of the engines was too real for a dream.

As Mike went through his checks, worry gnawed at his confidence. Despite a week of constant flying at Pax, he didn't feel comfortable with the aircraft. It was nothing like those he'd flown for so many years, and the aircraft configuration worried him. The Harrier had been stripped of its sophisticated avionics. The Litton AN/AS 130A inertial navigator had been replaced with a commercial Global Positioning System navigator. It was a handheld unit patched into the instrument panel. Mike doubted its accuracy and worried about its ability to survive the harsh aircraft environment.

He felt naked without the missiles carried on the Tomcats and Hornets he had flown. The Harrier's armament consisted of a five-barrel 25mm cannon on the port side of the fuselage fed by a 300-round container on the starboard side.

The Harrier was loaded to its maximum gross takeoff weight. The center station carried a large cargo pod. There were four 300-gallon fuel tanks mounted on the wing stations. Mike was making a 2600-mile round trip, and the ferry range was normally 2400 miles, but this Harrier's British configuration used the water-injection tanks for fuel, providing the added range he needed.

The weight made normal vertical takeoff and landing impossible, and there was no runway where he was going. The aircraft experts had assured him that with half the fuel gone, he'd be able to jump the Harrier into the air after a few yards' takeoff roll. They wouldn't say exactly how many yards: "Depends on terrain and atmospheric conditions."

The last item Mike checked was the timer. He watched it advance one minute, and a creepy feeling crawled up the back of his neck. The timer was wired to explosives laced throughout the plane. The timer would detonate the explosives in sixteen hours. A satellite signal, sent from an intelligence command post monitoring the operation, could override the timer and detonate the explosives on command. No one could stop the timer's inexorable march to destruction except Andy Staples, who was on the ship with a key—the only key that could turn the timer off—and he wouldn't be going along.

The elaborate precautions were designed to ensure

the aircraft did not fall into hostile hands. The plane would blow whether Mike was in it or not. Mike had the feeling the intelligence people would rather he be in it if something happened. That way he wouldn't be able to talk. They hadn't given him a cyanide pill, and his instructions were to tell the truth if he were captured—most of it anyway.

Andy's face had been grim, his eyes alert for any waver in Mike's resolve as he'd explained to him that he could expect to be tortured if captured—no matter how cooperative he was. It would be to his advantage to at first deny everything—hold out as long as he could to make his story convincing. Otherwise there would be nothing he could say to stop the torture. He was to admit that he was an American pilot on a covert mission to find out what had happened to the helicopters. It would cause a major diplomatic scandal, but he was to claim it was coordinated with the French. The French would be enraged, but they would get over it. Whether Pierre Desault would get over what the French would do to him was another matter. His bosses would be sure that he'd arranged the mission with the Americans during his trip to the States.

If the renegade operation went wrong there would be hell to pay. There would be no doubt in anyone's mind that once again the intelligence agencies had exceeded their authority and embarrassed the country. Heads would roll, but it probably wouldn't matter to Mike. He'd likely be dead or wishing he was.

Mike gave a thumbs-up to the deck officer and worked the engine-thrust controls. The Harrier trembled as vertical thrust increased. It felt as if it was going to dance off the deck despite the brakes. The deck officer dropped his arms, signaling that the restraints had been released. Mike went to full power and started his roll. He used up almost all of the LHD's 800-foot flight deck before he was able to urge the Harrier into the air.

Mike increased forward thrust and gained airspeed as quickly as he could. He hadn't flown the Harrier enough to shake the feeling he was teetering on top of a long pole when using vertical thrust, and he wanted to transition to normal flight as soon as he could.

When the Harrier gained enough speed to fly like a normal aircraft, Mike pulled it into a climb. He hoped the sea was calm when he brought the Harrier back aboard. He'd made over fifty landings during the week at Pax River, but forty of those had been onto a square painted on tarmac. He'd made ten landings on an LHD off Norfolk, but the sea had been calm. It had been seven years since he'd landed a jump jet on the deck of a ship pitching and rolling in rough seas, and that landing had been on the huge deck of an aircraft carrier. He wondered if he'd be better off taking Admiral Kittering's advice and ditching instead of landing if seas were rough. At least he wouldn't damage the ship or hurt anyone but himself.

Six more Harriers were orbiting the LHD at 20,000 feet, purposely making a fat radar target. Mike climbed to their altitude. The other Harriers were to give him navigation lead—tracking him with their IR sets until he broke off. He listened to the radio chatter, but did not join in. He maintained radio silence in order to reduce the possibility that he could be identified by radio-intercept gear and his absence noticed when the other Harriers returned to the LHD.

Mike took a fix with his jury-rigged GPS, and set a course for the Ethiopian coast. The Harriers drew into a formation tight enough to make it impossible for radar to accurately count the number of planes. Their course would threaten Ethiopian air space. While radars focused on that threat, Mike would be able to split off and dash for the Sudanese coast undetected. Two

F-117A stealth fighters were to rendezvous with him over Sudan. They would use their highly accurate navigation systems to escort him to the site. The F-117As didn't have enough fuel to provide cover while he was on the ground, and not knowing when he'd finish, they couldn't return to escort him out. They would ensure the area was secure; then he'd be on his own.

A hundred miles from the Ethiopian coast, Mike led the Harriers in a dive to 1000 feet and bored toward the shore at full power. Only a sophisticated airborne radar would be able to dig them out of the sea clutter. Every radar operator in the region would be convinced the Harriers were running under radar cover into Ethiopian airspace. Hopefully the diversion would cover Mike's sprint to Sudan.

Mike banked toward the Sudanese coast. He watched the instrument-panel clock. The other Harriers would be climbing now. They would level out at 10,000 feet and, clearly visible on everybody's radar, continue their dash toward the Ethiopian coast. While attention was focused on them, Mike would fly into Sudan.

Twenty miles from the coast, Mike reduced engine power. Ten minutes later the Harrier floated across the shore. Mike idled along for another ten minutes, then increased power and nosed the Harrier into a gentle climb. If the GPS was correct, he was heading for a pass through a range of coastal mountains.

Dawn revealed trackless desert below the Harrier. Mike checked the fuel gauges. Two ferry tanks were empty. He dropped them and checked the fuel gauges again. When he finished, he looked up and found an F-117A on each wing. They remained long enough to ensure he knew they were there, then climbed out of sight. They could cruise at high altitude without fear of detection.

Mike cruised at 1000 feet. The CIA experts had assured him there were no ground radars along his course and 1000 feet was below the radar horizon of anything but sophisticated airborne radars. The only such radars in this part of the world were a long way away and looking in other directions.

Chad

Mike and his escorts crossed into Chad and flew along its border with Libya. The site was in the mountains east of Aozou, just south of the border.

Mike topped a low ridge of mountains, and there they were: two Floggers. Mike didn't hesitate. He slammed on full power and jumped on the tail of the trailing plane. He put his pipper on the MiG's exhaust and armed and fired the 25mm cannon. There was a flash of fire from the Flogger's exhaust when the 25mm shells trashed the turbines. The Flogger turned into a huge blossom of flame.

Mike stood the Harrier on its wing and slammed into a six-g turn, but he didn't escape all of the debris. It rattled along the fuselage, and something swooped by the canopy. Mike stopped breathing, expecting the Harrier's engines to eat some parts and explode, but their roar didn't falter.

Mike allowed himself to breathe again, and looked for the other Flogger. He spotted it just before it turned into a shower of smoking junk. The F-117A pilot pulled up, and was more successful than Mike in avoiding the junk his weapons had created. The F-117A banked around and came up behind the Harrier, then eased in front. They were close to the landing site. The F-117A's navigation system would put them precisely on it. Would it be hot? The Floggers were not a good sign. Had one of the MiGs been able to get off a transmission? Mike didn't think so. It had all happened too quickly.

Even though he was less than a mile behind the stealth fighter, Mike had difficulty keeping it in sight; he kept losing it against the terrain background. He didn't know where the other fighter was—probably flying CAP and looking for more stray Libyan fighters. MiGs this far south were unexpected. The borders were quiet now that the main French force had pulled out. Maybe the French raid had stirred them up, Mike mused. Or maybe they were protecting a vital installation . . . maybe the nearby chemical plant.

Mike followed the F-117A from the flat desert into mountain foothills. The terrain below them was broken by jagged ridges and peaks. They climbed to 5000 feet to clear the mountainous terrain. Ten minutes later the F-117A slowed almost to stall speed. Mike checked his GPS. It said they should be on top of the helicopters, but when he rolled the Harrier to scan the terrain, he saw nothing. So much for the accuracy of his jury-rigged navagation system. How the hell was he going to find his way back to the ship?

The other F-117A dropped in front of him, alongside his wingman. Mike guessed that the pilot was reporting on the site. They were using covert transmitters, which probably employed spread-spectrum modulation and operated at some frequency no one else built radios for. He followed them over a ridge, and there were the helicopters.

Mike made a wide circle to check the area. He knew the F-117As had already checked. He would have been waved off if they had found anything, but doing it himself made him feel better.

The photo resolution hadn't been good enough to show the bodies. They were scattered along a ridge among the rocks. It was clear they'd been overrun. The helicopters appeared unscathed. An eerie feeling squirmed through Mike. The scene had all the earmarks of a CW attack, but that didn't explain the helicopters.

There were no bodies near them, and Desault had said they were prepared for chemical attack. Well, that was the mystery he'd come all this way to solve.

Mike decided it would be prudent to land some distance from the helicopters, in case guards were hidden among the rocks. He found a flat area just beyond a ridge. It was large enough to give him the short run he'd need to take off with the heavy load of fuel and cargo pod. The camouflage paint of the Harrier would make it hard to spot among the rocks. The surrounding ridges would hide the Harrier from aircraft, unless they flew directly overhead.

Mike lowered the gear, and fought the teetering feeling as he eased the Harrier down. The jet blast stirred up a storm of dust, and he lost sight of the terrain. He guided the Harrier toward the sandy surface using the plane's APN-194(V) radio altimeter. He had just decided his sink rate was too high when the gear slammed into sand. Mike shut off the engines. He worried about what the sand they had ingested had done to their innards.

Mike pulled off his helmet, released his straps and disconnected his g-suit. The dust had settled by the time he opened the canopy. He climbed from the cockpit and waved as one of the F-117As made a slow pass over him. It made another pass and then was gone— no roar, no smoke, no flare from an afterburner, just gone.

Mike had never felt so lonely. He got out of the g-suit. He wore a Marine combat uniform under it instead of a flight suit. He tossed the suit back into the cockpit and closed the canopy.

Mike took a step and sank into sand up to his ankles. It was going to be hell walking in the stuff, and it was hot—at least a hundred, and it felt like 210. He wondered if he'd made a mistake by landing so far away.

Mike crawled under the Harrier. The landing gear

was undamaged. The soft sand had saved him. But the tires were half buried in it. It was going to take a lot of power to lift them enough to roll. Mike scooted to the outsized cargo pod hanging from the center station. He took a wrench from a pocket, loosened an access panel and pulled a large backpack from the pod. He cringed at its weight. He *should* have landed closer.

Magazines for the 9mm Micro-Uzi strapped to his thigh were packed in the pod. He smiled grimly. They had provided him with enough ammo to kill an army. A bad feeling made him stuff a dozen magazines in the pack and find a space for six more in his pockets, despite their weight.

The pack contained bags with gas-proof and germ-proof seals for the samples. Two were several feet long, which when filled were going to be too large for the pack. Somehow he was going to have to carry both them *and* the loaded pack, or make two trips.

Mike lifted a large canteen of water from the pod and took a long drink. He debated leaving the heavy container. He hoped to return in two or three hours, and believed he could last that long without water. But probably not in this heat, he decided. He put it in the pack.

Mike replaced the panel and screwed down enough fasteners to retain it and keep out the dust. He wrestled the pack onto his back, tightened its straps and started for the ridge.

The walk through the soft sand proved as exhausting as he feared. Footing was firmer among the rocks. Walking there was easier but more hazardous, because of loose gravel and rock.

At the top of the ridge, Mike looked down on the deserted helicopters. They rested in a large sandy area. The bodies he'd spotted from the air were out of sight along the crest of a ridge beyond the machines.

Mike lowered the backpack to the ground, dragged

it into the shadow of a large boulder and removed the canteen. He fought off his thirst and limited himself to a few judicious swallows. Mike realized he'd underestimated the physical demands the harsh desert would make on him. He breathed hard from the climb up the ridge, and fatigue dragged at his legs. The hot air felt like the inside of an oven, and he knew there wasn't enough water in the canteen to keep up with dehydration.

Mike replaced the canteen, and removed a pair of compact binoculars. He squatted against a rock to steady himself, and slowly scanned the terrain around the helicopters. They were 50-power zoom glasses in a surprisingly light and small package: spook stuff, he guessed. Mike carefully examined each crevice for a concealed guard. He decided to wait another thirty minutes before approaching the craft; if anyone was out there, maybe they'd grow impatient and reveal themselves by moving.

Mike grew nervous as he waited. The silence oppressed him. He'd never been in such a barren place. No insects buzzed about. No vegetation. Just dust and rocks. No breeze stirred the searing desert air. It could have been the surface of the moon.

After twenty minutes, Mike decided there was more danger in waiting than getting on with it. He put on the pack and started for the helicopters. He carried the Uzi in one hand, his finger on the trigger.

When he reached the first helicopter, Mike scanned the surrounding ridges with the binoculars once again. He shrugged out of the pack and climbed through an open side door. He examined the cockpit first. Everything seemed to be in order, except that the mechanical gauges indicated the engines were running. Mike sat in the pilot's seat. He tried the stick and the pedals. He couldn't move them. He flipped on the power switches.

The instrument panel glowed dimly. He tried the starter. The lights went out. Spooky.

Mike left the helicopter and obtained a tool kit from the pack. He knew exactly what parts to remove. Scott had joined Mike at Pax River, and they had spent hours pouring over diagrams of the French helicopter furnished by the CIA. They'd selected mechanical and electronic parts most likely to have been damaged by their film agents.

Scott had believed microcircuit boards would be vulnerable to a variety of agents. There were the connector pins, printed-circuit interconnections and the microcircuit chips themselves. Each was composed of different materials, and thus a board could be disabled by a variety of agents. The microcircuit chips would be the most vulnerable, since the dimensions of their connecters and components were only a few microns. The microcircuits could be inserted into an automatic tester, which would pinpoint circuit problems: shorts, broken connections and dysfunctional semiconductors. Once the circuit problems were identified, high-resolution X-ray imagers could be used to pinpoint physical damage and provide clues as to what had caused it.

They had also selected a radio-transmitter circuit board and a key component of the flight control system: a multiplexer module. The module encoded signals from the pilot's manual controls and distributed them along the fiber-optic cables of the helicopter's fly-by-wire control system. Both were easily accessible. They had decided that bearing surfaces would be most likely to show mechanical damage. These mechanical and electronic parts spanned the effects of all of the agents they had considered for NESW.

Mike decided to start with the radio. He had difficulty loosening the panel fasteners. They appeared corroded, as if the helicopter had been operated for years in an ocean environment. Mike pried out the radio transmitter and extracted the board they'd selected. Even without any fancy diagnostic equipment, he could see the board was inoperative. The edge connectors were green with corrosion. No power or signals could reach the board.

The multiplexer module didn't show obvious damage. Its glass fiber-optic signal-cable connector parted easily. It, too, showed no obvious damage, but corrosion had made the module's metal power connecter useless.

Mike sealed the parts in bags, stuck the tools in his pocket and left the helicopter. He put the bags in the pack and got out the wrenches he needed to remove the tail-rotor shaft. Like the panel fasteners, the bolts securing the shaft were corroded. He broke half before he was able to loosen the bearing housings. It took a half hour to hammer out the shaft.

Mike unrolled a long bag and sealed the shaft inside. The bag had a carrying strap. He could hang it from his shoulder like a rifle, but carrying two was going to be difficult. They had decided to obtain duplicate parts from each of the Super Pumas in order to verify the nature of any damage.

Mike was exhausted by the time he extracted the parts from the other craft. Sweat soaked his clothes. The inside of his mouth was parched. His lips were cracked, despite a liberal coating of balm. His face was raw, and his eyes burned.

Mike collapsed in the shade of a helicopter and took long swallows from the canteen. He decided he'd rather be sick than so thirsty. The canteen was half empty before he controlled himself. His stomach felt queasy, but he didn't throw up.

Mike got to his feet, and stared up at the ridge where the bodies lay. His stomach turned over at the thought of what he'd have to do up there. He checked the seals on the bags containing the parts, and piled them under a helicopter. There was no point in lugging them up the ridge with him. He had to pass by the helicopters on his way back to the Harrier. He could pick them up then.

As Mike neared the top of the ridge, he found patches of bloodstained sand. Whoever had attacked the French had suffered a lot of casualties. They had removed their dead, but had left the French to rot in the sun.

The first bodies Mike found lay grouped in a small depression surrounded by boulders that offered cover. The stench was overpowering. Mike felt woozy, and leaned against a boulder to steel himself before he continued.

Despite their advanced state of decomposition, it wasn't hard to tell what had killed this group. Grenades had left gaping wounds, and several bodies were missing limbs. Lumps of rotting flesh dotted the sand. Mike fought down his nausea and continued along the ridge. He needed a body count, and he needed to find a body in good enough condition to provide usable specimens. Contemplation of what he'd have to do to get the specimens sickened him more.

Mike found three more clusters of bodies. There was a total of thirty bodies. All but six wore uniforms. The six civilians included two women. They had been well armed: heavy machine guns, grenade launchers and submachine guns. They should have been able to fight off a small army and escape in the helicopters, except that the helicopters couldn't fly. Even so, they should have been able to hold off their attackers until they ran out of ammo. They *hadn't* run out of ammo. The bodies were draped with bandoliers of it, and there were belts of 7.62mm ammo for their Mle 24/29 machine guns.

Mike picked up an MAS38 submachine gun and tried the action. It was frozen. He tried several other weapons. Same thing. That explained the unused ammo.

Mike shrugged off the pack and opened it. He wanted to stop and rest, but didn't dare. If he stopped and thought about it, he might not be able to do what he had to do. Mike tied a scarf around his neck and tugged it up over his nose. He took a medical kit from the pack and opened it. It contained specimen jars, two scalpels, a small pair of forceps and other instruments. A Navy doctor had instructed him in their use. The doctor had wanted him to practice on a cadaver, but there hadn't been time.

Mike and Scott had agreed with Staples that they had to rule out chemical or biological attack. The only way to do that was to collect specimens from the bodies.

Mike pulled on rubber gloves and selected a male who lay in the shade of an overhanging rock, which shielded the body from the ravages of the sun. What had been a young man lay on its back, so bloated that his uniform had split. The flesh had sloughed from his face, and rotting lips exposed his teeth in a macabre grin.

Mike tried to hold his breath as he cut away the shirt. He searched for a patch of skin that had not been completely devastated by decay. He found it under the breastbone. He outlined a square patch with scalpel cuts. The skin disintegrated when he tried to pull it away from the body. The wound oozed something dark and disgusting.

Mike picked what he thought was an area in better shape. He carefully peeled the skin away with the scalpel. He deposited it in a specimen jar and screwed on the top.

Mike paused a moment, bracing himself for the horrible thing he had to do next. He made an incision just under the breastbone and parted the flesh. The wave of stench made him gag, but he didn't stop. He dug through organs, almost frantic now. He needed to finish before he lost it, and he was losing it fast.

Mike found the lung. He started to tear it from the body, but managed to regain control of himself. He iced his mind and carefully cut away a section, and got it into a jar without it coming apart.

Mike removed a small saw from the kit and aligned it on the skull. The saw cut swiftly, and before he had time to think about what he was doing, the man's brain was exposed. Mike cut out a section, sealed it in a jar, then hurriedly loaded everything into the pack. He rushed away from the bodies at almost a run.

Mike was twenty yards away before he stopped himself. If he didn't pace himself, he would never make it back to the plane, and they needed to know what had happened to the weapons. Mike reluctantly trudged back to the bodies. He picked up a 9mm PA/5 automatic lying near an outstretched hand. He tried the action. It was frozen, as he expected. He sealed it in a bag and stowed it in the pack. He started off again, this time at a rational pace. Then he heard the unmistakable beat of helicopter blades.

Chapter Seven

Chad

Mike scrambled into a crevice underneath overhanging rocks, which almost formed a cave. Two helicopters came up over the ridge. One was a Hind-F gunship. The other was a Hip-H cargo craft. Both had Libyan Air Force markings. The Hip-H was rigged like a crop duster. Two long arms with spray nozzles had been attached to the external-stores stations.

The helicopters swept across the site toward the far ridge. Mike's heart sank. He was sure they would see the Harrier. But the helicopters stopped short of the crest, hovered and turned. The gunship climbed slowly while the Hip-H drifted back at low altitude. The spray came on, and it laid a deep carpet of blue mist behind it.

Mike got the pack off, opened it and searched frantically for the gas mask stowed in it. He found it and got it on just as the mist drifted over him. He breathed shallowly, hoping the mist wasn't some new agent capable of penetrating the mask or something like mustard gas that attacked the skin.

The Hip-H made two more passes. Mike breathed normally. The mist seemed to have no effect on him. The helicopters orbited the area for another ten minutes before landing. The Hip-H landed first, and six heavily armed Libyan soldiers jumped to the sand as the pilot shut off the engine and the rotor wound down. The Hind-F came in slowly and settled beside it. The men weren't wearing gas masks, though the air remained hazy. Mike pulled his mask off and shoved it back into his pack. Angry frustration filled him. He'd almost had it done! Now he was cut off from both the Harrier and the samples.

A civilian emerged from the Hip-H and carried a large aluminum suitcase to the nearest French helicopter. He shoved it through the door, then disappeared after it. A few minutes later he scrambled from the helicopter, waving his arms and yelling at the soldiers. He'd obviously discovered the missing parts. An officer ran toward the helicopter. A soldier yelled and pointed to the other French helicopter. He'd spotted the bagged parts lying beneath it. Mike crumbled inside.

The officer gave some orders, and the men took defensive positions around the French helicopters. The officer rushed to the gunship and yelled at the pilot. The rotors started turning. Mike's heart sank. If the gunship found the Harrier on the ground he was finished.

Mike pulled the Micro-Uzi from its holster and rested it on a rock. He was too far away to hit anything, but they would know they were being shot at, and that their adversary was in the rocks above them. As long as they were chasing him, they wouldn't find the Harrier. He might be able to work his way back through the rocks to the Harrier and get it in the air.

Mike aimed high and emptied the magazine. To his surprise, one of soldiers fell and a few rounds pinged off the gunship. The Libyans dropped to the ground and sprayed the surrounding rocks with automatic-weapons fire. They had no idea where he'd fired from, only that he was in the rocks above them.

The gunship engine screamed to life and the helicopter beat its way skyward. It swept a large arc before returning.

Mike scooted further back in the crevice and watched the gunship fly back and forth over the rocky ridges. It finally slowed and hovered over the bodies. Then it started to drift toward him. Mike's gut tightened. They'd spotted his tracks in the soft sand.

Mike shoved a fresh magazine into the Uzi, thinking what a pitiful weapon it was against a gunship. The sound of the rotors told him it had slowed to a hover. They'd lost his tracks in the rocks. The rotor beat picked up, and the helicopter passed over him. The overhanging rock shielded him from view. Its sound faded as the pilot searched along the crest, then grew again as the helicopter flew slowly back along Mike's side of the ridge. He felt cold in spite of the desert heat. They were about to find him. Hell of a place for a Navy officer to die, in the damn desert! He wondered what they'd tell his daughter and in-laws. There'd be no body.

Mike crammed a full magazine in the Uzi.

It happened suddenly.

He hadn't believed the helicopter was that close.

Hadn't believed it could come so close.

But there it was.

He stared through the gunship's windshield.

He locked eyes with the pilot's.

They were as startled as his.

Mike's body didn't wait for his brain. His finger squeezed the trigger, and the magazine was empty before he realized he was firing. The helicopter's windshield cracked. The helicopter tipped slowly backward, as if it were falling off a ladder. It didn't go far. The tail rotor struck the rocks. A screeching blast of sound deafened Mike. The gunship seemed to be dissolving into the rocks, tail first, spewing pieces of metal which spanged off the boulders. Then the rotors struck. A large piece clanged against a rock above Mike's head. The gunship turned into a fireball that washed a wave of heat up over the rocks and turned Mike's crevice into an oven. Mike squeezed his eyes shut and held his breath. He could smell his hair burning. He was sure his eardrums had burst.

When he dared breathe again, Mike opened his eyes. He knew his eyebrows were singed, and his face felt blistered. The shock wave had made him drop the Uzi. He found it and jammed in a fresh magazine. He couldn't see down the ridge. The burning gunship had covered the area with blinding, choking smoke.

Mike scrambled out of the crevice dragging the pack after him. He got it on and stumbled through the smoke, falling and climbing over rocks. He had to escape while the smoke still provided cover. The sound of the other helicopter taking off spurred him on.

Mike was gasping with exertion by the time he was far enough away from the burning wreck to risk crossing the open desert to the other ridge. He dropped behind an outcropping of rock to gather his strength and locate the other helicopter, which he could hear in the distance.

A pall of smoke still cloaked the top of the ridge. He could see the helicopter circling slowly, keeping its distance. It had taken off to fly out of danger rather than come after whoever had shot down the gunship. In his haste the pilot had taken off alone. The other Libyans were crouched behind one of the French helicopters, attempting to see through the smoke. One, with a 7.62mm RPK machine gun, scattered a few random bursts across the rocks, hoping to stir some movement or get lucky.

Mike got to his feet. His best chance to escape was while attention was riveted on the crash site. The Libyans had no way of knowing whether there was one man or a battalion of people hidden in the rocks. Mike tightened the backpack's straps and sprinted across the sand.

He thought he was going to make it unseen until he heard the fast-approaching helicopter. He looked back. The Libyans were running after him. The helicopter was coming down on him. Mike forced more from his tired legs. His breath came in desperate gasps. Then the helicopter was on him, stirring up a choking storm of dust. The dust saved him. The Hip-H pilot lost him in the swirling cloud. As the pilot pulled up, Mike stumbled in among the rocks. The pilot spotted him again, and came after him. Mike scrambled up the side of the ridge, seeking cover.

Mike's foot came down on a loose rock, and he spilled on his face onto gravel. He rolled onto his back. His face and hands were bloody, and he was blinded by the dust in his eyes. He pointed the Uzi at the helicopter's sound and loosed a long burst. The helicopter's turbines screamed and the sound receded in the distance.

Mike squeezed his eyes tight to produce tears, and managed to blink enough dust out of his eyes to see again. Things were blurry, but he could see the helicopter hovering in the distance. He hadn't done any damage, but after what had happened to the gunship, the Hip-H pilot was taking no chances. He'd contented himself with hovering at a safe distance and directing the Libyans on the ground to Mike.

Mike struggled to his feet and scrambled over the rocks. He knew he wouldn't make it. He was too tired, the pack too heavy and his pursuers too fresh.

A burst of automatic-weapons fire sent bullets buzzing by him to whine off the rocks and shower him with chips.

Mike rounded a boulder and stopped. He pulled the half-empty magazine from the Uzi and replaced it with a full one. He stuck another in his belt. He could hear the scrape of his pursuers' boots as they climbed over the rocks.

Mike stepped from behind the boulder and came face-to-face with a tall, lean Libyan who had outdistanced his companions. A burst from Mike's Uzi turned his chest to hamburger. He was so close his blood splattered Mike.

Instead of fleeing, Mike dashed toward the Libyans, firing. They were so shocked to see their quarry charging instead of fleeing, Mike was able to cut down two more before they could react and scurry for cover.

The Libyans recovered from their surprise and fired wildly. Mike rolled into a small ravine and slapped another magazine in his Uzi. He waited for a pause in the firing, then raised himself enough to rake the Libyans with another burst. He bolted to his feet and dashed to another rock. A storm of AK-47 rounds chased him. When the firing stopped, he stepped from behind his cover to loose another short burst. Two Libyans burst from behind a rock and ran for cover further down the ridge.

Mike turned and scrambled up the ridge. His surprise counterattack had provided him time enough to make the top.

As Mike crested the ridge, the helicopter closed in again, but it pulled up and hovered well out of range of his little Uzi. There was no gunner on board, or Mike would have been a dead man.

The Libyans on the ground resumed pursuit, but they moved cautiously and slowly, pausing frequently to carefully search the broken terrain ahead of them. The spray of 9mm slugs had punched holes in their radio, as well as their radioman. They had no communications with the helicopter. They could only guess Mike's position from the location of the hovering helicopter, and they feared Mike would step out from behind something and surprise them again. They were being so careful and slow that Mike believed he had a chance to make it—if only his body held out. His heart was trying to hammer its way out of his chest, and his legs were wobbly. Each breath felt like the flame of a blowtorch flashing into his lungs. His mouth was as dry as the desert, and his vision was none too clear. The pack made it difficult to maintain his balance, and its weight was crushing. But damn if he'd give up. He wasn't going to drop the pack, even to save his life.

Mike was lucky. The helicopter pilot was so intent on tracking him that he didn't see the Harrier until Mike was fifty yards from it. Mike drew strength from somewhere and sprinted the last yards. The helicopter pilot hovered, trying to decide what to do. He had no guns, and Mike's Uzi was too dangerous to let him get close enough to ding the plane with his landing gear. All he could do was hover out of range and hope the others would arrive in time.

Mike stripped off the pack and raised the canopy. The ground pursuers spotted the plane. They loosed a few bursts. They were beyond the range of their AK-47s, but a few rounds ricocheted perilously close.

Mike stuffed the pack between the seat back and the raised canopy. The pack prevented the canopy from closing, but there was no help for it. He clambered into the seat, sitting on his g-suit. The helicopter came for him again. The pilot believed Mike couldn't fire from the cockpit. Mike held the Uzi out beyond the canopy, pointed it skyward and emptied the magazine. There was no prayer of hitting anything, but it scared off the helicopter pilot.

It was cramped. Mike frantically worked the switches and got the turbine spinning. The engine started with a belch of flame. An AK-47 round popped a tire, which deflated with a loud hiss. Mike jammed on full power and vertical thrust. The Harrier plowed across the sand and jumped into the air. Mike fought for control. He rotated the craft toward his pursuers. They sent a storm of AK-47 fire after the Harrier. Mike armed the five-barreled cannon and pressed the firing button. The 25mm rounds exploded among the rocks. One of his pursuers disappeared in a cloud of bloody mist. The rest dove for cover. The helicopter climbed at full power.

Mike desperately juggled vertical and forward thrust and forced the careening craft to rise. He pointed the Harrier toward a gap in the ridge, and increased forward speed until the roar of wind told him his canopy was about to tear off. The added wing lift gave him better control, and the Harrier ceased its dangerous pitching and yawing. Mike twisted in the seat and managed to drag the pack over his head. He wedged it between himself and the top of the instrument panel.

Mike jammed an arm under the pack and felt for the canopy switch. He had to lift the pack to reach it. He crammed the pack back down as the canopy whirred shut. He could get more airspeed now, but he was wedged in so tight he could hardly move. He pushed the throttle forward. The Harrier accelerated to 200 knots and stabilized.

Mike struggled into a position from which he could do more than just keep the plane in the air. He searched for the Hip-H. It was fleeing the area at ten thousand feet. Mike went after him.

Mike zoomed up behind the helicopter and loosed a

short burst from his 25mm cannon. The Hip-H exploded into a shower of burning debris.

Mike spotted only two people when he made a low pass over the French helicopters: the civilian and a heavily armed soldier. He banked around a tight circle and saw them running for the rocks. He slowed almost to a hover, and sent a burst of 25mm after them. The soldier turned into a limp, burning rag doll. The civilian fell, staggered to his feet again and disappeared among the rocks. Mike turned the Harrier and headed back to the helicopters. The civilian was no longer a threat, and Mike had neither the fuel nor ammo to chase him.

Mike eased the Harrier toward the ground as slowly as he could. The pack blocked his view of the instrument panel. He had to land without the radio altimeter. Anxiety cramped his innards.

The Harrier jolted onto the sand and settled with a worrisome tilt toward the side with the trashed tire. Mike let out a long sigh of relief.

He opened the canopy and pushed the pack out of the cockpit. It fell to the ground. He followed it.

Mike ran to the helicopter under which he had stashed his samples. They weren't there. Even taking apart the rotting bodies hadn't made him as sick. Had they been on the Hip-H? Mike pushed away the shock and began a methodical search.

He found the sealed bags fifty yards away. They had been ready to load them onto the Hip-H when the exploding gunship had caused the pilot to bolt. He dragged the bags to the Harrier and opened the cargo pod. He stuffed everything in the pod, unwired a red-handled lever and yanked it. Nitrogen hissed into a plastic bag, which expanded to fill empty space in the pod and keep the contents in place.

Mike had just screwed down the last fastener when he sensed a presence behind him. Before he could react, a pistol barrel jabbed the base of his skull. "Do not move." The English was heavily accented. "Let me explain. I must decide whether or not to kill you. Do not make the decision for me by moving. My superiors most certainly would desire to ask you for some information. They might be disappointed if *I* kill you. But it would be safer. And it would make me feel much better. You killed my pilot. He was my friend. We flew together for many years. I am angry. Very angry."

The Hip-H copilot. The pilot had taken off without him, and he had probably been hiding in one of the disabled helicopters.

The Libyan was quiet for a long time. Mike's mind raced, searching for a way out. "I have decided," the Libyan finally said. "Now you must decide . . . whether to do exactly as I say or die now." He let the statement hang in the air. "You might wish to die now. I have decided not to kill you, because of the manner in which you will be interrogated. I have neither the skills nor instruments to make you suffer as much. However, you can spare yourself much pain," the Libyan suggested. "All you have to do is move before I tell you to, and your death will be quick. And I will have the satisfaction of killing you myself."

Mike stayed frozen. He breathed shallowly, tensed against the bullet that might splatter his brains at any moment. He couldn't help considering the Libyan's offer. He didn't know what he might say under torture, and it certainly would be an unpleasant way to die. Mike decided to die trying to escape, not screaming in pain. He had a chance. The man was a pilot, not a trained killer. He might make a mistake.

"Back toward me, *very* slowly," the Libyan ordered. The gun barrel jabbed Mike's neck painfully to emphasize the order, then withdrew.

Mike inched carefully backwards. As he cleared the plane, the gun jabbed the base of his skull again.

"Stop!" the Libyan ordered. "Now, stand up. Slowly." Mike complied. The gun barrel stayed against Mike's neck as he rose. He felt a glimmer of hope. The man wasn't trained in the use of small arms. Otherwise he would have backed off to put himself out of reach before he let Mike stand.

"Now, turn a—" The Libyan didn't have the chance to finish the sentence. Mike spun backward, jolting into him.

The gun barrel slipped to the side of Mike's neck.

An explosion filled Mike's head.

Agony seared his neck.

Mike smashed an elbow into the Libyan's gut.

The Libyan grunted and dropped his pistol.

Mike smashed a fist into the man's face. Bone crunched. The Libyan staggered backward. Mike followed, seized a shoulder and spun him around. Mike got behind him and wrapped his right arm around the Libyan's neck. The man struggled feebly, shocked and dazed by the sudden onslaught.

Mike had learned this tatic long ago in basic training, but had never used it. He placed his left palm against the side of the man's head, and gave a sharp push while tightening his hold around the man's neck.

The copilot's neck didn't break.

Mike choked him to death.

The man struggled a long time.

He made horrible gurgling sounds.

He defecated.

The stench was terrible.

Mike lowered the man to the ground, breathing hard from exertion and emotion. He heard yells in the distance. His pursuers were running down the ridge.

Mike climbed into the cockpit. He pulled on his helmet and started the engine while lowering the canopy. He could hook everything up later and do without the g-suit. Puffs of dust from bullet impacts marched closer. The engine whined into a roar. Mike jumped the Harrier into the air. He accelerated just above the ground to put distance between him and the AK-47s, then pointed the Harrier's nose skyward.

Foxbat

Colonel Muhammad Aziz flew the Foxbat at 40,000 feet. The Foxbat had been designed thirty years ago to counter the high-altitude threat of the Mach-3 B-70 strategic bomber then under development by the U.S. Air Force. Emphasis had been placed on high-speed, high-altitude capability and a radar-missile combination that would permit long-range attack. It was not a very maneuverable aircraft and not well suited for intercept of modern, highly maneuverable tactical aircraft operating at low altitudes. But it was still one of the fastest of the MiGs, capable of flying at over 123,000 feet.

Aziz's craft was a MiG-25M, a Foxbat-A converted to a Foxbat-E. Radar improvements and other equipment had been provided to give the E model limited lookdown/shootdown capability. The engines had been upgraded to 30,865 pounds of thrust.

Aziz wanted to see for himself what the biotech weapon had done to the French. He was also worried about security. Gadhafi knew nothing of the weapon and its testing. It would be fatal to Aziz if he found out.

Aziz had intercepted some puzzling radio transmissions that worried him even more. First there had been a noisy fragment from one of the two Floggers that he had dispatched to ensure no other aircraft strayed over the battle site. Then there had been a garbled transmission from the combat site which had been suddenly cut off. The Hip-H had a powerful radio on board, but

Aziz hadn't been able to contact it. He had the feeling that something was terribly wrong.

Aziz turned on his Fox Fire radar and climbed. He was at 20,000 feet, and could see the site when the radar picked up a target moving away at high speed. Aziz jammed the two Tumansky R-15BD-300 turbojets to full power. The Floggers wouldn't be streaking for Sudan at low altitude. It had to be an intruder. But what had happened to the Floggers?

Aziz pulled out of his dive five miles behind the intruder. The Foxbat was traveling at 600 knots, and the distance between the two aircraft shrank rapidly.

Aziz was shocked when he recognized the Harrier. Fear bolted through him. This had to be an intelligence-collection aircraft. How much did the Americans know? Aziz armed an Archer missile. Whatever they knew, the Harrier pilot wouldn't add to their knowledge.

The whine in his earphones told Aziz the Archer missile was locked on, but he hesitated. He could see the craft had no missiles, only three large pods. Intelligence craft were usually lightly armed, if armed at all. The Harrier should present little threat to the heavily armed Foxbat. Aziz decided to take a closer look before he blasted the Harrier out of the sky. He pulled the Foxbat into a vertical climb, demanding all the power the twin Tumanskys had to give. He hadn't seen any missiles, but he could be wrong, and no doubt the Harrier had a gun. Aziz didn't intend to take any chances.

Aziz looped behind the Harrier again. He cursed the Foxbat's lack of maneuverability, and decided jockeying for a closer look was too dangerous. He'd destroy it on this pass. Downing the low-flying Harrier with weapons systems designed for high-altitude intercept was not going to be easy. The clutter—false signals from the rocky desert background—made it difficult for his missiles to home on the target. The MiG-25 didn't have a gun. Aziz backed off the power and lifted the Foxbat's nose. The craft lost altitude. Flying the Foxbat at low altitudes was tricky, dangerous and awkward, but if he got below the Harrier, so that it was between him and the uncluttered sky, his missiles would have no trouble homing on the target.

Chapter Eight

Harrier

Mike checked the fuel gauges again, not wanting to believe what they told him. He'd barely make the coast. If he had to hunt for the LHD, he'd go in the drink.

When the MiG roared by, Mike's breath stopped. He recognized the aircraft climbing away as a Foxbat. A steel band clamped Mike's chest. His Harrier—designed for close support of ground forces—was no match for a hot fighter, let alone a sophisticated interceptor like the Foxbat. And his AV-8B had been stripped of avionics, had no missiles and was loaded with two ferry tanks and the cargo pod. It was a fat, lumbering, defenseless target.

The Foxbat disappeared behind the him, and Mike knew the pilot was lining up for a firing pass. Mike pulled the Harrier's nose up. It decelerated and lost altitude. He couldn't outrun the Foxbat, but he knew it would be virtually impossible for the Foxbat's missiles to hit a slow, maneuvering target against a terrain background. Maybe by some miracle, he'd get a chance to use his gun.

Foxbat

Aziz cursed. He was going to overrun the Harrier. He rolled the Foxbat into a port turn, the g-force crushing him in his seat and graying his vision. He flew perpendicular to the Harrier's course a few moments, allowing the gap between the two aircraft to widen. He snapped into another turn and crossed behind the Harrier before turning again to complete an S. He pushed up the nose to dump speed, and pulled behind the Harrier. He worked the Foxbat into a high yo-yo: he pulled the stick back and climbed. At 8000 feet, he rolled the Foxbat onto its back and pulled into a dive. When he rolled upright and pulled out, he had the Harrier against the sky, but it was slowing so rapidly he couldn't lock up a missile.

Harrier

Mike's skin crawled; he couldn't see it, but he knew the Foxbat's pilot was preparing to fire a missile up his ass. Mike deployed the air brake. Airspeed dropped to ninety knots. Mike knew the Foxbat couldn't fly much below 140 knots without falling out of the sky. He armed his gun.

The Foxbat went by, almost taking off the Harrier's wing. Its nose was high, and its engines were at full power, struggling to keep the Foxbat flying at low speed. Obsessed with getting off a missile, Aziz had made one of those stupid mistakes even the best sometimes make: he'd let his airspeed drop too far. Mike centered the Foxbat in his sight.

Foxbat

Aziz realized what was about to happen as he passed the Harrier. He felt as if someone had dropped an ice collar around his neck. His plane wasn't flying anymore, just falling through the air. He worked at the controls, and somehow got the Foxbat to fall away from the Harrier's guns.

Harrier

Mike fired his cannon, but the MiG surprised him by dropping instead of climbing. Before he could react, the Foxbat disappeared, but not before a 25mm round went through the Foxbat's spine. Others punched holes in a wing.

Foxbat

Colonel Muhammad Aziz fought the temptation to eject, and tried to push the Foxbat's nose down. It didn't respond. He had no real control now. He was just along for the ride. His airspeed was fifty knots less than needed, and he had only 2500 feet of altitude to get that fifty.

The Foxbat's nose finally *did* fall. It gained airspeed. Aziz kept the engines at full power as the ground rushed up at him. The Foxbat reached 150 knots at 1000 feet. Aziz eased back on the stick. The MiG responded slowly. At one hundred feet Aziz said what he thought was his last prayer. Suddenly the Foxbat leveled. Accelerated. The twin Tumanskys were finally able to gulp enough air to produce their 30,865 pounds of maximum thrust. The MiG rocketed up.

Harrier

Mike watched the MiG's upward rush with amazement and chagrin. He knew the Foxbat would be back, and its pilot would be a lot more cautious. He'd probably maintain a safe range and pump missiles at Mike until one found its way through the ground clutter.

Mike reluctantly went to full power and headed for a range of low mountains. The full-power dash at low altitude would use more fuel than he could spare.

The supersonic Foxbat caught him before he could reach the mountains. Mike sensed rather than saw the MiG-25 behind him. He pulled the Harrier into a chin-tugging, five-g turn. The Harrier's airspeed dropped to 300 knots.

Foxbat

Aziz cursed. He'd underestimated the Harrier's maneuverability again, and hadn't paid enough attention to his machine's lack of it. He had realized all that just after he'd fired an Archer. The missile bored a hole through empty air. By the time Aziz turned the Foxbat, the Harrier had hurtled in among the mountains, 3000-foot-high ridges of sand, broken by jagged spires of rock.

Aziz banked around behind the Harrier again. He attempted to use the Fox Fire radar to line up on the Harrier, but ground return from the mountains defeated its track mode. Aziz decided to try the high yo-yo again. He pulled up into a steep climb, inverted at 10,000 feet and pulled into a dive. While he was going up and down, the Harrier was going forward. As a result the Foxbat closed on the Harrier at a reasonable rate while maintaining high airspeed.

Aziz pulled out too low for the likes of a Foxbat and armed an Archer. It locked up.

The Harrier suddenly accelerated—straight at a spire of rock. Clutter broke the Archer's lock. Aziz continued pursuit, but he couldn't relock the Archer's seeker. Aziz followed Harrier's charge toward the mountain as long as he dared, then pulled into a climb.

The Harrier's pilot earned Aziz's respect. Only a highly skilled, experienced combat pilot would have known how to use background clutter to defeat the Archer, then use his maneuver advantage to lead the Foxbat into a crash.

Aziz rolled the MiG on its back and watched as the Harrier sprinted toward disaster. At the last moment it rolled into an impossible turn, then rolled back and went around the mountain.

Harrier

The MiG was nowhere in sight when Mike brought the Harrier around the mountain. He slowed the Harrier as close to a hover as he dared, then spotted a narrow ravine and accelerated into it. The rock-strewn channel would be a clutter nightmare for both radar- and IR-guided missiles.

Mike peered up through his canopy and saw the Foxbat, orbiting at 10,000 feet. The pilot obviously intended to wait up there until he was sure of a clear shot. Mike didn't have enough fuel to play that game very long. The violent maneuvering had already exhausted the fuel he needed to return offshore to the ship. Another few minutes of flying nowhere would use up the fuel he needed to make it to the coast where he had a chance of being picked up.

Mike kicked the Harrier out of the ravine and roared across the open desert. He watched the instrument-panel clock, counting off the seconds that he estimated it would take the Foxbat to get into firing position, lock up his missile and fire. He hoped what he'd read about the Foxbat was correct.

Time.

Mike deployed the air brakes, and brought the Harrier to a hover. He rotated the craft and, as he had expected, the Foxbat was screaming down on him, behind a missile. Mike couldn't see the missile itself, but he could see its bright exhaust plume. Mike didn't know whether it was possible to shoot down an air-to-air missile with a gun, but he was going to try. The Harrier's engine, running at full power to maintain the hover, produced a hot plume which made a giant target for what Mike guessed would be an IR-guided missile. It would head straight into his gunfire. If he survived the missile, he'd get a good shot at the Foxbat as it went by.

Mike raised the Harrier's nose and fought to keep it stable; it wanted to slide back on its tail. He held down the firing button.

The sky exploded in front of him. Things clanged off the Harrier, but nothing went into the intakes and trashed the engine. The Foxbat flashed in front of him. Mike's thumb never left the firing button.

The Foxbat flew through a hail of 25mm shells, and disappeared behind Mike.

Mike spun the Harrier. The Foxbat pulled out and climbed, apparently undamaged.

Foxbat

Aziz fought to keep the Foxbat from rolling. He didn't want to believe that he was going to have to let the American escape, but the fuel indicators didn't lie. Cannon fire had punctured a wing tank, and fuel was draining away at an alarming rate. Aziz cursed and turned the Foxbat toward the Libyan border.

Sudan

It was night when Mike crossed the mountains near the Sudanese coast and dropped toward the coastal plain. He was almost out of fuel and almost out of time. He'd dropped the last two ferry tanks before he'd crossed the Nile. He was running on fumes. The panel clock told him he had forty minutes left before the Harrier blasted itself into scrap metal. Mike was rigid with stress, and his head ached with the concentration needed to adjust the plane's flight to conserve fuel.

Mike searched the dark ahead of him. Points of light dotted the ground. He'd been led to believe the coast was desolate and sparsely populated, but there seemed to be people everywhere. He backed off the throttle and started a slow descent toward an island of darkness among the scattered lights. He hoped it wasn't a lake.

Mike thought he detected a change in the engine sounds. He stopped breathing. Then it seemed all right again, but he knew he had to get the plane on the ground while he still had enough fuel for a vertical landing. If he ran out of fuel and was forced to glide in he'd almost certainly trash the aircraft . . . and himself.

Mike steepened the dive, watching the radar altimeter. When he reached 2500 feet, he pulled up the nose and deployed the air brake. Airspeed fell to 120 knots. He cranked on vertical thrust. Speed dropped to twenty knots. The plane was light enough to hover now, but that would burn fuel at a tremendous rate.

Mike lowered the landing gear and reduced power. The Harrier sank rapidly. Mike teetered on the edge of terror, expecting the engine to stop at any moment. He braked the descent when the altimeter read one hundred feet, and turned on the landing lights.

He was over water.

Mike turned off the landing lights, and was shocked to see lights close ahead of him. Boats? The shore? The engine faltered. Its whine slowed. No more time.

The Harrier dropped. It splashed into the water with a jolt that snapped Mike's jaw open. He sat immobile for a moment, stunned and trying to come to grips with the fact that he still lived. There had been a huge splash, but the plane wasn't sinking. The clock still glowed. It gave him ten minutes to get out of the plane, extract the samples from the pod and put a safe distance between him and the doomed Harrier.

Mike tore off his helmet, clambered out of the cockpit just as the canopy finished opening, and jumped into water. He sunk into mud up to his knees. He could hear yelling in the distance. Mike fought despair. The landing gear had sunk into the mud, and the pod was submerged.

Mike dug the panel-fastener tool out of his pocket, and half crawled, half swam under the plane to the pod. He had to put his head underwater to reach the fasteners. The water was filled with dirt stirred up by the plane's impact, and it smelled and tasted like sewage.

The panel wouldn't come off. The water pressure held it firmly shut. Mike dug at the edge with the fastener tool. He finally forced a crack. Water rushed in. The panel slid off and sank in the mud.

Mike jabbed at the nitrogen-filled bag with the tool. Gas hissed out. It was deflating too slowly. Mike desperately pushed it aside. He struggled blindly to get a hold on the pack. Foul-smelling water went up his nose and got in his eyes. Coughing and sputtering, he finally got a grip on the pack and heaved it out.

Mike fought to extract the two shaft bags. He got them out, but discovered he couldn't pull everything away from the plane at once. He let the shaft cases sink into the mud, and dragged the pack away from the plane. He could hear excited voices in the distance, and flashlight beams speared the night.

It took two trips to get the shafts. He didn't take time to look at his watch, but he was sure he'd used up his ten minutes. With grim determination, he slung the pack on his back. The lights were almost on him now. He splashed away through the water as fast he could, dragging the bags.

The voices exploded into wild yells. The Sudanese had discovered the Harrier. They were so astonished, it was a few more moments before someone scanned a flashlight through the darkness and spotted Mike.

They splashed after him. Mike struggled harder, refusing to let go of the bags or shed the pack, even though he knew they would catch him in the next few seconds. He'd come this far, survived all the other shit; he wasn't giving up now. They'd just have to kill him.

Then the Harrier exploded with a deafening roar. A hot fist slapped Mike into the water. The explosion did more to his pursuers. Screams and moans filled the night.

Mike knew the survivors would be after him as soon as they recovered from the shock. He struggled to his feet and lurched through the water toward a dark stretch of shoreline, dragging his gear.

Mike came out of the water and plunged into a thick wall of vegetation. He burrowed in, dragging the bags and pack after him. He collapsed in the weeds and rolled onto his back. He struggled for each ragged breath. No strength remained in his tortured muscles. The foul smell of the water soaking his clothes made him want to throw up. The muzzle burn on his neck burned even more, no doubt seriously infected.

Mike's breathing finally slowed. His stomach decided it could stand the smell and the ugly taste in his mouth. He tried to stand. A wave of vertigo whirled him back to the ground. He had to rest before he could go on. And where would he go in the dark?

Mike took a Search and Rescue beacon from the pack. He believed he was too far from the coast for rescue, but at least they'd know that he'd survived and where he'd crashed. There might be something they could do. He extended the transmitter's antenna, switched it on and leaned it against a tree. Then he stretched out on his back and closed his eyes. He intended to try making his way to the coast on his own, but he'd have to wait for daylight. Exhaustion dragged him into deep sleep.

When the AK-47 barrel jabbed into his throat and jolted Mike awake, dawn was glimmering through the trees. The dark man prodding Mike wore a tattered khaki shirt, with stripes on one sleeve and some sort of medal hanging from his pocket. Out of the corner of his eye, Mike saw six other men surrounding him. Only one was armed. He also wore a khaki uniform shirt. The others wore long robes and sandals. All the men's heads were wrapped in turbans. Mike concluded the unarmed men were farmers and the others local militia or police.

The dark man took the AK-47 from Mike's throat and motioned him to his feet. Mike's muscles were impossibly stiff, and it took a major effort to just sit up. He was too slow for his captor. The Sudanese struck Mike in the back of the head with the barrel of his weapon. He fell on his face. The man kicked him in the side and gave an order in a language Mike couldn't understand. He backed off and raised the assault rifle. Mike struggled to his hands and knees, then slowly stood, expecting to be shot at any moment. He was too exhausted to be scared, but not too tired to be angry. Why the fuck had everything gone wrong? Mike glared at his captors, and in his rage was tempted to say the hell with it and charge the man who'd kicked

Robert Payton Moore

him. He was tired of this shit. The mission had failed, and the bastards would probably torture him to death. Maybe he could take one with him.

One of the unarmed men picked up the SAR beacon and examined it. Another started to open the pack. Mike's heart sank. They'd probably divide what looked useful and trash the rest. His captor yelled at the farmer and jabbed his AK-47 at him. The farmer dropped the pack.

Mike's two captors engaged in a long heated discussion. They finally ordered the farmers to pick up the pack and the bags. The dark man shoved Mike roughly into the brush. He stumbled through the tangled vegetation, urged on by painful jabs in the kidney with a gun barrel. After a few yards they came onto a well-worn trail.

Mike was near collapse when they finally reached a road. His captors shoved him toward a battered flatbed truck and pushed him onto the truck bed. The farmers threw his gear after him. While one man kept his AK-47 trained on Mike, the other "official" tied his hands behind him and secured them to a steel loop protruding from the back of the cab. He then settled down with his rifle across his lap to watch Mike. The other shoved his weapon into the cab and got behind the wheel. The farmers crowded onto the truck as the driver coaxed the engine to life.

The truck passed a dam and jolted its way down the steep, winding dirt road to the valley below, and Mike thought his shoulders would be jerked out of their sockets as he bumped around in the bed. The truck finally halted in front of a ramshackle building with a tattered Sudanese flag flying from a pole out front. An antenna sprouted from the roof. His guard untied Mike from the truck and shoved him from the truck bed. His hands still tied behind him, Mike fell to the ground with a painful jolt. The waiting driver kicked him. The kick angered Mike more than it hurt him. The two jerked him to his feet and marched him into the shack. The farmers brought in the pack and bags, then departed.

The shack had a dirt floor and contained two battered wooden tables, a few scattered chairs, and two cushions as dirty as the floor and covered by blankets just as dirty. One table held the stale remains of a meal. On the other sat a surprisingly modern radio. The open windows had no glass, only stout wooden shutters. Rank body odor haunted the air.

The Sudanese dumped Mike onto a wooden chair and tightly bound him to it with rope. The apparent leader stood in front of Mike and without ceremony slapped him. Blood trickled from the corner of Mike's mouth. His captor studied him a moment. Apparently dissatisfied with the damage, he swung his fist. He meant to break Mike's nose, but his aim was bad. Instead, he opened up a cut over Mike's right eye. However, the stream of blood running into Mike's eye seemed to satisfy him. He jabbered a question at Mike. Mike didn't understand the language, but he answered with name, rank and serial number. The man looked puzzled. He didn't understand English.

The two Sudanese men conferred for a few minutes. The leader sat at the radio. While he fiddled with the dials, the other left through the back door. Mike heard a generator start up, and the radio lights blinked on. His captor talked into the mike. Mike guessed that he was asking what to do with his prisoner, probably asking permission to dispose of him. The conversation ended with his captor looking angry and frustrated. He glared at Mike. He had probably been looking forward to disposing of Mike in a most unpleasant manner, and had been told to preserve his prisoner for interrogation.

They loosed Mike from the chair, tied his hands behind him and marched him outside. They were shoving him onto the truck when automatic-weapons fire broke out in the distance. Mike's captors froze, wide-eyed with shock.

A group of men backed over the crest of a hill 200 yards down the street. They were firing at something out of sight. Their uniforms identified them as Sudanese Army troops. Most fired AK-47s. Two struggled with a heavy machine gun. A Sudanese stopped, kneeled and attempted to install propellant in the launch tube of a RPG-2 antitank rocket launcher. There was a whistle, and the antitank gunner was flung out of a fiery explosion like a rag doll. Half the others fell, spurting blood from a rash of puncture wounds. As the survivors turned to run, they were mutilated by heavy automatic-weapons fire.

The sight of the Marines cresting the hill broke the paralysis of Mike's captors. One brought his AK-47 to his waist, intending to finish Mike before they fled. Mike flung himself at the man's knees. The AK-47 went off, but it pointed skyward as the man fell. Mike rolled and squirmed on top of him, depriving him of the space to use his weapon. Mike's other captor aimed his assault rifle at the struggling figures, seeking an opportunity to shoot Mike without killing his companion. An M-16 round went through the man's head, spraying brain matter. He jerked, eyes impossibly wide, then collapsed.

The Sudanese squirmed from under Mike, rolled away and came up on his knees. He pointed the AK-47 at Mike. Before he could squeeze the trigger, a Marine rushed up and swung the butt of his M-16 against the man's head. He fell to the street. The Marine sank his bayonet into his chest. The Sudanese grabbed the bayonet and the blade sliced his hands. He gurgled and fell back, blood bubbling from his mouth. His back arched. Then he went limp.

As the Marine withdrew his bayonet, a lieutenant approached at a run. "You Captain Boen?" he barked.

"What's left of him."

"Come on! We've got to get out of here! There's a lot more of these bastards in the hills, and they probably have mortars." He jerked Mike to his feet and cut the ropes binding his hands. "Daly! Brown! Help this man!"

"Wait!" Mike yelled. "We can't leave what this was all about!" Mike ran into the shack. The Marines followed. "The pack! And those two bags!" Mike directed.

"All right. Johnson! Peel! Hardy! Get 'em! Now let's get the hell out of here!"

An air-cushion landing craft—LCAC—waited fifty yards inland from the river. Its turbines screamed as it floated just above the street. An automatic weapon went off, and rounds chased Mike and the Marines. When a Marine groaned and fell to the dusty street, two others lifted him and carried him toward the LCAC. A heavy machine gun on the LCAC started up and shredded a shop front. A rifle grenade followed and turned the interior into an inferno.

The Marines hurried Mike onto the LCAC and followed with the pack and bags. The LCAC backed onto the river, rotated and accelerated away from the shore.

"You all right?" the lieutenant asked Mike, who leaned against a wall, gasping for breath.

"Helluva lot better than I was. You guys saved my ass—and the rest of me, too."

"Glad to oblige. Commander Barton, our LCAC captain, would like to speak to you."

"I'd like to speak to him, too, and thank him." Daly and Brown started to take Mike's arms. "Thanks, but I can make it." When he started up the ladder, Mike wasn't so sure he *could* make it, but he managed to pull himself up through the hatch.

The LCAC screamed down the nearly dry riverbed, its air cushion taking it over sandbars and mud flats.

The commander sat in a raised chair behind the pilot. "Captain Boen," he said without taking his eyes off the river in front of him, "I'm Jas Barton. I see we got to you in time. Get all your equipment?"

"Yes. All of it." Mike swayed and nearly fell when the LCAC swerved.

"Better have a seat, Captain," Barton suggested. "Up here." He directed Mike to a chair beside his. "Whatever you have, it must be pretty important to convince Commander Collins to send us into a foreign country without authorization. He could be court-martialed for this. Mind telling me what's so important?"

"Can't."

"Yeah, I guess you can't. Sorry I asked."

"How'd you find me?"

"We had an AV-8B up looking for you. Saw an explosion. Same time your plane was supposed to blow. We knew where to look. Made it easy to pick up your beeper, but we had to wait for daylight. The spooks had assets to keep track of you when the Sudanese caught up to you."

Red Sea

Commander Collins was worried and angry. He couldn't believe he had let himself be talked into this insane operation. But he couldn't leave Mike out there to die, knowing he had the means to get him out. And Andy Staples had convinced him it was a matter of national survival to recover whatever Mike was carrying—with or without Mike. But he suspected Staples would be of little help when the shit hit the fan. And he'd just made command! No doubt this would be his last command. He glared at Mike and Staples, who stood with him on the bridge. "So how long have I got before I have to explain all this?" he asked bitterly.

"Quite some time, I would guess," Staples answered. "Communications are poor in this part of Sudan. Be days, maybe weeks, before their government even becomes aware of this little imbroglio and figures out what happened. And once they do, they have to decide how to protest, what to demand, whether to go to the U.N., that sort of thing. It will be a while."

"A while won't help me. Only *never* would help me. Nobody gave me permission to invade Sudan, and I've got a wounded Marine I have to explain."

"You did what you had to do to rescue a downed pilot," Staples offered.

"Admiral Kittering will support you, Commander," Mike assured him.

"A spook?"

"The Navy's chief spook."

It didn't mollify him. "I don't know. Getting mixed up with spooks could make things worse—nobody trusts them. Well, what's done is done. A helicopter is on its way to pick up you and your stuff, Captain."

"Thanks." Thanks didn't seem nearly enough for the man who'd saved his life, but Mike couldn't think of anything more to say. The thought of what might happen to the young officer's career sickened Mike. He'd demand that Kinnebrew and Kittering use all of their influence to protect the young officer, but if the episode turned into a highly publicized incident, he doubted even two admirals could save the commander.

The Sea Stallion was on the deck within an hour, and Mike began the first leg of his trip back to the U.S.

Chapter Nine

Baltimore, Maryland

Mike felt Julie's eyes on him as he drove out of Baltimore and onto the parkway. He had been surprised when Julie had suggested an Orioles-Yankees game instead of the dinner he had promised.

"I'm a Yankee fan and proud of it," she'd declared. "And I have two tickets." It had been great fun: the crowd, the peanuts, the beer and Julie. Julie most of all. She really got into it: jumping to her feet and screaming at every hit and yelling insults at the umpires *and* the Orioles, drawing hostile looks from the Baltimore fans surrounding them. Her bubbling enthusiasm surprised Mike. This wasn't the calm, controlled, hostile Julie Barns he knew from their business meetings. This was a fun person to be with. He had spent more time watching her than the game.

He searched for the answer to his daughter's question: "Is she pretty?" Her face seemed too elegant for pretty—more like beautiful. Her dark eyes—Mike couldn't tell if they were really black—belonged in a beautiful face. Her thick black hair fell into a tangle of undisciplined curls at her shoulders. Mike wondered what a classy hairstyle would do for her, and decided he liked it the way it was. Her full lips made him think about kissing. She had a long-legged, athletic body made deliciously feminine by the flair of her hips, her taut bottom and the high thrust of her breasts. He'd felt a stab of lust whenever she'd stood up to yell. She intrigued Mike. He wanted to know her, know Julie Barns the *person*.

The heavy traffic thinned after the BWI Airport turn-off. The car rushed through the night, the thick wall of trees lining the parkway making it seem as if they were plunging through a dark jungle. Mike glanced from the roadway to catch Julie staring at his damaged face. He did look as if he'd lost a fight. Stitches closed a cut above a black eye. A scab perched on his cut lip, and he sported a thick bandage on the side of his neck. Carefully combed hair couldn't quite cover the bare patch on the back of his head and more stitches. She couldn't see the bruises under his clothes, or the cracked rib, but he walked a little funny and sat down *very* carefully. He'd obviously been involved in serious violence. He knew she probably wondered whether he was a brawler, whether she was safe with him. Violent men often assaulted women. Mike decided some kind of explanation was in order. "Julie . . ."

"Yes."

"I guess you're wondering how I got so beat up."

"I can't help being a little curious."

"It wasn't a barroom fight, or anything like that."

"Oh."

"Happened on duty."

"Get in many fights on duty?" He couldn't tell

whether the question was meant to be serious or humorous.

"None. This happened—" He struggled for an explanation that wouldn't violate security. "—when I landed an aircraft a little too hard."

"It crashed?"

"No . . . not exactly." Mike berated himself for not keeping his mouth shut.

"Something classified? Or something that would embarrass the Navy?" she asked, needling him.

The car phone interrupted them. It had been a joint birthday gift from his daughter and in-laws. He had thought it an unnecessary extravagance at the time, but now wondered how he'd done without it. The caller was Dr. Jack Temple, Head NESW Project Engineer. A classic workaholic, Temple virtually lived at the NESW laboratory—day, night and weekends. He supervised a staff of twenty full-time employees. Contractors did most of the NESW development. Temple's small government laboratory tested and integrated NESW subsystems produced by contractors.

"We have a problem, Mike," Temple said with concern.

"What kind of problem?"

"I don't honestly know, and that's what makes it so serious."

"I don't understand."

"It's not something we can talk about over the phone. We need you here right away."

"Tonight?" Mike couldn't imagine what could have gone wrong: an explosion, contamination, security violation?

"Tonight. Soon as you can. I've called Scott. He's on his way."

"Anyone else there with you?"

"Just about everyone. All going crazy trying to figure out what's happening."

"I'm on the BW Parkway. I should be there in about twenty minutes."

Mike hung up the phone, bewildered.

"Something wrong?" Julie asked.

"Apparently. Would you mind a little detour? I need to stop by the lab. Some kind of emergency."

"I don't mind. I know about lab emergencies," she said with a sigh. She dreaded just such a call, telling her the microbes had escaped.

"You won't have to wait. You can take my car. I'll hitch a ride from someone and pick it up tomorrow."

"See what the problem is. I can wait."

White Oak, Maryland

Mike turned off the Baltimore Parkway onto the Outer Loop of the Beltway, heading west. The NESW program lab resided in a building on the grounds of the Naval Surface Warfare Center (NSWC), White Oak, Maryland, just north of the Washington Beltway. The building was located in a remote corner of the Center grounds, away from the other buildings and laboratories. Abandoned shortly after the Second World War, the building had been built for some long-forgotten chemical-processing experiments. It had been designed to contain gas and other poisonous materials, and had been isolated from the rest of the installation for safety purposes. It was ideal for the NESW test program, which required the same sort of containment and safety facilities.

A few minutes' driving through the light night traffic brought them to the New Hampshire Avenue off-ramp, which Mike took north to the main gate of the White Oak installation. He parked the car and led Julie into the pass office. Mike waited anxiously while the security people completed the paperwork for Julie's temporary pass. He signed as her escort, and hurried her back to the car.

Mike completed more formalities at the guard gate, and drove into the secure area. The main building loomed in front of them at the end of a long driveway, which made its way from the gate through a broad expanse of grass-covered grounds. In the silver moonlight, the lawn was revealed for what it was, a golf course. Only laboratory personnel were allowed on the course, arousing the jealousy of developers who wanted to replace the Center with luxury homes and use the golf course to attract wealthy buyers. They likely would have an opportunity to do just that when bases were closed to consolidate and streamline operations.

Mike drove past the main building and turned onto a gravel road that wound through a thick stand of trees to the NESW laboratory building. The isolation, the forest and the dim moonlight made Julie feel as if she'd been spirited into a wilderness. Mike parked in front of the building. New paint and a new roof couldn't disguise its age.

The lobby was small and cramped. An armed guard sat behind a desk in front of a vault door with a cipher lock. Uncomfortable government-issue furniture, with stiff brown plastic upholstery, crowded the space. In front of a four-pillowed couch with cracked plastic upholstery sat a large coffee table; old technical journals covered its gouged top. A battered stand with a half-empty bottle of water stood in a corner.

"Hi, John," Mike said to the guard, a large black man who didn't appear to need a gun to protect the place. "This is Dr. Barns." Julie shook the guard's hand. "She's going to wait for me out here." Mike turned to Julie. "I'll see what's up. If it's going to take a while, I'll let you know, and you can take my car home."

"I don't mind waiting. I'll talk politics or something with Mr. Jefferies." She had read the name on the guard's badge. The guard smiled, instantly liking her. It got boring and lonesome sitting behind the desk all night.

Mike punched the cipher lock's buttons, and it clicked open. He stepped through the door into an airlock. He waited until the airlock cycled and the inner door's electrically controlled lock clicked open, then walked into an office crowded with desks and computer terminals. There was insufficient space to provide individual offices for all of the scientists and engineers. They shared offices with each other and the secretaries. The technicians lived at their benches in the laboratory work space.

Mike entered a second airlock; it separated the office area from the laboratory work space. He closed the outer door and waited. The inner door unlocked when air pressure rose enough to ensure air would flow into the laboratory. Mike pushed the door open and stepped into the laboratory. Rows of benches filled the large hangarlike room. The bench tops were covered with jungles of electronic equipment, chemical-testing apparatuses and optical benches. A large electron microscope dominated a corner.

Across the laboratory, another airlock led to a test facility, which consumed over half the building. In it staff and contractors performed subsystem and functional tests with small-scale models. The full-scale test problem had yet to be solved. They hadn't found a way to avoid the problems that Army chemical-warfare testing had encountered in Utah and other places. The NESW agents wouldn't kill anyone—or even make them sick—but they would raise havoc with machinery.

The NESW needed an isolated test site with predictable winds to ensure that the agents would disperse harmlessly before reaching populated areas. They hadn't yet found such a site. Use of large hangars or warehouses were under consideration, but the expense of sealing such large structures was prohibitive and they would not provide realistic testing. The test problem was another showstopper: a problem that could kill the program.

Mike expected to find the scientists busy at their benches. Instead, they were scattered about the lab in small groups. They appeared fatigued and discouraged. Mike found Scott and Jack Temple in intense conversation beside the electron microscope. Temple was a tall, bony man. His washed-out blond hair matched his pale skin and light-blue eyes. His face was always a little angry. Now frustration amplified the anger. His tie was loose, his white shirt dingy and sweaty and his baggy pants more rumpled than usual. Dr. Jack Temple was as difficult to get along with as he was brilliant— so difficult to get along with, he'd never married.

"Something really weird has happened, Mike," Scott informed him. "Nothing in here works anymore."

"What do you mean nothing works?"

"Just that. Electronics have died; mechanical stuff is frozen."

"Even the office equipment is starting to go," Temple complained irritably. "Lost two computers and a laser printer today. We thought it was a power problems. You know—surges, spikes or high-frequency noise that the regulators couldn't handle. But we've monitored the power lines and found nothing. Anyway, power problems couldn't cause the mechanical breakdowns."

"Mike, whatever's happening is happening at an increasing rate," Scott added with concern.

"That's why I called you," Temple explained. "We started losing a few pieces of equipment about a week ago, the day after you brought in the samples. Didn't think much about it. Thought it was a run of bad luck, happens all the time. But after a couple of days, we'd lost too much equipment for it to be just bad luck. Half the team was out of business. I shifted half of the idle people to analysis tasks and put the rest to tracking down the problem. Then today, everything stopped, and the problem spread out of the lab into the office. This is no longer a functioning facility."

"What about the NESW agents you've been testing?" Mike asked. "A leak maybe?"

"First thing we thought of," Temple replied. "But we're not fooling with anything we can't detect; we don't bring an agent into the lab unless we're sure we can detect even a few molecules of the stuff. We can't find traces of any agent we have in the lab or have ever had in the lab. And the effects are like nothing we've ever observed."

"There is one thing, though," Scott informed Mike, his face scrunched with puzzlement. "Take a look at these." Scott led Mike to a table stacked with photographs. He selected several and placed them in front of Mike. "These are microscope photos of surfaces of the shaft bearings you brought in." The photographs revealed rough, pitted surfaces, which at microscope magnification looked more like a mountain landscape than a bearing surface—that is, wherever they hadn't crumbled into a chalky substance.

Scott placed another set of photos in front of Mike. "These are bearings from one of our milling machines. Had to drive the shaft out, so it's scored. See any similarities?"

"Looks the same." Mike said in disbelief. He was getting a bad feeling, a *very* bad feeling.

"Now look at this," Scott said, laying another picture in front of him. "This is a precision-instrument bearing, from inside a chassis with a good air-filtration system. A technician removed it this morning when the dials jammed. This is a photograph of it this morning.'' The bearing surface was too rough for a bearing, but there were no chalky areas.

''Now look at this—the same bearing just twelve hours later,'' Scott said, replacing the photo with another. ''You don't really need a microscope to see the damage. These things are corroding at a tremendous rate. Same thing with electrical contacts and plugs. Conducting surfaces are being turned into insulators. It's now getting to the microcircuits. We don't have anything in here but conventional circuits with feature sizes—the width of the chip wires, so to speak—of anywhere from one half to three microns wide. The chip interconnections have just disappeared. I shudder to think of whatever this is would do to integrated circuits being incorporated into advanced systems. Some have interconnections which are less than a quarter micron.''

''Isn't just size,'' Temple put in. ''It depends on what kind of chip it is; one chip will be destroyed, and the one next to it left untouched. It's material-dependent.''

''Have any ideas as to what it could be?'' Mike asked.

''Wish we did,'' Scott lamented. ''Whatever it is attacks surfaces, like our NESW agents do, but our agents don't keep on attacking. They ruin the surface, are consumed in the process and that's the end of it. You can mill off a surface and use it again. This stuff just keeps on gnawing. Things keep crumbling away.

''What's really scary,'' Scott added anxiously, ''is that it seems to be spreading—like a disease. Acts like some kind of microbe that feeds off materials and multiplies.''

''That's crazy!'' Temple objected. ''I've never heard of such a thing.''

"I have," Mike stated. He felt poised on the edge of a nightmare. "You have, too."

"What are you talking about?" Temple groused.

"Lesatec's work." It *was* crazy. But it fit.

"Sounds pretty far-fetched to me," Temple declared, looking at Mike as if he was an idiot. Mike had the feeling that Dr. Jack Temple didn't think Naval officers were very smart. "I know you and Scott think she has something, but nobody's seen it yet. I think your Dr. Barns and her buddies are just high-tech con artists. Besides, how could her bugs get into our laboratory?"

Temple was right. Impossible. Still . . . "Do we have any other ideas?" Mike asked pointedly.

"No, but let me get back with my crew," said Temple. "We'll figure something out by morning."

"If you don't have any ideas, how can you expect to have the problem solved by morning?" Mike asked roughly, feeling a flash of anger. Sometimes the man's arrogance was too much. "You and your crew keep working, but I want Dr. Barns to take a look at the pictures," he insisted.

"We shouldn't waste our time on the impossible. We should—"

"Jack!" Scott interrupted, attempting to prevent an angry confrontation. "We *don't* have any other ideas, and this kind of thing is her field. She may recognize some agent that our people are not familiar with. Can't hurt to let her look at the photos."

"How can we do that?" argued a seething Temple. "She's not even cleared to come though the door."

"She doesn't have to know where the pictures came from, or even what they are," Mike explained, trying to control his anger. He kept telling himself he should treat Temple like a machine and ignore the bastard's abrasive manner.

"You have a lot of uncleared people working on this

program," Mike pointed out impatiently. "You use un-cleared university people and consultants without clear-ances. We'll handle her just like we do them."

"But they don't come into the laboratory," Temple objected stubbornly.

"We can fix up a package for her just like we do for college professors," Scott said quickly to head off another argument. "We only have to show her pictures of common parts that could be from unclassified lab equipment."

"Let's not waste any more time," Mike ordered. "Jack, Scott, put together a package of photos covering the entire range of damage."

Julie was arguing with the guard about the talents of a Redskins wide receiver when they emerged. Her eyes widened with surprise. "I'd like you to meet some colleagues of mine, Julie," Mike said. "This is Scott Corbett, my deputy."

"I'm the guy he vents his frustrations on," Scott kidded, smiling. He had a large manila envelope under one arm. Julie got slowly to her feet and shook his hand.

"And this is Dr. Jack Temple, our Head Project Engineer."

"Oh! Dr. Temple! I've read some of your papers," Julie said, taking his hand and smiling warmly.

"You've read some of *my* papers?" said Temple, surprised.

"Yes. We're trying to engineer organisms that produce thin films that attack material surfaces, and I've been trying to absorb some surface physics. The effects described in your papers are similar to what happens when our microbes attack surfaces," she explained.

"I see." Temple hated to admit to the possibility that Mike had stumbled onto something. The admission didn't do a thing for his ego.

130

"Sit down, Julie," Mike said. "We have some pictures we'd like you to look at."

Julie's face hardened. "I told you that I wouldn't have anything to do with your program."

"This is has nothing to do with what we've been discussing. We've had an emergency . . . a problem in the lab."

"A problem? More like a disaster," Temple groused.

Mike raked him with a warning glance. He fell silent, his eyes smoldering.

"I'll look at your pictures, Mike. But if I think you're conning me, I'm leaving."

Mike cleared the tattered magazines from the table, and piled them on a corner of the guard's desk. Scott extracted a dozen photos from the envelope, and arranged them in two rows on the table in front of Julie.

"What am I supposed to be looking for?" Julie asked.

"Characteristic surface damage," Scott answered. "The top row of pictures are microscope photographs of metal surfaces. The bottom ones are materials used in electronics. The photos on the left were made this morning or yesterday. The photos on the right were made this afternoon. They show how damage progresses with time."

Julie picked up a photo of a bearing surface and studied it. Her face clenched with concentration, and then filled with surprise. "What have these been exposed to?" she exclaimed.

"Look at the rest," Mike replied without answering.

She stared at him suspiciously a moment, then resumed her examination. By the time she finished, she was obviously shocked. "Is this what you do here?"

"This isn't our work," he answered evasively.

"Do you work with biological agents?"

"No, only chemicals." Mike's mind filled with the

image of the helicopter rigged like a crop duster. Dread chilled him.

"Where did you get these?" Julie demanded, getting to her feet. Mike and Scott looked at one another. Temple watched them with a growing anger. What had these two gotten the lab mixed up in?

"We can't tell you that," Mike said reluctantly.

Julie glared at Mike, then sat down and went through the photos again. When she finished, she was pale and her eyes were scared. "Does this have anything to do with the bruises on your face, Mike?" she asked. Temple stared at him with surprise. Scott tensed. The guard listened intently.

"If it did I couldn't tell you," Mike answered.

"I think a biological agent caused this," Julie said, a tremor in her voice, fear in her eyes. Mike felt as if he'd just fallen off a cliff. This could be worse than anything they had imagined.

Julie picked up a photo and studied it again. "Mike, have you been to North Africa . . . Chad maybe?" she asked. Mike couldn't have been any more shocked than if she had pulled out a pistol and shot him.

"I have to know, Mike!" Julie insisted desperately. "I think I know what this is and—"

"Julie! Don't say any more. We need to talk. *Alone.*" Anxiety twisted Mike's gut. He hadn't been able to stop her in time. Temple would figure it all out, if he hadn't already. And the guard . . .

"I need to take her inside, John," Mike told him.

"Sorry, Captain, I can't let you do that," the guard replied uncomfortably.

"This is an emergency, John."

"Sorry, Captain. I can't allow an uncleared person in the lab. I have strict orders. It would mean my job . . . maybe worse."

Temple's face had filled with anger. Critical information had been kept from him.

"Is something going on inside?" Julie asked fearfully. "If something *is* going on in there, Mike, you'd better let me help you. You don't know what you're dealing with."

Cold apprehension crawled up his spine. It seemed too incredible, but there were thirty bodies rotting in the desert to spur his fear. "What will it take to get her inside, John?" Mike persisted.

"I have to get approval from the NAVAIR Special Security Officer. He'll call the White Oak Duty Officer on a secure phone. Before I pass her in, he has to come out and verify that she's who she is and that she's with you. She'll be your responsibility. They'll hang you if anything is wrong."

"Well, get on it!" Mike burned with frustration, but he knew there was no budging the security people.

"There is one other problem," John said nervously. "The Special Security Officer can't make the decision himself. He needs flag-level approval, and it's 2300 hours. Nobody will be in their office."

Mike cursed the bureaucracy. "Who can okay it?"

"Probably the Commander of NAVAIR."

"He'll demand a briefing. Take forever. How about the Director of Naval Intelligence, Admiral Kittering?"

"I'm sure that would do it."

"Okay, get the NAVAIR Duty Officer. Have him contact the Special Security Officer at home and alert him. Tell him to expect a call from Admiral Kittering and to get his butt into his office. I'll go back inside and contact Admiral Kittering. Maybe we can get this settled before morning," Mike said bitterly.

"I don't see why we have to go through all of this—waking up admirals in the middle of the night," Temple objected. "We can take her to a secure space over at the main lab. You know, just off the lobby."

"Not secure enough," Mike snapped, "and I need her inside. Get the NAVAIR Duty Officer, John. I'll talk to him myself, and I'll call Admiral Kittering.''

Mike could see Julie struggling to keep herself together. It scared him to see her so scared. "I'm sorry, Julie, but you'll have to wait out here until we get this straightened out. I'll have some coffee sent out.''

"No! Don't have anything sent out!'' Her violent reaction startled him. "And don't let anyone come out.''

"We can't do that,'' objected Temple. "We—''

"We *will* do that,'' Mike interrupted harshly.

"Go do what you have to do, Mike,'' Julie said. "I'll be all right out here.'' She sat back down on the couch, her arms hugged about her as if she was cold.

Mike's conversation with Rear Admiral Kittering was short. Kittering obscenely expressed his irritation at being roused from bed. But he knew that if a senior officer with Mike's reputation said there was an emergency, there *was* an emergency. He agreed to contact the security officers.

It was after midnight, but Mike decided to call home anyway. They needed to know he might be gone for the night. A sleepy Susan answered the phone. "I might not be home tonight,'' he told her.

There was a moment of pregnant silence. Then: "You with Julie?''

"Yes, but—''

"It's okay. Really. You're consenting adults.''

"Susan, we're not—''

"You don't have to explain, Dad. It's all right.''

Mike sighed and gave up. "See you sometime tomorrow. Don't know when,'' he said, and hung up.

Two hours later Julie was allowed through the vault door. "Is there an empty office we can use, Jack?'' Mike asked.

"Use mine if you need to be alone,'' Temple answered resentfully.

"Mike, you want me to—" Scott started.

"No, I think it'd be better if Julie and I went over this alone first."

A couch, two straight-backed chairs and a cluttered desk crowded the small office. Mike sat beside Julie on the couch. "Why did you ask me about North Africa, Julie?"

Julie looked at Mike with tormented eyes. "The only things that I know of that cause damage like that are living organisms. They leave a residue that's like a fingerprint. I've seen the residue in those pictures before."

"Where?"

"At Lesatec . . . in my laboratory."

Mike had expected the answer, but it still jolted him. "Why did you ask if I'd gotten those samples from North Africa?" he asked.

Julie dropped her head. "I couldn't believe it. Didn't want to, I guess." She was talking more to herself than to Mike. "But it didn't make any sense—Omar stealing anything. Chad doesn't have the facilities to do anything with the technology."

"You're losing me, Julie. Who is Omar?"

"Was one of my team. Brilliant. Had a Ph.D. in chemical engineering and a master's degree in biotechnology, just the combination we needed. He devised the processing and engineered the equipment that makes living things out of our computer models.

"Omar was from Chad. Came on a student visa. Lesatec hired him after he finished graduate school. He had a green card and had applied for citizenship. A few months ago he disappeared. The private detectives that the company hired concluded he'd returned to Chad. He took his notes with him. He could have taken copies of software and microbe cultures, too; we have no way of knowing. It's obvious he took enough to duplicate the microbes. But I still can't believe Chad has computers and laboratories to do that.'' Her eyes suddenly widened in horror. ''You didn't get the materials from Chad, did you! Where—''

''Doesn't matter where and I can't tell you.''

Julie stiffened. Her eyes burned into him. ''You got them from Libya, didn't you? Omar was really a Libyan.'' Fright filled her face. ''Libya probably does have laboratories that could be used for bioengineering, and no telling what the Libyans will do with the technology.''

Mike winced at her rapid deduction. ''Don't discuss this with anyone, Julie. It's important that the wrong people don't find out about this.''

''I won't talk about it. I don't think I can bear to talk about it.''

''What do you think we have in the laboratory, Julie?''

''What you have in your laboratory is Doomsday,'' she said in a brittle voice. Anguish spilled from her eyes and splashed fear across her face. ''It's like the black plague.''

''Are you saying this is an epidemic of some kind?''

''Yes. A machine epidemic. Airplanes, cars, trains and ships will carry the microbes all over the world. If not neutralized, the microbes will disable all of the world's machinery.

''The world can't support its current population without machines. Just too many people. Suppose all of a sudden there were no trucks, airplanes, cars or ships? No power? No communications? No factories? How would people get food, water, medicine and all of the other things they need to survive?

''The world needs its machines. The microbes will destroy them. Kill civilization. Millions of people will die. It won't happen all at once. There won't be a big bang like with a hydrogen bomb. But it will be Doomsday all the same. A *silent* Doomsday.'' Her voice trembled with fear. The nightmare that had stalked her had become real.

Mike was appalled. What Julie had described was all too plausible. The NESW had been developed to do just what she had described—but not on such a mind-boggling scale. Her microbes could send the world back to the Stone Age.

"How well is this building sealed, Mike?"

"It's gas-proof."

"What about biological protection?"

"Nothing. We don't fool around with BW stuff. I've been ordered not to even think about it."

"We have to contain the microbes in the lab," Julie told him. "Then we have to determine if anything has been carried out. You can't let anybody in or out. How many people have gone home?" she asked fearfully.

"Two secretaries, an administrative assistant and a couple of the S&Es."

"You've got to find and quarantine them."

"There's no way to do that, and if we tried, we'd terrorize the whole East Coast."

"We'll have terror *and* a disaster if we *don't* do it," she argued.

"Julie, I've been exposed to this stuff, and I haven't spread it. I don't think we have to worry about people having carried it out of here."

"We do," she objected stubbornly. "You haven't been working intimately with the materials for extended periods like the others."

"Neither have the people who left. Only six people have, and they're still in the lab."

"You have to worry about everyone in there. The microbes we know about can infect watches, ballpoint pens, calculators, tools—anything containing the right materials. These could be different organisms. They might infect clothes, maybe people, too."

"All right, we'll keep everyone here. None of the

people who left worked in the lab with materials. We don't have to worry about them.''

"I *am* going to worry," she insisted, "but it's probably too late to do anything about it. We're going to need the decontamination equipment from Lesatec, and my people."

"Your people?"

"Yes. They're trained for just such an emergency."

"Do they have secret clearances?"

"No, but you got me in here, and I don't have a clearance," she pointed out.

"You don't understand, Julie. I put my neck on the line to get you in here, and I haven't heard the last of it yet. Getting a mob of uncleared people in is impossible. The security people would rather burn the place down first."

"You may have to do that," Julie retorted angrily.

"Look, we have a highly skilled group of scientists and engineers here. You can show them what to do."

"Okay, if you want to be responsible for a major catastrophe, we'll do it your way. But I have to have the equipment and chemicals. We'll need a truck or van."

"I can get a van, but getting approval to bring a van load of equipment and chemicals on base is going to take time."

"How much time?"

"Probably be tomorrow afternoon,"

"Tomorrow afternoon! You can't be serious!"

"Julie, you have to understand—"

"*I* understand! *You* don't understand! Tomorrow afternoon might be too late. I don't want to even think about what might happen. You have hundreds of people going in and out of White Oak. Half the state could be devastated by tomorrow."

"I'll do what I can, but there's no way around security procedures. No way I can get a whole van full of equipment in here before tomorrow. And how could you get your people out of bed and get the equipment here before morning?''

Julie suddenly realized she hadn't considered the difficulty of obtaining the release of equipment and chemicals from Lesatec. She couldn't just drive away with a van full of equipment. She would have to explain an emergency she hardly understood. She would have to admit presiding over a catastrophic technology theft— even protecting the thief.

Julie had fought desperately to convince Lesatec not to cooperate with the Navy; suddenly reversing her position would destroy her credibility. She envisioned days of wrangling.

Julie dropped her head in despair. ''It's going to get out of hand,'' she said desolately.

''We haven't lost it yet,'' he maintained. ''We'll work it out somehow.'' Mike believed there was solution or a way around every problem. ''First thing we have to do is tell the staff what they're dealing with.''

Chapter Ten

White Oak, Maryland

Mike ordered Temple to gather the laboratory staff in
a space used for experimental-system assembly. Mike
sat on a bench and waited, his insides churning with
anxiety. The lab staff regarded Julie with undisguised
curiosity. "I'd like to introduce Dr. Julie Barns," Mike
said when they had crowded around him. "As some of
you know, she manages an NSF program based on
technology we think is related to ours. She has reviewed photos of the surface damage, and will explain
what she thinks we have here."

Julie's explanation filled their faces with disbelief.
"You think germs are doing this?" exclaimed an in-
credulous electronics engineer. "With all due respect,
Dr. Barns, that is just too far out."

"You have a better explanation?" Mike asked pointedly.

"No, but that's no reason to grasp at the first fan-

140

tastic theory that comes along. We could spend precious time doing science fiction instead of the science needed to solve the problem.'' There were murmurs of assent from around the room. They weren't buying Julie's theory.

"How did the lab become infected anyway?" asked the same engineer.

Mike had put the question off as long as he could, but he knew he was going to have to answer it sooner or later. He needed these people's support, and they needed the information to do their jobs. He decided to stretch security as far as he could.

"The microbes came from parts I brought in last week for testing. They were obtained from a foreign source. The same effects were observed in that country. Now, I've probably said enough to get myself put in jail, but you all have top-secret clearances. Treat what I have told you as if it was classified at that level." Several stared meaningfully at Julie. They knew she didn't have *any* kind of clearance.

"We will do whatever you want, Captain," the engineer said. "I think this theory of hers is off the wall, but it would explain some things. Before the microscope focusing mechanisms froze up, I did notice a lot more microbes than usual scurrying about—like the materials had been dipped in sewage."

Mike's order confining the staff to the lab brought a wave of protests. "You have no authority to quarantine anyone!" Temple objected angrily. "We're civilians, and this is a laboratory, not a ship!"

"I'm going to tell the guard not to let anyone leave without my authorization because we have a security breach," Mike responded. They watched in amazement as he picked up the phone, dialed the guard outside and did just that. He also notified the front-gate guards.

Temple glared at Mike, but didn't protest further. He promised himself that as soon as he escaped the clutches of this madman, he was going to go home, update his resume and contact his colleagues in the university community about a job. He vowed not to work on another military program.

Julie, Mike, Scott and Temple crowded into Temple's office after the briefing. All were woozy with fatigue. "I think there *is* something we can do tonight, Mike," Julie told him. "We can slow the contamination process and reduce the possibility of microbes escaping the lab. Also, we could get the people out of here tonight. We need them out to complete the decontamination."

"How can you get the people out? Thought you were afraid of spreading the stuff," Temple pointed out.

"I am, but we can test and decontaminate the people before they leave. We've developed a portable detector. It uses an ultraviolet laser scanner to stimulate IR line emissions from microbe atomic structures. It provides an image highlighting contaminated areas. We can scan the people in the lab to determine if they've picked up anything. They probably haven't. The microbes don't seem to survive on skin. What we *do* have to worry about are their watches, ballpoint pens, pocket calculators, anything containing materials that these particular microbes like. That stuff can be left here. We also have portable decontamination units. We can spray people before they leave to be sure they're clean. I can call Saba, my software engineer, and have her bring out the equipment. Can you get it past the gate?"

"How big is it?"

"We carry the detector in a TV camera case. Looks like a camcorder. The decontamination unit is about the size of scuba gear."

"My uniform, White Oak pass and camera permit should get that in. Have Saba call when she gets to the gate. I'll meet her and bring in the equipment.''

Julie picked up the phone and dialed. Saba's answering machine had just clicked on when her sleepy voice came on the line. "Hello, who—"

"It's me, Julie."

"Julie?"

"Yes."

"Julie! It's three in the morning! You okay? You haven't been in an accident or something?"

"I am all right, Saba, but . . . there *is* sort of an emergency."

"What kind of emergency?" Saba's voice was alert now.

"I need you to do something for me, and I need to ask you for a big favor."

"Of course."

"I want you to go out to Lesatec and pick up the scanner and a portable decontamination unit for me."

"Julie, what—"

"The big favor is don't ask any questions."

"Julie—"

"Saba, please."

Saba was silent.

"I *have* to have that equipment, Saba."

"I'll do it," Saba answered reluctantly.

"This is not industrial sabotage."

"I hope not. Because of Omar, I get the feeling we're being followed by company detectives twenty-four hours a day. I don't have to take it to another company, do I?"

"No. The Naval Surface Warfare Center, White Oak."

"The what?" Saba exclaimed.

"The Naval Surface Weapons Warfare Center. I'll give you directions. A Navy captain will meet you at the gate. He'll bring the equipment in to me."

"Not Captain Boen?" Saba said incredulously.

"Yes."

"You swore you wouldn't have anything to do with his program. What changed your mind? And why at three in the morning?"

"This is different . . . an emergency."

"Then shouldn't I come in with him?"

"You can't."

"What *is* going on, Julie?"

"My big favor, remember?"

Saba sighed. "All right. No more questions."

"And not a word to anyone."

"There *will* be a word to somebody when the guard reports I took the equipment. Lesatec will go crazy when they find out it went to a Navy installation. When can I expect you tomorrow? I'll probably be fired before you get back—maybe arrested. I sure hope you have somebody's approval or an awfully good explanation."

"Don't worry. I'll take full responsibility for this. You can truthfully say you were just following your boss's orders and assumed I had Lesatec's approval. I'll take care of it when I get back," Julie said with confidence she didn't feel.

"I'll do it, but I *will* worry, and I'm not sure you *can* take care of it. The company is still upset about the Omar business."

"Call from the gate, and Captain Boen will come out."

"It will take me at least two hours."

"Just get here as fast as you can." Julie hung up the phone, staring at it, feeling as if she had just ordered a burglary and despising herself for making Saba an innocent accomplice.

Saba Saunders was pacing the lobby when Mike arrived. She reminded Mike of a leopard. There was the same impression of sudden strength, barely contained by her lithe body. Her breasts lifted her simple black dress, the nipples more than a hint. Mike wondered if she wore a bra. She had piercing black eyes, long, heavy black hair and dusky skin. She had the beauty of a dangerous wild animal. "Captain Boen?" she asked as he came through the door.

"Yes, and you are Ms. Saunders?"

"Yes. I have the equipment," she said, nodding to a camcorder case and what appeared to be a canvas backpack.

The suspicious security people insisted the cases be opened. Mike showed them his photo pass and constructed a complex technical description. Not satisfied, the security supervisor insisted Mike call and personally obtain the duty officer's approval. The duty officer approved only because he knew of Kittering's involvement.

"Please tell Julie to call as soon as possible, Captain," Saba said as she prepared to depart. "We are *both* going to be in a lot of trouble over this."

"If there's anything I can do let me know. I'll talk to your bosses if you want."

"I'm not sure that wouldn't make it worse. If anybody can get us out of this, it's Julie. Well, good night, Captain. I hope you're able to solve *your* problem . . . whatever it is." She shook Mike's hand, startling him with the strength of her grip. She left with the fluid stride of a panther.

Julie met Mike in the laboratory lobby. "Let's check the lobby first," she said anxiously. Julie knew that if the microbes had gotten past the air lock, the crisis had already turned into a disaster.

"Do you have a permit for that?" asked the alarmed guard when Julie removed the scanner from its case. "You're suppose to have a photo permit before bringing a camera on board." It did look like an oversized camcorder.

"It's okay, John," Mike said. "I have a camera permit." Mike extracted his wallet and flipped it open.

The guard studied it for a moment. "Okay, Captain. I guess it's all right as long as you stay with her," John said with resignation. He was worried. There had been more strange activity tonight than he'd seen the whole fourteen months he'd been at this post. He had the feeling that these people were about to make him lose his job.

The detector was a modified, repackaged infrared night rifle scope. The IR detectors had been replaced, and an optical filter allowed only microbe radiation stimulated by ultraviolet laser light to reach the detectors. The scope illuminator had been replaced by a laser that used an oscillating mirror to scan an invisible UV beam of radiation over the scope's field of view.

"Stand in front of John's desk, Mike," Julie said. "I'll check you and John first. That should tell us right away whether our problem has spread beyond the laboratory."

"Check me for what?" John exclaimed.

"Material that people may have accidentally carried out of the laboratory," Mike answered. "Could have gotten on their hands, shoes or clothes."

"What kind of material? Is it radioactive?" John asked fearfully.

"No, it's nothing to worry about," Mike reassured him. "Won't make you sick or anything. We just don't want it all over the place."

"Why?"

"It's something I can't talk about, but it's nothing for you to worry about either."

John's face said plainly that he didn't believe him.

Julie slowly scanned Mike from head to toe several times. Each scan increased his apprehension. "Now turn around," she requested. She repeated the procedure. "Hold out your hands." Mike complied, turning his hands first palms up, then palms down as she instructed. "Take off your shoes." He sat on the couch and removed his shoes. Julie placed them on the coffee table and scanned them thoroughly.

"Up with your feet."

Relief flooded Julie's face when she finished. "You're clean." Tension drained from Mike. Maybe it wasn't a catastrophe yet.

Julie went over the lobby with the detector, and finally scanned a very suspicious and reluctant John. "We're okay so far, Mike. In fact, more than okay. Seems people haven't carried anything out . . . though that's not one-hundred-percent certain. Could be a watch or calculator somewhere. Anyway, I feel a lot better. Let's go inside and see what we have."

Julie went over the office areas first. She found a printer, two computers and an old mechanical typewriter that were infected. Microbes had escaped the laboratory, despite the air lock. "Do people bring stuff from the lab out here, Mike?"

"Sometimes."

"That may be it, but what worries me is the office equipment, things only the secretaries use. Could mean the microbes are getting through the air lock on their own and could get through the lobby air lock next."

Julie removed two canisters from the canvas pack. They were attached to a frame with shoulder straps. She screwed a manifold and a long nozzle onto the canisters, then proceeded to fog the office areas.

"I didn't plan on this," she said when she finished. "There may not be enough left to do the lab and the people."

Inside the laboratory, Julie scanned the benches. Almost every piece of equipment was infected. Then she scanned the staff. She found the microbes had infected several watches, a pocket calculator and assorted rings.

Only one piece of clothing indicated contamination: a man's shirt.

"I don't understand it," Julie said regarding the shirt, which had been spread out on a bench. "We've never seen these organisms survive on fabrics. They're not engineered for fabrics. Of course, we don't know for sure that we're dealing with same organisms."

"Killian, you're a machinist, aren't you?" Mike asked the slender, gray-haired, now-bare-chested man.

"Yes," he answered, frightened and embarrassed.

"What was your last job?"

"I was turning a shaft for Dr. Jackson—at least I was until my lathe froze up. He wanted some surface material for analysis."

"Get any on your shirt?"

"Probably. Always get bits and pieces of metal turnings stuck in my clothes. Makes my wife mad as hell when she does the wash."

Julie picked up his shirt and studied it closely. "There are specks of material embedded in the cloth. I think that's it. I want you to stand as still as you can, Mr. Killian," she requested, adjusting the scanner. Julie placed the scanner very close to Killian's skin. She held it as still as she could, her eye pressed to the eyepiece. After thirty seconds Julie lowered the instrument. "His skin is contaminated, too," she concluded, biting her lower lip nervously. "The level is so low that the scanner can't detect it unless it's held still long enough to integrate the signal."

"He probably has specks on his skin," said Temple.

"Maybe," Julie responded doubtfully.

"There's no *maybe* about it," Temple snapped.

"I don't know," Julie said slowly, her face screwed up in thought. "We only *think* we know what we're dealing with here. Won't know until we analyze some samples.

"I need to try something on you, Mr. Killian," Julie told him.

"What?" he asked suspiciously.

"Please, just stand there. I'm going to spray some of the neutralizing chemical in the air and let the vapor drift onto you."

"Will it make me sick?" Killian's fright grew with each second. News accounts of accidental radiation and poison leaks ran through his mind.

"No, it's harmless," Julie assured him.

Killian stood rigidly while Julie sprayed several puffs of chemical in his direction. He seemed ready to bolt when the thin blue haze drifted over him. Julie spread Killian's shirt on a bench and repeated the process. She waited for five minutes, then scanned Killian and his shirt. Nothing.

Julie almost collapsed with relief. "I think we can still safely get people out of here," she announced, "but since we don't know what we're dealing with for sure, we have to decontaminate everyone and all of their clothes before they leave. The skin indications are so weak, normal scanning won't detect the contamination. I don't have enough chemical to treat everyone individually, and we need to fog the whole lab."

Julie hesitated, steeling herself for the reaction she knew her next words would bring. "There's only one way to make sure. Everyone has to strip—to the skin, everything off—before we fog the lab."

There was a collective gasp. "You got to be kidding!" someone exclaimed.

"I'm not kidding."

"Really, Dr. Barns," objected Temple with disgust. "There is such a thing as dignity. Even men have it," he finished sarcastically.

Mike surveyed the rebellious faces. He knew what was going through the men's minds. Walking around naked in a locker room was one thing, but being ordered by some woman to strip and be sprayed like a bunch of cattle was another.

"Is this the only way, Julie?" Mike asked.

"There's not enough in the tank to do it any other way. I can open up the canisters and fill the lab with vapor. That will take care of the people, their clothes and the equipment all at the same time. There's not enough to take care of all this equipment, but it should get most of the microbes outside cabinets. We can reduce the chance of microbes escaping the building before we obtain the equipment and enough chemical to finish the decontamination."

"We'll do it," Mike announced firmly. "We can't take any chances, people. Nobody, but nobody leaves this room until they are decontaminated. If you're too modest, you can wait until we have enough chemical on hand to do it privately, but that will be tomorrow, maybe the next day."

Angry murmuring rumbled through the room, and no one began undressing.

"Come on, let's get this over with," Julie urged. She unbuttoned her skirt and let it fall to the floor, revealing long tanned legs.

Shock swept the men's faces. Mike's breath caught.

Julie unbuttoned and discarded her blouse. She reached behind her and struggled with her bra clasp for a moment. It came loose, and she pulled the bra from her shoulders. She pushed her panties down over her hips and stepped out of them.

Julie faced the men, breasts pointed high and the dark tangle below her flat belly jutting defiantly.

Astonishment filled the room. Mike fought the urge to cover her. Temple's eyes bulged.

"Everybody spread their clothes out on the benches," Julie instructed, carefully arranging skirt, blouse and underwear on the nearest one.

An engineer nearby loosened his tie, pulled it off and

started to unbutton his shirt. Soon the room was filled with the rustle of clothes and angry muttering.

Julie picked up the tanks. "Mike, help me get these on my back."

"Let me do that, Julie."

"No, I'd better do it. I've practiced this procedure dozens of times as part of our safety drills." Mike helped Julie strap the canisters to her back. He winced at the angry red marks the straps made on her bare skin.

Julie filled the room with blue haze. "All right, everybody," she said when she finished. "We'll wait an hour and do another scan. If we don't find anything, you can dress and leave."

Dawn was breaking by time the staff filed out. Temple ordered task leaders and some technicians to remain to help with decontamination. Most went to sleep in chairs or on top of benches. Temple instructed the guard to inform arriving staff that they had been put on administrative leave because of ventilation problems—almost the truth.

Julie, Mike, Scott and Temple had gathered in Temple's office to plan how to complete the decontamination. "Do you need your management's permission to bring your equipment out here, Julie?" Mike asked.

"Yes, and that's going to be a real problem."

"Think it would help if I called?"

"No. You *are* the problem. You're the guy we've been fighting off. And what could you tell them? You say this is all secret."

"I guess somehow I'm going to have to convince NSF to force Lesatec to cooperate."

"But you've already tried that," Scott pointed out.

"This is an emergency—it has nothing to do with the program issue."

"Classification is still a problem."

151

"Not that much of a problem. The NSF people we deal with have clearances, so they can talk freely with military researchers. Besides, I've already broken enough security regulations tonight to get me tossed in jail. I'll do whatever else it takes. Unfortunately, I'm not going to be able to get hold of the right guy until about nine. Julie, while we wait, why don't you tell us some more about these microbes—how they propagate, what they attack, anything that might help us."

At 0830 Saba called. "They've gone crazy out here, Julie! I'm sure we're going to be fired, and we're probably going to be tossed in jail for grand theft. They shut the lab down and sent everybody home but me. Probably want to keep an eye on me until the cops get here."

The news jolted Julie. She hadn't expected repercussions so soon, or that they would be so extreme. "I'll be there as soon as I can and explain."

"I hope you can tell them more than you told me."

"I'll work it out with them somehow."

Julie had hoped to reach Lesatec before her management people discovered what she'd done. She'd believed she might have been able to talk them into being reasonable.

"We have a problem with my management people, Mike. They found out about last night and are really exercised. They're treating it like grand theft. There's no chance they'll give us more chemicals. They'll probably have me jailed for taking what I did."

"Could we get along without Lesatec's chemicals?" Mike asked, knowing the answer but hoping for a miracle.

"Afraid not. All we did was get exposed stuff. Maybe a little inside the boxes, but at the concentrations we achieved, it's likely the microbes are still in there multiplying. We need to seal the building, open up all cases with seals or filtration systems and fill the building with neutralizing vapor. We need to maintain a high concentration for several days. And even if Lesatec gives us all they have, it might not be enough.''

"I'll call NSF," Mike said. He hated to think about how long it could take to work through the bureaucracy.

As Mike reached for the phone it buzzed. It was Admiral Kittering's executive assistant. "Captain Boen, please."

"Speaking."

"Please hold for Admiral Kittering, sir."

"What the hell is going on out there, Captain?" Kittering bellowed.

"We had an emergency, sir."

"I know that," Kittering growled. "What I don't know is what kind of emergency."

"Sir, it can't be discussed over the—"

"Dammit! I know that! Get your ass in here and explain!"

"Yes, sir, but I'm having difficulty with a contractor that I need to straighten out first."

"The first thing you have to do is straighten things out with me," he growled. "Don't talk to contractors or anyone else before you talk to me. Understand?"

"Yes, sir."

"My EA will arrange for a Navy car to pick you up. There's always one somewhere in your vicinity. He'll bump somebody and have the car there in a few minutes. I'll see you in an hour."

"Yes, sir."

The EA came back on the line. "Come directly to the vault, Captain. We'll meet in the admiral's office."

Mike slowly replaced the receiver, feeling he was eyeball-deep in shit and sinking fast.

"Sounds like you have boss trouble, too," Julie commented.

"Yeah. Admirals take a long time getting over being called in the middle of the night by some captain with a problem. I have to scrape the admiral off the ceiling before I call NSF and get anyone else involved."

"I'll do what I can," Julie said in a discouraged voice. "But what can I tell my management people? I have to tell them *something*," she pleaded. "Can I tell them that there was a spill of infectious material?"

"No way!" exclaimed Temple. "If anyone thought we were working with anything connected with biological warfare, everybody would be fighting over who was going to cut our throats first. Can you imagine the lawsuits if anyone thought we had allowed infectious material to escape?"

"Jack's right," Mike agreed. "Take a long time to get to work, Julie, a *very* long time," Mike suggested. "Go home. Take a shower. Get some sleep." Mike wished *he* had time for a shower. He knew he looked and smelled like shit after being awake for thirty hours and being sprayed with disinfectant. Maybe the admiral would understand, but he doubted it.

"Don't answer the phone." Mike instructed Julie. "I'll call after I've talked to Kittering and NSF. You do have an answering machine with call monitoring?"

"Yes."

"Turn it on and listen for me."

The Pentagon

The EA escorted Mike to Admiral Kittering's office. His office was small by admiral standards. Vault office space was scarce, even for an admiral. A small conference table, six chairs and a couch took up most of the space.

"Captain, I take it you have a good explanation for calling me in the middle of the night to get some uncleared person I've never heard of into a sensitive area," the admiral said as Mike walked through the door.

"I do and it has to do with Illogic. Those helicopters were disabled by a biological agent, Admiral. We had no inkling of that, and microbes from the samples I brought back contaminated our laboratory. Put it out of business."

The admiral blanched. "Is that what killed the Frenchmen?" he asked fearfully. If lab people died from some BW agent they had obtained by means of an unauthorized covert mission, Congress and the public would demand more than his resignation. Kittering feared he'd end his Navy career in jail.

"No, sir. The French personnel were killed by conventional weapons. The CIA tested the tissue samples I brought back and found no BW or CW agents."

The admiral breathed normally again.

"These agents attack equipment, not people, just like the agents we are developing for NESW. But they're produced by micro-organisms. What we have is a machine disease. The samples I brought back infected the lab equipment." Mike went on to explain the situation as best he could. By the time he finished, the admiral was a frightened man.

"Knowing how sensitive all of this is, why did you bring in this Dr. Barns?"

Mike took a deep breath, and braced for a violent reaction. "The agents came from her lab."

"From her lab! How could they come from her lab?"

Mike described Julie's involvement and the suspected technology theft.

"This is a helluva lot more serious than I thought it would be, and I thought it would be damn serious," the admiral said grimly. "We're going to have to get SECNAV involved . . . probably SECDEF and the

White House, too. Can you imagine what terrorists could do with this?''

''We have a more immediate problem, sir.''

''What could be more immediate?'' the admiral snapped irritably.

''The lab decontamination is not complete. Until it is, the whole region is threatened. But we don't think Lesatec will give us permission to use its chemicals and equipment unless we find some way to force them.''

''But haven't they already given permission?''

''We didn't really have their permission, not management's permission. Dr. Barns recognized the seriousness of the situation and provided the equipment we used. She may get fired for it. May even be accused of theft.''

The admiral glared at Mike with hard eyes. Then the storm went out of his face. He'd taken the same kind of unauthorized action many times. ''How can we get our hands on the equipment and keep your Dr. Barns out of jail?''

''A call from you would help put them off until I can convince NSF to do something.''

''I think you've been up too long, Captain. You're not thinking. What would some executive in a company whose business is environmental protection think of a call from the Director of Navy Intelligence? He'd go straight to the press. I can see the headlines now. 'Navy lab performing unauthorized biological-warfare research has disastrous spill.' The whole Navy would be crucified.''

''What do you suggest, sir?''

''I suggest you figure out how to solve the problem, and get right on it.''

Mike fought to control his temper. How the hell was he supposed to solve the problem without any help from the Pentagon or from the admiral that had gotten him into the mess in the first place?

"I'm going to let the SECNAV people know what's going on, Captain. They'll be screaming for briefings. So expect a call any time, day or night. How long have you been up, Captain?"

"Thirty-six hours, sir."

"You look like hell. Smell like it, too. Take time to get yourself cleaned up."

"Yes, sir."

"Well, what are you waiting for?"

"Nothing, sir." Mike turned and started for the door, feeling more than a little abused.

"Captain." Mike stopped. "Helluva good job. You confirmed my worst suspicions, unfortunately, but helluva good job. I'll support you any way I can."

"Thank you, sir." Maybe Kittering wasn't such a bastard after all, Mike concluded. He started for the door again, then stopped and turned back when an idea struck him. "Admiral, could you get the CNR to help? His office does a lot of work with NSF. NSF funds this program and a lot of other Lesatec work. The Chief of Naval Research certainly has more clout than an unknown captain. He can probably convince NSF to pressure Lesatec into cooperating."

"That just might be possible. Sit down."

Kittering picked up the phone and buzzed his secretary. "Get me the CNR on the phone, and I want to talk to him secure, so get him on the scrambler."

"Boyce," Kittering said to the CNR when he came on the phone, "I have an emergency, and really need your help." He put the CNR on the speaker phone, and Mike explained the situation.

"I think we can fix it," the CNR said when Mike finished. "I had my EA get my environmental guy, Dr. George Gersch, up here while we were talking. He knows Lesatec, the NSF people and Dr. Barns. He's on the line."

Gersch then spoke. "Admiral, Captain, I think I can help you. I work with the NSF people who fund the Lesatec work. We've been tracking Dr. Barns's work, because the Navy is a big player in environmental-protection research. We have bases all over the world. Most are where they could pollute coasts and fisheries. Ships would also be big polluters if we didn't do anything. We've made a lot of advances in the area and support a lot of environmental research, including waste disposal. We can tell Lesatec that the Navy is investigating some new dumping techniques for R&D installations, and we've discovered micro-organisms are polluting our facilities."

"Will they believe that?" Admiral Kittering asked skeptically.

"Probably not, but it doesn't really matter. If NSF orders Lesatec to cooperate with the Navy, Lesatec will cooperate with the Navy—no matter what their contracts say. They can't afford to lose NSF support."

"What about Dr. Barns?" Mike asked. "She may lose her job."

"I don't see that happening," Gersch replied. "Lesatec's most promising contract depends on her. Fire her and it's good-bye contract. They won't do that.

"I should be able to get the NSF people out to Lesatec in a couple of hours, Captain. Meet me there, and we'll get things moving."

Mike concluded he'd finally found an office in the bureaucracy that could act swiftly and decisively. He could allow himself to believe that the situation would soon be in hand.

Mike walked out of the admiral's office feeling that he'd turned a corner. He used the EA's phone to call Julie. After six rings, the answering machine came on. He talked to it to let her know it was him.

Julie's sleepy voice interrupted the machine. "Mike?"

"It's me."

"Is there anything you can do?"

"Everything is being taken care of."

"Who's taking care of it?"

"Dr. Gersch at ONR and his boss, Admiral Boyce. They are going to work with NSF to get things going."

"How did—"

"I'll explain later. I'm meeting with the ONR and NSF folks at Lesatec in a couple of hours. I need you there."

"I'll be there."

Chapter Eleven

White Oak, Maryland

"I think that's it, Mike," Julie said as they finished with the last office PC and shoved it back in its case. Fatigue slurred her speech.

"What do you think?" Mike asked a red-eyed Scott.

"I think we've done all we can. Jack?"

"Any more would be a waste of time," Temple answered brusquely.

"Let's go home," Mike said, suddenly feeling the exhaustion. It was two a.m. "Maybe I can get a couple hours' sleep before the Pentagon starts calling." He knew Kittering had been to SECNAV by now. They would be screaming for a briefing, and it would snowball from there. "I'll drop you by your apartment, Julie. Julie . . . Julie!" She had fallen asleep in her chair.

Julie's head snapped up, and she stared at Mike with

bleary eyes. "What? I'm sorry. I must have dozed off." She smiled wearily.

"Come on. I'm taking you home."

As they crossed the parking lot, Julie stumbled. Mike caught her and swept her into his arms.

"Put me down," she protested weakly. "I can walk."

Mike ignored her and carried her to his car. He deposited her on the front seat and buckled her in.

Julie slept soundly all the way back to Crystal City, her head snuggled against his shoulder. He had the urge to slip his arm around her and pull her closer, but he didn't dare. If he got that comfortable, he'd fall asleep at the wheel, crash and probably kill them both.

Crystal City, Virginia

Mike woke Julie when they reached the underground parking garage. "I need your parking card to open the gate." She rummaged through her purse, found it and handed it to him. He inserted it into the slot, and the red-and-white arm snapped up.

Mike found a space near the elevator. After some more rummaging in her purse, Julie found the ring with the keys to the elevator and her apartment.

"Thanks, Julie," Mike said when they reached her apartment door.

"Thanks for what?"

"For preventing a disaster."

"A disaster I caused?" she responded bitterly.

"Don't blame yourself. Sometimes things just go wrong. Nothing you can do about it."

"But I could have done something about it," she argued miserably. "I could have dealt with the containment problem long before now. I kept putting it off, making myself believe the chemicals would do it. Same thing with Omar. Didn't want to believe he was a thief or that he could steal anything he could use.'' Anguish tortured her face. Her eyes were pits of misery.

She let Mike draw her against him. She laid her head against his chest. Mike searched for soothing words. He couldn't find any. He could only press her to him and hope it would help. He cared about this woman that he hardly knew. He wanted to protect her, care for her. She awakened feelings he'd thought he would never have for another woman.

"Why don't you stay here tonight, Mike," Julie murmured against him. "It's three in the morning. By the time you get home and to bed, it'll be time to get up and go back to work. If you stay here, you'll almost be at work when you wake up." It made sense. He had a fresh uniform in his locker at the Pentagon Officers Athletic Club, which was located in the Pentagon basement. He could shower there and change on the way to Kittering's office. The admiral would expect a full report first thing in morning.

"Thanks," Mike said.

The one-bedroom, one-bath apartment had a combination dining-living room and a large kitchen. It wasn't sleekly furnished like most Crystal City apartments. A mismatched menagerie of furniture, plants and fugitives from craft shows crowded her living room. The white naugahyde couch with impossibly overstuffed cushions didn't go with the solid oak table and its massive chairs. Julie bought and discarded furniture a piece at a time with little thought to coordination. Whenever she discovered something she liked, she bought it, then figured out where to put it and what had to go to make room for it.

The rest of the apartment contained only bare essentials. The one extravagance was her bed. Julie had purchased the largest bed she could find. She rolled around a lot in her sleep, and wanted to have all the room she could get for her nocturnal twisting and turnings. It had been different during her marriage. She hadn't rolled around much, just wrapped herself around the warm body beside her. Her ex-husband had liked that in the beginning, but had complained bitterly about broken sleep when their marriage had begun to fail. He'd grow angry and move to the couch. He moved there permanently when he began sleeping with his lady law associate. Julie tried to suppress the memories of her broken marriage. The memories hurt.

She'd been consumed by love, and had believed Thad loved her when they'd married. They'd been university students; she'd been in graduate school and he in law school. Living together had saved them from financial disaster. Julie wondered whether it had been a marriage of convenience for him—handy sex and help with the rent.

Mike closed and locked the apartment door and handed Julie the keys. "I'm afraid my couch is not the fold-down kind . . . small, too," she said hesitantly.

"It'll be all right."

"No, I'll sleep out here," she decided. "You're a lot bigger, you take the bed."

"I am *not* taking your bed, Julie," Mike said firmly.

"Well, I'll get you a blanket and sheet."

Julie's full bladder woke her before dawn. She dozed off again and dreamed she was wetting the bed. The realistic dream jolted her awake, and she hurried to the bathroom.

Julie came out of the bathroom lusting for a large glass of ice water. She put on a robe, and walked softly through the living room toward the kitchen. The dim night light illuminated Mike, who had given up on the couch and lay curled on the floor. The blanket lay crumpled by his side. He'd removed everything but his

163

jockey shorts. She hurried into the kitchen, hoping he wouldn't wake.

Julie couldn't understand why she was so thirsty. She drank until she felt nauseous. She refilled the pitcher, returned it to the refrigerator, turned out the light and left the kitchen.

Julie stopped and stared at Mike. He had stirred in his sleep. He had stretched out on his back, every muscle tense. He was having a bad dream, she surmised. Her eyes traveled over him. She liked his body: not heavily muscled, but obviously strong. A tangle of wiry hair spread across his chest. His black hair was mussed and tousled like a boy's. His face seemed as guileless as a child's in his sleep. What if he was hers? she speculated. What would he be like as a lover? Husband? Need built inside her, almost painful in its fullness. Not make-love need. To-have-and-to-hold need. The long emotion-torn hours had underlined how devoid her life was of close personal relationships. She realized that she couldn't identify a close friend: someone to reach out to when there was heartache in her life, someone that would seek her in a time of need. She had let obsession with her research rush her past life . . . maybe too fast. She'd always assumed that she would marry again and have a family. But a husband and family wouldn't happen unless she slowed down and did something besides root around in the lab. If she did slow down, would somebody like Mike Boen happen?

Mike groaned and rolled on his side, drawing his legs up. Julie stopped breathing. She didn't want him to wake and find her leering at him. Mike grumped a couple of times, pillowed his head on his hands and subsided back into deep sleep.

Julie let out her breath and hurried into her bedroom. She shrugged out of her robe, crawled into bed, rolled on her back and pulled the sheet up to her chin. She wondered about herself. She had never pictured herself as a woman who would stand there leering at a nearly naked man in his sleep. She'd have been outraged if he'd taken advantage of her like that.

Julie couldn't understand how a virtual stranger could affect her the way he did, send warm quivery feelings through her every time he touched her.

Julie fell asleep with her mind full of Mike Boen.

The Libyan Desert

Aziz had been switching his Fox Fire radar on and off for the last ten minutes—never keeping it on for more than ten seconds out of each minute. He didn't want to set off the Sirena-3 360-degree radar-warning system in the Foxbat-E that he knew would be escorting the dictator's MiG-25U Foxbat-C. The Foxbat-C was a two-seat trainer version of the MiG-25 high-altitude interceptor. It was combat-capable, but lacked the radar and other avionics of the interceptors. Aziz knew Gadhafi would be in the rear seat.

Aziz again cursed Gadhafi's seemingly supernatural luck. They had planned to kill him in his office, but when they had sorted out the bodies, Gadhafi's wasn't among them. Aziz had raced to the hidden airfield on the outskirts of Tripoli, but he'd been too late. The colonel had been already airborne, racing for a heavily fortified bunker hidden deep in the desert. It had taken Aziz fifteen minutes to secure another Foxbat and pursue him. Aziz had been very lucky himself. The plane had been fueled and armed, and the pilot they'd shot had been the same size as Aziz. His flight suit had been too full of holes and blood to be of use, but he hadn't yet donned his g-suit. It hadn't been damaged.

Aziz knew Gadhafi's escape route. He had flown escort a few times when it had seemed the Americans had finally been provoked into an attack. Gadhafi had always ridden in the back seat of an unarmed Foxbat-C, escorted by a heavily armed Foxbat-E. The Foxbats had been chosen for escape planes because of their speed and ability to climb faster and higher than anything else in the region.

Aziz's frustration grew. His radar showed nothing. Then a blip flashed on the display at the edge of the Fox Fire's range. Aziz risked leaving the radar on for an extra five seconds to make sure. He smiled with satisfaction as he shut down the radar and increased power. He was at 60,000 feet and could reach almost Mach-3. His prey flew at 2000 feet, hoping to stay below radar horizon. The Foxbats could barely make Mach-1 at that altitude, and Gadhafi's aircraft were flying at 400 knots to conserve fuel. They weren't expecting airborne pursuit. Aziz forced himself to be patient, and held his MiG to 1100 knots to conserve fuel.

When Aziz turned on his Fox Fire radar again, he was dismayed. The blobs on the radar display were only partially separated, but Aziz was sure there were three planes instead of the two he'd expected. A nervous band squeezed his forehead. He was confident that he could handle one Foxbat-E and the unarmed trainer, but *two* Foxbat-Es were going to be difficult—very difficult. Aziz knew who would be flying the escorts. There were only two pilots besides himself with knowledge of the secret landing strip and bunker buried deep in the Libyan desert. They were the best fighter pilots in the Libyan Air Force. They had trained in the Soviet Union and had flown combat missions with the Iraqi Air Force. Aziz had flown simulated combat against both pilots. He had always considered himself the victor, but not by a large margin, and the other pilots would certainly debate his assessment.

Fighting his way past both escorts to shoot down Gadhafi's plane was a task that daunted even Aziz's huge ego, but he didn't hesitate. He gently nosed the Foxbat over and accelerated to its not-to-exceed Mach-3 combat speed.

When Aziz pulled out at 2000 feet, the dense, low-altitude air and maneuver reduced his airspeed to 600 knots, still 200 knots faster than his quarry. He was only five miles away when the escorts reacted. The Foxbat off the two-seater's right wing banked into a high-g turn. He knew the pilot would attempt to escape and come around behind Aziz while Aziz chased the other aircraft. If Aziz followed the maneuvering craft, the other escort would break off and pounce on his tail. He'd be sandwiched.

The Foxbats in front of Aziz went to afterburner and pointed their noses skyward. He decided to take his chances with the plane attempting to get behind him, and went for Gadhafi's aircraft. He heard a frantic cry over the radio from the turning MiG: "Foxbat behind you! He is going after our leader's plane!"

Aziz armed the radar-guided Acrid missile. The clean MiG-25U could outrace his missile-laden aircraft. He had to get off a shot before it was out of range. He punched the firing button. Aziz heard the turning MiG's pilot scream into his radio: "Missile launch! Missile launch!" Gadhafi's pilot dove, trying to get down into the radar ground clutter. The missile followed. The Foxbat-C pulled into a seven-g descending turn. A ball of orange fire obscured Aziz's view. He held both his course and his breath.

The fireball faded to thin smoke, and a wave of frustration swept through Aziz as he watched Gadhafi's plane twist away low across the desert out of missile range.

Aziz could no longer ignore the jet behind him. He intended to survive, even if it meant letting Gadhafi escape. Aziz slammed the throttles to full power and stood the MiG on its tail. His plane leaped skyward.

The hairs on the back of Aziz's neck prickled. He imagined the pilot behind him arming an Aphid and locking onto Aziz's exhaust. Aziz pulled out of afterburner. His MiG shuddered through heavy buffet and fell awkwardly into a dive. The other MiG roared past so close its wake shook Aziz's craft. The pilot hadn't been able to follow Aziz's floundering maneuver.

Aziz pushed the throttles to the stops, and was barely able to pull out before slamming into the desert. He'd gotten behind the other MiG, but it sprinted out of missile range before Aziz's Foxbat regained speed.

The MiG looped out of its climb, rolled over and roared back at Aziz. Aziz pulled up his plane's nose and fired an Acrid before the other pilot could arm his missile. It was no contest. The radar-guided missile had no trouble locking onto a target with a clutter-free sky background. It slammed into an intake and turned the Foxbat into a plunging fireball.

Aziz banked into a hard turn to avoid the cloud of burning debris that swarmed by him, and pointed the Foxbat's nose after the fleeing MiGs.

The climbing aircraft shrank to specks and disappeared. Aziz's radar showed Gadhafi's plane had reached 70,000 feet, and it was roaring away at close to Mach-3. Aziz didn't want to believe Gadhafi could escape, but it was hard not to. The dogfight had used so much fuel, Aziz was likely to run out before he could catch Gadhafi's craft. To make matters worse, the surviving escort's radar return was increasing instead of diminishing. It was coming back to challenge Aziz. More fuel and time gone.

Aziz suspected that Jassim al-Amir was piloting the remaining Foxbat-E. He didn't fear risk, but he was a deliberate, careful man who did nothing that was not well thought out. Jassim had to be the survivor. He would have never allowed Aziz to draw him into the fatal head-on confrontation.

Aziz couldn't yet see Jassim's MiG; he had to rely on the Fox Fire radar, but it had no trouble locking onto the jet against the clutter-free sky background. Jassim's radar and missile-guidance sensors were going to have trouble separating Aziz's Foxfire from the ground clutter. Aziz knew Jassim wanted to stay in a lookdown/shootdown position, which would give him an advantage over Aziz's more awkward shoot-up situation.

Jassim pulled out soon enough to maintain a 10,000-foot altitude advantage. Jassim could shoot an Apex as he passed over Aziz, turn and shoot again while maintaining his lookdown/shootdown advantage. But it would be a beyond-visual-range engagement using the Fox Fire radar, whose lookdown/shootdown capability against low-altitude targets was limited. Jassim would have to reduce range dangerously in order to overcome the radar ground clutter.

Aziz hauled the plane into a tight loop, completing it at 5000 feet and leveling out. His Sirena-3 complained of fire-control-radar signals. He couldn't see him, but Aziz knew Jassim was diving after him, probably thanking Allah and Aziz's stupidity for giving him such an opportunity. Aziz kept increasing speed and descending, keeping his Foxbat just out of missile range.

Aziz pulled into a turn that dimmed the world despite his g-suit. Jassim's altitude advantage was now a disadvantage. He couldn't turn as fast in the thinner air. Aziz turned inside Jassim's turn and armed and fired his last Acrid without checking range to target.

The Acrid raced away. It didn't quite make it all the way, but exploded close enough for fragments to damage control surfaces. Jassim's Foxbat suddenly decelerated. It rolled and its nose dropped. Aziz armed and fired a short-range IR-guided AA-8 Aphid as Jassim's plane loomed in front of him. He hauled back on the stick and barely avoided slamming into the rear of the MiG. It exploded behind him. The shock wave jolted Aziz's plane.

Aziz turned onto the Foxbat-C's last observed course and studied the Fox Fire radar display. There was nothing within its fifty-mile range. Aziz refused to give up. He increased power of the twin Tumansky turbojets, but he didn't dare use the afterburner, which would rapidly empty his tanks.

After fifteen discouraging minutes, Aziz thought he saw something on the edge of the radar display. The blob was steadier than clutter, and it grew into a hard-target return. Two minutes later an elated Aziz knew he'd found Gadhafi's plane. It had slowed to search for the poorly marked airfield, giving Aziz time to catch up before it landed.

The Foxbat-C had no radar-warning system, and the pilot had no inkling he was being tracked. He was in his final approach when Aziz dove from the sky like a hawk. He fired his last missile, an Aphid, when he was almost on top of the Foxbat-C. Flaming debris tumbled the length of the runway.

Aziz circled the smoking smear of wreckage, filled with triumph. He, Colonel Muhammad Aziz, now ruled Libya, and would soon rule all of North Africa . . . maybe more. And it was because he was the best fighter pilot in the world.

Tripoli

When Colonel Muhammad Aziz strode into the late dictator's office, he stumbled over a bullet-riddled body lying in the doorway, slipped on the bloody floor and nearly fell. Automatic weapons rattled somewhere in the building. The stench of blood and excrement choked the room.

A band of steely-eyed men waited for Aziz. Aziz

regained his footing and surveyed the tense group. They were all heavily armed with automatic weapons. But not all were his co-conspirators. Aziz had killed Gadhafi, but he hadn't won yet. He and his grand scheme could perish in a careless burst of gunfire. It was one of those instants when history balances on the knife edge of a moment, waiting to be nudged off by a flick of emotion.

Aziz had counted on Gadhafi's staff to allow the coup to take place. Only the intricate security apparatus, fueled by mistrust and maintained by treachery, had prevented these men from disposing of Gadhafi themselves. They hadn't trusted one another enough to even speak of it, let alone organize to do it. Now that the deed was done, and Gadhafi's web of security smashed, they could look to their own ambitions. Those ambitions could fuel Aziz's own assassination.

Aziz stopped. Waited. Held a 9mm Stechkin AP machine pistol by his side. His men had positioned themselves in back of the dead dictator's staff. If Aziz had miscalculated, there would be bloody carnage, which he would likely not survive.

"Is he dead?" someone asked.

"He is dead," Aziz stated flatly.

"How?"

"His aircraft was shot down just before landing at his secret refuge in the desert." The eyes were suspicious. "*I* shot it down." His eyes challenged anyone to dispute him.

"You caught up with him then?" This questioner was one of Aziz's men.

"Yes."

"The other two MiGs also?" a wondering voice asked.

"All three."

There were elated eyes. There were suspicious eyes. There were hostile eyes. There were eyes which were

171

indecipherable. The room poised on the edge of violence.

"Brothers, the dictator is dead," Aziz announced again. "And there is a new order." Aziz paused. The eyes didn't change. "Not just here, not just in Libya, but all across North Africa Muslims are taking back their birthright from criminal dictators who have insulted the name of the Prophet. The corrupted will all be destroyed this day."

"What do you mean?" someone asked skeptically.

"Tyrants are dying this day in Chad, Sudan, all across North Africa."

"Planned?"

"And executed." His emphasis gave the word all of its literal meanings. Now there was more fear than hostility in the faces.

An Air Force major entered the room. He carried a large portable shortwave radio. "It's happening, Colonel!" he cried. He set the radio on the late dictator's desk and turned it on.

The information was fragmentary, but was sufficient to establish that upheaval was sweeping North Africa—from the Red Sea to the shores of the Atlantic. Fingers eased on triggers.

Aziz strode to the massive desk and lowered himself into Gadhafi's chair, signaling that he had assumed command. "We who have freed our country from the yoke of the dictator ask you, our Arab brothers, to join us and help establish a new world order, an order in which Arabs will no longer be the puppets of America and its lackeys. We will be the puppeteers. They will dance at the end of *our* strings." Invoking the ageless dream took Aziz past the crisis. His confidence surged. Then he saw her. His confidence slipped a little. That made him angry.

Fatima had materialized near the door. She stood silently against the wall, unnoticed, swathed in robe and veil from head to toe. Her incandescent eyes burned out at him.

The storm of excited discussion went on for almost an hour. Fatima stood as still as the wall behind her, seemingly invisible to everyone but Aziz. She nagged at his consciousness, a worry that shouldn't have been there. He vowed once again to rid himself of her at the earliest possible moment.

Finally the excitement waned enough to allow Aziz to order the room cleared. "The bodies?" someone asked.

"Leave them for a while. I need to read the messages my servant has brought me." Resentment flared in Fatima's eyes. Servant indeed! There were puzzled frowns; a woman messenger was unusual, but Gadhafi had used them.

"It is done!" Aziz exclaimed in elation when the door closed behind the last man.

"Yes, it's done," Fatima agreed, her voice charged with emotion. "It's the day we have long waited for. My only regret is that his body is not here. How did he die?"

"Too mercifully," Aziz answered.

Fatima removed the veil. Triumph filled her face, but rapidly disappeared behind the cold mask she used to hide her emotions. "The Americans know we have the technology," she stated.

"I know that," he replied casually. He enjoyed the surprise that ruffled her face.

"You know? How—"

"I also have my sources," he informed her.

"Doesn't it concern you?" she asked harshly.

"Of course it concerns me," he growled. "Don't persist in speaking to me as though I am an idiot," he said. "You need me more than I need you."

"That is debatable," she responded defiantly. "What do you think the Americans will do?"

"Nothing immediately. It will take their bureaucracy weeks to agree that there is a threat and even longer to decide what to do about it. Then they must debate the options. By that time, we will be in firm control."

"In firm control? I think not. There are Egypt and the others. You might have to actually use the weapon."

"Perhaps."

"Perhaps? Victory doesn't stand still. It leaves those who linger."

"Don't lecture me, woman." The *woman* was meant as an insult. "*I* will decide what is to be done, and when."

"Our agreement?"

"You can trust me."

"No, I can't."

"You know there is nothing to be done now," he chided. "The pronouncement you want would tear the coalition apart at this point."

"We will not wait much longer. The coalition means nothing to us unless it brings us freedom."

Aziz won the battle to hold his tongue. Death, not freedom, awaited her, but he still needed her and her band of bitches.

Chapter Twelve

Crystal City, Virginia

The phone dragged Julie awake. "This is Scott, Julie. Is Mike there?"

"Yes," she answered sleepily.

"I need to talk to him. It's super-urgent."

"I'll get him." Julie slipped on a robe and hurried into the living room.

Mike was still stretched out on his back asleep. The crotch of his jockey shorts bulged with a partial erection. Was he dreaming of her? She scolded herself for being a dirty old woman, untangled the blanket and covered him. She didn't know whether she was protecting his modesty or hers.

Julie shook Mike's shoulder. "Mike." He answered with a groan. "Mike!" She shook him harder.

His eyes snapped open and he sat up abruptly, the blanket falling to his waist. He looked surprised to see her, then remembered where he was. He groaned. "Time to get up already?"

"Scott's on the phone. Says it's urgent." She picked up a phone sitting on the coffee table, set it beside him and gave him the receiver.

"Scott?" he said into the phone.

"Admiral Kittering is screaming for you, Mike. Sounded like he's going to have you shot because you weren't in his office at 0700." Mike glanced at his watch: 0720. He'd had only three hours sleep. "I lied, Mike. Told him you were on your way. If you don't meet him in SECNAV's office in thirty minutes, I think he's going to have you court-martialed."

"But I need to stop by the POAC for a shower and clean uniform," Mike protested.

"How long will that take?"

"Too long."

"Why don't you shower at Julie's and skip the fresh uniform? I'll have a car out front by the time you finish."

"All right, but I'll never be an admiral if I show up in SECNAV's office with this gamy uniform." Mike hung up the phone and rubbed his eyes wearily.

"Trouble?" Julie asked.

"Admiral Kittering wants me in SECNAV's office immediately, and I'm a mess."

"I heard. Look, get in the shower," she ordered briskly. "Use my stuff—toothbrush, deodorant, anything you need. I have a Lady Schick you can use if you don't mind a pink razor. I'll spot off your uniform and press out the wrinkles. Well, don't just sit there! Get going!"

When Mike emerged from the bathroom, clad in his shorts, Julie waited by the bed with his uniform. She handed him his shirt. He put it on and hurriedly buttoned it. "Wait!" she ordered. She unbuttoned his shirt again. "You have it crooked." She rebuttoned his shirt, then reached up to straightened his collar. Her breasts pressed into him, and her lips were close enough to kiss. He had the urge to crush her in his arms and devour her.

"I put all your stuff back in your pockets," she said, going to the bed for his pants. He took his pants from her and pulled them on, racing to cover the swelling he couldn't control. She made him react like a horny teenager, and it was embarrassing as hell!

"Stand still," she ordered. She brushed lint off his shirt, then stood back and surveyed him critically. "I got most of the wrinkles. A few little spots I couldn't get, but you look okay to me."

"Too bad you aren't the admiral," Mike said dispiritedly. Kittering would spot every out-of-place thread.

"You look okay," she insisted. "Now, come on, I have a cup of coffee for you."

"No time."

"Just a small cup. You need it to stay awake."

Mike stopped in the living room long enough to gulp down the coffee. Julie unlocked and held the door open for him. "Thanks, Julie." He felt as though he was saying good-bye to a wife. He hadn't intended to kiss her, but it seemed such a natural thing to do, as if they'd been married for years. "Julie, I—"

"You'd better hurry," she said quickly, staring at him with wide eyes.

"I'll call."

The Pentagon

Rear Admiral Kittering was prowling SECNAV's outer office like a caged tiger when Mike arrived. "Where the hell you been, Captain?" he roared.

"I—"

"Never mind. Do you know what's happened in North Africa?"

"No, sir, I—"

"Don't you read the damn papers?"

"Yes, sir, but—"

"There have been coups across the whole damn continent. And guess what friend of ours got his," the admiral said, smiling smugly.

"Gadhafi?"

"Yep. The good colonel."

"How?"

"Not sure, but this Colonel Aziz wouldn't be broadcasting from Tripoli and proclaiming himself the new Libyan head of state if our boy was still alive. Aziz talks about a new world order. Arabs taking their rightful place in the world. The usual Third World crap."

Mike was surprised, but not very. The reunification of Germany, the Gulf War and the disintegration of the Soviet Union made it hard to be surprised by anything.

"Sir, what's the meeting with SECNAV about?"

"Your damn mission! What the hell else would it be about! I warned you yesterday."

"Yes, sir. But I didn't expect it to be elevated so quickly."

"This North African thing has put another spin on the ball," the admiral informed him. "But we don't know which direction the ball is spinning. Sit down, captain. You ought to get more sleep, and your uniform looks like something the dog dragged in." He eyed Mike with disgust.

"As soon as the Agency people arrive, the CNO will be called," Kittering continued, "and we'll meet him and SECNAV in a vault. When they've finished chewing me out, they'll decide what to do."

Kittering was right about the chewing out. "Admiral Kittering, do you realize that you have caused an in-

ternational incident, a shooting incident, for heavens
sake!'' the SECNAV bellowed. Burton Collins was a
large man with unruly, sandy hair and a lantern jaw.
His hazel eyes flashed from behind thick glasses.

The CNO sat silent and stony-faced. He hadn't had
any inkling of Kittering's operation until receiving
SECNAV's angry call. He was not at all pleased. If the
man weren't about to retire . . .

''Sir, the implications were such—''

''Such that you should have gotten clearance clear
up to the White House. Who the hell do you think you
are? Some kind of cowboy? This is the Navy, not a
damn rodeo!''

''Yes, sir,'' Kittering answered stiffly. Mike sat frozen in his seat, his stomach a knot, wondering when
his turn would come and whether the Secretary would
demand he be kicked out of the Navy.

''Mr. Secretary, Admiral Kittering *did* have the cooperation of my agency,'' said a wide, beetle-browed
man with slick black hair and steel-gray eyes. Carl Jacobs was Andy Staple's boss and a deputy director of
the CIA. A representative of the Defense Intelligence
Agency sat at the conference table, a tall cadaverous
man with an angry face.

''He might have had your support, Mr. Jacobs, but
he didn't have mine,'' SECNAV replied. ''Admiral
Kittering is in the Navy, not the CIA. He's supposed
to do intelligence for the Navy.''

''I understand, Mr. Secretary, but let's get on with
the business at hand. I think we have a crisis which is
orders of magnitude more serious than Admiral Kittering's bruising of the rules. And I might remind you, if
it hadn't been for Admiral Kittering, we wouldn't even
know we had a crisis . . . maybe not until it was too
late.''

''Well, I'm not convinced we do have a crisis,'' the
Secretary blustered.

"We do. And what's going on in North Africa may be connected. Why don't we let Captain Boen brief us on what he's found to date, so we can all start from the same baseline?"

"Fifteen minutes," the CNO ordered harshly.

Fifteen minutes! Mike raged silently. He held his anger in check and sketched a rough account. He was subjected to an additional thirty minutes of grilling, which Mike was sure had the sole objective of making him feel like shit.

"All right, gentlemen, enough," the Secretary finally announced, halting the discussion. "We"—and he really meant himself—"have to decide what to do with this information."

"It should go to the White House immediately," Jacobs said. "The Agency has held off, since the information was collected by the Navy and we should be coordinated on this."

"This is still a Navy affair at this point," the SEC-NAV responded coldly. "I think it should go up through the chain of command—JCS and SECDEF."

"It can't wait that long, particularly in view of what's taking place in North Africa," Jacobs stated. "The Agency is required to present such information to the White House as soon as we obtain it." It was a threat. The CIA was going to the White House with or without the Navy. If that happened, Navy management would be accused of withholding vital information for political reasons. The White House would be very unhappy with the SECNAV.

Collins glared at Jacobs for a moment. "All right, we'll take this to the National Security Advisor. *I* will call. Captain Boen will do the brief," Collins stated firmly. If the information was as important as Jacobs seemed to think it was, Collins intended to ensure the Navy got credit for collecting it, since it would get the blame for the Sudanese incident in any case. But regardless of how all of this turned out, Collins intended to ask the CNO to do something about Kittering... and that captain, too.

The White House

The SECNAV didn't accompany them to the White House. He would not involve himself personally unless the President himself became concerned. He did send them in his car, a huge black Cadillac with a forest of antennas sprouting from the trunk. The car whisked Kittering, Jacobs and Mike across the Memorial Bridge, past the Lincoln Monument and onto Constitution Avenue. The car turned at 17th Street and stopped in front of the ornate Executive Office Building, which sprawled beside the White House.

Their identification and uniforms didn't save them from an intense security check. They were escorted to a small conference room in the bowels of the building, ushered in and shown the coffee and cups. Then they settled into chairs to await Jason Goodson, the President's National Security Advisor.

Mike felt abused and pissed off. He'd been treated like a criminal, instead of a Navy officer trying to do his job. And the man who'd ordered him into this mess had been none too civil either. But Mike's personal affront was trivial compared to the apprehension haunting him. He believed the world could be standing on the edge of a holocaust.

It was a half hour before Goodson arrived. He was a tall, gawky man—a former college basketball player—with a narrow face, brown hair and alert brown eyes. He folded himself into the chair at the head of the small conference table. "Well, gentlemen, I guess this *is* important. We have *both* Navy Intelligence and the CIA descending on us. Burton seems to think so. Insisted I see you immediately. Well, what is it that can't wait? We *do* have a crisis going on, you know.''

"I think this might be related," Jacobs informed him.

"Oh. How so?"

"We think that Libya has developed a weapon that could make this new North African coalition more of a threat than anyone believes."

"We aren't yet sure there is a coalition," Goodson reminded him. "Nevertheless, Libya is a threat as always, so tell me what you have."

When Mike finished his account and presented his conclusions, Goodson leaned back in his chair, his chin resting on a tent of his hands, his face squeezed in thought. "I think Burton was right," he said. "We did need to be made aware of this immediately. Could eventually play a role in the North African business. The coups were obviously coordinated, and it appears that somebody is attempting to seize control of all of North Africa. Probably this fellow Aziz, who has evidently disposed of Gadhafi."

Goodson got to his feet, glancing at his watch. "The National Security Council is meeting with the President in ninety minutes to go over the North African thing. The service secretaries, SECDEF and the Chairman of the JCS will all be there. I'll make them aware of this."

"Shouldn't we take some kind of action?" Mike asked.

"What do you suggest?" Goodson snapped, no longer affable. "We don't know what's going on over there, and except for a few stuck helicopters, we have no evidence Libya or anyone else has developed any kind of new weapon, let alone a doomsday machine."

Mike couldn't suggest anything, but he believed *something* should be done, and quickly.

"We have higher priorities right now, Captain,"

Goodson said brusquely. "We'll just have to wait and see what develops. Thank you," he said, dismissing Mike, his mind already on another crisis. He hurried from the room.

The Pentagon

"Dammit, Captain! They're going to just sit on their asses, as usual!" Kittering stood angrily behind his desk. "Well, what are you going to do?" he suddenly asked Mike.

The question startled Mike. What the hell did Kittering think a *captain* could do that all the heavies couldn't do? "We'll get the lab back in operation and monitor Lesatec's effort to develop a counter."

Kittering sank into his chair. He suddenly seemed very tired, as tired and wrung out as Mike. "I guess that's it, then," the admiral said heavily. Then he managed a smile. "We did all we could, Captain. Got'm stirred up, anyway. You *do* realize that I've probably gotten you kicked out of the Navy. SECNAV is taking all kind of shit from SECDEF and JCS because of our little operation. CNO is spitting nails. Called me twice to chew me out."

"We did what had to be done, sir."

"That's what a lot of people in jail say, too. Hell with it! Go back to your job, Captain. They'll call you when the shit hits the fan."

Alexandria, Virginia

The walk from the King Street Metro Station had never seemed so long. Carrie heard Mike unlocking the door, and came down the hall as he entered. "Mike! Where have you been? You look awful! Like you're out on your feet."

"We had an accident at the laboratory, and I've been

up day and night trying to fix things. The rest of the time I've been trying to explain why I had to fix things. And I *am* out on my feet. I just want to go to bed.''

"According to Susan, you've already been to bed. That's probably why you're so tired," Tim Polaski said, laughing. He had followed his wife into the hall. His brown eyes leered from his craggy face. Salt-and-pepper-colored stubble sprouted from his face, the same color as his hair. Baggy pants and a stained T-shirt hung on his sparse frame.

"Tim! You and your nasty mind!" Carrie exclaimed. "Mike, you'd think someone his age would have mellowed a bit."

"Oh, I've mellowed," said Tim, giving Carrie's plump bottom a quick squeeze, "but not died."

She gasped and jumped. "Tim! Stop it! Go look at a dirty book or something while I fix Mike something to eat."

"Carrie, I'll eat later—that is, if I wake up. The way I feel right now, I might not even wake up for breakfast."

When Mike finally woke up, he felt as if he'd been run over by a freight train. His mouth tasted terrible, he had to piss and he was hungry as hell. He groaned and sat up. His eyes wandered to the clock. Six? Six in the morning? He couldn't believe it. He'd slept nearly twelve hours. The aroma drifting up the stairs made his stomach squirm and pulled him from the bed.

Mike hurried to shower and shave, prodded by his empty gut. When he arrived at the kitchen table, Susan was finishing her breakfast. She looked up at him with a smug smile. "Hi, Dad. Have a nice time?"

"Nice time? I was working. Had a hell of a crisis."

Susan's eyes said, "Oh, yeah, tell me another one," but she said, "Oh." She studied him speculatively. "How's Julie?" she finally couldn't resist asking.

"Fine, I suppose," Mike mumbled around a mouthful of eggs.

"You were at her place, weren't you?"

"Some of the time," Mike admitted uncomfortably. Carrie finished puttering with the dishes, and sat down at the table, her eyes filled with curiosity.

"Just business?" Susan asked with exaggerated casualness.

"Susan, you shouldn't pry into your father's affairs," Carrie scolded, despite her own burning curiosity. "What he and his lady friend do with each other is private." Mike wished Carrie had not used quite those words.

"Didn't mean to pry. I'd better get going," Susan apologized, rising from the table. "Going to be home tonight?" she asked meaningfully.

"Yes."

"Talk to you then," Susan said as she departed.

Mike knew Carrie was filled with questions, but she contained herself. Questions filled Mike, too. What were the disturbing emotions roaming around inside him, all having to do with Julie Barns?

Crystal City, Virginia

Mike walked into the office two hours late. "Dr. Corbett needs to see you right away, and Dr. Barns has called about four times—says it's urgent," Lila announced in greeting. "And Dr. Temple called—sounded like he was going crazy. Dr. Corbett talked to him, but I don't think he'll be satisfied until he talks to you."

"Send Scott into my office. I'd better find out what's going on before I talk to anyone else."

* * *

"Doesn't look like we are going to get the lab back into operation any time soon, and that may be the least of our worries," Scott informed Mike.

"Is that what Temple called about?"

"Yeah. Seems like the microbes got through the outer air lock into the lobby."

"Oh, shit!"

"Oh, shit is right. Temple's pretty sure they stopped it there—this time."

"Pretty sure! If the microbes escape the lab and spread into the surrounding area, it'll be like a hydrogen bomb going off!"

"Well, nobody's reported anything unusual. If the microbes had escaped, they would have gotten into the Center's instruments, and we'd have heard about it by now.

"I guess all we can do is keep spraying the lab and hope we can contain the microbes until Lesatec comes up with neutralizing organisms," Mike said, his stomach queasy. "But we can't allow people to go in and out."

The intercom buzzed. Mike punched the talk button. "Dr. Barns is on the phone again, Captain. Says she has to talk to you—line five."

"Julie—"

"I've been trying to get you all morning," Julie complained. "I need samples of the contaminated materials. We need to analyze them to make sure we're dealing with the Lesatec microbes. We don't want to develop antidotes for the wrong organisms."

Mike knew he shouldn't let any of the materials go to an uncleared facility, but there was too much at stake to let regulations stop him. They would just have to put him in jail. "I'll have Scott select some samples and bring them out to you, but he has to stay with them all of the time. He can't let them out of his sight for even a second, and he'll have bring them back as soon as the analysis is done.''

"Have him call when he gets here. Either Saba or I will come out and escort him into the lab.''

"How close are you to developing a neutralizing microbe?''

"I wish I knew,'' she answered despondently. "I thought we were close months ago. If we could find the program bug, we could run the model and come up with the genetic code for the neutralizing microbe in twenty-four hours, assuming the synthesis and culturing processes Omar developed work for the anti-microbes. Searching for a program bug is like playing the lottery: mostly chance, no real methodology and no way to predict when you'll win. If you play any game long enough, you'll win, and we've been playing for a long time. Saba and I are going to live at Lesatec twenty-four hours a day until we find the problem. We'll go through every line of instruction code if we have to,'' Julie vowed.

Chapter Thirteen

Springfield, Virginia

Scott had difficulty locating the Lesatec building. He had expected a multi-storied office building. Instead he found himself driving through an industrial park bordering Shirley Highway, the main artery south from Washington. The park was a sprawl of low one-story warehouse-like buildings. They were home to everything from off-road vehicle shops to aerospace laboratories. Scott was surprised that Lesatec carried out potentially dangerous research in such a densely populated area in a bustling commercial business center, surrounded by apartments and homes. Of course the Lesatec lab wasn't the only one in urban areas handling virulent organisms; there were the medical labs engaged in production of vaccines, and those using animals for contagious-disease research. Besides, Lesatec's work had not been considered dangerous. Their microbes didn't cause disease, just made things rot. No one had considered the potential for disaster.

Scott extracted the hermetically sealed aluminum suitcase from the trunk and carried it into the Lesatec lobby. The receptionist called Saba to announce his arrival.

Panther was the word that came to Scott's mind when Saba entered the lobby. Her dancer's stride drew his attention to her strong legs, and Scott was captivated by the tantalizing length of firm thigh revealed by her short black knit dress. The snug dress amplified the thrust of her breasts, the sharp flare of her hips and her deliciously rounded bottom. Her hair was black, long and straight. It went with her dusky skin. "Dr. Corbett?" Saba said as she approached, regarding him with piercing black eyes. She struck Scott like a kick in the gut.

"Yes, and please call me Scott," he answered, a little embarrassed. She couldn't have helped but notice him leering at her legs. She smiled. If she had noticed, she didn't seem offended.

"Those are the samples?" she asked, eyeing the case.

"Yes."

"I'll take them in. We'll start the analysis immediately." She reached for the case.

"I'll carry it," Scott said, stopping her.

"Oh, that's right." She smiled politely. "Julie said you had to stay with the samples at all times. Are they classified?"

"No. But security regulations require it anyway," Scott said, reluctant to continue the discussion in the lobby with all sorts of people milling about.

"All right, this way." Scott followed her through a door that opened into a long hallway, at the end of which sat an armed guard. His desk was crowded in front of a heavy steel door with a cipher lock. "Lesatec

189

has really tightened up security—become paranoid is more the term for it,'' she complained.

''What happened?''

''You people happened. Of course they had already become nervous about the security of their trade secrets before all this came up. Julie's a very modest, save-the-world type person,'' she explained as they walked toward the guard. ''She doesn't concern herself with profit potential, and Lesatec hadn't realized the commercial value of what has been accomplished by Julie's team.''

''You mean the waste-disposal systems? They think they can sell a lot of them?''

''Not the systems, but licenses to use the process and the software. There will also be money in disposal-system design and consulting,'' she explained as the guard closely scrutinized Scott's identification. He asked for Scott's driver's license to cross-check against Scott's DoD pass.

''They *really* have gotten serious about security,'' Scott commented, surprised.

''Would you believe this is just a day old?'' she asked as the guard checked Scott's name against a computer printout sheet. ''Hired a contractor that provides security for the Defense Department. Really upset our staff.''

The guard made Saba show her ID, even though he'd just seen her emerge a few minutes ago and knew she was staff. It was a new contract, a new location, and he was a new guard. He went by the book.

''We didn't mean to trigger all this—the guards and all,'' Scott said, but he felt good about it.

''Well, I guess you could say you triggered it,'' Saba responded doubtfully, ''but this business with the government just accelerated a review that would have happened anyway. Lesatec management has just realized what the full range of commercial applications are. For example, law-enforcement people have been using DNA matching in criminal cases. But the accuracy is still being debated. There are no standards, and only a few labs are trusted enough to perform tests that could send someone away for life or to their death. There's only one company and the FBI lab in this area that can do the DNA matching. The tests can take weeks, and are very expensive. We've accelerated that process enormously. Also, because our equipment is cheap and easy to operate, this research has the potential for putting a DNA matching kit in the hands of every law-enforcement agency. That's a worldwide market.''

Scott was astounded. He was surprised there weren't more guards. The implications for medicine, drug development and a host of other applications were mind-boggling.

Saba led Scott around the guard's tiny desk and punched numbers into its cipher lock. ''Scott, we have a safety procedure that you might find a little embarrassing. No clothes or anything else goes in or out without special decontamination procedures. You'll have to remove your clothes—underwear and all—in the first chamber. Then you can proceed to a second chamber which establishes positive air flow into the lab and decontaminates people and things on the way out. We will go through one at a time to save embarrassment. I'll go first and set up the locks. Whenever you see a green light, just push the next door open. You'll come out into a curtained-off area. There are coveralls hanging on hooks labeled with size. Put one on. I'll be waiting outside the curtain.''

Saba waited beyond the curtain with a pretty blond young woman. Her large blue eyes stared at Scott from behind large black-rimmed glasses that seemed about to fall off the end of her nose. ''Sally, this is Dr. Scott Corbett from the Navy. He has the samples we're to analyze.'' Sally politely shook his hand.

"I'm going to leave you with Sally, Scott," Saba informed him. "I have to get back on the software. You can stay with her while she and the others work on the samples. Sally, as I explained to you, Dr. Corbett has to stay with the samples all the time."

Sally looked at Scott with a mixture of puzzlement and suspicion, then smiled. "That won't be a problem."

Scott followed Sally though a maze of equipment and passageways to a laboratory, where several other people were waiting. "First we have to extract the microbes from the surface of your samples," Sally explained after introductions. "We will use some to start cultures for later use, and the rest we will use for DNA profiling. Once we have those, we won't need your samples anymore. You can return them to your laboratory, if you like."

"No, I think I'll stick around." Scott smiled, lifting the case to a bench top. "I'd like to see how you do this, if you don't mind." And keep close tabs on the analysis results, he said to himself.

"We don't mind. We're glad to have you," she said proudly. "We think we've done some great things here, and we like to show off. With all the new security, it looks like we aren't going to get to show off much." Frustration filled her face. "I thought when I came to work here, I'd be able to get my name on some papers. Now it looks like all I'll get my name on are some patent applications," she said bitterly.

Scott worked the case's combination lock, and was about to flip the case latches. "No, no!" Sally stopped him. "You'll let the little beasties loose in here and contaminate the place. Or they could pick up some of our stuff. We'd have a mess and not know what is what. We need to open this in a clean room and scrape off the microbes, so to speak. We have a room with equipment especially designed for that, but there's space for only one person.'' She saw the frown on his face. ''You can watch through a window. The person in there can't go anywhere.'' Scott reluctantly relinquished custody of the case.

''What we need is the genetic code of the microbes infesting your samples—you'll see why we call them codes when we're finished,'' Sally said as Scott watched another staff member process the samples through a window. ''It's like a bar code. What Steve is doing right now is extracting microbes from the surface of your samples. It's like extracting blood cells from a crime scene, only these cells are alive and need to be contained until we're sure they're dead. Next we'll extract the DNA from the cells.

''Would you like to see what we expect the DNA to look like?'' she asked. ''We can use the desktop computer here by the door, and keep watch on your samples. It's connected to our local area network, LAN. The models we play around with are stored in the LAN's file server. It has more capability than a lot of mainframes still in use, but not enough to generate the models we use. I'll call up a model we have stored on a CD. Unless we connect to the supercomputer, it would take forever to generate the images I'm going to show you. Once the supercomputer generates the model, the server can handle minor modifications and gross simulations. We have high-resolution monitors on all PCs hooked to the file server. We get good color displays of the DNA models. Can't get the whole thing at once, but enough.''

Sally worked at the PC for a few minutes, and the screen filled with what appeared to be two winding strings of beads. The strings were linked to each other to form what looked like a rope ladder. There were four different link colors. It was beautiful in a weird way, Scott thought, like an abstract painting.

"These are pretty much what human DNA looks like, too," Sally observed. "Each of these," she said, pointing at the links connecting the two strings, "are composed of four chemical units that always bond crosswise in pairs: adenine to thymine to make one link, guanine to cytosine to make another. Lengthwise, the four units can bond in any sequence. The sequences are unique. What we're going to do with your microbes is to cut their DNA into pieces with enzymes coded to look for specific sequences. We use a process similar to that used by the FBI forensic lab. Their enzymes sever the string every time it sees the sequence guanine-guanine-cytosine-cytosine. Our process extends that process to look for sequences of sequences, because of the nature of the cells we're looking at. It does a lot of other things for us that it would take too long to explain.

"Our enzymes are different, too. We designed and synthesized them ourselves. Our DNA profiling is enormously fast compared to what is done in other labs. It's a byproduct of the genetic engineering. We needed a rapid process, not only to design the microbes, but also to identify them."

She smiled proudly. "It's amazing what can be accomplished by the right combination of people," she said with wonder. "It's sort of like casting for a TV sitcom. Some shows are successful because the people just click. Science is like that. All the people on a team can be brilliant, and still nothing will happen. Put the right people together, and they can be pretty dumb, but things will happen. I'm not saying we have any dumb people here, but we do have the *right* people.

"Take the gel we use in the analysis procedure. Negatively charged DNA fragments are placed into a gel, and a positive pole is introduced. The fragments move toward it at speeds depending on fragment size. After a while, the fragments distribute themselves along a line according to size. That takes time, and sometimes the fragments don't spread like you expect. We needed more precision and predictability than we could get with conventional gels. And we needed speed.

"We just happen to have a person on the team who was interested in the gel and fooled around with it when he was in college. It's a detail geneticists are not *that* turned on about, but it is this guy's secret passion. He developed a gel without which we probably wouldn't be where we are today. There are a lot of key developments like that in this program, the probes for example—somebody else's secret passion.

"The DNA fragments are blotted onto a nylon membrane after they've spread through the gel," she continued. "We then introduce probes that are bits of radioactive, synthetic DNA with known sequences. The probes bind only to complementary sequences. The excess probe material is washed away, and the membrane is placed on X-ray film. The radioactivity exposes the film wherever the radioactive probes are bound. What we get on film is a fuzzy bar code which uniquely identifies the cell. Our gel solves another problem, too—'bandshifting.' The fragments in ordinary gel sometimes don't drift at predictable rates. Bits of DNA from the same sample can look different, and DNA from different samples can look the same. This gel doesn't let that happen.

"Synthesizing the DNA probes to fit our unique sequences just happened to be something another person on the team was interested in and had the knack and experience to do. His probe development depended on Omar's synthesis work. I miss Omar. Don't know how we'll get along without him. Julie is very good on that stuff, but Omar was a genius like you wouldn't believe." Her eyes told Scott she missed more than Omar's technical prowess.

"What happened to Omar?" he asked.

"No one knows," she answered sorrowfully. "He just disappeared. That's one reason the company laid on all of the security. They think he might have taken some trade secrets, and don't want it to happen again. They all of a sudden think they're going to make a lot of money off this stuff. But Omar wouldn't have stolen anything. He wasn't a dishonest person," she said with conviction. But Scott knew Omar had stolen something. Omar was not only a dishonest person, he was a spy. Scott wondered what he'd gotten from this young lady—evidently her heart, probably her body, and maybe some technology.

"You can see why we call DNA profiles genetic codes," Sally said, adjusting the focus of the projected images. The X-ray film had been scanned into the computer, and now the stored codes and the codes from Scott's samples were projected onto a large movie screen by a digital projector. They were crude versions of the bar codes found on grocery labels, which were scanned by a laser at the checkout counter.

"They are the same, no doubt about it," concluded Saba, who'd joined them and other researchers in the small conference room. "Computer says there's only one chance in fifteen billion that they're not the same. Where did these samples come from?"

Everyone in the room stared at Scott expectantly. "I can't say," he answered.

"Saba, I need to discuss something with you and Julie privately," Scott said abruptly, cutting off further questioning. He got to his feet with the samples, which he had locked into their case again, and followed Saba out.

Chapter Fourteen

ASSOCIATED PRESS: TRIPOLI

AT A PRESS CONFERENCE TODAY THE
NEW LEADERS OF SEVEN COUNTRIES
CONFIRMED THAT THE COUPS IN THEIR
COUNTRIES HAD BEEN COORDINATED,
AND THEY ANNOUNCED FORMATION OF A
COALITION LED BY LIBYA. THEY SAID
THAT THE AIMS OF THE COALITION ARE
TO UNIFY ARAB POWER, AND TO USE
THAT POWER TO HALT AGGRESSION AND
EXPLOITATION BY THE U.S. AND ITS AL-
LIES. LIBYAN AIR FORCE COLONEL MU-
HAMMAD AZIZ, WHO IS RUMORED TO
HAVE ASSASSINATED THE PREVIOUS LIB-
YAN HEAD OF STATE, COLONEL MOAM-
MAR GADHAFI, CLAIMED THAT LIBYA
HAS DEVELOPED A NEW WEAPON THAT
ALTERS THE WORLD BALANCE OF

POWER, AND DECLARED THAT ANY COUNTRY THAT ATTACKED A MEMBER OF THE COALITION WOULD PAY "A TERRIBLE PRICE."

ALGERIA AND TUNISIA CALLED THE NEW LEADERS "A BAND OF ASSASSINS." BOTH COUNTRIES PROMISED SWIFT EXECUTION OF ANY PLOTTERS ASSOCIATED WITH THE COALITION. EGYPT WARNED THE COALITION THAT IT WOULD RESPOND MASSIVELY TO ANY INCURSIONS INTO ITS TERRITORY OR ANY ACTS OF TERRORISM. EGYPT AND ALGERIA MOVED ADDITIONAL TROOPS TO THEIR BORDERS WITH LIBYA.

MOST OBSERVERS DOUBTED THE STRENGTH OF THE NEW COALITION, COMPOSED AS IT IS OF POOR COUNTRIES WITH LITTLE MILITARY POWER. EXPERTS DISCOUNTED LIBYA'S CLAIM TO HAVE MADE A WEAPONS-TECHNOLOGY BREAKTHROUGH. LIBYA HAS LONG BEEN ACCUSED OF DEVELOPING CHEMICAL AND BIOLOGICAL WEAPONS, BUT HAS INSISTED THAT EVEN ITS NEWEST CHEMICAL PLANT—BUILT UNDER A MOUNTAIN—IS DEVOTED TO PRODUCING CHEMICALS FOR PEACEFUL USE. LIBYA'S NEW LEADER, COLONEL AZIZ, DENIED HE WAS THREATENING THE USE OF CHEMICAL OR BIOLOGICAL WEAPONS, AND SAID THAT HE WAS WELL AWARE THAT IF SUCH WEAPONS WERE USED, THE WORLD WOULD UNITE TO DESTROY LIBYA AND ITS COALITION.

THERE WERE CAUTIOUS RESPONSES FROM OTHER COUNTRIES AROUND THE

WORLD. NONE HAS YET RECOGNIZED THE
NEW GOVERNMENTS, BUT IT IS EXPECTED
THAT SOME MIDDLE EAST COUNTRIES
WILL SOON DO SO. U.S. STATE DEPART-
MENT SPOKESPERSON GEORGE TENNISON
SAID THE U.S. UNDERSTANDS THE ASPI-
RATIONS OF THE ARAB PEOPLES, BUT DE-
CRIES THE INTRODUCTION OF NEW
WEAPONS IN THE REGION, AND WILL
TAKE STRONG ACTION IF THE COALITION
ATTACKS ITS NEIGHBORS. MR. TENNISON
SAID FURTHER COMMENT WILL HAVE TO
AWAIT ANALYSIS OF THE SITUATION.

Camp David

Saturday night the President made the connection as
he watched CNN in bed. He called for an early Sunday
morning meeting. The hastily called meeting was attended by the Vice President, Secretary of State, SEC-
DEF, SECNAV, National Security Advisor, Chief of
Staff, heads of assorted intelligence agencies, Admiral
Kittering, and Captain Mike Boen, who was still reeling from the call and the helicopter ride. He was thoroughly intimidated, and sure he was going to make a
fool of himself. He hadn't any notes, and it seemed he
couldn't remember a thing.

"Jason, you brought up the possibility of a new Libyan weapon at that NSC meeting," the President said.
"Now this Aziz claims to have a doomsday machine,
and he seems to be in control of most of North Africa.
Is this the new weapon you briefed us on or just another chemical-warfare threat?" The President was a
gruff, square-featured man whose white hair had once
been blond. His azure eyes could be charming or frightening. They were frightening now, Mike noted. The
President was trim, and wore tan canvas pants, a green-

striped polo shirt and sneakers with no socks. Staffers who'd accompanied the President to Camp David also wore casual clothes. The new arrivals had hastily pulled on suits and uniforms.

Jason Goodson, the National Security Advisor, had been at Camp David with the President, and had no additional information. He hadn't even seen the CNN report. Nevertheless, he attempted to say something wise: "Sir, I think this announcement confirms our suspicions. They have at least *attempted* to develop some sort of terror weapon based on the technology we discussed. How real the threat is, we don't know yet."

"All right, you intelligence people, what have you got?" the President demanded.

"We have something from HUMINT," answered the Director of the CIA, Anton Carlson. "We have what amounts to a transcript of the Coalition meeting. I believe you have it in front of you."

The President picked up the papers and riffled through them, and then angrily flung them down. "Meeting transcript!" he exclaimed disgustedly. "This is the same as the news reports. What about this, Admiral? You're the one that brought this to everyone's attention in the first place."

"We've been working on it, sir."

"Working on it! What the hell does that mean! Everybody is always *working* on every damn thing and never getting a damn thing done!"

"Remember, sir, we agreed that there was nothing we could do until the situation clarified," Goodson reminded him.

"Well, it seems to have clarified. Captain, what the hell did they bring you along for! Why get you up at this ungodly hour? You have something to say about all this?"

"Sir, I—" Mike felt as though he was going to choke and fall over on the table. Blood roared in his ears, and he was having difficulty breathing. The President glared angrily at him.

Mike got his mind working again. "Everything confirms what we suspected, sir. They have a biological version of our NESW technology—"

"NESW! What the hell is that? You damn DoD people and your frigging acronyms. Why don't you speak in English, for heaven's sake?"

"It's non-explosive-strike-warhead technology, sir." Mike briefly described the technology. The President seemed fascinated, and listened intently.

"All right," the President finally said, "what you are telling me is the Libyans have a new biological-warfare weapon. Stole it from us! That's a hell of a note! Once again, what *exactly* are we *doing* about it?"

"Developing a biological defense, sir." Mike went on to explain the crash research effort, and what had occasioned it.

"Well, I finally found someone who's *doing* something. Jake, Art"—General Jake Thompson was chairman of the JCS and Arthur Johnson was the SECDEF—"I want the Navy program to have anything and everything it needs: money, priorities, whatever. And I want the captain in charge—he seems to be way out ahead of everyone else—and I don't want this done by any damn committee. You hear that, Captain?"

"Yes, sir."

"That means you don't sleep or eat until this problem is solved, if that's what it takes. You have direct access to me whenever you need it." A wave of angry expressions swept around the table. Giving a Navy captain more access to the President than four-star admirals and generals was not only unprecedented, but a slap in the face to the people sitting around the table.

The President had anticipated the reaction. Knowing people and how to handle them had been one of the abilities that had made him President. He now attempted to soothe egos. He needed these men, and he needed them in good spirits. "Gentlemen, I know this seems extreme, but I believe we have an extreme situation here. This technology scares the pants off me. I think genetic engineering has finally created the Frankenstein monster we always feared it would, and it's in the hands of one of the most dangerous nations in the world. Extreme measures are required. We may be facing a catastrophe. I feel it in my gut."

The cabinet and staff around the table had never seen the President so stirred. "Paul, Sam, we have to decide what we're going to release to the public." Paul Jasper was the President's Press Secretary, and Sam Moon was his Chief of Staff.

"Sir, if we aren't careful, we could cause a panic," Jasper warned. "Escaped microbes causing a plague, doomsday just around the corner, all that sort of thing. You know what the media will do with this."

"I know, Paul, but maybe that's what we need—a panic."

"Sir?" Jasper gasped incredulously.

"Let me think a moment." The President made a tent of his hands, leaned back in the leather high-backed chair and stared off in the distance for what seemed like minutes.

Finally the President's eyes came back to the room. "What I don't like about this is that it smells cover-up to high heaven. We could be accused—as the government always is—of hiding a danger that *we* caused from the public. And it will happen. Curious neighbors, one of your scientists who feels he has to save the world or one of the uncleared Lesatec people will talk to the press. We can't contain it and shouldn't try. But we *can* manage the information flow.

"We need to convince the country and our allies that there is indeed a threat. Best way to do that is scare the hell out of them. You should like that, Jake. This time it's not the military that's loosed a technology monster; it's the environmentalists. You're going to be the good guys.

"This incident will also support our efforts to halt transfer of critical technology," the President continued. "This is a tremendous example, waste-disposal technology turned into a doomsday machine."

Paul Jasper looked sick. How the hell was he going to manage this? No one around the table looked happy, and nobody was unhappier than Mike. He could see himself submerged in a sea of reporters, video cameras and microphones. The program office, the lab and Lesatec would be flooded with media people. They'd never get a damn thing done. "I think we should give this some more thought, sir," Paul Jasper said, daring to risk the President's famous wrath.

"Think about it!" the President exploded. "That's why our damn bureaucracy never gets anything done! Everyone wants to think about *every* damn thing!"

"But sir, how can we maintain security with the media hounding everybody?" the CIA director objected.

"And the press will crucify NSF, Lesatec and that Dr.—what's her name?—Julie Barns for creating a monster and letting some foreign student steal it," Jasper pointed out.

Mike felt ill. Jasper was right. And Julie had a hard time suppressing her guilt as it was. How could she handle this? "Mr. President, dealing with the media is certain to slow our work," Mike dared to offer.

The President fixed him with a searing stare, but didn't say anything for what seemed like an eternity. Tension filled the room. "You're right. We can't let it get out of hand," the President finally said slowly and firmly. He shifted his hard eyes to Paul Jasper. "Manage the information flow, Paul, but don't hide anything unclassified."

"Yes, sir," Jasper responded reluctantly. He turned

to Mike. "We need to prebrief everybody involved on what they can and can't say, although I'm not sure it will do any good. Any suggestions on security? How do we keep reporters out of the Lesatec laboratory?"

"They have tight security. That shouldn't be a problem, but we need time—a week or so."

"Give them as much time as you can, Paul," ordered the President. "But do it before we have a leak." He got abruptly to his feet, signaling the end of the meeting. "I'm going to church. Sam, get the captain in whenever he needs to see me. Keep your superiors fully informed, Captain, but don't let that delay you telling me anything I need to know." He looked at the others with fierce eyes, warning them not to interfere. Then he strode from the room.

Tripoli

"The Americans have given us what we needed!" Colonel Muhammad Aziz cried triumphantly. "Credibility." He waved the newspaper like a victory banner. Its front page was filled with accounts of the President's news conference at which he announced the existence of the biotech-weapons threat and accused Libya of stealing the technology to develop an instrument of mass terror.

"This will strike terror in the heart of the world," Aziz crowed with a broad grin.

"Strike terror in the heart of the world?" Fatima responded sarcastically. She hated Aziz's penchant for flowery language and exaggeration. She thought it clownish, but had to admit it played well in the Arab world and Western media. "I don't think the world is prostrate with terror just yet," Fatima continued caustically. "The Egyptians mass on our border. Algiers threatens us. Even little Tunisia swears it will not be intimidated. The Americans may have succeeded in frightening the world into acting against us. I'm sure that's their intent.''

Aziz's glow of triumph dimmed and winked out. He knew her assessment was correct, and that enraged him. His dependence on her stoked a smoldering rage that grew with each passing day. Omar now led the genetic engineering program, but Fatima retained control by withholding information needed to complete and deploy a weapon. She made sure Aziz needed her.

''However, if we're clever, Colonel, perhaps we *can* exploit the American announcement—be a bit more clever than they,'' she suggested. ''Maybe we *can* use it to strike terror in the heart of the world. You will hold a press conference. I will prepare your notes and a press release.''

Aziz started to object, then checked his anger. Her mind was devious and brilliant. Why not use it? At least until he could afford to kill her.

REUTERS: TRIPOLI

COLONEL MUHAMMAD AZIZ, LEADER OF THE NEW NORTH AFRICAN COALITION, TODAY HELD A PRESS CONFERENCE TO SUMMARIZE THE COMMUNIQUE HE HAS SENT TO NATIONS AROUND THE WORLD. HE EXTENDED THE ''HAND OF PEACE'' TO HIS NEIGHBORS: EGYPT, ALGERIA AND TUNISIA. HOWEVER, HE EMPHASIZED THAT HE COULD NOT IGNORE THEIR PREPARATIONS FOR AGGRESSION. HE THREATENED TO STRIKE THEM WITH THE ''HAND OF ALLAH'' IF THEY CONTINUED TO THREATEN THE TRUE DEFENDERS OF ISLAM, AND EXPRESSED CONFIDENCE HE

WOULD BE SUPPORTED BY THE REST OF THE MUSLIM WORLD.

HE SAID HE HAS INFORMED THE EUROPEANS THAT HE HAS NO TERRITORIAL AMBITIONS, AND IN NO WAY INTENDS TO THREATEN THEIR COMMERCE OR ACCESS TO OIL. HE OFFERED TO TAKE A LEADERSHIP ROLE IN MODERATING OIL PRICES, AND OFFERED LIBYAN CRUDE AT REDUCED PRICES. HE EMPHASIZED THAT THE POTENTIAL CONFLICT IS PURELY A NORTH AFRICAN AFFAIR, AND HE THREATENED TO USE HIS NEW WEAPONS TECHNOLOGY TO WREAK ECONOMIC HAVOC ON ANY COUNTRY THAT INTERFERED.

HE NOTED THAT U.S. DISCLOSURES HAVE SUBSTANTIATED THE EFFECTIVENESS OF LIBYA'S NEW WEAPONS TECHNOLOGY, ALTHOUGH HE CALLED THE AMERICAN ACCUSATIONS OF THEFT NONSENSE. HE DEMANDED THAT THE U.S. STAY OUT OF ARAB AFFAIRS AND STOP "SICCING ITS DOGS" ON THE TRUE BELIEVERS OF ISLAM. HE NOTED THAT WHILE THE AMERICANS ARE "DEDICATED TO DEATH AND DESTRUCTION," LIBYA'S WEAPONS ARE INTENDED TO STOP THE ENGINES OF DEATH, DESTRUCTION AND GREED. BUT HE WARNED THAT MUSLIMS NOW HELD THE POWER TO DESTROY THE ECONOMIES OF WHOLE NATIONS AS SURELY AS IF THEY WERE STRUCK WITH HYDROGEN BOMBS. HE WARNED, "WE WILL NOT HESITATE TO BRING AGGRESSORS TO THEIR KNEES, BUT UNLIKE THE AMERICANS, WE WILL

NOT KILL THE INNOCENTS THESE TY-
RANTS GRIND UNDER THEIR HEELS. WE
WILL FREE THEM.''

EGYPT'S PRESIDENT STATED IN RE-
SPONSE THAT AZIZ WAS CONTINUING
GADHAFI'S TRADITION OF TERRORISM,
AND THAT AZIZ'S THREATS WERE THE
SAME CHEMICAL-BIOLOGICAL-WARFARE
THREATS OF HIS PREDECESSOR. HE SAID
THE GULF WAR PROVED SUCH WEAPONS
ARE INEFFECTIVE AND THAT THE WORLD
WOULD NOT TOLERATE THEIR USE. HE IN-
FORMED AZIZ THAT THREATS TO USE
SUCH WEAPONS INVITED THE ANNIHILA-
TION OF LIBYA AND ITS ALLIES. HE PROM-
ISED THAT EGYPT WOULD NOT STAND
IDLY BY AND LET CONTROL OF NORTH
AFRICA BE SEIZED BY A TERRORIST
STATE. MEANWHILE, EGYPT CONTINUED
A MILITARY BUILDUP ALONG ITS BORDER
WITH LIBYA.

ALGERIA'S REACTION WAS LESS STRI-
DENT, BUT ITS PRESIDENT SAID HIS
COUNTRY WOULD NOT BE FRIGHTENED
INTO YIELDING TO AGGRESSION OF ANY
KIND AND REFUSED TO BE TERRORIZED
BY CLAIMS OF POSSESSING A DOOMSDAY
MACHINE. ALGERIA'S GOVERNMENT HAS
BEEN LOCKED IN A DESPERATE STRUG-
GLE WITH FUNDAMENTALIST GROUPS,
AND NARROWLY ESCAPED A COUP AT-
TEMPT EARLIER IN THE YEAR. THE FUN-
DAMENTALISTS ARE DEMANDING THAT
ALGERIA JOIN ITS ARAB BROTHERS IN
THE COALITION. OBSERVERS BELIEVE
THE ALGERIAN PRESIDENT IS BEING
FORCED TO SERIOUSLY CONSIDER JOIN-

ING THE COALITION TO DEFUSE THE INTERNAL POLITICAL SITUATION.

TUNISIA CALLED AZIZ AN OUTLAW, AND ACCUSED HIM OF ATTEMPTING TO SUBVERT ITS GOVERNMENT. IT CALLED ON OTHER NORTH AFRICAN COUNTRIES TO BAND TOGETHER TO THROW AZIZ OUT AND BREAK UP THE "UNHOLY ALLIANCE HE HAS FORMED BY MURDER AND ASSASSINATION." TUNISIAN TROOPS CRUSHED FUNDAMENTALIST DEMONSTRATIONS IN SUPPORT OF THE COALITION, AND MARTIAL LAW HAS BEEN IMPOSED THROUGHOUT THE COUNTRY.

OTHER WORLD REACTION HAS BEEN MUTED. MIDDLE EAST EXPERTS ARE GENERALLY OF THE OPINION THAT THE U.S. DISCLOSURE HAS GIVEN MORE CREDIBILITY TO THE COALITION THREAT, BUT THAT AZIZ'S CONCILIATORY STANCE WILL BLUNT THE REACTION THE AMERICANS HAD HOPED FOR: SUPPORT FOR SWIFT ACTION TO REMOVE THE LIBYAN THREAT. INSTEAD, THE SITUATION THREATENS TO DRIVE A WEDGE BETWEEN THE U.S. AND ITS ALLIES.

EUROPEANS SEEM FEARFUL OF SUBJECTING THEMSELVES TO THE THREAT OF MASS TERROR BY INVOLVEMENT IN A CONFLICT THAT DOES NOT APPEAR TO AFFECT THEIR VITAL INTERESTS. ALSO, THEIR EXPERTS HAVE EXPRESSED CONSIDERABLE DOUBT AS TO THE REALITY OF THE THREAT. ALTHOUGH THE AMERICAN DISCLOSURES REVEALED A BREAKTHROUGH IN GENETIC ENGINEERING,

TRANSFORMATION OF SUCH TECHNOL-
OGY INTO WEAPONS IS A FEAT THESE EX-
PERTS DOUBT LIBYA CAN PERFORM. THE
EUROPEANS HAVE MADE IT CLEAR THAT
THEY WILL NOT PARTICIPATE IN OR AL-
LOW THEIR TERRITORY TO BE USED FOR
MILITARY ACTION TO NEUTRALIZE A
THREAT THAT IS UNVERIFIED AND NOT
AIMED AT THEM.

WASHINGTON POST

THE PRESIDENT ANNOUNCED DURING HIS
PRESS CONFERENCE THAT HE HAS OR-
DERED TWO MORE BATTLE GROUPS TO
THE MEDITERRANEAN TO CONDUCT EX-
ERCISES. THE PRESIDENT VOWED THAT
THE U.S. WOULD NOT BE PARTY TO "AP-
PEASEMENT OF YET ANOTHER DICTA-
TOR." WHEN ASKED ABOUT DEFENSE
AGAINST LIBYA'S DOOMSDAY MACHINE,
THE PRESIDENT SAID DEVELOPMENT OF
COUNTERMEASURES ARE BEING RUSHED,
AND HE EXPECTED THE U.S. WILL SOON
HAVE THE MEANS TO NEUTRALIZE THE
COALITION'S NEW WEAPON. BUT VET-
ERAN WASHINGTON WATCHERS BELIEVE
THE U.S. WOULD NOT TAKE UNILATERAL
MILITARY ACTION AGAINST THE COALI-
TION IN THE FACE OF THE OVERWHELM-
ING OPPOSITION OF ITS ALLIES.

Springfield, Virginia

Dr. Julie Barns sat at her desk, her tear-streaked face
full of rage and frustration. She had been able to hold

back the tears until she'd reached her office, but now she couldn't seem to stem the flow. That they could make her cry made her so angry. The mob of reporters in the conference room had made her feel like a witch who deserved to be burned at the stake.

The press conference had been the most horrifying experience of her life. Spots still danced in her eyes from the camera lights, and her ears still rang from the barrage of questions thrown at her. She had felt smothered by the forest of microphones thrust in her face. If it hadn't been for Mike, she would never have survived. She would have burst into tears, fainted or gone berserk—probably all three. Mike had been a rock. He had patiently answered questions for her, fending off the reporters, until she got over her initial shock and could speak for herself. Despite Mike's help, Julie felt the reporters had manipulated her like a fool. She must now be known as the "Witch of Springfield."

Why had the President elected to announce to the world that Dr. Julie Barns had developed biological-warfare technology that she had then allowed to be stolen and turned into a doomsday machine? *Silent Doomsday Machine,* that was what the media were calling it. The media had invoked all of the fears of meddling with the creation of life. Even members of the scientific community were calling her research irresponsible. The White House press release had shattered her life and career.

Camera crews and reporters were still camped outside, waiting for her to emerge—as if they hadn't savaged her enough during the press conference. Mike had warned her to expect others to be waiting to ambush her at her apartment building.

As he watched her now at her desk, he realized that his calm had been a thin facade that had threatened to shatter at any moment. The press conference had been like watching Julie being gang-raped. He had barely resisted the urge to snatch away the microphones and smash them in the reporters' faces.

Now Julie slowly rose to her feet, as if feeling for balance. She pulled a wad of tissues from the box on her desk and blotted her face dry.

"You okay, Julie?"

"I'm okay. Just angry, I guess. My first press conference, you know. Sort of overwhelming—different than watching on TV. But I shouldn't have let it get to me that way—crying and stuff.

"I better get back to the lab, Mike. The staff must be going crazy. I owe them an explanation, and I've got to help Saba with the software." Determination hardened her face.

"I'd better get going, too. I hate to leave you surrounded by the media sharks, but I have two more press conferences today, and a bunch of admirals to pacify. Then I have to untangle my office and lab from the media and get the program running again."

Julie started toward the door, stopped and suddenly put her arms around his neck, looking deep into his eyes. "Thanks, Mike," she said gratefully. "For helping me through this. I don't know what I'd have done without you."

Mike slipped his arms around Julie and drew her closer. Their lips touched, launching a tender exploration that turned into searing urgency. Her lips parted, and his tongue ravaged her mouth. Her hand pressed the back of his head, and urged him to deepen the kiss.

They broke apart, startled, minds reeling from the sudden flood of desire.

"Julie—"

She stopped him with a finger on his lips, then backed toward the door. "Mike . . . thank you." Then she was gone.

Robert Payton Moore

Mike stared after her, his mind too foggy to find a clear thought. He didn't understand what made him feel as if he wanted to spend a lifetime with a woman he hardly knew.

Chapter Fifteen

Alexandria, Virginia

"Dad, it's your girlfriend," Susan called from the living room as Mike searched the refrigerator for a beer his father-in-law might have overlooked. "She sounds excited."

"She is *not* my *girlfriend*," Mike objected, taking the phone from his daughter.

"I think we have it," Julie told him, voice bubbling with excitement. "It's like a computer virus. Everything would be fine when we initialized the program, then—it's too hard to explain. I'm not sure I understand myself. Saba found it."

"That's great!" Mike was as elated as she sounded. Tons of apprehension dropped from him. He knew how far they had to go from a program bug to a defense system, but at least they were finally on the road.

"It's more than great," Julie bubbled. "I feel like I can live again."

"What you can do is go home and get some sleep."
It was almost midnight.

"Can't. Have to run the models and put the codes
on tape."

"Anything I can do? Want me to come out?"

"Nothing you can do, but . . . I would like to have
you here," she said hesitantly.

"How 'bout I bring a bottle of champagne?"

"And a pizza?"

"And a pizza. Bring cheap champagne."

"I don't know good from bad, and Saba doesn't
drink."

Springfield, Virginia

Mike found Julie and Saba at a computer. They were
so engrossed they didn't notice him walk in. A twisted
ladder, its rungs attached by colored beads, filled the
screen, slowly rotating, changing colors and expanding.

"Champaign and pizza time," Mike announced.

"Oh, Mike!" cried Julie. She scrambled from her
chair and rushed to him. She clamped her arms around
his neck and kissed him, making him almost drop the
food.

Saba sprang to her feet and saved the pizza. Julie
took her lips from a startled Mike. "You don't know
how great this is, Mike. I feel like the world has been
taken off my back."

Saba took possession of the champagne. "Why don't
we take this out to a lab bench where we have more
room?" she suggested.

Julie drank too much champagne, and when they finished the pizza, she sat with a silly smile on her face
and a piece of cheese stuck in the corner of her mouth.
The alcohol and twenty-four hours without sleep had
left her dazed. "Why don't you let Mike take you
home, Julie?" Saba suggested.

"No, I'm all right."

"You're exhausted," Saba insisted.

"But we're not finished."

"I can finish up. All I have to do is watch the computer and make tapes. Today is Wednesday—Thursday now. I'll have the tapes ready for the lab people in the morning. They can work over the weekend, and we should have cultures started by Monday."

"You've had less sleep than I have, Saba. You've been working around the clock for two months."

Saba's endurance impressed Mike. She had worked longer and harder and with less sleep than Julie, yet she looked as fresh as if she had just stepped out of a shower.

"I don't need much sleep," Saba said. "Besides, what could you do? It only takes one person to check status once in a while and run the tape machine. No use you just sitting around being miserable, and you won't be any help half asleep."

"What you mean is I'll just be in the way."

"Julie, you know that's not what I meant."

"You don't have to lie to make me feel better, Saba." Julie turned to Mike. "This has been her show, Mike. I'd never have found that bug."

"Don't believe it," Saba objected. "I couldn't have done it without her."

"Hold it, you two!" Mike laughed. "Let's not fight over who's the heroine. Julie, I think Saba is right. You don't look so good. I'm taking you home."

"Is that an order, Captain?" Julie grinned.

"It is. A direct order. Now, will you come quietly, or does it have to be in chains?"

"Saba, you're sure—"

"Go!" Saba ordered.

"Call me if—"

"Julie!"

"I'm going! I'm going," she groused.

Robert Payton Moore

Crystal City, Virginia

Julie slept soundly all the way to Crystal City. Mike rummaged through her purse and found the garage access card. He drove up and down the lanes of the crowded garage, and almost gave up before he found a space in a dark corner.

"You're home, Julie," he announced, shaking her shoulder gently.

She responded with only a break in her gentle snore.

Mike smiled. She was not only exhausted, but probably a little drunk. He got out, went around the car and opened her door. He attempted to lift her into his arms, but the cars were parked too close. He had to wake her. "We're home, Julie."

She moaned and her eyes opened slowly.

"Come on, just a little way further. Up the elevator, down the hall and you can go back to sleep."

She looked at him blearily, finally comprehending where she was. "Just let me stay here," she mumbled. Her chin dropped to her chest. "I'll sleep in the car. You take the keys. Use my bed."

"Julie, I'm not going to leave you down here in the basement."

"I'm so tired, I won't even notice."

"Come on, Julie," Mike insisted. He grasped her arm and guided her from the car. She stood swaying while he locked the car door.

"I can walk," she protested when he started to lift her into his arms. "It's too far for you to carry me." He put an arm around her and guided her uncertain steps to the elevator. When they reached the apartment, Mike took the keys from her and unlocked the door. He closed it behind them, and steered her into the bedroom. She dropped heavily onto the huge bed.

"All right, into bed with you," Mike ordered.

216

She stared at him. Then her eyes closed and her head dropped.

Mike put his hand under her chin and lifted. Her eyes opened, but were uncomprehending. "Julie, get your clothes off and get in bed."

"I'm too tired," she mumbled.

"If you don't undress, I'll do it for you," he threatened.

She didn't answer. Just stared at him. Her eyes started to close again.

"I mean it, Julie." He knelt in front of her and loosened the first two buttons of her blouse, expecting a protest that would jolt her awake. Her eyes just blinked sleepily. Mike unbuttoned the blouse to her waist. Her hands lay limply at her side. He stopped. She wasn't going to stop him.

Mike sat back on his heels. He considered just letting her lie back on the bed and covering her with something. But why? She wouldn't sleep well, and she had already stripped in front of him and a room full of people. He decided to put her to bed properly.

Mike had difficulty getting Julie out of her skirt and blouse. She kept wanting to fall over. He unhooked her bra and slipped it off.

Julie fell back on the bed. Lying on her back didn't diminish the thrust of her breasts, and the thin strip of nylon between her parted legs didn't hide much. But her body didn't stir his lust; she looked too painfully vulnerable for that. He *did* think about holding her in his arms while she slept.

Mike couldn't understand what she mumbled when he lifted her legs onto the bed and pulled her panties from her. She curled on her side and pillowed her head on her hands. He unfolded a sheet lying at the foot of the bed and spread it over her. He kissed her lightly on the forehead and started from the room.

"Mike," she called sleepily. He stopped and turned back. "Where are you going?"

"Home. Got a busy day tomorrow."

"Stay here. Too late to go home," she said, her speech thick and slurred.

At three in the morning, Mike didn't feel like going *anywhere*. And he did have to go to Lesatec with Julie in the morning to check the status of Saba's work.

"You're right, I'll stay." He walked to the door.

"Where are you going?" she called again.

"The living room. I'll sack out on the floor like last time."

"Don't be silly," she admonished. "This bed's big enough for four people. It'll be like sleeping in two double beds with no space between them."

The bed did look inviting. "You're sure?"

"I'm sure."

Still he hesitated.

"Go ahead, take off your clothes."

She heaved a heavy sigh, lay back and stared at the ceiling. "I am *so* tired. . . ." Her voice trailed off, and her eyes closed. Her breathing slowed. Exhaustion, aided by the champagne, had hit her like a baseball bat.

Mike stripped to his briefs, turned out the light and slipped under the sheet. He stretched out on his back, as far away from Julie as he could get without falling off the bed. But as he was falling asleep, he felt a warm body roll against him.

Sleep left Mike slowly. Comprehension came even more slowly. Belief trailed far behind. This wasn't his bed, and somebody was in bed with him.

Julie.

She lay on her side, a breast flattened against him. In her sleep, she had flung an arm and leg across him.

Mike lay absolutely still, hardly daring to breathe, unable to control his swelling arousal.

Julie stirred, mumbling incoherently. She buried her head deeper into his shoulder. Her pelvis moved on his hip. The arm lying carelessly across him tightened. She felt unbearably exciting, even smelled exciting—a musky woman smell, spiced with perfume.

Mike stopped breathing, his muscles so tense they ached. Hot need filled his groin.

Julie awoke suddenly. Her body stiffened. Shock widened her eyes. She lifted her head and stared at Mike. Disbelief, dismay, embarrassment, chagrin and finally acceptance chased each other across her face.

Julie suddenly slid on top of him and sat up, her hands braced on his chest, her thighs straddling his hips. She searched his eyes, found what she sought and moved back.

Mike slid into her warm, moist depths.

Julie gasped. Stiffened. Then sank forward onto him, her firm breasts pressing his chest.

He groaned, and thrust deeper into her.

She moaned and closed her eyes.

Mike enclosed her head in his hands and drew her lips to his. He kissed her. Softly. Tenderly.

Julie moved her hips.

Her body's deep, warm caress choked Mike with desire. He slipped his arms around Julie and crushed her to him.

She thrust.

He thrust.

Julie pulled her lips from his, and pushed up enough to peer at him with bright eyes. He saw his urgent desire reflected in those eyes.

They moved slowly and carefully at first. Then quickened. Driven by growing urgency, the tempo of their desperate rhythm spiraled out of control.

His hoarse cry mingled with her soft scream.

They slid down a long slope of melting desire and plunged into a serene pool of fulfillment.

Julie softened against him, her cheek resting on his shoulder. Mike stroked her hair. "Do you think you could ever love me?" she suddenly asked, startling him.

"I already do." He surprised himself with his answer. It had come without thought. Could he have fallen in love so quickly? Didn't seem possible.

Julie pushed to her elbows. Her gaze penetrated his eyes and sought his heart. "I feel that way, too. Like I love you. But . . ."

He waited for the rest, but it didn't come. "But what?" he asked when he couldn't wait any longer.

"All this . . . makes it hard to know what we feel."

"All what?"

"The Libyan mess and the emotional roller coaster we've been on—at least the one I've been on."

"I know what I feel."

She kissed him lightly, then laid her cheek on his shoulder again, her face turned away from him. "We have to get up," she mumbled.

"I know."

"We have to get out to the lab and see if Saba made the tapes.

"I know."

"I have to make sure the culture process gets started."

"I know. And I have to stop by my house, shower and put on a uniform."

"You do?"

"Yes, and you have to come with me. We left your car at the lab last night."

"We did, didn't we." Her voice had grown sleepy.

"Julie!" He grasped her arms and pushed her up.

"We make beautiful love," she said, a silly smile on her face. She looked drunk.

He drew her down to him again and kissed her urgently.

"We have to go," he said firmly when their lips parted.

"We have to go," she repeated tiredly. She dragged herself off him, and sat staring blankly at the wall.

"Julie—"

"I'm going, I'm going." She struggled to her feet. "You sailors are all alike. Make love to a woman, then kick her out of bed."

"I am not kicking you out of bed," he protested.

"It's all right, sailor. A woman who sleeps with a seafaring man shouldn't expect any more." Her humorous tone didn't quite hide the serious undercurrent in her voice.

"Julie, I—"

"Shhhhhhh." She put a finger on his lips, smiling crookedly. "Don't spoil the memory." She backed from the room, her eyes imploring him to be silent.

Mike stared at the door for a long time after Julie disappeared, even after he heard the shower start. Stared and tried to sort out the emotions tangling his mind.

Springfield, Virginia

"I don't see how you can stay on your feet, Saba," Julie scolded. The four of them, the two women along with Mike and Scott, were standing in the lab conference room. Saba had just completed briefing them on the status of the neutralizing microbe engineering. The supercomputer had generated the DNA codes, and Saba had copied them onto tape. Sally Smith and the other scientists were using them to produce the microbes.

"It's time you had a vacation," Julie insisted to Saba.

"Well, maybe this afternoon—"

"That's not long enough. You haven't been away

221

from this place for more than a day in two years.''

"Maybe I *could* go for the weekend.''

"At least," Julie said, her hands on her hips.

"I know just the place—a lodge in upstate New York," Scott said. "We can catch a commuter flight, rent a car and be there tonight. We can make a three-day weekend of it. You can sleep the whole time, if you want." Scott saw the sudden question in Saba's eyes. "Don't worry, we'll get separate rooms."

She stared at him for a moment, then smiled. "All right. And we don't need to pay for two rooms. We're adults, and I think I can trust you."

Scott wondered if he could trust himself.

Julie slipped an arm about Saba's shoulders and gave her a quick hug. "You and Scott leave now. Have fun, but get some sleep, too," she said, her voice heavy with implication.

"I'll call and make the reservations," Scott said. "We can catch a shuttle this afternoon, pick up a car in New York and be in bed before ten."

Alexandria, Virginia

"Wow, what's in this one?" Scott exclaimed when he lifted a large shoulder bag. "You aren't taking a computer, are you?"

"No." Saba laughed. "Just . . . my stereo tapes and stuff."

Scott put her luggage into the trunk and slammed the lid shut. He turned to find her regarding him somberly. "Scott, would you be real angry if I say I've changed my mind?"

"Changed your mind?"

"I haven't changed my mind about going, just about going to New York."

Scott was annoyed, very annoyed. It was too late to

cancel his hotel reservations. It was going to cost him $200 if he didn't show up.

"What I would really like to do is go someplace warm and just lie on the beach in the sun. Maybe walk along the shore at night . . . look at the stars and listen to the surf . . . get to know each other." She smiled seductively.

"Why didn't you say something before?" he complained, irritated despite the seductive images she painted.

"I just now decided. I'm sorry," she said contritely, dropping her eyes like a little girl. "I'll make it up to you," she promised. She put her arms around him, and her body told him how she intended to make it up to him. "Please," she pleaded.

Her plaintive tone melted Scott. Making her happy was more important than the lousy $200 reservation deposit.

"Where?" he asked.

"Florida. Miami Beach."

"All right, let's go back in and call for reservations. We'll probably have to wait till tonight for a flight."

"No, we won't. We can leave right now."

"And how are we going to do that?"

"Private aircraft. I love flying. I rent a plane and go up every chance I get. I don't go anywhere. I just like being free of the earth. I love it when the clouds pile up like mountains. Makes me feel like I'm flying through another world. An unspoiled world." Her eyes sparkled. "You told me you like to fly, too."

Scott was surprised. He had mentioned that he had a private pilot's license, but she hadn't indicated that *she* was a pilot. "Where are we going to get a plane we can take to Florida on such short notice?" he asked skeptically.

"The flying service at Manassas Airport. I'm one of their best customers. Don't be mad at me, but I called before you got here. They have a Beechcraft Turbo Bonanza available. Fueled and ready.''

"Sounds like you didn't decide just now."

Saba dropped her eyes. "You *are* angry. I'm sorry."

Scott couldn't bear her forlorn look. "It's all right," he said quickly, putting his arms around her and drawing her closer.

"I know it will be expensive," she murmured against him. "I'll pay for the plane and for whatever you lose on your credit card in New York."

"You don't have to do that."

"I want to. I'd feel rotten if I didn't."

"We'll talk about it later." He might just let her pay; it *was* going to be damn expensive. On a GS-15's salary, you couldn't afford to just rent a plane on the spur of the moment and pop off to Florida. But then again, GS-15s like Scott Corbett didn't meet women like Saba Saunders every day. He could get more money; he might never get another Saba.

"I'll lock our stuff in the car and we'll go back in," Scott said.

"Why go back in?"

"To use the phone, cancel the reservations and let people know where we'll be."

"No. Let's just go. It's too late to cancel the hotel reservations, and the airline can take care of itself. And it'll be better if no one knows where we are. I don't want to be called about a computer bug or something. Let's just go," she pleaded.

Scott couldn't deny her anything with her lithe body pressing his, and what she said did make sense. "Okay, we'll do it your way."

Her fierce kiss startled him.

She squirmed out of his arms before he could react, leaving him dazed and wondering what the kiss promised. He thought he knew, but he couldn't wait to find out.

* * *

Manassas Airport, Virginia

Saba screamed the Bonanza down the runway and rotated as if she were lifting off a carrier deck. She climbed at such a steep angle, Scott feared the aircraft would stall. She didn't back off the power until they reached their assigned altitude. She handled exchanges with the air controllers with the confidence of an airline pilot. Despite thinking he might need a g-suit, Scott had to admit Saba was a skilled and evidently very experienced pilot who loved flying.

Crystal City, Virginia

"We've just completed background checks on all the people at Lesatec who've had access to the biotech data," said one of the two hard-eyed men in Mike's office. Neither had taken a seat. They were in their early thirties, clean-cut, serious and dressed in dark suits. Their ties were solid black, and their shoes' polish would have passed military inspection. Kyle Howard was FBI and Glenn Adams was Naval Investigative Service.

"Miss Saunders was the last, unfortunately," Howard continued. "Her father was an American—dead now. He worked in the Libyan oil fields up until a few years ago. Married a Libyan woman and returned to the U.S. with her. Saba Saunders was their only child. Her mother eventually divorced her father and returned to Libya without Miss Saunders. The mother died a year after returning, but despite her mother's death, Saba Saunders has made frequent visits to Libya over the years. She has spent extended periods there, as long as two years. She has always stayed with an aunt, whom she frequently traveled abroad with. That in itself is puzzling. Single Libyan women like her aunt don't often travel abroad alone unless they come from rich, powerful families. Her aunt's family is neither, but she stays in expensive hotels, gambles at Monte Carlo and generally lives the life of a jet-setter. The source of her funds is a mystery. She's probably some powerful man's mistress.

"That aunt has recently been seen with Colonel Aziz, the leader of the new coalition, which worries us. We may have a close relative of Aziz's mistress working on the program from which the technology for his biotech weapon was stolen. Saba Saunders was probably working with Omar Salim all along, and helped him steal the genetic-engineering data."

Mike's mind reeled. "But Saba just made the breakthrough we needed to neutralize the Libyan weapon," he protested. "Wouldn't make sense for a Libyan agent to do that."

"Things in this business often don't make sense. We're going to talk to her today, but we need you to fill us in on what she's doing with Dr. Barns before we do—so we can ask intelligent questions."

Cold grew in Mike's belly. "You won't be able to talk to her today. She left yesterday afternoon for a three-day vacation in New York."

"Alone?" Their two men's faces were alarmed.

"No. With my deputy, Scott Corbett." The look that passed between the two men was not comforting.

"Do you know where?" Their faces were filled with suspicion, and Mike knew that he and Scott were in for a real grilling, probably lie-detector tests and the whole bit before it was over. If they thought Scott had been sleeping with a foreign agent—innocently or not—they might yank all his special clearances. And they'd want Mike to explain why he hadn't known, and if he had, why hadn't he done something or reported it?

NIS was relentless in its investigations, and left no details or anybody untouched. The thought of them grilling Julie chilled him. Working so closely with Saba would make Julie highly suspect. And *he* was sleeping with Julie. Mike shuddered. These guys were sure to believe they had another Walker spy case on their hands.

"I have the phone number and address of the lodge they're staying at," Mike said, feeling quite unwell. He searched through the mess on his desk and came up with a scrap of paper. He handed it to the FBI agent. "Want me to call them?" Mike offered.

"Absolutely not. If she *is* into something, we don't want to spook her, make her run. May I use your phone?"

"Yes." Mike pushed the phone across the desk to him.

"I'm going to set up surveillance on the lodge," the FBI agent said. "We'll just watch. To make sure they don't run." The "they" shocked Mike. Surely they didn't think Scott—but why wouldn't they? Suddenly Mike felt very weary.

"We won't do anything until they return," the NIS agent told him. Mike knew that wasn't technically correct. They undoubtedly had already obtained court orders allowing them to tap everybody's phones, including his.

"We need some more background information," Adams continued. "We need to know how all this started, how the Libyan connection was first made and what part Dr. Barns and Saba Saunders played in that. We need to know about whatever foreign information sources were involved."

"Sorry, can't tell you that," Mike replied curtly. He was a little angry. The NIS agent knew he was asking for information for which he hadn't established a "need to know." He was testing Mike.

"We have the clearances, Captain," Adams persisted. "You can check, if you have any doubts."

227

"I don't have any doubts. You do *not* have the right clearances. If you have any problems with that, I suggest you have your bosses take it up with Admiral Kittering and Mr. Goodson at the White House," Mike said stiffly. "I'll be glad to talk to you about anything they give me permission to."

The room filled with hostility. No counterintelligence agent liked to be denied access to anything he asked for. "I'll call Dr. Barns, and tell her you're coming out," Mike announced. "You *do* want to talk to her, don't you?"

"Yes, we want to talk to her. No, we don't want you to call her—warn her that we're coming," Howard said. Mike bristled at the implication, but managed to control his temper. "We would like you to come with us, though."

"I suppose one of you will ride with me."

"Yes. I think that would be best."

The next time he and Julie made love they had better search for hidden microphones and cameras, Mike noted.

Springfield, Virginia

Julie met them in the lobby and escorted them to a large, empty office. "These gentlemen are from the FBI and the NIS, Julie." Her face paled. "They need to ask you some questions about Saba."

"Saba? Has something happened to her? Did she and Scott have an accident?"

The phone buzzed. Julie picked it up. She listened for a moment. "Is one of you Mr. Howard?" she inquired.

"I am." Howard took the phone. As he listened, consternation filled his face. "Yeah, I understand. We'll decide what to do when we finish here." He stopped and listened for a moment. "No, I don't have the slightest idea where to start looking. Maybe we'll get some idea here.'' Howard hung up the phone, obviously angry. "Seems like your Miss Saunders and Dr. Corbett never showed up at the lodge,'' he informed them sourly. "Didn't cancel. Just never showed up.'' Mike felt sick.

"But I heard Scott phone for reservations,'' Julie protested. "Something must have happened to them.''

"Maybe to Dr. Corbett,'' Adams commented dryly.

Chapter Sixteen

Miami Beach, Florida

"Scott, would you get the soap out of my case?" Saba
called from the bathroom through the sound of the
shower. "I hate these bitsy bars of hotel soap."

Scott rose from the bed, where he'd been stretched
out half asleep. He groggily unzipped the heavy shoulder bag.

"Scott. Can't you find it?" she asked after he'd fumbled through tape cassettes and wrestled with a thick
stack of computer printout sheets. He was startled.
Why had she brought this stuff with her?

"No. It's not in your shoulder bag. Wait and I'll—"

"Not the shoulder bag! My overnight case. The little
square one." Scott wondered why she sounded so upset.

"Oh." He left the shoulder bag and found the overnight case sitting on the dresser. "Sorry, wrong case.
Just a minute." He snapped open the lid and dug

through the usual women's stuff to find the bar of fragrant soap.

Scott carried it into the bathroom. "This is tasty-smelling soap," Scott observed as he approached the shower. "Don't be surprised if you get eaten from head to toe."

"I think I'd like that." She pushed back the curtain and grinned at him, reaching for the soap. She saw the heat in his eyes, and snatched the curtain closed again. "I thought I could trust you," she said, laughing.

Back in the bedroom, Scott remembered he hadn't closed her shoulder bag. When he tried to zip it shut, he found that, in his haste, he'd made such a mess of things that it wouldn't close. He took the tape cassettes from the case, and rearranged the printout sheets. He started to replace the cassettes when he noticed they were labeled. He recognized them as program-module names for the genetic-engineering computer model. There were also cassettes labeled "DNA CODES," with what appeared to be serial numbers.

These were definitely not stereo tapes. They were digital-data storage tapes. They were the kind often used to back up computer data. All computer memories and storage disks eventually crashed, trashing their data. Duplicate, backup storage was essential. Every computer installation—and PC user, if he was wise—had a back-up routine that periodically stored programs and data on high-capacity disks or digital tapes. Digital tape cassettes such as Scott held in his hand had become popular backup instruments because of their small size and low cost. A machine the size of an audio tape deck could replace a computer-tape machine the size of a twenty-cubic-foot refrigerator, and their cassettes could hold as much data as a two-foot-high stack of fifteen-inch-diameter reels of conventional digital tape. The same technology was used in digital audio tapes. There were enough tapes in Saba's shoulder bag to hold a huge computer program and vast quantities of data.

Scott retrieved the printouts from the bag. The header shocked him: *GMU Lesatec SYSTEM DOCUMENTATION: ADA SOURCE CODE INDEX*. She seemed to have the entire genetic-engineering program in her bag. Why?

Scott heard the shower go off. His gut tight, he repacked the bag and zipped it shut. He sat on the bed, and fought with the suspicions pummeling him. He told himself he was being paranoid. She had just made the breakthrough they needed to defeat Aziz's biotech weapon. She probably just couldn't bear to stop working. But how could she use the tapes without a computer?

"Is something wrong, Scott?" she asked as she emerged from the bathroom. She was still damp, her hair a long tangle of wet midnight. The towel she held around her barely covered her breasts, and failed to cover a long leg and hip.

"Nothing's wrong." He decided to ask her about the tapes later. "I'd better get in the shower. I can smell myself and I don't like what I smell."

"I like the way you smell." Her eyes smoldered. "Please make love to me, Scott," she said abruptly, in a voice so low and husky he couldn't believe what he'd heard. Astounded, he watched the towel drop from her body. Fire coursed through him, exploded in his groin and left him rigid and aching.

She walked to where he sat on the bed and stopped in front of him. He grasped her hips and pulled her to him. He pressed his face against her firm belly. Her skin felt cool and moist, and smelled like flowers. He touched her with his tongue.

Her belly tightened. She gasped. Jerked. Then abruptly pulled away. "No! Wait!" she said.

He reached for her. ''Please,'' she pleaded, backing away, ''not yet.'' Scott dropped his arms. She came close again, and pushed him onto his back on the bed.

Scott filled with mindless desire as she slowly undressed him. When she finished, she stood by the bed and caressed his body with her eyes. Her face held an almost innocent expression, as if she'd never seen a nude man before. Her gaze roamed his lean body and studied its well-defined muscles. They weren't the muscles of a bodybuilder, but those of a person born with strength. Her eyes traveled across his ridged stomach and paused at his middle before surveying his long-muscled thighs. Scott sat up and pulled her down beside him, moved over her and sank between her thighs.

She smiled gently and kissed him. Softly. Her tongue found his. Her hand grasped him and guided him into her. There was resistance. Her hips surged, and he sank deep inside her. Her arms tightened around him. She locked her legs behind his calves and wouldn't let him move.

Saba took her lips from his, and studied his face.

Scott gasped when she tightened around him.

Still she wouldn't let him move. She squeezed him again.

He moaned.

Saba smiled and began to move. She seemed to know his body better than he did. She knew how to make his flesh scream for release, then squeeze it back from the edge.

When Scott exploded inside her, he felt as if a grenade had gone off in his groin and spewed hot, liquid shrapnel.

Scott collapsed on her, then rolled off her onto his back. He breathed raggedly, drained of strength but filled with wonder.

When his sanity returned, Scott started to pull Saba

into his arms again. She scooted away. "Go take your shower," she ordered. "We need to go eat—build our strength for later," she said mischievously.

When Scott came out of the bathroom, Saba was fully dressed and holding a silenced automatic. The bore looked enormous for a .22. Her face was sorrowful, but her eyes were flinty with determination.

"Too bad you found the tapes," she said with disappointment. "I might have found a way to keep you out of this." She took a deep breath before she went on. "Scott, I wanted to know what it's like to love a man, not just fuck him. Now I know. Makes it hard to kill you. I don't think the pain will ever go away."

"Don't do this, Saba!" He started toward her.

"Don't!" she warned sharply. Her finger tightened on the trigger. "Don't make me kill you, not yet. I might find a way to let you live. I'd like that . . . to know you're still alive . . . even if you hate me. I am very good with this gun, Scott, and I've killed many times before. So don't try to be a hero. Just get dressed. We're going to the airport."

"I'm very good at this sort of thing, had lots of practice and training," she informed Scott when he finished dressing. "You can't escape or warn anyone. You'll die the instant you try.

"You carry the shoulder bag," she directed. "I will be behind you—out of reach. Go down the stairs, through the lobby and out to the car. Open the doors on the passenger side—both of them. Put the case on the floor in the back. Then crawl onto the front seat on your hands and knees. Remain there until I tell you to get up and drive. I will be in the back with the gun.

"Don't try to be a hero. I'll just put a bullet in your brain, take the case and escape before anyone realizes what's happened. You will have wasted your life for nothing."

She made him back out of the hotel room with one hand behind his back and the other wrapped with the shoulder-bag strap. There was no chance to slam the door and bolt.

"You're going to take me to the plane, Scott," she announced once they were settled in the car. "I'll decide then whether I can let you live." He didn't believe her. She had already decided to kill him.

Springfield, Virginia

"Julie, can you think of anything she might have said that would give us a clue?" Mike pleaded urgently.

"No, I can't think of a thing. Nothing."

"Any place nearby she visits regularly?" asked Howard, the FBI agent. The two agents, Mike and Julie had gone through Saba's papers page by page. They had examined her phone pad for impressions. Julie had called up Saba's computer files and examined them record by record.

"Corbett's car is missing," Howard said. "We searched all the airport car lots—nada. Makes us think wherever they went, they drove there."

"Did you search the private airports?" Julie asked absently, still struggling to think of something.

"No, but we checked the charter flights."

"What about flying clubs?" Julie asked.

"Flying clubs? I don't understand."

"Saba loves to fly. She flies almost every weekend. Insists on flying us to conferences." Julie's face brightened. "That's it! Bet you'll find Scott's car at Manassas Airport. She belongs to a flying club there that has all sorts of aircraft. Bet she talked Scott into flying rather than taking an airline. The number is probably on her computer Rolodex." Julie went back to the computer, called up Saba's personal-management program and asked for flying service. The name and number crawled onto the screen. "Want me to dial?" she asked.

"Yes."

"Pick up the phone," she instructed Howard. Julie used the screen cursor to highlight the number and entered it.

The conversation was brief. The excited agent dialed another number. "Johnson, Howard here. We've picked up their trail. Saba Saunders filed a flight plan for Miami yesterday. Instead of taking the airline shuttle to New York, they flew a rented plane to Florida. Contact our Miami people. Get them to the airport to secure the plane. Then get the cops to put out an APB on them and have our people start checking hotels.

"All right, let's get moving!" Howard said to the NIS agent as he hung up the phone. "We'll get a Bureau plane to take us down there."

"You're treating them like criminals already," Julie protested. "We don't know if they've done anything more than change their plans."

"If they haven't done anything wrong, it will all be over in a few hours, and they can go about their business," Howard lied. The agents rushed from the office.

"Can't we do something, Mike?" Julie asked, staring after the departing men. "They could get killed in an accidental shooting or something. They haven't the slightest idea anyone is looking for them. I know what I'd think if a bunch of men in civilian clothes burst into my room."

Mike was worried, too. His instincts told him Scott was in danger. "Have you inventoried Saba's stuff to see if anything is missing, Julie?"

"What is there to inventory? She just has what's in

the office, and we've been through everything.''

"What about GMU?''

"Nothing there.''

"Nothing at all?''

"Well, there *are* the backup tapes. Our programs are automatically downloaded every twenty-four hours. They're piped to recorders in a special air-conditioned vault.''

"Check them.''

"But—''

"Omar left here with tapes.''

Fearfully Julie dialed the university computer center. As she listened, her face twisted with horror. When she hung up the phone her hands were shaking, and she was pale. "Mike, Saba copied the supercomputer-program backup tapes, which means she undoubtedly copied the genetic-code and PC-program tapes. She also printed copies of program documentation. It's happened again, Mike!'' Julie moaned. Her eyes filled with tears.

Mike gripped her shoulders and held her rigidly. "Look at me, Julie!'' he ordered. She refused to meet his eyes. "I said look at me!'' he ordered again.

Her tear-filled eyes reluctantly met his.

"Guilt trips aren't going to help right now, and we need your help. Make a list of everything you think Saba might have taken.''

Miami International Airport

"Scott, I'm sure you don't want to be responsible for the deaths of innocent people,'' Saba said as they left the car and walked toward the terminal. "Seven, I would think. There are nine rounds in this weapon. I would need the first for you, seven for them, and a spare . . . maybe for me.'' Cruel determination hardened her voice, leaving no doubt that she would kill without hesitation. Kill anybody. "If you don't do exactly as I tell you, people will die, people that don't have to die, and you will be responsible for their deaths. Could you live with that? I don't think so," she answered for him.

"Saba—"

"Don't tell me I wouldn't kill innocent people," she rasped. "I have and I will again. I'll carry the bag this time. The pistol will be under this scarf. You'll do all the paperwork."

She stood close behind him at the desk, carefully watching as he filled in the forms. The flight plan was for Nassau—a flight that would never be completed, Scott thought bitterly. Her sharp eyes and the gun pressing the small of his back gave him no opportunity to try anything. He wondered when she planned to shoot him. Just outside on the ramp? Or would she walk him out to the plane first? Probably by the plane. It would be a long time before anybody noticed him lying on the tarmac.

He was right. The Bonanza sat in the front row of the crowded tie-down area. As they approached the plane, Scott decided he couldn't wait any longer. He slowed and gathered his strength to jump backward into her. He knew he was going to be shot, but he hoped it wouldn't be a head or heart shot. He might be able to keep going long enough to bring her down. It wasn't much of a chance, but the odds were better than waiting to be executed.

"Hold it right there!" Someone shouted the time-honored cliché behind them. Scott stopped, but his relief was premature. Saba's pistol coughed, and there was a hoarse cry in the distance.

Saba smashed the gun across the back of Scott's neck and shoved him under the fuselage of the nearest plane. His head hurt like hell, and his legs wobbled out of control.

Two guns barked, and shattered pavement sprayed his legs.

Scott struggled to regain control of them.

Saba yanked him to his feet. Her strength surprised him. She spun Scott around and shoved the gun into his spine. "Move!" she ordered harshly, and gave him a shove that sent him stumbling.

Pounding steps raced toward them.

She pushed Scott toward another plane.

Scott heard scrabbling under the aircraft behind them.

Saba shoved him to the ground, his weakened legs offering little resistance. Her automatic coughed twice. Two nine-millimeters exploded back. Fuel splashed out of the plane in front of them. An automatic weapon ripped off a burst from another direction and stitched holes across the craft. The fuel went up with a whoosh.

A wave of scorching heat staggered them.

Scott gathered his legs under him and rammed Saba like a linebacker. The gun clattered from her hand as she fell.

Scott pounced on her.

She fought like a cat. She was all squirm, elbows and knees. Her thigh thudded against his testicles. The pain stiffened him. She slammed a fist into his solar plexus. Breath and strength deserted him.

Saba squirmed away from him. Scott tried to get to his feet, but he kept falling down, and the world wouldn't stop tilting.

Saba found her gun in the light of the building inferno. Soon other planes would catch fire. Scott heard a siren wail in the distance. He finally managed to struggle to his feet.

Saba aimed her gun at his head.

He saw death in her eyes.

The gun was rock steady as she got the bag's strap on her shoulder.

Saba suddenly hit his shoulder with the palm of her hand spinning him on weak legs, which threatened to drop him to the tarmac.

She shoved him straight at the flames, then allowed him to stagger around the edge of the roaring inferno. She followed. They surprised two men in torn, singed suits.

"Drop your guns!" she screamed.

The shocked men froze for a moment, realized they had no chance and let their weapons clatter to the pavement.

"Your hands! Up!" she barked.

They complied.

She shot them. She was quick. Holes seemed to appear simultaneously in both foreheads. They crumpled to the tarmac.

Sick rage consumed Scott. He whirled. "You didn't have to do that!" he roared. He leaped at her. She shot him twice in the gut.

The twin lances of agony were unbelievable.

He struggled to stay on his feet and keep moving, but agony defeated him. He jolted to the pavement.

She pressed the barrel into the flesh between his eyes.

He looked into the eyes of death.

Her finger tightened on the trigger.

"I love you, Scott Corbett," she said softly.

Scott waited—suspended between life and death.

The hard steel left his forehead.

She stood and looked down at him, her face tragic. "You might live," she stated simply. "They're only twenty-twos . . . copper-jacketed . . . not hollowpoint."

Then she was gone.

The sirens were very close now. There were shouts among the planes.

Scott heard the Bonanza's engine sputter to life nearby. He tried to get up. Dizziness overcame him, and fire slashed his gut. Damn, it hurt! He tried again. This time he made it to his feet. The world stabilized, but the pain worsened.

The engine sounds moved toward the runway. Scott staggered after them, stumbled over a body, and fell to the tarmac. Incredible pain jolted him into a black void.

Bethesda Naval Hospital, Washington, D.C.

Mike, Julie and the doctor stood watching the nurse fuss with the tubes and wires connecting Scott to bottles, instruments and devices Mike couldn't identify. Scott had been stabilized and flown to Bethesda. He had not regained consciousness.

"Technically, he should be dead," the doctor commented. "Damn near lost all of his blood—it leaked inside, which is even worse. Two bullets bounced around inside him. Small-caliber, high-velocity bullets do that. Only good thing is that the holes are small. Your friend was lucky, the shooter used copper-jacketed bullets. Still, he's far from out of the woods. We're going to have to fight massive infections. Stuff from his guts is spread all through his stomach and chest cavities."

"When will we know whether he's going to be all right?" Julie asked in a shaky voice.

"Don't know . . . a week, maybe. Depends on what kind of bugs he's got in his guts, and how often they counterattack. I don't expect him to regain consciousness for another day or so. Captain, I'll call if there is any change," the doctor said, ushering them from the room.

The White House

The long black limousine glided through the East Gate and stopped at the White House entrance. "I'm not up to this, Mike," Julie complained. Her face was gaunt and pale. The stress had been enormous. She'd had to fight off the press. Lesatec had informed her in no uncertain terms that her employment would be terminated as soon as the company could find a way to extricate itself from the government. And she was personally supervising every step of the desperate effort to produce neutralizing microbes. She slept on the couch in her office—mostly catnaps. Omar's and Saba's defections had made her afraid to leave the lab for an instant. She wanted to be there—or any place—instead of meeting with the President, who would likely order her shot for creating a holocaust.

"The President needs a damage assessment, Julie, and he wants to get it directly from our best expert," Mike said. "That's you. He needs your estimate of the damage Saba might do with what she stole."

"But I'm too shaky and tired to think straight. I feel like I don't even know where I am, what I'm doing or whether I'm sane. You do it, Mike. I need to get back to the lab."

"I don't know enough to do it." Mike took Julie's chin in his hand and forced her to look at him. "I'll be right there with you. You can hold onto my hand, if you want. The President just wants your opinion. Nobody blames you for anything. They are not going to have you shot."

Julie smiled wanly. "All right," she said, "but if I faint or throw up on the rug, it'll be your fault."

"So you are the lady who let all of this loose on the world," the President said to Julie when he swept into the room with the Vice President. Mike winced and watched Julie fearfully. Horror flooded her face. The President couldn't have used worse words.

The President shook her hand briefly, then went around his desk and sat down. Julie stood staring at her hand. Mike tensed. Resignation replaced the horror in her face, and Mike relaxed a little.

"What I need to know from you, Dr. Barns, is what Libya can do with the technology that woman stole. The Europeans are trembling in their boots—raise a fuss every time one of our planes takes off. And despite all his tough talk, I think the Egyptian President is wavering. We lose Egypt, and we'll find ourselves in another war. The Coalition will go after Israel next. We can't allow Israel to go under, but we'll be in it all by ourselves this time. We need to know what we're facing. Dr. Barns, do we have a new threat?"

"Sir, before this, they only had copies of genetic codes for the three strains of microbes we had developed," Julie managed to say. She realized her voice trembled, and paused to steady herself. She carefully measured each word before speaking. "They now have genetic codes for microbes that can neutralize those three strains. They can protect themselves and limit the area and severity of a counterattack.

"Saba also took the modeling software needed to create new organisms. They didn't have that before. Omar Salim didn't have access to it. Also, the software Saba took is far more advanced than what we used for the original genetic engineering. It reduces engineering time by orders of magnitude and makes practical the creation of many more varieties of organisms."

"So they can not only control what they have, but now they can produce new agents," the President concluded.

"No, sir, I don't believe so," Julie responded.

"I don't understand."

"The software Saba took is of no use without a supercomputer like the one at GMU. The programs are much too large and require too much processing to run on anything but a large machine with parallel processing."

"And you don't think they have such a computer?"

"No, sir, but then I'm not an intelligence person."

"What about that, Anton?" the President asked the CIA Director.

"There is no evidence they have a supercomputer, or the expertise to use one."

"But this Saunders woman has the expertise."

"Yes, sir, but no machine."

"Are you sure, Anton?"

Carlson hesitated. "Reasonably sure." He flinched at the President's thunderous look. The President hated the term "reasonably sure." "We are aware that Gadhafi's people approached a Japanese manufacturer a few years ago. We investigated, but the company has gone out of the supercomputer business. Their machines were good, but not good enough to compete with American machines. Since they couldn't win big, the Japanese gave it up. Pieces of the equipment went everywhere, test models and all. It's possible the Libyans obtained a test model. Nothing is ever one-hundred-percent certain."

"Sure as hell is true in the intelligence business," the President commented dryly. "Dr. Barns, are you assuring me that they can't do anything more than neutralize the microbes they have?"

"No, sir. I'm not sure of anything anymore."

"I'm glad I have company," the President responded. "I appreciate your candor, Dr. Barns."

"We shouldn't underestimate the impact of their having the capability to neutralize what they have," the Vice President pointed out. "Aziz and company no longer have to worry about fratricide and can move in after an attack."

"You're right, but there doesn't seem to be a damn thing we can do about it. Doesn't seem to be a damn thing we can do about a lot of things," the President grumbled. "How's our defense against this stuff coming along?"

"We've cultured and tested the neutralizing microbes," Julie answered. "They do destroy all three strains of the original microbes." Pride filled her voice. Despite the disaster, she was proud of how well her team had performed under terrible pressure.

"We have used the priority you gave us to get pharmaceutical companies under contract to DoD to produce the defensive microbes," Mike added. "Dr. Barns and her people are working out production procedures now."

"Fine. That's all I need for now," the President said, dismissing them.

Julie left the White House in a daze, and climbed into the rear of the Navy sedan that had replaced the limousine. She had talked to the President. She should be experiencing exuberance, exhilaration, importance—something other than the feeling of floating through a nightmare. Her stomach burned and felt tight as a drum. She couldn't shake the sense of impending disaster.

"You okay?" Mike asked. The rigid set of her pale face worried him.

"No, I feel like hell."

Mike slipped an arm about her shoulders and squeezed her, ignoring the eyes of the driver in the rearview mirror. "You shouldn't feel like hell. You did great. The President liked you."

She relaxed against him. She forced microbes, computers, spies and everything else from her mind, and concentrated on how good his arm felt around her.

Julie was nearly asleep by the time they reached Crystal City. "How about lunch?" Mike asked as they emerged from the car.

"No, I've got to get back to Lesatec." Her anxiety grew every minute she was away from the lab. Did she have another spy on her staff? Suddenly, returning to the lab seemed a matter of life and death.

Chapter Seventeen

Bethesda Naval Hospital, Washington, D.C.

When Scott awoke a gang of demons were tearing at his insides with hot pitchforks. A nurse's face swam into view. "Well, Dr. Corbett, you're back with us again," she said, smiling. "I'd better call the doctor." She disappeared.

Memories exploded in Scott's mind—every bit as agonizing as his wounds. Saba! The tapes! He tried to sit up, but a shock of pain pinned him to the bed, making him sweat and gasp for breath.

"Well, Dr. Corbett, you've rejoined the land of the living," a voice boomed. A large man with a fleshy, cynical face leaned over him. "I'm Dr. Brassert. I've been assigned to resurrect you. You weren't quite as far gone as that Lazarus fellow in the Bible, but damn near." The doctor scanned the instruments hooked up to Scott.

"I have to talk to Captain Boen," Scott gasped. "I

have to tell him about—'' A cough choked off his
words and drenched him with pain.

"Captain Boen knows all about your lady friend and
whatever she took," the doctor assured him. "You can
talk to him in the morning. You've been out of it for
three days, so I think he can wait another few hours."

"Three days!" Scott couldn't believe it.

"I think he's over the hump," Brassert told Mike
the next morning as they reached Scott's room. "Being
in such good shape probably saved him, and he'll heal
fast."

"I really fucked up, didn't I?" Scott rasped when
Mike sat down beside the bed.

"What are you talking about?"

"If I had been thinking with my brain instead of my
dick, I could have stopped her."

"I doubt it. She's a highly trained agent, and was
probably on her way out of the country before you ever
thought of going to Florida with her."

"I could have," Scott replied bitterly. "I found the
stuff before she pulled the gun. I—''

"Cut it out, Scott! You would have probably just
gotten yourself killed. Anyway, feeling guilty won't
change what happened. You need to concentrate on
getting out of that bed and back to work. You've done
more operational analysis of nonlethal weapons than
anyone in the world. We need you to help design defensive systems and tactics. Aziz and his bunch can
drop that weapon anywhere—even here—and we don't
have any kind of defense."

"We have Julie's defensive microbes."

"But no way to use them—no system, no tactics."

"If you get me a computer with an encryption board
and a modem, I can hook up to our network and get
things started."

"Maybe in a couple of weeks—if the doctor okays it."

"A couple of weeks! I don't intend to be in here a couple of weeks!" He tried to sit up, but fell back with a groan.

"Scott?"

"I'm all right. Just a little sore is all."

"A little sore? I guess so."

A nurse came into the room with a tray of syringes and bottles, followed by the doctor. "We need to do a little work on our patient, Captain, so tell him good-bye," the doctor said.

Mike gave Scott's hand a squeeze and got to his feet. "You really scared me, old buddy. Don't you worry about anything but getting well. I'll call, come by whenever I can."

Egypt

The war started by accident, as wars often do.

Tank Company Commander Captain Majeeb Zaid led his ten M60A3 tanks toward the Libyan border through the desert south of the railroad that paralleled the Mediterranean Coast from Marsha Maturah to Salum. If war came, the railhead at Salum would be crucial to the Egyptian push along the coast planned as a response to Libyan provocation.

Captain Majeeb Zaid had been ordered to probe along the border for Libyan incursions. He wished he knew for sure where the hell he was. Zaid ordered the column to pivot north and form a skirmish line. The bad feeling gnawing at Zaid's guts caused him to order his crews to lock and load.

They had just turned and formed up when Zaid's tank came up over a small rise and collided with a parked truck. Zaid was flung forward against the hatch's side and almost fell back into the tank. As he fought the pain in his ribs and struggled to regain his balance, his nose filled with diesel fumes. A fuel truck! "Go! Go! Full speed!" he screamed to the driver.

The M60A3 roared ahead, smashed aside a BMP armored personnel carrier and mashed a startled squad of infantry into red mud. The fuel went up with a roaring whoosh. Zaid dropped back into the tank and slammed the hatch shut as the tank was sheathed in flame. The driver kept the throttle wide open despite the crashes and jolts. He knew that the wind of speed was the only thing that would smother the flames and prevent them from roasting to death.

Machine-gun rounds rattled off the armor. "Gunner! Fire to the rear! Platoons! Fire! Fire!" Zaid yelled into the radio.

Zaid's gunner fired. Despite the roar and clank of the tank, Zaid thought he could hear the other tanks fire.

Zaid looked to the rear through the extension. There were still flickers of flame streaming off the tank, but they were dying. The encampment they'd burst through was enveloped in flame and smoke, but as he watched, one of the third platoon's tanks disappeared behind an intense white flash. When it became visible again, black smoke was belching from a gaping hole in its side, and it was tipped at an odd angle.

Antitank weapons!

"Disengage," Zaid yelled over the radio. "Keep going. Get out of range! Go! Go! Go!" he screamed at his driver.

Zaid's tanks were now rushing headlong into Libya, but Zaid didn't know that. He believed he had discovered a Libyan armor and mechanized infantry team moving into Egypt to cut the coast railroad.

Zaid switched to the battalion net, and broke radio silence. "We have engaged invaders! At least two companies. We are under attack. We need air support!"

"What are your coordinates?"

Zaid rattled off coordinates—rough guesses. "Locate us by the smoke!" he added.

Zaid's message snowballed at each echelon. The battalion commander reported his patrol had encountered armed intruders bent on cutting the rail line. The message reaching the CINC reported a full-fledged Libyan invasion.

The Egyptian CINC had standing orders for a counterattack, and he initiated it without further consultation. The Egyptian President was quite surprised to learn that his country was at war with Libya. An Egyptian armored column had closed on Tobruk, and 300 Egyptian tanks were tearing across the Libyan plateau toward Benghazi.

Tripoli

Colonel Muhammad Aziz hadn't believed the Egyptians would attack without provocation. He had watched the Egyptian President's political situation deteriorate, and had been certain the country would soon oust their President and join the Coalition.

Aziz's position was desperate. He hadn't sufficient forces to even slow the Egyptians. Aziz had no choice but to order use of his biotech weapon, but given this miscalculation, there was no certainty it would stop the Egyptians. It might just anger them further and harden their resolve to destroy him. Giving the order was like jumping off a cliff into the night. He didn't know whether the bottom was two feet or 2000 feet below.

Egypt

Major Fethi Bahar jinked his MiG-29 Fulcrum along the Egyptian coastline, using his Infrared Search and

Track set to follow the shore. It wasn't the first time he'd made the flight, but this time he would go further than he ever had before. He had followed Colonel Aziz on a previous flight. It had been a training flight: a very dangerous one, since they were violating Egyptian airspace. Aziz had personally taught Fethi the radar-evasion techniques that Aziz had used so successfully in Iraq. He'd taught Fethi which terrain and coastal features provided the most concealing clutter returns. For a realistic demonstration he had led Fethi on a flight along the Egyptian coast. They had not been detected by AWACS or other radars. Aziz's technique was a poor-man's stealth. Aziz had learned the technique from a lustful Soviet engineer in Iraq whom Aziz had supplied with young girls. The man had been a rising star in the Soviet technocracy until he'd been caught sleeping with the wrong wife. He'd been sent to Iraq for punishment. His superiors had thought it a fate worse than death.

Fethi thought it was too easy when he popped up from his twenty-foot sea-skimming altitude and streaked across Alexandria, leaving a hail of popping bomblets behind him. It *was* too easy.

The Egyptian F-16 Falcons were too late to prevent weapons release, but they were determined that the MiG would not escape. A Sidewinder took off a wing tip, and tracers rent the sky in front of Fethi's canopy.

Fethi inverted the Fulcrum, pulled it through a crushing loop and rolled out to blaze across the city just above building roofs. The missing wing tip made control a desperate struggle.

Fethi gained the sea before the Falcons could turn, but it was becoming harder to control the Fulcrum. He didn't need gauges to know the Fulcrum was hemorrhaging hydraulic fluid.

It took the Egyptian Falcons ten minutes to catch him. By that time he was sixty miles out to sea.

Another Sidewinder exploded just aft of his tail. Its fuse had been triggered prematurely by confusing signals from the sea surface, but it finished the Fulcrum. Fethi barely had time to eject.

East of Tobruk

Even inside the Fahd armored personnel carrier the noise of antiaircraft fire deafened him. Debris clattered onto the deck of the vehicle. Then he heard nothing but engine and gear sounds.

Egyptian Tank Battalion Commander Lieutenant Colonel Tariqu Hussein opened the hatch of the APC and stood up to survey the damage to the tank column spearheading the attack into Libya. He couldn't see anything but bits of burning junk flaming on the tops of some APCs and tanks. He radioed for a SITREP. No one reported damage. Only a single plane had attacked. It had sneaked up a canal at twenty feet, turned onto the road and swooped along the column. The SU-24 Fencer had been turned into a cloud of junk shortly after releasing a ten-kilometer trail of bomblets. The bomblets seemed to have done no damage. The only casualty was from falling aircraft debris that killed a tank commander who had been tardy in closing his hatch.

Hussein settled back inside to report the attack to division. Five minutes later the tank jolted to a stop. The engine refused to turn over, though the displays showed fully charged batteries.

Suddenly the radio crackled with voices reporting disabled vehicles. Then the radio died. Alarmed, Hussein fiddled with the knobs. He was shocked when they froze.

Hussein climbed out of the hatch and stood on the deck of the Fahd. The chaos horrified him. The column

253

had turned into a tangle of stalled armor. If they were attacked, they would be helpless.

Recovery vehicles brought up to clear the highway failed. The devastation spread along the column, and the attack along the coast came to a confused halt.

REUTERS: ALEXANDRIA

AN ATTACK BY WHAT IS REPORTED TO BE A SINGLE AIRCRAFT HAS PARALYZED THIS PORT CITY AND PLUNGED IT INTO CHAOS. ALL TRANSPORTATION AND UTILITIES HAVE CEASED TO FUNCTION.

THE DAMAGE HAS BEEN COMPOUNDED BY TERROR. MOBS HAVE LOOTED STORES AND WAREHOUSES. ARMED GANGS ROAM THE STREETS, ROBBING AND KILLING. FIRES ARE RAGING OUT OF CONTROL. RELIEF VEHICLES ATTEMPTING TO ENTER THE CITY HAVE BEEN ATTACKED AND ROBBED. ARMY AND POLICE UNITS WERE OVERWHELMED WHEN THEIR VEHICLES AND WEAPONS BECAME INOPERATIVE. OBSERVERS ARE PREDICTING THOUSANDS OF DEATHS FROM THIRST, STARVATION AND RIOTING.

THE EGYPTIAN GOVERNMENT HAS MOVED TO QUARANTINE THE CITY, BUT EXPERTS SAY THAT QUARANTINE OF SUCH A LARGE CITY IS IMPOSSIBLE. POTENTIAL SPREAD OF THE CONTAMINATION THREATENS THE SOCIAL AND ECONOMIC FABRIC OF THE WHOLE COUNTRY. EXCEPT FOR ABSENCE OF PHYSICAL DESTRUCTION, THIS ATTACK HAS BEEN AS THE DEVASTATING AS THE DETONATION OF A NUCLEAR BOMB. EXPERTS

NOW CONCLUDE LIBYA HAS DEVELOPED THE LONG-SOUGHT POOR NATIONS' AN-SWER TO NUCLEAR WEAPONS.

TRANSCRIPT OF CNN REPORTS FROM EGYPTIAN ARMOR UNITS ON THE ROAD TO TOBRUK:

THE EGYPTIAN ATTACK ALONG THE COAST HAS HALTED IN UTTER CHAOS. TANKS, TRUCKS, WEAPONS AND COM-MUNICATIONS EQUIPMENT OF FORWARD UNITS HAVE BEEN DISABLED. EGYPTIAN ARMY UNITS STRIKING TOWARD TOBRUK ARE PARALYZED AND DEFENSELESS. TER-ROR IS CAUSING A SERIOUS BREAKDOWN IN DISCIPLINE.

TRANSCRIPT OF CNN REPORT FROM THE EGYPTIAN UNITS ADVANCING ON BENGHAZI:

SEVERAL LIBYAN ATTACKS ON THE AD-VANCED ARMOR UNITS HAVE BEEN RE-PULSED. THOUGH A NUMBER OF TANKS HAVE BECOME INOPERATIVE, THE LOSSES HAVE NOT MATERIALLY REDUCED THE EGYPTIANS' CAPABILITIES. SPEED AND DISPERSAL SEEM TO BE EFFECTIVE COUN-TERS TO THE LIBYAN WEAPON.

The Oval Office

''Well, they did it.'' The President announced what everyone in the room knew. Mike had been hastily summoned by Sam Moon to the meeting with the Vice President, the SECDEF, the Chairman of the JCS, the

Secretary of State, the CIA Director and other key members of the Administration. Mike thought he ought to feel a tremendous sense of prestige to participate in a meeting with the President, bypassing a gaggle of four-stars. He didn't. He felt like an intruder.

"What do we have, Jake?" the President asked the CJCS.

"What we have is a strike by a single aircraft which has destroyed a whole city and its port. It's the equivalent of a hydrogen-bomb attack without the physical destruction and death. A single plane ran along the coast skimming the waves and caught the Egyptians by surprise."

"I hope to hell we weren't surprised!"

"We ID'd the threat and warned the Egyptians," the CJCS hedged, "but they couldn't respond in time."

"Were you able to warn them in time?" the Vice President persisted.

"Not in time to stop weapons release. It's extremely difficult for even the most sophisticated radars to detect a sea-skimming target close to land, and our systems had to pick the target out of heavy Egyptian air traffic in the area. Took a lot of signal-processing time. By the time our computers dug out the threat and we could get through to the Egyptians, the weapons had been dropped.

"The Egyptians did have time to scramble F-16s and engage the bomber over the city. Splashed him off the coast. Pilot survived. Carrier SAR picked him up."

"He give you any useful information?" the CIA Director asked.

"No, he's tough and dedicated."

"Get him here as fast as you can," the CIA Director urged. "He might know the location of the biotech-weapons-production facility."

"Will do, but I doubt he knows that. They probably

loaded his plane somewhere else. He probably didn't even know what he was carrying.''

''Well, we need to decide what we're going to do about this,'' the President said.

''I'm afraid there isn't anything we *can* do about it,'' responded the Secretary of State.

''What the hell you mean we can't do anything!''

''We do not have a mutual defense treaty with Egypt, and furthermore, Egypt is the aggressor. Egypt attacked Libya, and the Libyans haven't threatened us. Been very careful to stay away from American ships. Our allies are dead set against any interference. They claim it's a North African problem.''

''We didn't let that stop us from bombing the hell out of Libya before.''

''Not the same situation. We would be supporting the aggressor in the face of the violent opposition of all our European allies. Congress would raise holy hell.''

''Be even worse if all we did was precipitate attacks on Europe,'' the CJCS added. ''To prevent that we need to destroy the biotech-weapons-production facilities and stockpiles, and we don't know where they are.''

''What you are telling me is that Aziz has found out how to get away with mass terrorism,'' the President concluded bitterly.

''I'm afraid so,'' the Secretary of State replied.

The President paused for thought. ''I guess we'll just have to wait,'' he finally said. ''I don't like it. This damn Coalition is going to bite us in the ass if we screw around too long. How near are we to deploying a defense against this thing, Captain?''

''Sir—'' Mike started to say they were working on it, but remembered the President's aversion to the term. ''We are designing a delivery system and—''

''In other words, you're *working on it*,'' the President interrupted sarcastically. "Hell, Captain, why should you be any different than anyone else around here. Don't apologize. At least you're doing something concrete that might get us out of this mess—not sitting around with your thumb up your ass complaining."

Mike left the White House depressed. The whole world could go down the drain before anybody decided to act. He entered the cream-colored Navy sedan waiting for him outside the White House. He dreaded debriefing the Pentagon brass on his latest White House meeting. They were enraged by the idea of a Navy captain bypassing the top admirals, generals and SECs. He was going to take a lot of abuse. He'd never be an admiral now, and forced retirement loomed.

ASSOCIATED PRESS: TRIPOLI

IN A COMMUNIQUE ISSUED FROM A HIDDEN BUNKER, COLONEL MUHAMMAD AZIZ CALLED FOR A CEASE-FIRE AND TALKS BETWEEN THE COALITION AND EGYPT. HE OFFERED TO FLY TO CAIRO FOR THE TALKS ONCE THE CEASE-FIRE IS IN EFFECT. HE ALSO OFFERED TO NEUTRALIZE THE EFFECTS OF THE COALITION WEAPON ON ALEXANDRIA AND PREVENT ITS SPREAD TO THE REST OF THE COUNTRY. HE SAID THAT FURTHER AGGRESSION BY EGYPT WOULD GIVE THE COALITION NO CHOICE BUT TO ATTACK THE SUEZ, AND THEN THE WHOLE WORLD WOULD SUFFER.

CNN: CAIRO

UNDER PRESSURE FROM THE INTERNATIONAL COMMUNITY, PARLIAMENT AND

A TERRORIZED POPULACE, THE EGYPTIAN PRESIDENT RELUCTANTLY ACCEPTED THE COALITION'S CEASE-FIRE TERMS.

CNN: CAIRO

COLONEL MUHAMMAD AZIZ ADDRESSED THE EGYPTIAN PARLIAMENT TODAY AND SPOKE OF A NEW WORLD ORDER LED BY ARABS. HE INVITED EGYPT TO PARTICIPATE, AND PROMISED TO NEUTRALIZE THE EFFECTS OF HIS WEAPONS AS SOON AS EGYPT BECAME A MEMBER OF THE COALITION. HE CALLED UPON EGYPT TO EXPEL ALL AMERICANS, POINTING OUT THAT AMERICANS WERE UNABLE TO PROTECT THEM. MANY MEMBERS OF PARLIAMENT GREETED AZIZ AS A HERO. A VOTE OVERWHELMINGLY IN FAVOR OF COALITION MEMBERSHIP IS EXPECTED TONIGHT.

ASSOCIATED PRESS: CAIRO

ALL AMERICAN MILITARY PERSONNEL HAVE BEEN ORDERED TO LEAVE EGYPT. THE STATE DEPARTMENT IS ADVISING AMERICAN CITIZENS TO DEFER NONESSENTIAL TRAVEL TO EGYPT.

REUTERS: ALEXANDRIA

LIBYAN DECONTAMINATION TEAM ARRIVED IN ALEXANDRIA TODAY, AND WERE GREETED AS SAVIOURS, DESPITE LIBYANS BEING RESPONSIBLE FOR THE DEVASTATION. BOTH HELICOPTERS AND

AIRCRAFT WERE USED IN THE OPERATION. A LIBYAN FENCER MADE NUMEROUS PASSES OVER THE CITY, RELEASING DEVICES IDENTICAL TO THOSE USED IN THE ATTACK. FOREIGN EXPERTS ON THE SCENE SAY THE RESULTS HAVE BEEN DRAMATIC. VEHICLES CARRYING FOOD AND MEDICINE HAVE BEGUN ENTERING THE CITY, AND HAVE NOT BECOME IMMEDIATELY INOPERATIVE LIKE THEIR PREDECESSORS. HOWEVER, IT WILL TAKE MONTHS TO RESTORE BASIC SERVICES.

Washington, D.C.

"It's certain now that Saba Saunders did reach Libya with the tapes," Dr. Julie Barns announced to the people assembled around the table in the White House Situation Room. The meeting—hastily called by Jason Goodson, the President's National Security Advisor—was attended by White House Chief of Staff Sam Moon; CIA Director Anton Carlson; Chief of Naval Intelligence Admiral Jake Kittering; and Captain Mike Boen. "It's the only way they could produce the neutralizing microbes," Julie concluded.

"Do you think they've developed any new agents?" Goodson asked.

"Not without a supercomputer, but that's something you would know more about than I."

"I wouldn't bet on that. How's the defensive system coming, Captain Boen?"

"We're almost there. We've rigged together parts from chemical weapons and cluster bombs. We have an air-dropped version under test. Of course we can't use real organisms, and we aren't sure how it's going to work for cities. The pharmaceutical companies will start production of small quantities in two weeks."

"I hope we have two weeks," Goodson said, worried. "Any word on location of the lab producing this stuff, Anton?"

"Nothing definitive."

"What about the Tarhunah plant? It's constructed in tunnels under a mountain."

"We've been watching that for a long time—continuously. We have HUMINT in there, and our people were members of the international inspection team Gadhafi let tour the plant. Nothing has indicated he's managed to get equipment needed for genetic engineering in there. We suspect that because of the publicity and our threats to bomb the place, he's given up on that site.

"There are other chemical plants we've known about for a long time, and we suspect the Libyans have been experimenting with biological agents at the same sites. And there are probably sites we don't know about buried in the desert somewhere.

"We're using satellites and remotely piloted vehicles to map every square inch of Libya and Chad, and we're running a massive computer analysis of data we've collected for the last ten years. We've got every analyst familiar with the area working on it—CIA, DIA, NSA and all of the services. With the help of French and German intelligence organizations, we've managed to identify engineers who have worked on construction projects in Libya. Like Iraq, Libya has spent billions of its oil money on hardened hangars, underground command centers and the like. We hope to find people who have worked in computer and genetic-engineering labs. But it's going to take time— weeks, maybe months. By the way, the fact that the French and German intelligence people are helping us is not to be disclosed to anyone. Their governments would have them shot. Please, Sam, no public thanks for assistance."

"I think I have enough to brief the President," Goodson said unhappily, "but not enough to satisfy him. We are in deep shit, and it's getting deeper every day. That damn Aziz is also proving to be one helluva politician, too. Sounds very reasonable while terrifying the hell out of everyone. He's every bit the equal of Gorbie in the early days of glasnost. We're losing NATO and the whole Middle East. Nobody, but nobody, in the region is going to do anything that might provoke an attack. They're terrified.

"Captain Boen, the President wants a briefing from you as soon as you have a working defense system. You'd better come along, too, Dr. Barns. He always likes to talk directly to the experts. Thank you, gentlemen—I'm sorry." He smiled ruefully. "*Lady* and gentlemen, or should I say people?"

Julie smiled. "Don't worry about it. Just call me one of the boys, if you want."

They filed out of the conference room with a deep sense of foreboding.

ASSOCIATED PRESS: ALGIERS

SUPPORTED BY A TERRIFIED POPULACE, THE FUNDAMENTALIST ISLAMIC TRUE BELIEVERS FRONT HAS OVERTHROWN THE REGIME OF PRESIDENT QUSSEN TIBI AND ANNOUNCED THAT ALGERIA IS JOINING THE NEW ARAB COALITION LED BY LIBYA.

REUTERS: TUNIS

TUNIS ANNOUNCED IT HAS RESOLVED ITS DIFFERENCES WITH LIBYA AND IS JOINING THE NEW COALITION.

REUTERS: TANGIER

KING HASSIEM III HAS ANNOUNCED MOROCCO WILL JOIN THE NEW ARAB COALITION.

ASSOCIATED PRESS: BRUSSELS

THE EGYPTIAN CONFLICT APPEARS TO HAVE WIDENED THE BREACH BETWEEN THE U.S. AND ITS ALLIES. ITALY, GREECE AND SPAIN, WHICH ARE WITHIN EASY STRIKING DISTANCE OF LIBYA, TODAY CALLED UPON THE AMERICANS TO STAY OUT OF NORTH AFRICA, AND HAVE SHARPLY RESTRICTED OPERATIONS OF AMERICAN FORCES USING BASES IN THEIR COUNTRIES. THEY THREATENED ARMED INTERVENTION IF AMERICANS ATTEMPT TO USE THOSE BASES TO SUPPORT MILITARY OPERATIONS AGAINST THE LIBYAN COALITION.

VETERAN OBSERVERS BELIEVE THE COALITION HAS SUCCEEDED IN TERRORIZING ALL OF WESTERN EUROPE. THEY BELIEVE THAT COLONEL AZIZ'S CONCILIATORY GESTURES, WHILE AT THE SAME TIME DEMONSTRATING THE ABILITY TO DEVASTATE A CITY AND THREATEN THE ECONOMIC AND SOCIAL STRUCTURE OF AN ENTIRE COUNTRY WITH A SINGLE AIRCRAFT, WILL DETER ACTION BY THE EUROPEAN COMMUNITY.

ASSOCIATED PRESS: TRIPOLI

IN WAKE OF A WHIRLWIND TOUR OF THE
MIDDLE EAST, COLONEL MUHAMMAD
AZIZ HAS ANNOUNCED THAT SAUDI ARA-
BIA AND THE OTHER PERSIAN GULF
COUNTRIES HAVE AGREED TO JOIN THE
LIBYAN-LED COALITION. THE COALITION
NOW INCLUDES ALL ARAB COUNTRIES IN
THE MIDDLE EAST. SOME WERE ANGERED
BY IRAQ'S MEMBERSHIP, BUT EVEN THE
KUWAITIS ACQUIESCED IN THE FACE OF
THE COALITION'S MILITARY THREAT. IN
ADDITION TO ITS "DOOMSDAY MA-
CHINE," THE COALITION NOW CONTROLS
A VAST ARSENAL OF CONVENTIONAL
WEAPONS AND HIGH-TECH SYSTEMS,
MOST OF THEM FURNISHED BY THE U.S.
AMERICA'S ABILITY TO DEFEND ITS MID-
DLE EASTERN ALLIES NO LONGER AP-
PEARS TO BE CREDIBLE, AND AS A
CONSEQUENCE THE AMERICAN MILITARY
SEEMS CERTAIN TO BE FORCED OUT OF
THE REGION.

CNN: TRIPOLI

AT A NEWS CONFERENCE, COLONEL MU-
HAMMAD AZIZ DETAILED THE AGREE-
MENTS REACHED AT THE FIRST MEETING
OF THE EXPANDED ARAB COALITION. CO-
ALITION MEMBERS HAVE AGREED TO
DOUBLE THE COST OF OIL AND LIMIT
PRODUCTION. THE COALITION THREAT-
ENED MILITARY ACTION AGAINST ANY
MEMBER WHO VIOLATED THE AGREE-
MENT. FEAR OF LIBYA'S BIOTECH

WEAPON IS EXPECTED TO ENSURE THERE
WILL BE NO SUCH VIOLATIONS.
   SHOCKED EUROPEANS HAVE ACCUSED
AZIZ OF BETRAYING THEM, BUT STILL
STRONGLY   RESIST   RETALIATION   AS
URGED BY THE AMERICANS.

Gaza Strip

   The woman glided silently into Yasir Arafat's office
and over to his desk. Only Asrar was allowed to enter
his office without his bodyguards—men and sons of
men who'd been with him through the early days, when
he was a hunted terrorist. She'd been there, too. She
was completely veiled in black except for a narrow slit
for her eyes—so narrow, he'd never been able to dis-
cern her eyes' color, let alone what was in them. He
idly wondered what kind of person floated under the
silk—what she felt. Did she feel? She had no husband.
No children. The veil muffled the emotion in her voice
when she spoke, which she seldom did. She most often
did his bidding without verbal response. Anything he
wanted.
   A disturbing thought ran through Arafat's mind. He
had no way of telling who the black cloth hid, whose
face the veil obscured. Could be anyone. Maybe not
Asrar at all.
   Suddenly his survival instincts—intuition, premonition, almost psychic powers—raised the hair on the
back of his neck.
   Had he taken leave of his senses! he screamed silently
at himself. He should never be alone with anyone these
days. Too many extremists were calling for his blood
because he'd refused to embrace Libya's Coalition.
   So swift. She was so swift. He stared at the knife
sunk into his chest, not quite to the hilt, but far enough
to penetrate his heart.

Arafat felt more disappointment than pain. More disgust with himself than fear of death. To have survived so much to die like this. Carelessness. To be killed by such carelessness. Killed by an old habit—trusting this woman. Almost like committing suicide.

Arafat expected the guards to respond to his reedy scream. He wanted to see her precede him in death. None came. And he knew why. They were dead. She hadn't come alone.

He only had time to wonder who they were before he died.

ASSOCIATED PRESS: TEL AVIV

YASIR ARAFAT HAS BEEN KILLED IN A COUP BY A GROUP CALLING ITSELF "THE HANDS OF GOD." THE LEADER, YOUSSEF SALEM, HAS ASKED TO JOIN THE NEW LIBYAN COALITION. ISRAEL'S PRIME MINISTER WARNED ISRAEL WILL NOT ALLOW A COALITION-CONTROLLED GOVERNMENT TO RULE THE PALESTINIAN TERRITORIES, AND THREATENED TO REOCCUPY THE WEST BANK.

REUTERS: TRIPOLI

ON BEHALF OF THE LIBYAN COALITION, AZIZ VOICED WELCOME AND STRONG SUPPORT FOR THE NEW PALESTINE LEADERS, AND WARNED ISRAEL THAT THE COALITION WOULD NOT ALLOW REOCCUPATION OF THE WEST BANK OR ANY OTHER MILITARY ACTION AGAINST THE NEW PALESTINE.

WASHINGTON POST SPECIAL
CORRESPONDENT: JERUSALEM

ISRAEL LAUNCHED A SURPRISE ATTACK
THAT OVERWHELMED GAZA AND PENE-
TRATED TO RAMALLA. THE ISRAELI
PRIME MINISTER CLAIMS ISRAELI FORCES
HAVE DETECTED LARGE ARMS SHIP-
MENTS MOVING INTO PALESTINE FROM
JORDAN. HE CLAIMS SUCH SHIPMENTS
CAN HAVE ONLY ONE PURPOSE—PREPA-
RATION TO ATTACK AND DESTROY IS-
RAEL.

CNN: TRIPOLI

LIBYA'S COLONEL AZIZ HAS SENT A MES-
SAGE TO ISRAEL'S PRIME MINISTER GIV-
ING ISRAEL TWO WEEKS TO WITHDRAW
FROM THE PALESTINIAN TERRITORIES ES-
TABLISHED BY THE PEACE ACCORD. HE
HAS ALSO DEMANDED THAT THE ISRAE-
LIS GIVE UP JERUSALEM AND REMOVE
ALL WEST BANK SETTLEMENTS. IF IS-
RAEL DOES NOT COMPLY BY THE DEAD-
LINE, COLONEL AZIZ VOWS TO PARALYZE
ISRAELI CITIES ONE BY ONE, STARTING
WITH TEL AVIV. IF ISRAEL RETALIATES IN
ANY MANNER, AZIZ THREATENS TO DE-
STROY THE ENTIRE COUNTRY. HE EMPHA-
SIZES THAT HE IS NOT THREATENING THE
DEATH OF INNOCENT WOMEN AND CHIL-
DREN, ONLY THE ECONOMY OF AN OUT-
LAW STATE WHICH REFUSES TO ABIDE BY
INTERNATIONAL LAW.

THE U.S. STANDS ALONE IN ADVOCAT-

ING DEFENSE OF ISRAEL AND MILITARY RETALIATION FOR ANY COALITION ATTACK. BUT UNTIL THE U.S. DEMONSTRATES THE ABILITY TO DEFEND AGAINST LIBYA'S BIOTECH WEAPON, IT IS UNLIKELY TO FIND SUPPORT FOR ITS POSITION.

Crystal City, Virginia

"Scott, what are you doing here?" Mike exclaimed.

"I work here."

"You're not due back for another six weeks."

"Another six weeks lying around my apartment would drive me out of my mind."

"Lying around? You've been on your computer night and day ever since I got you the secure modem. You shouldn't be out of the hospital, never mind working at home. And you certainly shouldn't be here." Scott was pale, and his suit hung loosely on his gaunt frame. Mike estimated he'd lost twenty pounds.

"You need me here," Scott said. "Aziz has already clobbered Egypt, and we still don't have a damn thing to stop him."

Mike did need him—desperately. The chaotic effort to field the technology needed Scott's broad systems-development experience to successfully integrate the pieces and make them work together.

"Okay," Mike relented, "but pace yourself. You won't be worth a damn to us if you overdo it and collapse."

"I run marathons, remember? I know all about pacing myself," Scott said, grinning.

Chapter Eighteen

The White House

Secret Service agents roused Mike from his bed at three o'clock in the morning and drove him to the White House. He found a dazed Julie Barns and key members of the President's cabinet and staff assembled in the Oval Office: National Security Advisor, White House Chief of Staff, Secretary of State, Chairman of the Joint Chiefs and CIA Director. Everyone stood when the President and Vice President entered.

"Fill the others in, Anton," the President ordered the CIA Director.

"We believe an attack on Israel is imminent, perhaps within twenty-four hours. I think you all know about the Coalition threat to take out one Israeli city at a time until the Israelis vacate the West Bank or are destroyed. If the Israelis retaliate, the Coalition threatens a mass attack that will send Israel back to the Stone Age."

"You can imagine the consequences," the President

said grimly. "If the Egyptian experience is any indication, the biotech weapon will leave the Israelis defenseless. Coalition forces will overwhelm them and slaughter the Jewish population. It would be the holocaust all over again. We cannot allow that to happen.

"Israel is the final barrier to this so-called Coalition, which I believe will turn out to be a massive dictatorship run by Aziz. If Israel goes, Turkey will be next. It has its own bunch of fundamentalists who want to take it out of NATO and put it back into the fold of true Islam. Once that happens, the Muslim regions of the former Soviet republics will be pulled in, then Afghanistan and Pakistan. They'll be in position to crush India. They can take the rest of Africa whenever they please. Aziz's empire will stretch halfway around the world. It will have control of most of the world's oil reserves, strategic materials, critical sea lanes and a big chunk of the world's population. No telling where it will lead, maybe to a holy war to destroy the U.S.

"We have to stop them in Israel. Anton, tell them why we're here."

"The Coalition is putting together a tremendous air armada. Planes are fueled, armed and sitting on runways in every Arab country. We've never seen so many Arab countries coordinate a military operation like this. Israel will be hit from every direction. It could be a devastating multi-axis attack, even without this new weapon."

"I'm surprised the Israelis haven't launched preemptive strikes," the Vice President said. "Why? They have never hesitated before."

"The country is divided . . . terrorized. There is little doubt that the Coalition can make good on its threat to ruin the country, even if they can't blow it up," explained Winston Dudly, Secretary of State. "More and more Israelis are saying the West Bank is not worth the whole country."

"And what would the Israelis attack?" Carlson pointed out. "No one knows where the production facilities are for Aziz's doomsday weapons, and the weapons themselves are probably dispersed all over Libya. Be impossible to find them all."

"There is also another terrifying aspect to this," the President warned. "If all else fails, the Israelis might retaliate with the nuclear weapons they claim not to have. We have no idea how the Russians would react to that. It could escalate into World War Three, and in any case there would be millions of casualties.

"Captain Boen, I've come to the conclusion that the only way out of this is to neutralize the effects of that weapon. Can it be done?"

"Yes, sir. If we can install the delivery system in a B-1B, we can be in Israel within twenty-four hours."

"The B-1B you can have," the President said firmly. "Jake, I want you to get a plane to Israel as fast as you can. Station it there. Keep equipping and sending aircraft until there are enough to protect the whole country."

"Sir, you do realize that's putting those aircraft at risk. They might be destroyed on the ground, or their technology fall into the wrong hands—"

"I *realize* all that, Jake. What you need to understand—and what everybody in this room needs to understand—is that more is at stake than a few aircraft and their classified technology. Now, get going! I want the plane, Captain Boen and whatever he needs in Israel yesterday!"

B-1B

Fatigue blurred Mike's vision, but the adrenaline pumping through his veins kept him awake as the B-1B plunged through the night. Julie slumped asleep in her seat. He was surprised she hadn't collapsed before.

Julie had been with Mike every minute since they had left the President's office. Scott's weakened condition had finally caught up with him, and Julie had taken charge of final preparations.

Mike worried about the hardware. The dispensers were converted chemical weapons, which no one had ever considered dropping from a B-1B. The racks had been hastily installed by Navy lab people, and there had been no time for flight testing. Final assembly and loading of the dispensers had been done in a hanger at Andrews AFB. Mike had no idea whether the hastily assembled, untested system would work.

Mike and Julie had used the flight time to work out delivery patterns with the B-1B crew. They had studied maps of Tel Aviv, and programmed the plane's weapons-delivery computer. They planned to land, re-fuel and remain in the aircraft, ready for instant takeoff.

"Flash message coming in," the communications officer announced, and switched the incoming message to the internal communications system. The encrypted message was being relayed by MILSTAR, the advanced military satellite communications system operating at extra-high frequencies, which made possible jam-proof, secure communications using small antennas.

"Red Lion, this is Hen, acknowledge." The encryption electronics gave the voice a tinny, robotic sound.

"This is Red Lion. Your transmission is clear, over."

"The balloon has gone up. They hit Tel Aviv. Snuck a Fitter in low along the coast under radar coverage while the Israelis were diverted by feints. The Coalition filled the air with planes."

"All right, keep us advised."

"You do the same. Out."

"You understand what we have to do, Colonel Halloran?'' Mike asked the aircraft commander. "There's no time to land and refuel."

"I understand, but I don't like it. I'm not sure we can do the runs witnout refueling."

Tel Aviv

"We have fifteen minutes, Captain Boen," the plane commander informed Mike. "Then we glide, and this thing glides like a rock."

"Stand by to give control to the computers," Mike responded. "Are you ready, Lieutenant Jones?"

"As soon as we get over the reference."

"Two minutes," the plane commander responded.

Lieutenant Jones flipped the red cover off a switch.

"Now!" the plane commander announced. Jones flipped the switch.

The plane rolled sharply into a turn. The engines roared. Mike held his breath. The plane nosed over, then leveled. The engines settled back to a steady drone. Jones pushed the arming and auto-release buttons.

"Locked on course," Jones announced proudly. Mike felt the thud of bomb-bay doors opening, then slight jerks at ten-second intervals as the bomb-release mechanisms did their things ... or sounded like they did. He didn't want to think about what the jury-rigged system might *actually* be doing.

The computer flew the plane in twelve sweeps over the city. Lights signaled the completion of the mission.

"Handing control back to you, Colonel," Jones informed the plane commander.

The engine sounds suddenly whined down to silence. "Everybody check their harnesses," the colonel warned. "This is going to be a dead-stick landing. More like a crash."

The pilot lined the plane up on the Tel Aviv-to-

Jerusalem highway. The plane was sinking too fast for him to make the airport. No vehicles moved on the highway. The threat of a Coalition attack had cleared the traffic.

The Colonel had been right: It was more a crash than a landing. The jolt slammed Mike down in his seat. The landing gear crumpled, and the fuselage slid along the concrete with an awful screech. A wing touched an embankment, and the plane spun violently.

An unearthly silence descended on them. Mike began breathing again. He'd cheated death once again.

The Oval Office

"It worked, Mr. President," reported the Joint Chiefs Chairman. "The city was paralyzed for most of the day, but more from terror than actual damage. They lost quite a few cars, a TV station and power plant. The microbes ruined a lot of small stuff—radios, cash registers, that sort of thing. Scared the shit out of people, but the city is almost back to normal."

"I agree with the Israelis," the President said. "We have to respond. We have to press home the fact that their biotech weapon does not deter us in the least. I want to hit Libya hard. What do we have out there, Jake?"

"Three battle groups. One is in the Gulf of Sidra. We could get two more in a couple of weeks."

"I said now!" the President barked.

"We should make sure we get the chemical plants," said CIA director Anton Carlson.

"Will that take care of the production facilities for the biotech weapon?" the Vice President asked.

"We don't know for sure," Carlson answered. "Dr. Barns doesn't think those plants have the right equipment to do genetic engineering, but it's a possibility."

"Then do it," the President ordered.

Tripoli

A dismayed Colonel Muhammad Aziz shuffled through the pile of news reports in front of him once more, not wanting to believe the Coalition could unravel so rapidly:

WASHINGTON POST FOREIGN SERVICE:

IN THE WAKE OF THE ABORTIVE ATTACK ON ISRAEL AND THE DEVASTATING RESPONSE BY U.S NAVY AND ISRAELI AIRCRAFT, EGYPTIAN AND SAUDI ARABIAN ENVOYS HAVE VISITED THE WHITE HOUSE. PUBLICLY BOTH STATED THAT THEY ARE SEEKING WAYS TO AVOID FURTHER ARMED CONFLICT, BUT MIDDLE EAST EXPERTS BELIEVE CONFIDENCE IN THE NEW COALITION HAS BEEN DEEPLY SHAKEN AND MEMBERS ARE SEEKING WAYS TO SAFELY LEAVE IT. THE U.S. HAS DEMONSTRATED THAT IT HAS DEVELOPED TECHNOLOGY TO NEUTRALIZE THE NEW LIBYAN WEAPON, AND IT IS WIDELY BELIEVED THAT ATTACKS ON LIBYAN CHEMICAL PLANTS HAVE DESTROYED ITS CAPABILITY TO PRODUCE THE BIOTECH WEAPON. MORE COALITION MEMBERS ARE EXPECTED TO SEEK THEIR OWN PEACE TERMS, AND THE EUROPEANS ARE TAKING A HARDER LINE AGAINST THE COALITION. THESE EXPERTS BELIEVE THE COALITION WILL SOON UNRAVEL.

The raid had stunned Aziz, but not paralyzed him as a previous attack had paralyzed his predecessor. For weeks after the American raid, Aziz had watched him wander around like a zombie. Aziz believed the tyrant had never fully recovered. Otherwise, Aziz's plotting would have never escaped the notice of the old dictator, whose instincts had seemed supernatural. Aziz was dazed, but not paralyzed. He was going to act. What he contemplated terrified even him, but didn't deter him. Terror was his life. He regarded it almost with affection.

Aziz laid the news dispatches back on the table with calculated carelessness, adding to the pile of papers that he had used to conceal the fifteen-shot 9mm Beretta before Omar Salim and Fatima Sudari had arrived. Now the three of them were alone in the room and seated at a long conference table. Omar's face was filled with fear, as it always was in Aziz's presence. Aziz examined him with smoldering resentment. It irritated Aziz to have to depend on this weak young man who was only concerned with preserving his miserable life. But Aziz needed Omar's expertise. He was key to freeing Aziz from dependence on Fatima and her bitches. At least Aziz didn't have to worry about the fool's loyalty. His cowardice guaranteed that.

Aziz played it out in his mind. He didn't want to miscalculate; it would mean his life. He visualized the Beretta under the papers: where the trigger was; what the motion of arm and hand would be to seize it and fire. He reviewed how long that would take and where he would aim.

Fatima Sudari was the most dangerous person he'd ever encountered—man or woman. Even now, the anger smoldering in those hard, merciless eyes chilled him. A mistake would be fatal. She would see to that.

"We must attack the continental United States," Aziz announced. "It's time the Americans realized that they can be struck in their homeland."

Omar blanched. "But they have hydrogen bombs!"

he gasped. "Look what they've done to us already, what they did to Iraq. They'll destroy us."

"Not before we destroy their heartland," Aziz replied stubbornly. Omar found that scant comfort. He didn't want to be a martyr. He just wanted to live.

"You can't be serious," Omar persisted.

"Why can't I be serious?" Aziz asked dangerously. His terrible eyes made Omar slump in resignation.

"They have developed a defense," Fatima stated coldly.

"Only against the original microbes," Aziz responded. "We will use new strains." Suspicion dawned in Fatima's eyes. His new knowledge of the technology worried her. "We have the technology to produce as many different strains as we need," Aziz said confidently.

"Not unless I decide to give it to you, and I don't intend to unless you fulfill your pledge," she said. "Our patience is at an end, Colonel. You will get nothing more until you do as we agreed."

"You know that's impossible," Aziz argued. "This could not be a worse time. We already have defections." He pointed at the pile of news dispatches. "What do you think would happen if in the midst of all this I issued such a proclamation? Be reasonable."

"My good colonel, what would you do in my place?" she asked caustically. "Be reasonable? No, your weapons are now useless. If you want weapons that will defeat the American defenses, you will have to do what you promised, and do it now. Regardless of the consequences. Your survival depends on us."

"My dear Fatima, how sadly mistaken you are. Explain, Omar."

Omar choked on fear. Both people terrified him, and he was caught between them, like a rabbit torn between a lion and a panther.

"Omar!" Aziz spoke sharply, his eyes never leaving Fatima.

"I . . . we . . . have programs for the models. I have a staff of my own that can do the genetic engineering. Saba doesn't know." Upon her return, Saba had taken control of biotech weapons development from Omar.

"And where would *you* get such a staff?" Fatima asked.

"They are experts who were convinced it was in their best interests, and those of their families, to return to Libya," Aziz answered for Omar. "Just as Omar thought it best to return."

"They have been working with Saba," Omar continued. "And secretly for Colonel Aziz."

It was the first flash of fear Aziz had ever seen in Fatima's eyes. "But you still need the passwords to use the software," Fatima insisted, but her voice was unsure. Her knowledge of the technology was limited.

"No," Omar said, "Just the software design concept, and that was obtained by working as Saba's staff. We have brilliant software designers who have attended the best American schools. Some have worked on large computer-software development projects for American companies. They have re-created the software by using what they learned by working with Saba. Our software will do everything hers does, and more." Omar's voice was filled with pride. He'd outsmarted the filthy bitch who'd humiliated him, and he wasn't through with her yet.

"We don't need to run Saba's programs," Omar informed Fatima. "We can run our own. We have been testing them at night and whenever Saba is out of the lab. We're ready for production."

"I don't believe you!" Fatima raged, but she did. She also realized that she wouldn't leave this room alive. But she would see that Aziz didn't either.

"If you don't believe that," Aziz said, "I have

something else you won't believe." He punched the intercom button. "Send her in," he ordered.

The woman who entered the room was Fatima's first cousin. Eqbal Charaa and Fatima had been recruited at the same time. Together they had given birth to the "Movement." The "Movement" was as much Eqbal's as Fatima's. She was Fatima's second in command, and the Sisterhood members would obey her without question.

Eqbal's ravaged face spread cold fear through Fatima. Eqbal's eyes were filled with agony. A thick scab covered a split at the corner of her mouth, and she walked with difficulty.

"I think you two know one another," Aziz said sarcastically.

Eqbal dropped her head and refused to look at Fatima.

"What have they done to you, Eqbal?"

"Many rather unpleasant things," Aziz answered for her, smiling nastily. "But we have come to a certain accommodation."

"I'm sorry, Fatima," Eqbal sobbed. "I—I couldn't help it. I had to."

"What have you done to her!" Fatima raged.

"Show her, Mrs. Charaa."

"No!" Eqbal's head came up. She pressed the manilla envelope she carried to her breast.

"No? Mrs. Charaa, I don't believe you are in a position to use that word unless *I* tell you to." His eyes glinted dangerously.

"Please," she begged, shaking her head.

"Would you like us to take additional photos for your collection?"

Trembling, Eqbal dropped her head, withdrew six eight-by-ten photos from the envelope and laid them on the table. "Spread them out," Aziz ordered. "I'm sure Fatima will enjoy them.'' Tears streaming over her cheeks, Eqbal did as she was told.

Fatima had seen many horrors, had visited many horrors on men and women, but never on a child. Eqbal's daughter was nineteen, but her slender, delicate body was childlike. The photographs detailed her rape by a huge, hairy giant, and there were pictures of even more horrible things being done to the young girl.

Fatima's eyes filled with a red mist of rage. She fought the urge to spring at Aziz. The smirk on his face made restraint nearly impossible, but she had to make sure she killed this monster instead of just committing suicide.

''She was not damaged too badly,'' Aziz informed Fatima, enraging her further, if that was possible. ''She has a strong mind. I believe she will be returning to school next month. In Paris. Her brother and sister are already there. Her sister is still a virgin, but that could change. And I know those who love young boys. But their mother will not allow anything to happen to them.''

''I couldn't help it, Fatima!'' Eqbal cried. ''They are my children!''

''We have all the names of those in your Sisterhood, as you call it,'' Aziz said. ''But we won't kill them. They have a new leader—one with more realistic expectations. You *do* have different expectations, don't you, Mrs. Charaa?''

She answered with a sob.

''There will be more women in school. I will find places in government for some. We may even have a women's Olympic team. I have promised you all that, haven't I, Mrs. Charaa? That and the cost of three college educations in Paris. That would be hard for a poor widow to manage, wouldn't it, Mrs. Charaa? Mrs. Charaa will be a heroine, and of course your Sisterhood will continue to serve Libya.''

"Don't trust him, Eqbal," Fatima said angrily. "His promises are nothing but lies." She poised with glittering eyes.

Aziz realized that somehow Fatima knew about the pistol. "Keep your hands on the table," he ordered her.

She sat very still, studying him. Aziz knew she was calculating whether she could reach under her robe quicker than he could reach under the papers. He had already made the calculation. She had to push the robe aside. She would lose by at least a tenth of a second.

He knew she knew it was hopeless.

He knew she would try anyway.

She suddenly slipped from sight under the table.

Aziz scooped up the pistol as he dove across the top.

Two bullets shattered the back of his now empty chair.

He rolled along the tabletop.

Holes splintered the wood after him.

He heaved himself from the table to a desk along the wall. He sent three discouraging rounds through the table.

Neither could see the other now. She was hidden under the table. He was out of her line of sight on top of the desk. Omar and Eqbal sat frozen in their chairs.

Aziz could hear her moving under the table.

Aziz gathered his legs under him and leaped to the floor as bullets punctured the space behind him.

Aziz rolled once on the floor and came up firing.

Fatima was an elusive blur moving behind a tangle of chair legs.

A bullet burned across Aziz's temple, and a hot poker drilled through his left shoulder.

He kept firing.

There was a hoarse scream from under the table and return fire stopped.

Aziz paused, steadying his weapon.

A chair shot from under the table, smashed into his legs and sent him reeling backward.

He struggled to hang onto his weapon and recover his balance.

Fatima sprang from under the table, put an arm around his neck jammed the barrel of her gun against his head.

He jerked away.

An explosion filled his head.

His scalp felt as if it had been ripped off.

He dropped his pistol to get both hands on her gun.

Her gun exploded again as he yanked at the hot barrel.

He yanked again. She dropped the pistol and they fell to the floor. A knife blade ripped his flesh and skidded along a rib.

He saw her throat exposed in front of him.

He bit.

His mouth filled with flesh.

He clenched his jaws.

Blood spurted into his mouth.

He shook his head.

A large piece of flesh tore loose.

A great spout of blood filled his eyes and nose.

Fatima went limp.

Aziz pushed Fatima's body off him, and struggled to his feet. The floor was slippery with blood. He fell. The guards outside pounded on the door. Aziz had locked it from inside.

Omar vomited.

Eqbal sat frozen in horror.

Aziz got to his feet again, being more careful this time. He reached across the table and punched a button to unlock the door. Guards streamed in.

Chapter Nineteen

Washington, D.C.: Doomsday 1

The National Airport control tower had given the twin-engine Beechcraft Super King Air B200 permission to land from the northwest. The plane had been rented from a flying service that specialized in skydiving. There was room for thirteen parachutists in the stripped cabin, but it was now occupied by only two women. The rest of the space was crowded with twenty gray canisters, secured to rungs in the floor and to rails along the walls by web straps with quick-release buckles. Each canister contained one hundred bomblets. The bomblets weren't filled with explosives. Their bursts were powered by compressed gas that would balloon a cloud of fine mist out 300 feet. Each canister was capable of laying down a mile-long path of virulent material, which would expand as it floated to earth and be spread for miles by wind. Once the microbes touched a vulnerable surface, they would multiply and spread over it with lightning speed. When infected surfaces touched other surfaces, the infection would spread. In a world of fast-moving, far-ranging vehicles and aircraft, the machine epidemic could expand with frightening speed.

The two women in the cabin could change and fire a canister every fifteen seconds. They had practiced until their movements were swift and sure.

The Beechcraft's landing approach took it over the Metro tracks as they emerged from deep under Rosslyn. The tracks ran on the surface past Arlington Cemetery before plunging underneath the Pentagon. The plane was at 1000 feet when it passed over the Pentagon. No one noticed the tiny white puffs trailing from the Beechcraft. The first hint of disaster was the Beechcraft's call to the tower. "National, this is Beech Twenty-seven. I seem to have a problem with my landing gear," the woman pilot calmly informed the air controllers. The Beechcraft was now at 200 feet, an eighth of a mile from the end of the runway. The controller could see the plane now. Its landing gear was not down.

"Beechcraft Twenty-seven, abort! Your gear is not down!" Adrenaline poured into the controller's bloodstream, and images of impending-disaster churned through his mind. The other controllers were transfixed by the transmissions. The controller saw the white puffs trailing the Beechcraft as it flew low over the field. His heart caught in his throat. He had a seriously damaged aircraft on his hands!

"Beechcraft Twenty-seven! You may have a major problem! You're shedding something! Are you flying okay?"

"Fine. Instruments show nothing."

The controller debated his decision. He had to get the plane out of populated areas as quickly as possible and onto a field where there was adequate emergency equipment to handle the wheels-up landing and the fire and explosion he feared would follow. "Beechcraft Twenty-seven, I want you to turn south and stay over the river until you reach Broad Creek. Do you know the landmark?"

"Yes." The plane banked over Bolling AFB, just south of the huge Defense Intelligence Agency building. The two women had changed canisters in less than twelve seconds. Bomblets streamed from the aircraft.

"Come to heading three-one-five until you cross highway five. Then come to heading zero-zero-zero and use the main runway. Andrews will have equipment waiting."

The controller had issued the instructions before notifying Andrews Air Force Base, confident they'd cooperate. Another controller was on the radio with the Andrews tower: "We have an emergency. A Beechcraft King Air is unable to lower gear. We have directed aircraft to your main runway. Estimated TOA ten minutes. Can you clear it?"

"Roger that."

"You'd better have all of the equipment out. We saw something fall from the aircraft. It may have serious damage, maybe to some controls."

"We are rolling the equipment."

The National Tower halted traffic and spewed a stream of instructions taking aircraft away from the Beechcraft's course.

The Beechcraft pilot smiled with grim satisfaction as the bomblets trailed out over the Naval Research Laboratory, the nation's premiere military research facility. She could see the open Wilson Bridge ahead of her. They had planned the flight to coincide with the bridge's regularly scheduled opening.

"Target!" the pilot called as the craft approached the raised spans. The two-mile-long backup would grow to ten miles in minutes, and ramps onto the beltway would be clogged. Traffic between Maryland and Virginia would be strangled.

The invisible mist, alive with microbes, had settled onto the Pentagon and National Airport, and was now drifting onto the Metro and train bridges crossing the Potomac. A Metro train dashed through the cloud of contamination and carried the microbes into the District. At the L'Enfant Plaza and Gallery Place stations, other trains picked up the microbes and spread them east and west through the city. Another Metro train picked up microbes at the Arlington Cemetery Station and carried them under Rosslyn into the Potomac tunnel.

As the Beechcraft approached Andrews, the pilot could see fire trucks poised along the runway and other vehicles racing across the field. A blanket of foam had already been laid down. The pilot acknowledged the Andrews tower instructions, assuring the controllers that the plane was under control.

Twenty seconds from touchdown, the pilot leveled the plane and, despite screams from the tower, flew lazily across the base, laying down a trail of bomblets. The emergency crews watched in astonishment. Astonishment turned to fear when they realized the white puffs could mean they were under attack, but there were no explosions, no fire, only faint pops. They stared at the mist drifting down, bracing for the effects, knowing it was too late to escape.

An MP in a jeep was the first to react. "I think we've been attacked," he screamed into his radio microphone as the plane gained speed and disappeared beyond the trees. "Maybe chemicals! We need some medical personnel, or whatever you got for chemicals!" The MP's call precipitated more confusion than action. Andrews was not an air-defense base, and a chemical air attack on the continental U.S. was beyond comprehension.

*   *   *

Lieutenant Jeff Jones, U.S. Air Force, sat in the cockpit of his F-15 Eagle on the apron in front of a hangar when the Beechcraft passed over. His wingman was parked beside him. Andrews was an overnight stop on their training flight. They had delayed engine start because of the emergency.

The sound of the Beechcraft's engine drew Jones's eyes up past his raised canopy. He was surprised. What was a civilian aircraft doing on such a course over the field? Then he saw the white puffs and thought he heard faint pops. His breath caught, and his chest tightened. His combat instincts had been honed in the Gulf War, and they told him that they were under attack— with chemicals. It was crazy! But he was sure of it. The sudden flood of voices from his radio confirmed his instinctive conclusions.

Jones reacted swiftly. He closed his canopy, much to the consternation of the crewman on the ladder beside his plane. He radioed warnings and orders to his wingman. He was incredulous, but he responded immediately without question. Jones radioed the crew chief to clear for engine start. He wasn't cleared for takeoff, but he wanted to be poised to escape if the chemicals began taking effect.

Jones listened with growing apprehension to the confusion on every net he switched to. No one was sure they *had* been attacked, and they were even less sure what to do about it. When the base commander requested information about possible pursuit, Jones broke in. "I have two F-15s turning, sir. Request permission to follow intruding aircraft. Definitely witnessed the drop of chemicals of some kind."

"Identify yourself," the base commander ordered.

"Lieutenant Jeff Jones, sir. We are on a training flight."

"Permission to follow granted. *Follow* only. Update position continuously, and we'll get the right people to be there when this aircraft lands. Repeat! Follow only! We don't want a crash in urban areas.''

"Understand, sir. Bat Two, we're rolling.''

Jones released his brakes and eased the throttle forward. Nothing happened. Startled, he eased on more power. The plane shuddered forward a few yards with screeching brakes, then halted, its nose shoved toward the tarmac by the engine thrust. An astonished Jones backed off the throttle.

"Bat Two, you'll have to do this one without me,'' Jones informed his wingman. "I have a problem. I think my brakes are frozen.''

The engines of the other plane roared, but it didn't move either. "Bat One, this is Bat Two. I've got the same problem,'' an incredulous voice informed him.

There was an ear-shattering screech as turbine-shaft bearings froze and burst into flame. The shaft sheared. Turbine blades sawed through the engine wall. Jones scrambled from the cockpit just ahead of the flames that engulfed the Eagle.

The Beechcraft pilot shut off the plane's radar transponder and flew at one hundred feet over the city, below radar coverage. They had strewn the last bomblets across the Capital, Union Station and downtown D.C. before anyone realized where they were. A train departing Union Station as the Beechcraft passed over carried the devastation north. The pilot avoided the White House, fearing hidden air defenses, but the expanding cloud of virulence drifted onto it in minutes.

The pilot jinked the plane low up the Potomac, still out of sight of radar. She banked away from the river at Great Falls, skimmed the treetops and landed in an isolated field in rural Loudoun County. A nondescript blue Ford Escort had been hidden in the trees.

The three women sat in the car with engine idling until the timer ignited the explosives wired throughout the plane. A fiery explosion shattered the aircraft. The concussion rocked the car, and debris pelted it. For a moment they thought they'd parked too close.

Satisfied with the destruction, they followed a bumpy track to a paved road and drove away at five miles under the speed limit—three young ladies skipping work to enjoy the quiet countryside.

Heartbeats slowed in the National Tower. There'd been only minor disruptions in traffic. "United Four Six Seven, you are cleared for takeoff," the controller informed the impatient pilot of the 737 poised at the end of the runway.

The United captain watched the flaps through the cockpit window as he worked the controls. Nothing happened. Hydraulic pumps screamed somewhere and a warning light flashed. "Josh, what the hell is going on?" the copilot exclaimed.

"Damn if I know. Shit! Everything was fine a second ago. The damn flaps—see any movement on your side?"

"Nothing."

"Shit! Looks like we won't be going anywhere soon.

"Tower, this is United Four Six Seven. We have a major control problem. Hydraulics are going crazy. Request taxi instructions and gate assignment. We are going to have to discharge passengers."

The tower came back with the information, and the captain released his brakes and eased on the power.

The plane didn't move.

He cautiously eased the throttles forward. Engine roar increased, but the plane still refused to move.

"I fucking don't believe this," the captain said as he did everything he could think of to release the brakes. Finally he sighed and gave up. "Tower, this is Four Six Seven. Problem is worse than we feared." He felt sick. What a hell of a mess this was going to make.

He was blocking takeoffs. His passengers would want to lynch him—as would the pilots of the planes behind him, even if it wasn't his fault. "This pile of junk won't move an inch."

"Won't move!" came back the controller's amazed response. "Please don't tell me that. You have ten flights behind you and more waiting to leave the gates."

"Sorry about that, but my brakes won't release."

Three minutes later the controllers knew they had a major disaster on their hands. Reports of airliners frozen in place poured in. The tractors had failed, as had the buses sent to pick up passengers. The controllers hastily diverted all incoming flights to Dulles and BWI. Then they had the problem of extracting the passengers from planes that were rapidly turned into steamy ovens as engines failed—sometimes violently—and ventilation systems shut down.

They ordered the passengers to be guided to the terminal on foot, but the aircraft doors couldn't be opened. The passengers were forced to use the emergency exits. The passengers streamed from the planes—sliding down chutes and jumping off wings. There were injuries: broken bones, sprains, and two serious head injuries. The injured were carried by stretcher to the terminal, which was in chaos.

Telephones had died when the big switching center in southeast D.C. shut down. Medevac helicopters were unable to take off. Two ambulances were stalled out front. Taxis were frozen in place.

One of the passengers with head injuries expired, and the other remained in a coma as deep as death. Hysteria began to sweep through the crowd milling about the terminal and frantically searching for transportation. There were long lines in front of the Metro station. There hadn't been a train for over forty-five minutes. There were reports that the Yellow Line was stalled at L'Enfant Plaza and that a Blue Line train was stuck under the Potomac.

New York City: Doomsday 1

The twin-turboprop Cavenaugh Cargoliner had made an overnight stop at the Linden, New Jersey, Municipal Airport. The small cargo craft's woman pilot filed a flight plan the next day for a short hop to La Guardia Airport. The plane took off to the west, and released the first bomblets as it passed southwest of Newark International Airport. It passed over the Military Ocean Terminal and crossed the Upper Bay without anyone noticing anything unusual. The plane banked onto an approach that brushed Manhattan and took it along the East River, where its virulent cargo drifted down onto the bridges.

The plane crew worked frantically to load and fire the canisters. The pilot radioed warning of gear problems a half mile from the end of the runway. The tower personnel verified the problem as the plane passed over at one hundred feet. The pilot ignored instructions to fly out over Long Island Sound and attempt to get the gear down. Instead, after passing over the Whitestone and Throggs Neck bridges, the pilot climbed to 1000 feet and banked onto a course that took the plane over the Bronx and Yonkers. She ignored the air controllers' threats.

The air controllers frantically warned other aircraft as the Cargoliner turned and flew over White Plains. It dove on Kensico Reservoir and skimmed across it at 200 feet. It banked sharply and dashed to the Hudson River. The pilot flew north fifty feet off the water. The plane disappeared from radarscopes.

Thirty minutes later La Guardia Airport shut down. So did Newark International. Bridge traffic stalled.

Subways ground to a halt. The city slid into paralysis.

The scene replayed itself up and down the coast.

Washington, D.C.: Doomsday 1

"Captain Boen, this is Admiral Kittering! We've been attacked!"

"Attacked!" Mike was sure he hadn't heard what he thought he'd heard.

"Yes, attacked!" the admiral insisted angrily. "The Pentagon's a mess."

"Attacked by whom? With what?" Mike still couldn't believe what he was hearing.

"Attacked by terrorists with that damn biotech stuff! I'm sure of it. Everything mechanical has malfunctioned in the building—typewriters, escalators, computer printers, even hinges and locks. Electrical systems are failing, and the phone circuits are going—don't know how long this line will be up. I don't think it's just the Pentagon. Had word that the switching center in South East has failed, and we can't get any emergency medical equipment over here.

"I'm going to notify the White House, SECNAV, SECDEF, JCS and anybody else I can while I still have communications. See if you can get some kind of reading on this, and get word to the White House and to me. Get yourself to where there is hardened communications. SPAWAR has them. Tomahawk program office—down where they do mission planning—has them, too. We had better get those B-1Bs we got stashed around the country with your defensive stuff in the air—high in the air. Don't want them stuck on the ground. Am I getting through to you, Captain? You do understand?"

"Yes, sir," Mike lied. "I'll get right on it and get back to you."

"Use the secure, hard circuits. I don't think anything

else is going to survive." He hung up, and Mike stared at the phone in astonishment. The admiral was a sane man—last time Mike had talked to him, anyway—but. . . .

Mike's secretary, Lila Jones, rushed into his office, her breath coming in strangled gasps. She leaned with both hands on his desk, her head hung down, while she tried to recover from her dash up the stairs.

"What's wrong, Lila?" Mike exclaimed. He left his chair, came around the desk and put his arm around her shoulders. "Here, sit down." He led her to a chair and held her arm as she collapsed on it.

Lila threw her head back, her eyes closed. "You all right?" he asked.

"No! I'm damn near dead," she gasped. "I think I almost gave myself a heart attack running up the stairs."

Lila's breathing finally slowed enough to talk. "Have you heard, Captain? The whole city is falling apart. National's shut down. The Metro's stopped running, and there's the biggest traffic jam you have ever seen out front. The elevators are stuck with people in them!"

A chill washed over Mike. He walked to the small television sitting on a corner table and switched it on. Channel Nine was in the midst of a special report that confirmed Kittering's conclusions. National had ceased operation. The Wilson bridge was stuck open, halting Beltway traffic. Stalled cars blocked all major arteries leading out of D.C. Downtown traffic was frozen.

The camera panned over crowds of people milling in the District streets. Office equipment, air conditioners, computers—all the machines and gadgets Washington needed to function—were failing. Office managers were dismissing their staffs, but there was no way for them to go anywhere. The report went on to detail calamity after calamity, until it suddenly winked off the air.

"What's happening?" Lila asked in a frightened voice.

"I'm not sure, but I think we've been attacked."

"Attacked? I don't understand. What kind of—"

"Do you know what's happening outside?" Scott asked as he rushed into the office.

"Yeah."

"I just came from outside," Lila said, "and we were watching on TV until it went off. Captain Boen says we've been attacked. But Captain, that doesn't make sense. What kind of attack? What could do this?"

The red secure phone on Mike's desk rang. It was the President's National Security Advisor. "Captain Boen, get over here immediately!" Goodson ordered. He sounded on the edge of hysteria. "How much do you know about what's happened?"

"Just what's on television and what's happening at the Pentagon. I just talked to Admiral Kittering."

"He called here. Scared the shit out of everyone. That's why we need you here. Now! The President is frothing. You have *any* idea of what's going on?"

"I think Admiral Kittering is correct. We underestimated Aziz. It appears that he's managed to smuggle enough biotech-weapon material into the country to mount a terrorist attack."

"Terrorists? It would have taken an army of them to do this. The whole city's paralyzed, and we're getting similar reports from New York and cities all up and down the coast."

"I'll see what I can find out before I leave."

"No! Don't take the time to do anything but get your ass over here. Run across the bridge on foot if you have to, and you may have to. I don't think the Metro, buses or anything else is moving, and there is no way to get a car through the mess down here."

"I'll be there ASAP."

"Sooner!" Goodson ordered and hung up.

"See if you can get me a car to the White House, Lila," Mike ordered.

Lila got to her feet, still breathing heavily. "All right, but I think we're going to have trouble. Nothing, but nothing, is moving outside."

"Give it a try anyway."

Lila hurried from the office.

"It's hard to believe Aziz could pull off something on this scale," Scott said, shaking his head in disbelief. "Or that he'd even dare."

"Seems like he did dare. We'd better see how much decontamination equipment Lesatec can come up with."

Mike dialed Julie's number. "Mike!" she said. "Do you know what's happening? It sounds like—"

"I know," he interrupted her. "That's why I'm calling. You'd better assemble all the decontamination kits you have."

"We don't have enough here to do any good—only about six portable units. You need the aircraft." Three B-1B bombers had been equipped, loaded and stationed with trained crews at Wright Field. The craft were poised to respond to a biotech-weapons attack anywhere in the world—except the U.S.

"The President controls the aircraft, and I'm on my way there now. We may need you at the White House, Julie. The President considers you his personal expert. He'll probably want to talk to you soon as everyone retrieves their sanity. I'll call."

There was no response. "Julie. Julie!"

"The phones are dead," Lila announced from the door, "and you're going to have to walk."

"Figured as much. You and the staff stick here, Scott. Your fiber-optic link to the Navy Yard computer should be okay, and the tempest seals on your workstation computers should keep out the bugs for a while. I'll have the White House use its clout to get your operation moved into one of the intelligence vaults downstairs. Their chemical-warfare protection should protect the equipment, and you can use their secure data links and communications.

"Run your *what-if* programs, and see what kind of damage predictions you can come up with. Try to figure out how to use the aircraft to give us the best shot at containing this stuff."

Mike walked out of the front door of Crystal Plaza Two onto Route One. Stalled cars and angry, frustrated people jammed the highway. Some drivers had their cars' hoods up and were tinkering with the engines. Others stood beside their vehicles with dazed looks. A mass of frozen traffic blocked the Fourteenth Street Bridge.

Mike jogged to the bridge. Frustrated drivers and passengers crowded the space between the stalled cars. Mike pushed his way through the tangle of people, who were in no mood to get out of anyone's way. They weren't afraid yet, just angry and frustrated.

Traffic was stacked solid in front of the Bureau of Engraving and as far up Fourteenth Street as Mike could see. It wasn't until he reached the broad grassy expanses of the Mall that he could run again.

Mike sprinted across the grass toward the Ellipse behind the White House. People were streaming out of the Main Commerce Building, adding to the gridlock at 15th Street and Constitution Avenue. Office operations had ground to a halt, and supervisors—hearing about the Metro and traffic problems—were allowing employees to leave early. People jammed the sidewalks and streets.

Mike ran across the Ellipse to Executive Avenue. By the time he reached the East Gate of the White House grounds he was breathing hard, and his uniform was damp with sweat.

There was a long delay while the guards verified Mike's identity and that the President himself wanted to see him. Still, they refused to pass him through until someone came to escort him. With all the turmoil they weren't about to take any chances.

Sam Moon himself hurried up to extract Mike from the guards. "What the hell took you so long!" the White House Chief of Staff groused as they hurried toward the White House.

"I had to walk all the way."

"Walk? What about the Metro?"

"Not operating. Nothing's moving."

"Damn! Seems like everything in the whole world has stopped."

When they walked into the Oval office, Jason Goodson, the National Security Advisor, was briefing the President. Mike was waved to a chair. The tension filling the room bordered on hysteria.

"That's what we know about the Washington area," Goodson said, concluding his report on the local situation. "Only bright spot is that the disruption hasn't spread south of the Beltway into Northern Virginia. Traffic is still moving there. Fort Belvoir hasn't been affected, and Dulles is still operating. Maryland is another story. As you know, the plane overflew Andrews. Shut it down, and it looks like the disruption is spreading from there. Routes Four and Five are blocked with stalled vehicles.

"We have enough reports to believe that this could be happening in every major metropolitan area between here and New York. We've got the most information on New York. The city is paralyzed. Manhattan and Long Island are cut off. The Navy terminal is no longer functioning, and they've got some looting and rioting."

"Can you explain any of this, Captain Boen?" the President barked. He was an angry man.

"There is no doubt as to what it is—the Libyan bio-tech weapon."

"How the hell did they get it into the country!"

"Probably the same way dope gets in," said the FBI Director as he entered the room. Cal Doddson was panting from his struggle through the crowded streets on foot.

"How could they smuggle in so much?"

"It wouldn't take much," Mike pointed out. "The microbes replicate themselves and cover large surfaces in a matter of milliseconds. Our simulations indicate that a few microliters dropped on the wing of an aircraft will spread through the whole structure in under a minute—get into everything: bearings, brakes, engines, electronics."

"Well, what the hell are we doing about this?" the President raged. "We protected Tel Aviv. How come we haven't protected Washington!"

"We weren't expecting this, and we still aren't certain what we're facing," Goodson explained, "and we need your permission to use the B-1Bs."

"Need my permission!" the President yelled. "The country's going down the drain, and you need my permission to save it? Lord save us from bureaucracy! People don't ask my permission to blab to the press or issue insane regulations. Why the hell do you need permission to save the country?"

"Sir, your instructions were explicit," Goodson protested shakily. "Use of those planes is a major policy decision that you explicitly reserved for yourself—just like the use of nuclear weapons."

"Well, why didn't you ask me, dammit!"

"We weren't sure we'd been attacked, or with what."

The President shook his head in disbelief. "You

can't be telling me that we've just had another Pearl Harbor!''

"I guess it could be put that way. We hadn't planned on a massive attack on the continental U.S.," Goodson responded.

The President stared at Goodson hard for a moment. Then his face fell and he slumped in his chair. "We underestimated Aziz and his bunch. We didn't believe our own warnings," he said bitterly. "We've been so busy hollering at other countries to do something about this big terrorist threat, that we forgot to protect ourselves, figured Aziz wouldn't dare attack the U.S. because he knew he'd get his balls blown off. Well, I guess he dared." The President's face hardened. "And I guess he's going to get his balls blown off. But first, we have to do something about this disaster we've allowed to happen." He stiffened. "Get those planes in the air immediately," he ordered. "And where the hell is the Chairman and SECDEF?"

"Their helicopters are disabled and the streets are jammed," Sam Moon answered. "I advised them to stay in the Tank where we can reach them. Our strategic communications links are hardened against BW/CW and nuclear effects. It seems to be working for this stuff, too."

"You're right. They'll be more useful where they are. Jason, you and Captain Boen get down to the Situation Room, contact JCS and tell them to get those planes in the air."

"It's going to be a while before we can do that," Mike informed him.

The President greeted his announcement with the explosion Mike expected: "What the hell do you mean it's going to be a while!"

"We need time for mission planning. We don't have plans for protecting U.S. cities, and we don't know where all of the attacks have occurred. We have only a limited amount of counteragent, and it's essential we optimize its usage.''

''How long?''

''Three hours, if my analysis people are still linked to the computers at the Navy Yard and NRL, and if those computers have survived. If not . . . I don't know.''

The President looked for a moment as if he would burst, then subsided. ''Do the best you can,'' he said in a resigned voice. ''But what does this mean in terms of damage? You told us once that the defensive organisms needed to be there almost immediately.''

''That's correct, sir. It's probably been four hours since the attack and another three will make seven. The damage will be massive.''

The look in the President's eyes chilled Mike. ''Sam, go on down to the Situation Room with Jason and the captain. I'll be down in a few minutes, and I want a video conference set up with the JCS Chairman and SECDEF when I get there. Tell them I want to talk both conventional and nuclear options for blasting Libya off the face of the earth.''

''You should think about leaving, Mr. President,'' Moon recommended. ''We have no idea what's going to happen. It may get dangerous here.''

''I'm not going anywhere. Hell, Aziz doesn't have a hydrogen bomb. He's managed to screw things up, not blow them up. We're not in that much danger.''

Mike wasn't so sure.

Chapter Twenty

The White House: Doomsday 2

Mike spent the night in the Situation Room, watching reports of expanding disruption pour in. The information was fragmentary—only hardened military communications systems still operated—but the messages painted a grim picture of an expanding holocaust. Industry and transportation were shut down. Disabled vehicles clogged streets and highways. Emergency medical care was unavailable, and hospital death tolls mounted as life-support equipment failed. Power had failed, and water supplies were spotty. Phones were dead, and radio and television stations were off the air. Firefighting equipment couldn't move, and large fires raged out of control in New York and other cities. The looting and rioting that had begun when the lights went off continued into the daylight hours. Food distribution had halted. Panicked people had emptied the grocery-store shelves, sometimes by force.

Mike searched through the reports for some effects of the neutralization effort. He found nothing. Anxiety squeezed his insides. He feared that the six jury-rigged systems were too little and too late to save the whole East Coast. The attack had occurred hours before the defensive operation had started. The attacking microbes would be everywhere and into everything. It could be days, even weeks before the defensive microbes caught up with them. Mike just hoped that they could confine the destructive microbes to areas already infected.

Mike had been deliberately vague in describing his neutralization strategy to the President. The President wanted to save the East Coast, but Mike had ordered that the operation be concentrated on containment. The President would not be happy when he found out. It appeared the strategy had been effective: No damage had been reported west of the Appalachians, south of Alexandria or north into New England. But damage continued to increase rapidly inside the infected areas. Mike worried that what looked like containment was actually temporary, a natural phenomenon or the results of their quarantine measures. He feared it would be only a matter of time until the devastation spread to the rest of the country.

"Put me through to Dr. Corbett," Mike ordered a communications specialist. Scott had moved into an intel vault in the bowels of Jefferson Plaza, where he had access to hardened communications lines and data links.

Scott sounded exhausted. Despite his frail condition, he had been working desperately around the clock for days. Mike feared he'd collapse at any moment. "Scott, you don't sound so good. You need to take a break."

"A break! Now? You got to be kidding. Don't worry, I won't die on you before this is over."

"Scott, shouldn't we be seeing some effects of our defensive operations?"

"Probably too soon. The planes have only been in the air for six hours."

"But we saw immediate results in Tel Aviv."

"We were there within an hour of the attack."

"What about Egypt? The decontamination of Alexandria didn't start until two weeks after the attack, but within a day traffic was moving again."

"Uncontaminated vehicles were moving *into* Alexandria. Nothing already there moved. The situations aren't comparable. Our cities are much more complex, and these microbes were dispersed over hundreds of miles. By now they've burrowed into everything. May take days, weeks, even longer before our defensive microbes catch up with them."

"Maybe so, but in Tel Aviv, anything still operating kept operating. That's not happening here."

"I still think it's too early to worry."

"I guess there's nothing we can do but wait."

By late afternoon, Mike's unease had turned into dread. The operating hospitals, power plants and other critical facilities they had tried to protect had gone down. Something had to be wrong: maybe the defensive microbes had been stored too long and died. Maybe the dispensers had screwed up. Maybe . . . Mike shuddered as his mind filled with possible disasters.

Jason Goodson, the President's National Security Advisor, walked into the room. "Does it look like we're getting things under control, Captain?"

"Too soon to tell, but there are no reports of damage south of Alexandria or over the mountains into Ohio or Pennsylvania."

"So we've contained it."

"Appears so."

"But what about New York, Philly and here? Have we reversed the damage?"

"Can't reverse damage, just stop it from increasing."

"Have we done that?"

"I hope so, but the reports have yet to show any impact of the bomber operation."

"Nothing at all?"

"Not yet. Scott says it's too soon, but—"

"But you think something's wrong."

"Just a gut feeling. Things don't seem to square with our Tel Aviv experience, or what went on in Egypt."

"What does Dr. Barns think?"

"Lost contact with her three hours ago. The northern Virginia phone circuits must be failing."

"We can fix that. I'll have the Quantico Marines take a secure satellite terminal to Lesatec and patch her through to us. Ida, get me the commanding officer at Quantico," Jason ordered a senior communications technician.

"Mike! Thank God!" Julie exclaimed, as soon as she recognized Mike's voice. "I've been going crazy trying to reach you, reach the Pentagon, the White House, somebody. Mike, they've used new strains of microbes." Mike's guts froze. "What you have on the planes won't touch it. We obtained samples from the car of one of our VPs. He had returned from Washington just before everything stopped. His car stalled in the parking lot."

Mike switched the phone onto the speaker system. "I have you on the squawk box, Julie. Mr. Goodson is here with me. Go ahead."

"I just wanted to check," she explained. Everybody in the room stopped what they were doing to listen to the phone conversation. "It's a thing with me, checking. I didn't expect we'd find anything different, but we did. The genetic codes are different, not much different, but enough different that our neutralizing organisms won't work. We tried the defensive microbes on the samples. Doesn't affect them at all.''

"Can you produce organisms to neutralize this new stuff?'' Mike asked.

"Yes, but do you know how long that will take?'' she answered dejectedly.

"How long?''

"Three days is the best we can hope for—that is, if our link to the GMU computer survives, and if I can convince the GMU computer lab people to keep working. It will take twenty-four hours to run the models and synthesize the first microbe material. Then we have to culture it and get it to the pharmaceutical companies. I don't know how long it will take them to produce enough agent to do any good. Mike, I hear the entire East Coast is affected and it's spreading. The whole country could be ruined before we can do anything!'' Her voice bordered on hysteria.

"Listen to me, Julie,'' Mike said firmly. "Don't go to pieces on us. We need you.''

There was a long silence. All eyes in the room focused on Mike. "Julie?''

"What should I do?'' she asked plaintively.

"Work as fast as you can.''

"We'll take care of the logistics, Dr. Barns,'' Goodson said. "You get us those cultures, and they'll be at the pharmaceutical companies within a few hours. We'll send someone to see the university people. They will keep working, even if we have to post Marine guards to keep them there. In fact, I will have Quantico send some Marines to your place and GMU. You need some security.''

"Julie, you'd better send a team with chemicals to GMU,'' Mike recommended. "You can't afford to have the computer shut down.''

"I'll get somebody over there right away, but the supercomputer's environmental controls should protect it."

"What about the computer link?" Goodson asked. "Will it survive?"

"It's fiber-optic. I think it will. Anyway, if worse comes to worst, I can work at GMU and bring the data back on tape."

"The Marines will maintain communications with us, Dr. Barns. If there is anything you need, call immediately and you'll get it," Goodson told her.

The staffers in the Situation Room were already on phones and radios making things happen. Only the best worked in the White House, and being best meant knowing what to do without being told.

"I'll be here, Julie, if you need to talk to me," Mike added.

"Thanks." Julie sounded embarrassed by her previous lapse of composure.

"Keep us posted," Goodson said.

"How bad do you think it will get in three days?" Goodson asked Mike after Julie went off the radio.

"Pretty bad. I think you had better get the National Guard out to control population movement. If we can reduce that, we can at least slow the spread. Lots of things are still functioning outside the Beltway. Population density—I should say machine density—is a lot less; that could mean it won't spread rapidly outside of urban areas. If we can limit travel, we may be able to keep it from spreading between urban areas for a while, which will give us time to neutralize the microbes before they spread clear across the country."

"Well, let's go see the President," Goodson said dispiritedly. "He will not be happy."

Springfield, Virginia: Doomsday 3

It had taken most of the night to set the computer program up. Julie closed her weary eyes and leaned back in her chair. The computer display screen in front of her glowed with confirmation that the GMU supercomputer had digested all of the program parameters and adjustments, and had begun the massive processing task. Julie wished she was more certain about what she'd done. She didn't fully understand the program. She was following a menu developed by Saba. Exhaustion dragged her into restless sleep.

She escaped one nightmare only to face another—not a dream this time. The screen was filled with gibberish. Stunned, Julie typed in commands for status reports. The machine refused to respond. She stabbed the reset button. The screen cleared, and she allowed herself to breathe a little. Maybe it was a terminal problem. The terminal was actually a microcomputer, employing one of the newest chips.

The machine went through a hot boot, displaying its configuration: memory availability, communication port assignments, and a series of self-test results. Nothing seemed amiss.

The screen cleared except for a blinking dash, prompting her for instructions. Julie hesitated. She was scared. This wasn't a terminal problem.

Julie typed commands reestablishing communications with the GMU supercomputer. The GMU machine asked for her password. She typed it in. It digested that and requested a personal identification number, one that changed with date in a manner only she knew. She typed it in and waited.

Gibberish filled the screen again.

She felt as though she'd been splashed with ice water.

Her insides writhing with fear, Julie shut the terminal off and left the office. She walked down the hall to Sally Smith's office. Sally sat with her head on her desk. It seemed incongruous that such a pretty woman snored so loudly. Julie touched her shoulder. "Sally. Sally!"

"What," Sally responded groggily, pushing herself up from her desk, rubbing her eyes.

"I need to use your terminal, Sally." Julie waited impatiently while Sally woke up enough to struggle out of her chair and give Julie access to the terminal on her desk. "Is something wrong, Julie?" she asked sleepily.

"Yes, I'm getting gibberish on my terminal. I hope it's the terminal." Julie lowered herself into Sally's chair and turned on the terminal. She waited, tight with anxiety, while the display brightened and the machine went through a cold boot, displaying screen after screen of data of no interest to her. After what seemed like hours, the machine's blinking cursor signaled it was ready for Julie's instructions.

Julie established communications with the super-computer again.

The results were the same.

Julie stared at the screen, her mind numb with horror. "What's wrong?" Sally asked.

"The program won't run. Blows up every time I start it. Doesn't make any sense. We haven't changed a thing. This just cannot be happening! Not now!" she moaned. Frustration poured through her and exploded into anger. "Damn computer just can't do this to us!" she raged. "I won't let it!"

Sally watched apprehensively as Julie pushed the chair back, got to her feet and started for the door. This wasn't the calm, controlled Julie she knew. "Is there anything I can do?" she asked as Julie walked out.

"No. Get some sleep. And don't let anyone leave." Most of the staff was sleeping, waiting for the super-computer data. They dozed on bench tops and couches and slumped in chairs.

Julie marched out the front door and approached two

white-helmeted Marine guards standing by a Hummer. "Take me to George Mason," she ordered, climbing into the vehicle. She snapped the seat belt across her, and looked up to find the two guards staring at her in astonishment. "I said I need to go to the university."

"Ma'am, we are assigned to guard the entrance. We can't leave our positions," a guard explained nervously. Julie realized she must look a little crazy.

"Listen, I don't care what you've been assigned to do. Give *me* the keys if you can't leave." Julie's rage and frustration overwhelmed her. The whole damn world and its machines seemed to be conspiring against her, and it was making her fighting mad.

A lieutenant approached. "Is there a problem, Dr. Barns?"

"Yes, there's a problem. I need to go to George Mason immediately."

"All right. Hunter, drive. Jackson, ride shotgun. I'll be right behind you." He waved at two other Marines, who jogged over to take Hunter and Jackson's places at the entrance.

Julie marched into the office of the computer center's night supervisor to find him working his way through a program printout to keep himself awake. "Abe, I need to get on one of your terminals, one wired directly into the big machine. I want to bypass all the communications stuff."

Two hours later, Julie's worst fears had been confirmed. The program had self-destructed. She copied the archive tapes and reloaded the program. The program self-destructed again. Saba had embedded a virus in the program.

Julie rose from the terminal numb with despair. She had to catch the edge of the desk to keep from falling. She was so tired! And so discouraged.

She stood still for a moment, while her body adjusted to standing and her mind stopped reeling. She finally got her mind and body working well enough to make her way toward the exit. Abe intercepted her, but Julie refused to answer his questions. "I'll explain later," she promised as she reached the door.

"Shall I keep the crew here?"

"Yes. No place they can go anyway."

"Some of them have families they'd like to check on."

"Keep them here, Abe," she snapped.

Julie made her way to the waiting Hummers. "Do you have a radio that can get through to the White House, Lieutenant?"

"In my vehicle." He opened the door for her, and got in beside her. She waited, trying not to feel anything, while he established contact with the White House Situation Room. He handed her the mike.

"I need to speak to Captain Boen," she said.

She waited impatiently for him to come on the line. "Julie, how—"

"The program blew up, Mike. Saba left a virus in it. My guess is that it was triggered when we tried to generate a new code. It ate the program."

"How much will it delay us?" Mike asked, shocked.

"I don't know," Julie replied despondently. "Maybe forever."

"What are you going to do?"

"I don't know what to do," she answered despairingly. She felt terrible. Sick. Scared. Discouraged. Everything bad a person could feel. Her eyes dampened.

"You'd better come to the White House, Julie—as soon as you can find a way here. They'll want a brief."

The thought of being near Mike helped. He'd gotten them out of awful jams before. Maybe he could get them out of this one. She wiped at her damp eyes. She didn't like the expression on the lieutenant's face: *poor emotional woman who should be home with the babies*. The thought pissed her off, motivated her to pull herself together. Anger had become an effective defense mechanism. She had been angry more times in the past few weeks than she had in all of the rest of her life put together. In her few quiet moments, she wondered what was happening to her. Was she changing, or was the real Julie Barns finally emerging?

"Where are you, Julie?" Mike asked.

"At GMU."

"Okay. Wait there. A helicopter will pick you up in about fifteen minutes. You have any decontaminating chemical left at Lesatec?"

"Yes."

"Have the pilot swing by Lesatec and give the helicopter a going-over, or it will never get off the ground again. Better bring a kit with you."

The White House: Doomsday 3

Mike and Goodson were waiting for Julie in a small conference room in the bowels of the Old Executive Office building. "That will be all," Goodson told the staff assistant who'd escorted Julie from the entrance. He departed, leaving the three of them alone.

Julie's face was grim, and she struggled to maintain her composure. Mike wanted to take her in his arms, but contented himself with a quick squeeze of her shoulders before he pulled out the chair at the head of the table for her. "Start from the beginning, Julie," he requested.

"I think we'd better brief the President," Goodson said when she finished. "Can you give any kind of time estimate for fixing the problem?"

"Not now," she said dispiritedly. "Not until I get some software experts to analyze the program. It will take days, maybe weeks for them to just get familiar with the program. And we can't trust the program documentation. Saba prepared that, too. I'm sorry." Her head dropped and shoulders slumped.

"You can only do what you can," Goodson said grimly.

The Oval Office: Doomsday 3

Aziz's call interrupted the crisis meeting. The President fought his anger before he picked up the phone, and finally calmed himself enough to speak coherently. He put the phone on speaker. "Colonel Aziz, do you realize that your country has committed national suicide?" the President grated.

"No, Mr. President. We have only retaliated for your uncalled-for attack. You had no reason to kill our innocent women and children."

"And you had no reason to attack Israel."

"Mr. President, we were only implementing U.N. resolutions and peace agreements—as you did in the Gulf. Besides, our weapons didn't kill anyone. Do you know what the death toll of innocent civilians was in Tripoli alone?"

"We have the means to make you pay for this attack on our country, Colonel Aziz. We can wipe your country from the face of the earth, and we intend to do just that."

"But we can halt the devastation in your country. We won't be able to help you if you destroy us."

"The United States will not be blackmailed. *I* will not be blackmailed."

"I have not called to blackmail you, Mr. President," Aziz responded smoothly. "I have called to offer you the hand of peace, to offer aid in stopping the destruction your attack on us has brought to your innocent citizens."

The President seethed, but he resisted the urge to slam the phone down.

"We can neutralize the organisms, and are quite willing to do that for a few small concessions . . . despite what you've done to us, despite your murder of our innocent citizens, despite the destruction of our industry. My Coalition brothers demand vengeance, but I have said no. We want peace. So I am asking you for peace. We will always hate each other, but that is no reason to destroy one another. We ask only that you stay out of our affairs, and Israel is our affair, not yours."

"Israel *is* our affair! We will not abandon a faithful ally. We and the rest of the world owe Israel a debt for protecting our vital interests from tyrants like you!"

"Hear me out, Mr. President," Aziz requested calmly.

"Go on," the President said tensely.

"We will send you genetic codes for organisms that will neutralize the agents destroying your country. Of course, you can develop the codes yourselves, but that will take a long time. Can you wait that long? I don't think so.

"Let us help you. In return we only want what you can easily give. Renounce Israel. Cease military aid to them, and demand that they withdraw from the occupied territories. And we want you to agree to a U.N. peace conference to decide whether Israel should continue to exist.

"We want all of your military forces out of the Mediterranean area. That includes Italy, Spain, Greece and Turkey. You must also agree to cease providing these countries military aid."

It was moments before the President could calm himself enough to answer. "That's preposterous! You know we would never agree to such terms," he said in a tightly controlled voice. "Colonel, the American people will demand that you pay for this attack, and you will. Just as Iraq did.''

"Mr. President, positions are reversed this time. It is *your* country that is facing devastation.''

"Colonel Aziz, this conversation is ended,'' the President informed Aziz coldly. He hung up the phone.

The President didn't explode as they expected. He knew the situation demanded tight control of his emotions. But he didn't trust himself to speak immediately. He had just been subjected to the most audacious blackmail scheme in American history. Colonel Aziz believed he could hold the entire United States for ransom. Mind-boggling. Unreal. But unfortunately, not that unreal. The man could reasonably expect concessions from the U.S. to prevent countrywide devastation. But he didn't understand the depth of American resolve, or its abhorrence of appeasement for any reason.

The President put Aziz's insane demands out of his mind and focused his attention on Julie. "What's the situation, Dr. Barns?'' he asked.

The President sat stony-faced and silent while Julie briefed him. "We have to repeat much of the software development,'' she finished.

"How long did it take the first time?''

"A year for the part we're working on.''

"A year!'' the President exploded.

"It won't take that long this time,'' Julie explained. "We know exactly what to do, and we already have program code and documentation. Still, it could take several months. I won't know until we get some software-systems experts to go over the documentation and program code.''

"Months! It's only been seventy-two hours, and the Eastern Seaboard has already been devastated!'' the President pointed out. "What will it be like in two weeks? A month? Two months? Isn't there anything you can do?''

"Only if we had the genetic codes for the defensive microbes, or a copy of the uncorrupted program. Those only exist in Libya. If by some miracle we could get into their lab and copy the codes and software, we could produce neutralizing organisms in a few days."

"That miracle might be possible," said Anton Carlson, the CIA Director.

"What do you mean?" the President asked suspiciously. He knew he was about to be treated to one of Carlson's wild, high-risk schemes. Ever since he'd gotten Carlson confirmed as Director, the agency had been under attack for maverick operations.

"We've found the biotech-weapons facility. We're sure that the delivery aircraft, the weapons and laboratory are all there. The aircraft are not dispersed as we feared."

"Not dispersed?" the CJCS asked skeptically. "That doesn't make military sense."

"But it makes technical sense," Julie said excitedly. "To do the genetic engineering, culture the microbes and incorporate them into a system requires a team of highly trained people located together with their equipment. They need precise control of the environment, a supercomputer, sophisticated laboratory instruments—a lot of stuff you can't find just anywhere. The Libyans haven't had the time to develop and operate more than one facility. They don't have enough people or equipment."

"That wouldn't stop them from storing the completed weapons at dispersed sites," General Thompson argued.

"That's not practical," Julie countered. "The microbes can be stored only for a week or two at most, and keeping them viable in the Libyan desert would require elaborate equipment to control their environment. The Libyans have not had enough time to equip multiple sites."

"How did you find it, Anton?" the President asked.

"By hard work and analysis, mostly hard work. Hundreds of people worked on this—the most we've ever had work on a single project. We also had a lot of help from the French and Germans, whose nationals have worked on high-tech projects for the Libyans.

"Our analysts collected records of Libyan aircraft flights tracked over the last ten years and created a computer database of Libyan air-traffic patterns. We've been trying to verify the existence of Libyan chemical-and-biological-warfare-weapons factories, so there's a lot of surveillance data. I won't go into detail, but our analysts found a number of flight corridors that seemed to go to nowhere. We concluded that the *nowheres* had to be concealed air facilities. Flights left one site just before the attacks on Egypt and Israel. Surveillance photos show no airfield at the site. Just rocky desert. Large boulders block the only strip of land long and smooth enough to land a jet aircraft on. However, we think the rocks have been put there to conceal the airstrip's existence, and a pilot who knows their precise arrangement can probably squeeze between them.

"While this was going on, our French and German counterparts were tracking down engineers, architects and construction workers who have worked on Libyan high-tech projects. They located a German civil-engineering firm that had designed a Libyan facility capable of supporting a supercomputer installation and sophisticated laboratories. The design work was done in Germany, but the Libyans built it themselves at a secret location. The company has provided plans and a model with details like underground railways, elevators and secret entrances.

"We also reopened the Japanese-Libyan supercomputer investigation. The Libyans purchased enough pieces to assemble a complete machine. No one noticed, because the equipment appeared to be just odds and ends of hardware. The Libyans also hired Japanese engineers who had worked on the computer development. The engineers went to Libya and were never heard from again—probably killed to prevent them from divulging the supercomputer's existence. The Libyans probably feared we wouldn't tolerate their possession of a machine that could be used to design nuclear weapons.

"We also compiled information on components, instruments, lab equipment, building materials and other things that the Libyans have imported that could be used to construct the German-designed facility and support a supercomputer-installation and genetic-engineering lab.

"We've obtained information on operations, work routines and security from Libyan defectors who have worked at similar installations. All have secret entrances that are opened with key cards. The cards work like bank ATM cards—they require personal identification numbers. We know how to make passkey cards for the type the Libyans use. Those entrances provide a covert way in."

"Why wasn't I informed sooner?" the President asked angrily.

"We wanted to be sure. Now we don't have time to be sure."

"Do you believe we can get somebody in there to obtain what we need?" the President asked incredulously.

"It's a long shot, but the only shot we have."

"Have you put together a team?" Goodson asked.

"No. We need to send someone who is intimately familiar with the software and the technology." His eyes focused on Julie.

"When can you get me in there?" Julie asked.

"Julie, no!" Mike protested. He admired her bravery, but it was out of the question. "I'll do it," Mike told Carlson. "I've flown a similar mission and know a little something about the technology."

"A little something is not enough," Julie objected. "You don't know the software, the computers or the genetic engineering. I'm the only one with the familiarity and expertise Mr. Carlson needs."

"She's right, Captain," Carlson agreed. "The whole country is at stake. We have to use whoever gives us the best chance of pulling this off. There is no question that Dr. Barns is that person."

"We'll do it," the President declared. "With Dr. Barns. Anton, how do you propose getting Dr. Barns in there and back out with the information?"

"We think we can slip a single aircraft in under cover of a Navy air strike."

"Why a single aircraft? Why not a Special Forces team?" the Vice President asked.

"We can't afford to alert the Libyans. If the installation is attacked, they'll destroy the data. All it takes is the push of a button."

"This is pure fantasy," Goodson protested. "You're sending this woman to her death based on unsubstantiated assumptions. She and whoever goes with her are going to have to figure out how to penetrate a heavily guarded base, find a computer buried somewhere under the desert, hook up to it with equipment you don't know is compatible and get free long enough to transmit data back. That's insane."

"You have any other suggestions?" Carlson countered. "Even if this has only one chance in a million of succeeding, it's better than doing nothing."

Goodson didn't answer, just glared at Carlson.

"I'm going with her," Mike announced.

"Indeed you are," Carlson agreed. "We think a long-range, supersonic, carrier-based aircraft has the best chance. That pretty much means an F-14. You fly F-14s and you've flown a similar mission."

"Do you really think an F-14 can land on that strip without being detected?" the Vice President asked skeptically.

"No. They'll have to eject far enough away to avoid detection and approach on foot."

"How the hell are they going to get the data out?" Goodson asked, more certain than ever that Carlson was mad.

"Satellite link. We've developed a miniaturized MILSTAR terminal. It's smaller than anything DoD has, because it only has to transmit one burst of data. Our engineers used the Japanese design data to find a compatible miniature digital tape recorder. We have everything needed to copy and transmit the data."

"How do you plan to extract Captain Boen and Dr. Barns?" Moon asked.

Carlson looked uncomfortable. "We haven't worked that out yet. We'll . . . have to see what we can do when the time comes."

"Dammit, Anton," Goodson stormed, "you intend to send these people on a suicide mission!"

Mike froze. Shock filled Julie's face.

"Anton, that isn't true, is it?" the President asked.

Carlson choose his words carefully. "Mr. President, we'll do everything we can, but I don't want to minimize the risk. There is a good chance they won't come back."

The President stared at Carlson with hard eyes, and then at Julie. "Dr. Barns, you *do* understand what Anton is saying? This is, for all practical purposes, a suicide mission," he said bluntly.

Julie hesitated. A choking feeling rose in her throat. "I understand," she heard herself say. She understood, but didn't yet comprehend. These were only words; reality was still out there somewhere, poised to fill her with fear.

"And?" The President had noticed a tremor in her voice.

"We shouldn't waste time." She wanted to do it before panic caught up to her.

"Captain Boen?"

"We'd better get started," he said, though he doubted he'd be able to fly the woman he loved to her death.

"Jake, plan a coordinated cruise-missile and aircraft strike on that installation," the President ordered the CJCS, his face bleak. "We can't risk the Libyans escaping with the capability to start up again somewhere else. How long will their mission take, Anton?"

"Roughly eighteen hours plus flight time."

"Give them twenty-four, then launch the strike. Dr. Barns, Captain Boen, this strike will be launched regardless of whether or not you transmit. You understand what that means in terms of your survival?"

"Yes," Julie answered, voice wavering. Reality had begun to sink in and push fear to the surface.

"I understand," Mike said, feeling cold and clammy. He understood, all right. It was a death sentence.

"We will send a Special Forces team in after the strike," General Thompson said. "It will look for you."

His words didn't comfort Mike.

Chapter Twenty-one

Tomcat, Libyan Desert

In twenty minutes Mike and Julie would eject from the Tomcat. The Tomcat's modified autopilot would guide it another 200 miles before the explosives laced throughout the airframe turned the craft into unidentifiable debris.

Mike worried about Julie. Ejection was risky for even well-trained, experienced pilots, and all Julie had to go on was a few hurried instructions. Serious injuries during ejection were common, but if she suffered so much as a turned ankle, they would be in serious trouble. They had to move swiftly once they were on the ground, and Julie had to carry her share of the equipment.

"Twenty minutes, Julie," he informed her. She didn't respond. "Julie?"

"I heard you," she answered in a scared voice.

"Do you remember everything?"

"No."

"Julie—"

"I remember how to sit straight and stuff. I remember how to pray. I'm really scared, Mike. I don't think I can do this."

"You don't have to do anything. I'll do it. I'll tell you when."

Mike had pored over the recon photos with CIA spooks to choose their landing area. Its position had been programmed into a GPS navigator. Mike would drop the pod and punch them out when navigator's destination light came on. The pod's parachute would open only a hundred feet off the ground, not giving the wind a chance to drift it far from the planned impact point. The pod contained the MILSTAR transmitter, digital recorder, weapons and other equipment.

"Three minutes," Mike warned. "I'll start counting at ten seconds."

When Mike began his count, Julie's mind went blank. She couldn't remember anything she was supposed to do. When he reached three, she held her breath.

Julie couldn't believe the jolt. Couldn't believe the noise. Couldn't believe she would live through it. She had no idea of what was happening, but it was more violent than anything she had ever experienced . . . or imagined.

Julie found herself swinging under a parachute, which spiraled toward the ground like an out-of-control aircraft. She reached over her head and got her hands on dangling handles. She tried to remember what she was supposed to do with them. She couldn't, but she pulled anyway. Her descent seemed to slow. She remembered to put her feet together and bend her knees.

Julie crashed into the ground and tumbled onto her face. The parachute dragged her across the desert. She tried to get up, but kept being pulled off her feet. She couldn't remember how to release the harness.

Mike caught Julie, stopped her painful trip across the rock-strewn sand and released her harness. She collapsed on the sand, her chest heaving from exertion and fright.

Mike corralled Julie's chute, dumped out the air and made sure the light wind wouldn't blow it away. Then he ran back to her. She still lay facedown, her breath coming in heaves. He knelt beside her and put a hand on her back. "Julie." No answer. "Julie—"

"Don't you dare ask me if I'm all right!" she gasped.

Mike let out a breath of relief. At least she wasn't hurt seriously, or in too much pain to be pissed. "Nothing broken or sprained?"

She rolled over and sat up. "No, but I feel like I ought to be dead." Mike pulled her to him. He held her against him until her breathing slowed and trembling subsided.

Mike gave her a last squeeze, released her and got to his feet, pulling her after him. "We have to get the parachutes folded and out of sight. Then we have to locate the pod. Can you fold yours?"

"I can manage."

"Might as well get out of these g-suits and leave them with the parachutes." The g-suits had been worn over Marine combat fatigues instead of flight suits.

They folded the chutes, scraped sand over them with their hands and put rocks on top to hold them in place.

Mike didn't need the covert beacon to find the pod. It had landed almost on top of them. "Julie, we better get the pod chute out of sight, too." They concealed the parachute with sand as they had the others.

Mike felt naked. It was daylight and they were in plain view of any aircraft passing overhead. He worried that someone had observed their approach, although the spooks had assured them the area was deserted.

Mike worked the access hatch off the pod, and extracted the backpacks containing the digital equipment and MILSTAR transmitter. He also took out two folding shovels. They used the shovels to dig out a shallow depression for the pod. It was hot, exhausting work. The sand seemed to pour back into the hole almost as fast as they shoveled it out. Mike halted their efforts after a few minutes. It was taking too long, and they couldn't afford to exhaust themselves digging a hole. "That's the best we can do," he said, calling a halt to the digging. They pushed the pod into the shallow depression they'd scraped out. Mike stood and stared at it. He threw a few shovels of sand on it. The sand immediately slid off. "No use trying to cover the damn thing up," Mike said with disgust, "but maybe we can break up its regular shape. With the camouflage paint, it'll be damn hard to spot."

They went to work again, piling irregular mounds of sand and rock against the pod. Mike still wasn't satisfied. The first brisk wind would blow away the sand, but it would have to do. He hoped their mission would be concluded by the time anyone discovered the pod.

Mike pulled a handheld GPS navigator from his pack and turned it on. He waited until the circuitry inside deciphered the signals from the satellites passing overhead. It emitted a small beep and the LCD display flashed their position. They were where they were supposed to be. Their luck made Mike nervous. He'd found good luck often just meant that bad luck was being stored up to happen all at once.

They were five miles south of the hidden runway and 200 yards to the east of a dry streambed along which they would walk. It snaked its way past the airstrip, cut deep into sandy terrain millions of years ago by an ancient river. Using it for cover, they would only be visible from an aircraft flying directly overhead.

*   *   *

Daylight had faded to a hazy red glow when Mike finally stopped. The GPS navigator said they were a half mile from the end of the airstrip. "Julie, I think this is as far as we'd better go before dark." Julie sank gratefully onto the sand. She didn't move to take off her pack. She just sat there, resting her back against it. Her hands lay limply beside her on the sand. She was sweating profusely and breathing hard. She was in good shape, but the pack was heavy, and the soft sand had made for hard going.

Mike released his pack and lowered it to the ground. He took Julie's pack off for her. She stretched out on her back, her eyes closed. "We have about an hour before we try to get through the intrusion-alarm system," Mike informed her. He stretched out beside her and went over in his mind the procedure for getting through the intrusion-alarm system. CIA experts had identified a number of such systems purchased by the Libyans. They had concluded that the site was protected by a sophisticated German infrared system. It consisted of a network of passive infrared sensors that detected the presence of any object whose temperature differed from the terrain.

The spooks had provided Mike with an IR imager. It was similar to a video camera, but it detected long-wavelength infrared light—light with wavelengths longer than twelve micrometers. Long-wavelength IR radiation is emitted day and night by all objects. The amount of radiation emitted depends on the object's temperature and material. The imager could detect temperature differences between objects of less than a thousandth of a degree centigrade. The desert cooled faster than the alarm-system sensors, and just after sunset, the sensors would stand out like beacons when viewed through the imager.

Once he'd located the sensors, Mike would use a smart laser jammer to flood the sensors' fields of view with IR radiation. The jammer would raise the terrain's apparent temperature to that of the human body. Mike and Julie would look like terrain to the sensors and be invisible to the intrusion-alarm system.

When night chased twilight over the horizon, Mike and Julie struggled up the side of the dry riverbed. It was steep, and the loose sand and heavy packs made climbing difficult. Mike stopped just before they reached the top. "Wait here until I scope out the alarm system," he instructed. They slipped off their packs again, and Mike dug out the imager. It was the size of a standard video camera, but much heavier. The sensitive focal-plane-array detectors had to be cooled to minus 146 degrees centigrade. They were cooled by mounting them in a device called a cryostat, which was filled with liquid nitrogen. It had been filled before they left the carrier deck, and would cool the detectors for eight hours before its liquid nitrogen evaporated.

Mike switched the imager on and brought the eyepiece to his eye. After three minutes, the screen flashed a ready signal. There was a bloom of light—then he was staring at a ghostly landscape. The alarm sensors stood out like bright lights. When Mike tried to scan the imager across the landscape, the image dissolved into a white-streaked blur. "You need time to integrate—build up—the signals," the engineers had explained. "It's like taking pictures with slow photographic film: Both you and the object have to be stationary."

Mike surveyed the field of sensors in chunks. The display had crosshairs, which he moved to each of the sensors and pressed a button to record its position. The imager's microprocessor digested the position data and flashed bearing and range for optimum placement of the deception jammer. Mike entered the numbers into the GPS navigator before wiggling his way back down the bank to Julie.

When they reached the mound disguising the elevator that took aircraft to the underground hanger, Mike extracted night-vision goggles and an IR flashlight from his pack. He put on the goggles, which responded to the mid-IR light of the flashlight. The light was invisible to the naked eye and its wavelength was different from known IR surveillance systems. It would not be detected by other night-vision systems. The experts had assured Mike that the IR radiation would also reveal the hidden entrance.

As they hunted their way around the structure, Mike discovered why it appeared to be just another sand dune. The surface was real sand, and its grains were held together and to the underlying structure by an adhesive that did not affect surface appearance. The fake sand dune was just high enough to accommodate the elevator doors.

As they made their way around the false dune, Mike carefully scanned the surface with the IR flashlight. They completed two circuits of the fake dune without finding anything remotely resembling an entrance. Julie's fatigue worried Mike. She stumbled a lot, and breathed hard.

Mike started a third circuit, and had walked only a few yards before he realized that Julie wasn't following. He turned to find her on her knees in the sand. Alarmed, he put the IR light on her. The IR illumination made her face look ghastly, but the fatigue ravaging it was not an illusion. Mike hurried back to her.

Mike got her pack off and gently helped her lay back on the sand. She lay still, eyes closed, chest heaving. A sinking feeling dragged at Mike. Once they were inside, the going would be easier, but according to their drawings, they still had to hike five miles through tunnels to reach the lab. Then they would have to hunt their way through a maze of passageways to find the supercomputer. If she was already exhausted, she'd never make it. Mike settled to the sand beside her. She had done a lot of running, and he hoped she could get her second wind.

While Mike waited for Julie to recover, he studied the exterior plan. He fought a sinking feeling: What if the construction didn't match the plans he carried? They still had no evidence that this really was the bio-tech weapons facility, let alone a structure matching the German plans. Maybe it didn't *have* a hidden entrance.

Mike put away the IR light and goggles. He removed the imager from its case, switched it on and directed it at the dune. He hoped its greater sensitivity and resolution would detect more detail. It did. The mass of imperfections revealed startled him. If there was an entrance, this thing would find it.

"You all right?" Mike asked after fifteen minutes.

"Yes." Julie slowly got to her feet. Her breathing had returned to normal. She'd recovered quickly, Mike noted with relief.

"Rest here while I search for the entrance," Mike said.

"I'm *not* staying here by myself while you wander around the desert," she replied stubbornly. She pulled on her pack and started off.

"Julie! Wait!" She stopped. "I'm going to use the imager. We have to stop each time we want an image— about every fifty yards."

"That will take forever!" she objected.

"Only thing we can do. The light's not working."

Mike's discouragement grew as they tediously worked their way around the false dune. The display began to blur, and Mike knew the cryostat, batteries or both would be exhausted before they completed their circuit.

An irregular patch bloomed on the display. But before Mike could examine it, the display blinked off. That was all for the imager. Frustration choked him. They might have failed before even getting started. Dammit! Mike raged to himself. They *had* to get into this damn place somehow. He wasn't going let them die out here for nothing. He'd blast in through the hangar entrance if he had to.

Mike put the night goggles back on and shined the IR flashlight on the dune. He made his way to where he thought he'd detected the patch.

"Is this it?" Julie asked hopefully.

"Don't know. Maybe." Mike moved the IR light slowly across the surface and found nothing. Angry frustration flooded him. He yanked off the goggles and dug a penlight out of his pocket. "I'm going to chance using a regular flashlight. This IR thing doesn't have enough resolution to see small stuff. Stand beside me and block as much of the light as you can."

Mike found a faint line, barely visible under the dust. It appeared to be an irregular crack, but it formed a closed figure. Mike restrained his belief: too lucky. He found a small adjacent patch outlined by a wider crack, and pressed it. It sank into the dune and disappeared, revealing a card slot and number pad. The sudden success stunned Mike.

"You found it!" Julie exulted.

"Looks like it. Lets see if our pass card works." A ribbon cable attached the card to a small box. The box contained a small special-purpose computer, designed to produce number combinations at a tremendous rate. Hopefully one of those numbers would match a valid PIN. Mike inserted the card and switched on the computer. Thirty seconds later motors whirred, and the irregular section of surface slid out of sight, leaving a dark, gaping hole. The IR flashlight revealed a small elevator.

The elevator was a tight squeeze for the two of them and their gear. Mike slipped a Micro-Uzi from a holster in his pants leg. He pulled another from Julie's holster and put it in her hands. Both had silencers.

Julie stared at the weapon with frightened eyes. "Mike, I couldn't kill anybody."

"Just hold it. I may need to grab it if I empty my magazine." Mike made sure that the doorway was clear, and then pushed the down button. The door closed. The elevator dropped swiftly, then came to a smooth stop. Mike's finger tightened on the Uzi's trigger as the door slid open. Pitch blackness greeted them. Mike switched on the IR flashlight. It revealed a windowless passageway with a sliding door at the far end. Mike searched the wall beside the elevator, found a switch and turned on the lights. The row of television monitors along one wall surprised him. All were off. "Looks okay," Mike said. "Let's get the stuff out."

After they'd removed their equipment, Mike let the elevator door slide shut. "Which way?" Julie asked.

"Through the door at the end of the corridor. According to our plans, it should open into a rail tunnel, about a hundred meters from the hangar."

Julie lifted her pack. "Hold up a minute," Mike said, stopping her. "I want to take a look at these monitors." He perched on a high stool in front of the dark screens. He found a bank of switches labeled in both Arabic and French. He could understand very little of it, but he did understand "on" in French. He flipped switches, and the monitors came to life.

The cameras were strategically placed to provide a view of the entire hangar interior and the tracks approaching its loading dock. Six aircraft were parked in the hangar: two Foxbats, two Fulcrum fighter/attack aircraft, and two SU-24 Fencer ground-attack aircraft.

Mike noted that one of the Foxbats was a MiG-25U Foxbat-C, a combat-capable trainer with two seats. It could take both of them out, he thought, but he immediately gave up the idea. They would have to somehow find their way back and get the plane up the elevator, and he would have to figure out how to fly the damn thing. Not a promising escape route; but their future wasn't promising either, Mike thought sourly.

"Mike, how are we going to get out of here with all those people out there, and what if a train comes?"

He didn't have a good answer. He studied the track monitor. The rails curved sharply, and he could see no evidence of an entrance into the tunnel. He concluded their exit was beyond the curve. "I think we've around the bend in the tracks. Would make sense. If Aziz or somebody like him wanted to arrive unannounced, they wouldn't want to pop out of the wall in plain sight."

"Probably so, but the tunnel is so narrow if something comes down it, there's nowhere to hide," Julie pointed out. "And the plans indicate we have as much as five miles to go. Over an hour of walking. Something's bound to come by in that time."

"I don't think so. According to Libyans who've worked in places like this, everything should be shut down by now. Shouldn't be any more tunnel traffic until morning."

Motion drew Mike's attention. The guards were gathering on a loading dock at the end of the rails. A rail cart emerged from the tunnel and halted at the dock. It carried two men in Libyan Army uniforms.

"Mike, I hope the rest of our information is better than this," Julie said ruefully.

After enthusiastic greetings, the new arrivals handed the guards baskets and bottles from the cart's cargo bed.

"Julie, I think we have a ride! Save us a helluva lot of time and save us from lugging these packs." They needed all the time they could get, and if they could commandeer the cart, he wouldn't have to worry about Julie collapsing from exhaustion before they reached the computer center.

"You don't mean take the cart!" she exclaimed in disbelief. "Those people have guns."

"So do we. Come on, let's get our stuff together."

"Mike, we just can't—"

"We can and we're going to. Now hurry."

The night goggles and IR flashlight went back in the pack. Mike pulled a pin from the side of the IR imager and set it against a wall. Wisps of vapor curled from its case as hydrofluoric acid dissolved its insides. A timer had by now done the same to the IR deception jammer still outside. No intelligence agency could exploit what was left.

Julie followed Mike to the tunnel door; he pushed a button, and the door slid open. He'd been over it with her, but he wanted to make sure. "You know what to do?"

"Yes, and I don't like it a bit. I'm supposed to stand out there in front of a moving train and wave."

"With one hand. Keep the gun behind you. Is the safety off?"

"Yes, but I don't know how to use it, even if I could kill somebody with it, which I can't."

"All you have to do is point and pull the trigger, but you won't have to." He prayed he was right. "They'll freeze as soon as they see the gun, and I'll come out behind them. With you in front of them and me yelling at them from behind, they won't do anything but put up their hands. Julie, maybe you can't kill anyone, but you *have* to convince them you can and will, or I might have to kill them . . . or they might kill us."

She stared at him bitterly for a moment, then jumped from the door to the rail bed without speaking. She walked twenty yards further into the tunnel, before stopping and turning to stand rigidly facing the direction from which the cart would come.

Mike closed the door and hurried back to the monitors. He watched as the two men took seats at what was now the front of the rail cart. He rushed back to the corridor door. He pressed his ear against it, and suddenly realized he didn't know whether he could hear the cart through the door. Anxiety gripped him.

Mike waited for some sound. Nothing. It had been too long. He had to chance it. He pushed the open button. The rear of the cart was in front of him! They'd stopped short.

The men sat frozen, staring down the track. One caught the door's movement out of the corner of his eye. He jerked to his feet and brought up his Stechkin machine pistol. There was a rip of coughs, and he was slammed back over the seat to sprawl across the cart's flat bed.

Mike brought up the Uzi, but the other man slumped and fell part way out of the cart.

Mike stared at the dead men, frozen in shock for a moment, then leaped into the tunnel. Julie stood like a statue. Her finger still squeezed the trigger. But the gun was silent. She'd emptied the magazine.

"Julie! Quick! We've got to get away from here!"

"I didn't mean to," Julie said numbly, her eyes filled with horror.

"You did what you had to. Now, let's get moving."

"He . . . he jumped. He shouldn't have moved like that," she moaned.

"Julie—"

"It was an accident," she choked out, ignoring him. "He surprised me, and I pulled the trigger. It started shooting and wouldn't stop," she sobbed. "Mike, why didn't you come! Why did you take so long? Why did he move like that?" She looked at the gun in her hands and threw it down in horror.

Mike scooped up the little Uzi, took her hand and pulled her toward the cart. She stumbled and almost fell, but regained her balance and followed him like a robot. He pushed her into the passenger seat. Her eyes were vacant, and she trembled violently. Mike knew how it felt to kill for the first time, and her first time had been up close and personal, without any preparation or training. It went against everything she believed in and had worked a lifetime for. She was dedicated to saving people, not killing them. Mike could feel her pain as if it were his own.

By the time Mike got the packs from the corridor, he thought he could hear excited voices from the hangar. He wrestled the two bodies onto the cart's cargo platform. Then he shot out lights along the corridor. He hoped no one heard the cough of the silenced Uzi, and hoped the darkness would cover the blood. Mike got onto the cart and cranked on full power. The electric motor accelerated the cart down the tunnel.

When the rail line split, Mike braked to a halt. He dug a map from his pack and studied it. He knew he should take the right branch, but he wanted to be sure. They had less than a mile to go. Mike left the cart and cranked the manual track switch toward their destination.

Mike studied Julie as he returned to the cart. She sat rigid and silent, staring at nothing. She hadn't moved or spoken since he'd pushed her onto the cart. He knew her blank features hid a tortured mind. He wanted to take her in his arms and soothe her agony, but there was no time. He had to get her back on her mental tracks without derailing himself. Their lives and the mission depended on it.

It had been the same with some of the young strike pilots he'd commanded. A few had gone into shock when they'd first realized how many people they'd killed and how many of those were noncombatant women and children. He'd had to save them from themselves, make them get back in their aircraft and do it again, instead of taking off their wings.

"Julie, you have to help me," Mike said firmly. He put a hand on her shoulder and squeezed. She looked at his hand with a frown. Then she looked at him. She didn't seem to recognize him.

"You have to help me," he tried again. She stared at him, but said nothing, just trembled. "I can't do it without you," Mike persisted. "We can't give up now and just let them kill us. The country is depending on us. Julie?"

"What do you want me to do?" she asked mechanically.

"There are guards up ahead. We have to get near enough to prevent them from firing their weapons. You have to put on one of these guards' uniforms and get close to them." Her face filled with horror. "Julie, both uniforms are too small for me."

She shook her head violently.

"Julie, it's the only way we can get close enough to avoid a shooting."

Julie's chin dropped to her chest. Her body went limp. "We're going to have to kill them, too, aren't we?" she murmured.

"Not if we can get close enough to surprise them."

Her head snapped up. "That's what we were supposed to do back there," she cried angrily. "Don't lie to me!"

Mike felt he was losing control. He couldn't predict her emotions or her reactions or what she'd do or not do. "If you get close enough—"

"I should kill them," she said suddenly.

"Not if they put their weapons down."

"They won't," she said with conviction. "Do I need to take off my stuff?" It looked like she was going to be sick, but Mike was relieved. She was back with him again, and she wasn't quitting. There was steel under that soft exterior.

"No, the uniform will fit over your clothes." Mike turned to survey the corpses.

"Mike, you know, I actually killed those men a long time ago . . . back in the U.S." Mike didn't like what he heard in her voice. "I killed them in the lab when I invented those damn microbes. None of this would have happened; we wouldn't be here, and they wouldn't be dead, if I hadn't been trying to save the world from trash. Mike, if you ever see your daughter again, tell her not to go around trying to save the damn world! People who do that just screw it up more." She teetered on the edge of hysteria again.

"You're not to blame for this, Julie. Even if you are, it doesn't matter anymore. What matters is that we stop this before it goes any further, and I can't do it alone," he said harshly. He didn't like lashing out like that at her, but both of them needed discipline if they were to survive.

She regarded him with hostile eyes. "I'll do whatever has to be done. What choice is there? Kill a few people or let thousands die," she said bitterly.

Reassured, Mike turned to the rail cart. She was hating herself—he wondered if she was hating him, too—but she had regained her composure. She could function, and she was still committed.

Mike pushed the bodies apart and studied them. There were only two holes in one uniform coat, and it wasn't very bloody. Mike guessed the Libyan had done all his bleeding internally. Mike was sure of it when he rolled the man on his back and saw the mess soaking his pants. The movement stirred a terrible stench, and something gurgled deep inside the corpse. Its open eyes were accusing.

The other man's pants were not in much better

shape. The coat would have to do. The Libyans' pants were almost the same desert camouflage color as his and Julie's. The difference wouldn't be noticed until she was close. Mike wrestled the coat from the body and climbed from the cart.

Julie stood staring down the tunnel, as rigid as stone. "Put this on," Mike said gently. "It's too big, but I don't think they'll notice until they get close to you." How close would they have to get to notice the blood-rimmed bullet holes? Mike asked himself.

She turned and stared at the coat. Her face filled with revulsion.

"Julie—"

"All right," she whispered hoarsely. He helped her into the coat. She looked as though she was going to be sick when he buttoned the coat for her.

"Julie, there's a slight bend just before the track ends at the door to the lab. It will provide cover until we get about fifty yards from the door. There are garage doors in back of a loading dock. There are supposed to be only two guards at this time of night, but I wouldn't count on it.

"I'll stop just out of sight around the bend. You stagger toward them as if you are wounded. Make sure they see you, then collapse. Don't go to far. Make them come to you. Curiosity will probably bring any visitors, too."

"You're going to kill them, aren't you," she stated flatly.

"If I have to." She stared hard at him with loathing. He wondered whether, if they survived, their relationship would survive.

Julie climbed back onto the cart, and Mike followed. She wouldn't look at him. Wouldn't say anything. Just stared frozen-faced at the tracks in front of them.

Mike stopped the cart as the tracks started to curve. He shut off the lights. A dim glow leaked around the bend. "This is as close as we'd better get. They may have already heard us. Julie . . . I'll be right behind you." She left the cart without looking at him. The light was too dim to see her face, and he wasn't sure he wanted to see it, or see what was in her eyes.

Julie started off down the tracks. "Wait!" Mike hissed. "Take this." He handed her a 9mm Beretta pistol.

It took her a moment to realize what it was. "No! I don't need this," she said vehemently. "I don't want it." She let the gun clatter to the track bed.

Mike picked it up. "You have to take it. And use it if you have to!"

Julie stared at the instrument of death. She didn't want to touch it, but her mind went limp with resignation. She took the gun from Mike. Its weight surprised her. She almost dropped it.

"Careful. The safety is off," Mike warned. "All you have to do is point and pull the trigger."

She looked at him as if he were the devil incarnate, then stuffed the pistol in the waistband of her pants under the coat. She turned and marched off.

Chapter Twenty-two

Julie walked through a haze that made everything blurry. She knew the haze was in her mind. She tried not to think, and concentrated on putting one foot in front of another.

She rounded the bend in the tunnel. The loading dock was brightly lit. A guard slumped half asleep in a chair behind a desk. A 9mm Spectra M-4 submachine gun lay on the desk in front of him. Another guard squatted with his back against a wall. A cigarette dangled from his lips. His AK-47 assault rifle leaned against the wall beside him. Both men were numbed by boredom.

Julie walked toward them without breaking stride. They didn't notice her. She was getting too far from Mike. She let out a hoarse scream.

The guards jerked alert. Their eyes widened with shock. Julie let out a loud moan, stumbled a few more steps, then slumped facedown onto the rail bed.

The guards grabbed up their weapons, jumped off

the loading dock and ran to her. When they reached
her, they were too shocked by the bloody holes in the
back of her coat to notice that she wasn't wearing the
right pants.

Mike's breath stopped when he heard Julie's hoarse
scream. Ice gripped his heart. He slipped swiftly along
the tunnel wall, his heart pounding. Julie's pitiful moan
slammed him with agonizing guilt: he'd sent her to her
death—and it didn't sound quick and merciful.

Mike sprinted into the light. A storm of bullets tore
the air around him. He scrambled back around the
bend.

Julie jerked upright in time to see Mike scramble out
of sight. They almost killed him! she screamed to herself.

The guards were terrified. They were convinced the
person they'd seen had shot Julie, who they still believed to be one of them. Julie slumped back to the rail
bed. She watched them from slitted eyelids as they desperately slammed home fresh magazines.

Mike eased cautiously around the bend, his finger
tight on the Uzi's trigger. Another hail of bullets drove
him back. He was stymied. They were standing in front
of Julie. He couldn't fire without hitting her. He wondered how many other guards had been alerted by the
gunfire and were on their way. He had a sinking feeling
inside.

The guard with the AK-47 loosed another burst, then
turned and sprinted for the loading dock. The remaining guard screamed angrily after him. The first guard
stopped, swiveled and nervously aimed the AK-47
down the track to cover their escape.

Julie's determined ''rescuer'' slung his weapon on

his shoulder, squatted and lifted Julie. She stayed limp as he struggled to get her across his shoulders. He finally managed it, and then carried her down the tunnel in a stumbling run.

Her rescuer slung Julie onto the loading dock and dragged her across it into the corridor. The other guard loosed a precautionary burst, scrambled onto the loading dock and backed toward the entrance.

Julie's rescuer reached for a wall phone. She couldn't let him call! She rolled against his legs. The phone clattered from his hand. He staggered and fell against the wall, hitting his head. He swayed on his feet, as much from surprise as injury. The other guard's eyes were riveted on the tunnel. He didn't see Julie's assault.

Julie scrambled to her feet and slammed a knee in the first guard's crotch. He screamed. His companion spun, instinctively bringing up his AK-47. Julie hurled herself at him. She crashed into his legs as the AK-47 went off over her head. The 7.62mm slugs tore through the man behind her, splattering the wall with his blood.

Julie's momentum carried her and the other guard across the loading dock to crash onto the tracks in a tangle of arms and legs. The impact jolted the air from Julie's lungs. The guard's finger was still clamped on the trigger. The weapon kept firing until it was empty.

Julie tried to get to her feet. The guard brought her crashing back on the tracks. He climbed up her body, screaming curses. She punched him furiously with no effect. He crushed her into helplessness underneath him. Shock shattered his face when he realized she was a woman. He screamed at her in Arabic. His eyes were insane with anger. He drew a large knife from somewhere. She had an odd thought: She had always pictured Arabs using knives with curved blades. This one looked like a large Bowie knife.

He locked a hand in her hair, and jerked her head

back, exposing her throat. He pressed the knife against her flesh.

He paused.

She knew she was bleeding already.

His eyes glittered with a killing light. There was a strange smile on his face. He was going to saw her head off . . . slowly.

Mike had seen the knife come out. He couldn't see what the guard was doing to her with it. He was sitting astride her, his back to Mike.

The guard hunched his shoulders, gathering his strength.

Mike felt as if he were running in slow motion.

The guard leaned forward.

Mike knew he was too late.

He crashed into the Libyan.

The impact sprawled them off Julie's body.

Mike was blind with fury.

He got his arm about the Libyan's neck. He tried to tear the Libyan's head from his body. He wasn't strong enough, but he kept trying, even after a sickening crack.

The Libyan went limp.

Mike had trouble getting to his feet. He'd used all of his strength killing the man. He made himself take deep breaths. His eyes were full of tears. He didn't want to turn around. Didn't want to see her. Didn't want to see what the Libyan had done to her.

It wasn't as awful as he feared, but the sight made him cry. Julie lay on her back. Blood seeped from a long slash across her throat. The pain in her face hurt Mike terribly. If she had to die, she shouldn't have had to die in agony.

Mike sank beside her. He stared at her, full of anguish. Even with the welling line of blood across her throat, she was beautiful. Almost as if she was alive.

She *was* alive! She was breathing!

He'd been so sure the Libyan had—

Her eyes snapped opened. Her arms locked around his neck. She buried her face against him.

Mike was dizzy with relief, but he held her for only a moment. She clung to him as he got to his feet. "Julie, I was so afraid. . . ." he murmured into her hair.

She didn't reply, just hugged him tighter.

Mike reluctantly grasped her arms and took them from around him. He made her tilt her head so he could examine the cut. Mike shuddered. Another instant . . . The blood was already clotting. It might bleed a little when she turned her head, but it wasn't serious.

Mike let her head drop. "Julie, we've got to move. Someone must have heard the shooting. Take this and wait here while I get the equipment." He slammed a fresh clip in the little Uzi and shoved it in her hands. She looked at it with revulsion, as though she might drop it. "Julie—"

"It's all right." She tightened her grip on the weapon and put a finger on the trigger. Her face hardened. "Go!"

Julie wondered about herself as she watched Mike run back along the tracks. How could she feel so calm? She shouldn't feel so calm—so cold. Was it that easy to become hardened to killing? The cold steel biting into her throat had pushed her over the edge of desperation and dropped her into the horror of a nasty death. The impact had smashed something inside her, whatever it was that should have made her weep when she looked across the loading dock at the torn body of the man who'd risked his life attempting to save hers. She only felt cold determination.

Mike stopped their sprint down the corridor at the first door they came to. He threw himself against it.

The lock gave. He pulled Julie into the utter darkness, and they fell over a pile of boxes. They could hear shouting and running feet very close. Mike scrambled to the door and shoved it closed. He held his breath as what sounded like an army pounded past.

He waited a few seconds, then cracked the door. Through the thin crack, he could see down the corridor to the loading dock. He estimated there were at least a dozen heavily armed men piling off the platform onto the tracks. They'd discovered the bodies. "Come on!" Mike ordered, swinging the door open. Julie followed him into the corridor. He took off running again.

Julie skidded and fell as they rounded a corner. Mike jerked her to her feet again, and she followed as he plunged into a crossing passageway. He sprinted to a door fifty feet away. This door was also unlocked. They plunged in, and Mike slammed the door shut after them. He released the spring lock—something someone had forgotten to do.

Julie stood still until Mike switched on his flashlight. He kept his hand cupped over it to dim the light. It was an electrical shop of some sort, filled with benches on which sat big voltmeters and ammeters. A large electrical motor lay disassembled on one bench. Its innards were still attached to meters. Mike guessed that this was a maintenance room for the rail-cart power systems.

Mike switched off his flashlight, sat on the floor and pulled Julie down beside him. More feet pounded past. Someone stopped and rattled the door knob. A fist pounded on the door. Mike tightened his finger on the Uzi's trigger. Other hurried steps approached the door. There was a rapid exchange in Arabic, and the footsteps hurried away in the direction of the rail tunnel.

"Julie, they certainly know we're here now, but it sounds like they think we're still in the tunnel. I tied down the speed control and sent the cart back. It might go all the way to the hangar before they discover we aren't on it. Maybe we can make it to the computer center before they figure out that we've gotten by them.''

Mike spread a CIA map on the floor behind a bench and turned on his flashlight. The tracks made it easy to locate where they were. The spooks had marked the best route to where they thought the computer center was, but it was going to be hard to follow through the maze of passageways.

Julie followed Mike to his feet. ''Sounds like everyone ran to the tracks,'' he said. ''Let's go while we have a chance.''

''Stop!'' Julie gasped as they jogged down a corridor. Mike could hardly believe they'd gotten so far without encountering anyone, but he was sure they were lost.

Julie was gasping. She leaned against the wall to drag in enough air to talk. ''See that channel up there?'' She pointed to the large rectangular structure suspended from the ceiling of the corridor that intersected the one they'd been running along. It looked like a heating duct, but it was fabricated from heavy steel instead of flimsy aluminum. ''That's the kind of channel they lay computer cables in, especially when you want to be able to shift your equipment around. Can you boost me?''

''Yeah.''

Julie slipped off her pack and lowered it to the floor. She put her foot in his hand and he heaved. She teetered, then braced herself against the wall. She pushed herself toward the duct and caught the edge.

''Computer cabling, all right,'' she announced. Mike lowered her to the floor, and helped her hoist her pack onto her back again. ''There's a computer at the end of that somewhere: a very large computer.''

"Which end?"

"I wish I knew," she said, her voice filled with exasperation.

A door opened in front of them, and a man stepped into the hall. He glanced at them, then went about the business of locking the door. He was slender, thirty, Mike guessed. He carried a bulging beat-up leather briefcase.

The Libyan finished locking the door, straightened, then stiffened. He suddenly realized that Mike and Julie weren't staff members. He examined them fearfully, eyeing their weapons. He started to challenge them, but the weapons changed his mind. He turned without a word and started to hurry away.

In two strides Mike caught him. Mike clamped his hand on the Libyan's shoulder, jerked him to a stop and slammed him against the wall. The man said something angry in Arabic. "Do you speak English?" Mike asked.

The man shook his head no. Mike fixed him with hot eyes. The man had understood the question. "He doesn't understand English," Mike said to Julie. "He's no good to us. We may as well kill him."

"No!" the man cried, trembling.

"I can't understand you," Mike told him. "You don't speak English." He shoved the Uzi's muzzle into the man's gut. The man shrank against the wall. Terror filled his eyes.

"I speak English!" he admitted. "What do you want? What are you doing here? Who are you?"

"Whoa," Mike said. "I have the gun, so I'll ask the questions. Where's the computer center?"

"We want to know where the supercomputer is," Julie added.

"I don't know what you're talking about," the Libyan protested stubbornly.

"Then I guess we will shoot you," Mike said.

"Why! I've done nothing to you!"

"You can't lead us to the computer, and we can't have you telling people we've been here."

"No! I know where the computer is!"

"Sorry. I don't believe you," Mike responded. "You're lying to save your life."

"I'm not lying! I work in the computer center!"

"How many megaflops does the machine run?" Julie asked, her eyes dangerous.

"Gigaflops! Not megaflops. It runs gigaflops. It runs—"

"Which way?" Julie snapped.

The Libyan dropped his eyes. He was ready to lie.

"We have three minutes to find the computer," Mike announced. "We will shoot you in three minutes. This gun will be against your spine, and my finger will be on the trigger. Three minutes and you're dead."

"You'll kill me anyway."

"No. We will tie you up and leave you."

"How do I know—"

"We've wasted enough time," Julie interrupted him. "We can follow the cables. We don't need him. Shoot him."

"Wait! The cable channel splits. You do need me!"

"Three minutes," Mike said.

"Not enough time!" the Libyan cried. "It's at least a five-minute walk."

"Five minutes. No more."

"There! The double doors!" the Libyan exclaimed, pointing ahead of them. They had been walking quickly for seven minutes, almost at a run. Mike did not trust the Libyan, but had decided to let him live two more minutes.

"How many on the night shift?" Julie asked.

"There is no night shift."

Mike and Julie examined the door suspiciously. "If

347

there's anyone in there, I will shoot you immediately,'' Mike told him.

The man blanched. "There is someone," he admitted, terrified. "A guard. At a desk in front of the door." Mike's eyes filled with murder. "I was going to tell you," he pleaded. "I'll help you get past him," he offered, desperately trying to avoid the death he saw in Mike's eyes.

Mike nodded.

The Libyan reached for the door handle.

Mike pressed the Uzi's barrel harder into his back.

The Libyan turned the handle and drew the door open. The room was dark, except for glowing CRT displays and the guard's desk lamp. The guard was a burly man seated behind a desk directly in front of the door. He had obviously been asleep. He stared at them with bleary eyes. "These are specialists from Baghdad," the Libyan said quickly.

The guard's eyes widened with shock, and he reached for the machine gun lying in front of him on the desk. The engineer had spoken in English.

The engineer spun, knocking Mike's Uzi aside, and scrambled into the darkness.

The guard raised his weapon.

They fired at the same time.

A searing fist slammed into Mike's ribs.

A gout of blood burst from the guard's throat.

Mike staggered backward into Julie.

The guard fell forward on his desk.

Blood dyed the papers scattered across the desk red.

"Mike!" Julie screamed. She put her arms around him to steady him. He fought off the shock and pushed away from her. "He shot you," she moaned. The blood wetting her hands horrified her. She reached for him again. Mike pulled away.

"We have to find that bastard," Mike growled. Damn, it hurt! And shit, he couldn't afford to be dizzy.

The bastard probably knew where there was a gun back there.

Mike started around the desk.

The Libyan hurtled out of the darkness and smashed into Mike's back, sending him to the floor. The Libyan tightened an arm about Mike's neck, and pushed at the side of Mike's head. This engineer was combat-trained—maybe not an engineer at all.

Then the terrifying pressure was gone.

It was a moment before Mike recovered, and realized there was a furious struggle behind him. He tried to get up, but his body was reluctant to obey him. He heard a sharp cry of pain.

Julie!

Mike staggered to his feet. The two figures were entwined, straining. There was a thud, and Julie's breath whooshed out. The sound of a fist impacting her flesh jolted Mike. Julie reeled backward and fell heavily. Mike leaped onto the Libyan from behind. They crashed to the floor. The Libyan squirmed with surprising strength. Mike couldn't get an arm around his neck. An elbow stabbed Mike's gut and a hand sought his testicles. Mike rolled away. The Libyan started to his feet. Mike rammed his head into the man's gut. Mike's legs pumped until they slammed into a locker. The Libyan was stunned, breath gone.

Mike smashed his fist in the man's face and felt the spatter of blood. He pushed the man's head back with the heel of his hand. The Libyan's struggles were weak now. Mike measured the blow carefully, then stabbed his extended fingers into the man's windpipe. They penetrated flesh and felt as if they'd been plunged into something hot and sticky. The flesh clung to Mike's fingers when he pulled them out of the man's throat. Mike let go, and the body fell heavily to the floor.

* * *

Mike stumbled through the dim light and almost fell over Julie huddled on the floor. She was curled in a fetal position. Her breath came in choking gasps.

Mike knelt beside her. He put his hand on her shoulder, but he was afraid to crush her in his arms the way he wanted to. She might have broken something, might have cracked her back. Moving her could do serious damage.

"Julie, where'd he hurt you?"

"Bastard punched me in the stomach," she croaked. "In the eye, too," she gasped. "Banged me against everything. I probably look like shit! I *feel* like shit." Relief washed through Mike. She was angry. She couldn't be seriously injured.

"Stay right there." Mike got to his feet, found his Uzi and made his way swiftly to the door. It was hard to believe the shots hadn't been heard.

Mike pressed his ear against the door. Nothing. He eased it open. He still heard nothing. He opened it enough to see down the corridor. No one. He stepped out into the hall, ready to fire. It was empty. He dared to hope that everyone had rushed to the rail tunnel and no one had heard a thing.

Mike closed the door and rushed back to Julie. She had sat up, and was trying to struggle to her feet. Mike shoved the Uzi back into its holster and helped her up. "Julie, are you—"

"Mike! He shot you!"

"Just a scratch. Nothing to worry about," he lied.

"Let me—"

"No! We don't have much time. You've got to get on that computer. I'll be okay. Now go."

Julie stared at him for a moment, then reluctantly turned and started for the computer console.

Julie recognized the prompts. She'd spent two years staring at them with Saba. The menus to get her on-line were the same. Saba hadn't changed the environment. She called up the directories, and stared at them in dismay. She recognized none of the names, and there were many more files than used by the original program. She held her breath and typed in the request to see the first file. It requested an access code.

Julie felt brittle. She'd expected to have to break access codes, but it was still frustrating. They had so little time. Her head felt unbearably tight. She realized she was about to explode. She had to hold on to her cool.

Julie took her hands away from the keyboard, closed her eyes, leaned back in the chair and took deep breaths. She tried to think of nothing but how comfortable the chair was. It worked. The pressure bursting her skull subsided.

"Mike, would you please drag my pack over here?"

She rummaged through the pack and found the digital tape cassette that the spooks from the National Security Agency had given her. It was in a sealed black case. She broke the seal. Once the seal was broken, the cassette would self-destruct in three minutes. After she fed the program into the computer, she had thirty minutes to decode the access codes; then a virus would destroy the program.

Julie shoved the cassette into a digital recorder sitting beside the CRT display. A lazy operator had marked the tape's port on it, making it easy for her to direct the computer to the tape machine. Her fingers danced over the keyboard, and the tape machine's lights flashed. Damn noisy machine, she thought to herself as the machine whirred digital data into the supercomputer.

Julie decoded the access codes of over a hundred files in the next thirty minutes. She stored the decoded information in a new file she created. She was searching for other files of interest when the decoding program self-destructed. A set of crazy symbols fled across the display. There was a burst of color, and then a little triangle calmly blinked at her.

Julie's shoulders slumped. She felt very tired. Her left eye was nearly swollen shut. Her stomach ached, and she felt like a sore muscle from head to toe. She gathered her resolve and forced herself to go on.

Julie was able to reject some files on the basis of their names and labels. Others required her to scroll through hundreds of lines of code before she was sure they weren't what she was looking for. She had to go through thirty of the one hundred files before she found what she was looking for. "I found it, Mike!" she cried. "I see how Saba labeled them. I can find all the strains they've been working on."

"Great! But we're running out of time," Mike warned. He was both relieved and worried. They had beaten almost impossible odds, but he had a feeling their luck was about to run out, and Mike's strength was draining out through the wound in his side. He was feeling a little faint. He had tried to stop the blood, but the jagged tear kept leaking around whatever he pressed against it. If it didn't stop he'd have to be carried out the door. He hadn't asked for Julie's help. It would upset her, and she needed to spend every second they had extracting the data from the machine.

"How much longer, Julie?"

"I don't know . . . maybe another two hours." Frustration had replaced the elation in her voice.

"Two hours!"

"At least. I've got to verify and copy genetic-code files. Then I've got to find all the program modules and copy them. Are you all right, Mike?" She'd caught the strain in his voice. "Are you bleeding?" She started from her chair.

"I'll be okay. Just hurry."

"Mike—"

"Julie, hurry!" She reluctantly sat back down.

Thirty minutes later the power went off. The displays blinked out, and the room was plunged into inky blackness. Fans and drive motors whined to a stop.

Shock froze Julie. This couldn't be happening! Not now! She hadn't dumped the files on tape yet. They were in random access memory. She'd have to start all over again.

Mike fell off the desk he was sitting on, and crashed to the floor. He hadn't realized how weak he was. The door burst open. Mike tried to get up, but fell on his face again.

The lights flashed on again, and heavily armed men poured into the room. Julie thought about going for a weapon, but dismissed the thought immediately. It would be suicide. But maybe suicide would be preferable to what they faced. No! As long as you were alive, you had a chance. She saw Mike on the floor, his shirt soaked with blood. He struggled to rise. She screamed and started for him. She was slammed back against the console. A sharp edge seemed to fracture a vertebra. She screamed when someone kicked Mike.

Unbelievable pain exploded in Mike's side, and he couldn't breathe. He heard Julie scream. He was yanked to his feet. His legs wouldn't hold him. He fell back to his knees. A gun barrel was shoved in his mouth.

"Stop it!" someone yelled authoritatively in English. "Don't kill him! Colonel Aziz would not be pleased to be deprived of his chance to interrogate the good Captain Boen."

Mike was shocked. He didn't know the handsome young man who was neatly dressed in black pants, white shirt and tie. How could the man know who he was?

"Omar!" Julie gasped behind him.

"Yes. Your slave, who slaved so hard for so little in your laboratory. This is quite unbelievable: I would have never pictured you as a commando. Astounding! Haven't you anything to say to your former pupil? Hello, good to see you again . . . something?"

Julie remained silent.

"All right, bring them over here," Omar ordered.

They were shoved to the center of the room. Mike fell to one knee. Julie gave a little scream. "Omar! Can't you see he's hurt?" she cried. "He needs a doctor!"

Mike put his arm around Julie's waist and dragged himself to his feet.

"Don't worry, we will take care of him," Omar assured her. "Colonel Aziz would be upset if he was deprived of the opportunity to kill Captain Boen himself . . . very slowly." Omar smiled cruelly.

"Now, undress," Omar ordered them. Julie stiffened. "Don't worry, Dr. Barns—or can I call you Julie, since our positions are somewhat reversed—no one is going to rape you . . . not yet. This is the only way we can be sure you haven't hidden any James Bond–type weapons. You have proved quite dangerous, you know. How many of our people did *you* kill, Julie?" She couldn't hide the stricken look. "I see. More than you like to think about." He shook his head. "You never know what people are capable of—all the more reason for us to be cautious. Quickly now!"

They complied.

"Everything!" Omar ordered viciously when they stood in their underwear.

"She isn't hiding anything," Mike protested.

"I suppose I have your word on it—as an officer and a gentleman," Omar replied sarcastically. "Captain, if you don't do as I say in the next five seconds, you will both die."

"It's all right, Mike," Julie implored. "Don't get us killed for nothing."

Julie unhooked her bra and let it fall from her breasts. She quickly pushed her panties down and stepped out of them. She stood rigidly, defying the eyes crawling over her body, devouring her high breasts and attempting to penetrate the thatch of dark hair curling from her pelvis. She clenched her hands at her sides. She made no attempt to cover herself. She refused to give them the satisfaction of making her grovel.

"My, Julie, you do have a nice body," Omar observed. "Strange . . . as long as we worked together, I never thought of you sexually. I must have been blind." He reached out and rolled a nipple between thumb and forefinger.

Mike lunged. A rifle butt smashed the back of his head. He jolted to the floor. Lightning raced through his skull and seared him with agony.

Julie dropped beside him, and tried to shield him with her body. "Stop them, Omar!"

"Wait!" Omar shouted, halting the next blow. "Your captain seems to have a death wish, Julie. Colonel Aziz would be unhappy, but we will kill him anyway if he troubles us too much."

Mike tried to rise. His legs wouldn't cooperate. Julie helped him.

"Captain, if you insist on being uncooperative, we will just kill you and do whatever we want with her after you're dead," Omar informed him.

"Omar, I'll do whatever you want," said Julie. "There's no need to hurt him."

"Julie, you sound like an old American movie heroine, and old American movies make me sick. Chadi, Said, search their clothes—thoroughly. Jassim, put the packs and weapons in that storage cabinet over there. We will look at them later. And Ali, get something out of your kit to stop the leak in the captain's side.

Maybe you can get some practice with sutures.''

Mike was allowed to sit on the edge of the desk while Ali tended to him. Ali was a dark, very young man who was eager to try out his field dressing kit. Mike clenched his jaws while the youth experimented with the sutures in the kit.

"There," Ali said in English when he finished. "We give you an antibiotic now, and you will be fine." Mike's side was on fire, and he had to struggle to keep from falling off the desk. Julie steadied him. She looked sick, about to throw up.

Ali dug into the kit, searching for the antibiotic. His eyes brightened, and he brought out two syringes. "We have some painkiller, too," he enthused. "I'll give you that, also. Up, up!" he ordered. "This goes in butt."

Julie pulled Mike's arm around her shoulders and helped him stand up.

The two jabs were nothing compared to the sutures. "There. As good as MASH," Ali said proudly.

"Much better than he deserves," Omar commented dryly. "We should do something about your neck, Julie. Take care of her, Ali."

"No! I don't need sewing up!" Julie protested, horrified.

Omar chuckled. "A little tape, Ali. Julie, you bleed when you move your head." Julie stood apprehensively while Ali painted her with stinging antiseptic and stretched tape over the slash.

"Now, Julie, you and the captain get dressed," Omar said when Ali finished, "and we'll take you to meet an old friend of yours." He grinned smugly.

Chapter Twenty-three

The Libyans roughly pushed Mike and Julie through a massive steel door into a corridor between a steel-reinforced concrete wall and the doors of a long row of six-by-eight steel cages. There were no walls between the cages, only closely spaced bars. There was no furniture in the cells, and only an uncovered hole against the concrete-block back wall of each cell for sanitation. The pits weren't very deep; the smell was overpowering. There were other smells, too: of unwashed bodies and decayed flesh, the smell of death.

The block of fifteen cells held only one occupant—a woman. She was huddled under a filthy blanket against the back wall of her cell. Her knees were drawn up, her face hidden against her thighs, her hands clasped on top of her head.

The guards halted them in front of the cell next to the woman's. A guard pushed a card into the cell door's cipher-lock card slot. The cipher lock was part of a sophisticated security system. The guards outside had cards that opened the door to the cell block, but not the cell doors; they had to call a superior to open the cells in an emergency. It prevented guards from aiding escapes.

The lock clicked and the door swung open. The guards shoved Mike and Julie into the cell, sending them sprawling to the floor. Pain exploded in Mike's side, and he almost lost consciousness. The guards slammed the door behind them. The electric bolt clicked home, and the guards marched out.

Julie got to her knees and helped Mike sit up. "Mike? Are you okay?"

He looked at her, and grinned through the pain. "Hell, no! Why do you keep asking that?"

She stared at him startled, then smiled crookedly. "Touché." The smile disappeared. "But this isn't funny. I know Navy pilots laugh in the face of death and all that, but I'm scared. When Aziz arrives, I think we'll be tortured." Tears spilled from her eyes and crept down her cheeks. She turned her head away.

"I'm sorry," she choked out. "Crying is silly. Won't do a damn bit of good. But . . . I'm just not very brave."

Mike ignored the pain in his side, and drew her into his arms. "You are brave, as brave as any shipmate I ever had. And thinking about being tortured makes me want to cry, too. We'll figure a way out."

"Now I understand why they give spies cyanide pills. If I had one, I think I might use it."

"Julie! Cut it out!" He took her by the shoulders and held her at arm's length. "Look at me! Julie!" He shook her slightly when her eyes refused to meet his.

She reluctantly raised her devastated eyes to his.

"As long as we're alive we have a chance," he said.

"That's right." The determined voice from the next cell startled Mike. "Otherwise I would have made them kill me, or I would have killed myself, long ago."

Julie stiffened, then broke free of Mike's embrace and scrambled to her feet. "Saba! Is that you?" Julie exclaimed incredulously. She rushed to the bars separating the cells and gripped them.

"Yes, Julie. It's me, Saba." The two women stared at each other in astonishment. Julie knew she should hate her, but she didn't feel anything. Pity maybe.

Saba was naked, her hair tangled and dirty. Bruises mottled her skin. One blackened eye was swollen almost shut, and she smelled. Her eyes sent a shiver along Julie's spine. They burned with insane light, and brimmed with the most intense hatred Julie had ever seen.

"You'll have to excuse the way I'm dressed," Saba said dryly. "Omar thinks keeping me naked humiliates me. I encourage it. I beg for clothes whenever he comes."

"He comes here?"

"Yes. He should have killed me long ago—the day he took over. But he has this obsession. I humiliated him once, and he loves to humiliate me now. Then there's sex. He's addicted to it, and I'm very good at it."

"He rapes you?"

"No. I screw him." She smiled at Julie's shock. "It's as your captain says, Julie. As long as you are alive, you have a chance to survive. So that's what I do, screw for my life."

Julie's skin crawled.

"It's quite a shock to see you two here," Saba said. "I'm still not sure this isn't a dream."

"I wish it was a dream," Julie said hopelessly. "We came after the codes and the program."

"I can't believe you got this far," Saba said, shaking her head in disbelief. "Doesn't seem possible."

"Obviously it is possible to get this far," Julie pointed out. "It's also obvious that it's impossible to get any further."

Saba studied them. She seemed to make up her mind about something. "I see they left you your clothes," she remarked.

"Yes," Julie responded, and shivered. She wouldn't like to have to live naked like an animal.

"I suppose they searched you well?"

"Very well. They made us take off all our clothes, and they examined every seam, anywhere that might hold any kind of weapon."

"Did they search your body cavities?"

"No!" The thought horrified Julie. Then she wondered why they hadn't. On the other hand, what could they hide inside their bodies that would get them through a thick steel door with a cipher lock?

"Did you conceal anything inside your bodies—a weapon? Something that could be used to help you escape?"

"No," Julie replied. The idea disgusted her.

"What kind of weapon?" Mike whispered suspiciously.

"Anything. But I really need a knife."

"What would you do with it?"

"Kill Omar."

"That would only get us killed sooner," Mike pointed out. "That doesn't sound like trying to stay alive. Sounds like plain old revenge. Suicidal revenge."

"Killing him is the only way to get out. We need his lock card."

"That won't get us past the guards."

"There is another way. I need the knife for that, too, but any sharp piece of metal might do. Doesn't have to be very sharp. Don't you have a metal button, a pin, something?" Saba asked desperately.

"How would you use it to get us out of here?" Mike asked, still suspicious. He could see the crazy light in her eyes.

She seemed reluctant to tell him. His suspicion grew. "Look at the back wall," she finally said. The wall had been built with what appeared to be two-by-three-foot blocks of concrete. "It's a double wall, designed for blast protection. A penetrating warhead could be detonated by the first wall and the second would absorb the blast. It'll crumble, but damage will be limited to perimeter rooms, and nothing of value is kept in them ... only things like prisoners. Even a smart fuse can't handle the large space between the walls. As soon as a fuse senses that it has passed through the first wall, it will detonate the warhead, which will dissipate most of its energy in the space between the walls."

"How do you know so much about it?" Mike asked.

"I was screwing the German civil engineer who designed this complex. Having sex with him for our Great Leader. I screwed the German to find out if the German was screwing our Leader."

"That still doesn't explain how you plan to get us out of here."

"The space between the walls is also used for cables—mostly power cables. There are access panels in almost every room. I found them useful when I was in charge—for observation, for showing up where I wasn't expected. Made people think I could teleport myself.

"This area was not always a prison. There was computer equipment in here at one time. When it was converted, the construction people were too lazy to replace the access panels with concrete. They just cemented them in place and painted them over. There's one in my cell. There. Near the floor in the back," she said, pointing.

Mike walked to the wall. The block she had pointed out was too smooth to be concrete. "It's metal—cemented in place with the same mortar used for the concrete blocks," Saba explained. "I've been working on it. They made the mistake of leaving me this." She went to the blanket crumpled in one corner of her cell, and returned with a small sliver of metal. "It was on a chain around my ankle, and they didn't notice. It used to be a silver heart." The metal was worn to a useless lump. "I have been using this to dig out the mortar. I dig it out and then mix it with saliva and put it back so no one notices. That's what has kept me alive, kept me from trying to kill him or kill myself. I knew if I could be patient, I could escape.

"If we can get between the walls," Saba continued, "they won't be able to find us. I know many ways out of this place. We can get out, steal a truck, aircraft, or something and get away."

Saba's face filled with frustration. "I almost have the panel loose, but this won't work anymore. I've been waiting for a chance to steal something from Omar—a pin, cuff link, something. But there isn't much time. The beatings are worse each time. I think he'll kill me soon."

Mike allowed himself to hope, but he kept his face impassive. Saba had betrayed them once, and she was a cold-blooded, merciless killer. He didn't trust her. "If I give you something, how can I trust you to free us, too?"

"You *do* have something!"

"You haven't answered me."

"I won't leave you. I need your help, and if I help you escape, I think your government will reward me well—for that and the information I can provide. There's nothing for me anywhere in the Muslim world, except a very unpleasant death. Without your help, I have nowhere to go."

Mike wasn't quite convinced, but it was their only chance. He pulled off his shirt, and felt along a seam. Nothing indicated that there were two layers of cloth.

The searcher had been in a hurry and hadn't noticed the stiffness.

Mike tore the seam open and extracted an impossibly thin blade. "It's made out of a metal-matrix composite," he explained. "It's used for advanced-engine turbine blades and even gun barrels. This blade is sharper than a razor and as hard as diamond. It's serrated. It can cut through steel like butter and saw through concrete, too."

Saba reached desperately through the bars for the knife.

"Wait. You need a handle." Mike tore the collar from his shirt. A plastic insert stiffened it. He tore the plastic from the cloth. He folded it and pressed it hard to activate a catalyst. The material became warm and soft. Mike molded it around the knife handle. The plastic rapidly hardened.

"Be careful," Mike warned as he handed Saba the knife. "That blade is sharper than a razor and this is not much of a handle."

They heard the bolt on the door at the end of the hall click open. Saba looked wild for a moment, then buried the blade in her long hair. "That will be Omar," she said. "I expected him. I'm sure he's anxious to humiliate me in front of you two, and he undoubtedly wants you to think about what's in store for you, too, Julie."

Omar stood just inside the door, hating the lust boiling in his loins. He hated not being in control of himself. He felt like a pervert yielding to some obscene obsession.

Omar had physical control of Saba, but somehow she was still humiliating him, insulting his manhood. He always felt dirty going into her cell. He felt dirtier when he left—and full of rage. Omar promised himself each time he'd kill her, but he couldn't. He was addicted. Omar could no more kill Saba than a crack addict could flush his dope down the drain.

Sex was unbelievable with Saba. He'd never experienced anything like it. She could do incredible things with her body, and she could play his body like a symphony. But if it had been only the sex he might have been able to break his addiction and order the guards to kill her if he couldn't do it himself. But there remained the unfinished business of vengeance—for that night in America.

The nightmares stalked his sleep, and he hadn't been able to have normal relationships with women since. She had taken part of his manhood, and only proper vengeance could restore it.

Omar wanted Saba to feel the humiliation he'd felt— and more. Pain would not suffice. Death was too merciful.

Omar had abused her body in every way imaginable. He'd been disappointed to discover how few ways there actually were to sexually abuse a woman's body. But it wasn't her body he wanted to abuse; he wanted to abuse *her*. He wanted to make her feel shame and humiliation and hate living. That he'd failed to do.

She pretended humiliation. She screamed, begged and did incredible things with her body. But in her eyes there was nothing. Behind those eyes was an icy observer, affected by nothing he did to her. He could tell—she didn't care. The obscene acts, the words, even the pain meant nothing.

Omar wanted to make her care. He didn't want to end it until he made her care. But lately he'd begun to believe it impossible to make her care. Each visit, he came closer to killing her. He'd begun to think that he *could* live with the feel of hollow vengeance. With her gone, maybe he could bury the humiliating memories in a hidden corner of his mind and get on with his life.

Maybe without access to her body, he could become normal with other women again.

Omar made a decision. If having the Americans witness her abuse had no effect on Saba, he would kill her before he left her cell. He smiled. Julie would surely be affected, driven to the edge of insanity. Maybe extracting his vengeance from Julie would be sufficient.

Omar had left his machine pistol and anything that might be used as a weapon with the guard. He carried only the card that unlocked the cells. Only the guard could open the corridor door. Omar didn't fear Saba would assault him physically. Deprivation and abuse had weakened her, and she knew assaulting him would be committing suicide. He knew she wanted to live, wanted to keep hoping.

Saba lay huddled on the floor under her pitiful blanket as Omar unlocked the cell.

"Omar, how could you do this to her?" Julie asked with a strangled voice as he entered Saba's cell. "Abuse her like that? You must be insane!"

"Saba. Naughty girl," Omar chided, smiling. "You've been discussing our personal life with the good doctor. Shame." The smile left his face. "Get up, bitch! And get that damn rag off you."

Saba rose, letting the tattered cloth drop from her.

"Magnificent, isn't she, Captain? If you'd like her after I'm through, I'm sure she wouldn't mind."

"What I'd like is to tear you into little pieces and flush you down the toilet with the rest of the shit!" Mike growled.

Omar laughed. "I'm afraid you won't have that opportunity." His face hardened. "I'm going to enjoy watching Colonel Aziz interrogate you.

"Now . . . Saba and I want to enjoy ourselves a bit. You should watch, Julie. Saba's quite incredible. You can learn a lot watching her, and you will have ample opportunity to use what you learn. I can guarantee you that.''

Gorge rose in Julie's throat.

Omar quickly stripped off his clothes, heedless of their presence. He had the body of a muscular ballet dancer. Under other circumstances Saba and Omar would have been a beautiful matched pair.

Julie turned away, went to the far side of the cell, and sank to the floor with her back to them. She drew up her legs and clasped her arms around her knees. She hoped the sounds of Omar's assault wouldn't make her throw up.

Saba obediently spread the blanket on the floor, and urged him to lie on it, her eyes full of promise. Omar's eyes were glazed, deeply submerged in his obsession, like a crack addict taking his first hit.

Mike didn't want to watch, but forced himself to. He had to know if and when she killed him, but watching made him feel dirty.

Omar lay back on his back, his eyes closed. Saba straddled him.

The lance of pain snapped Omar's eyes open. Saba smiled. The smile filled him with horror.

Omar tried to rise. The knife sliced deeper.

Omar stiffened and screamed in agony, eyes bulging.

"Omar, remember our discussion back in Virginia?"

All Omar could do was croak.

"I still can't decide, so I'll do them all.''

The knife slid in easily. Blood filled Omar's mouth. It was all Saba could do to stay on his bucking body. She extracted the knife and jerked up his chin.

She slowly drew the knife across his throat. The extraordinarily sharp blade sliced deep.

Omar's horrible gurgles made Julie vomit. Mike couldn't force himself to watch.

Omar's heels pounded the floor. Desperate choking sounds. Horrible bubbling. Silence.

Mike looked. Wished he hadn't.

Omar's blood covered Saba. Blood ran across the cell floor.

"It is done," Saba pronounced firmly.

"Hurry, Saba. The guard may have heard."

"No, this area is soundproof, but we should hurry. After an hour or so, the guard will expect him. He'll come looking for him. We need time to get as far away as possible."

Mike heard Julie being sick behind him, but he didn't take his eyes off Saba. The moment of truth had arrived. Would she leave them?

Saba searched through Omar's clothes for the cell's key card. She found it, went to the door and used both hands to reach around the bars and get it into the slot. The door clicked open.

Saba pushed out of her cell and inserted the card in Mike and Julie's cell-door lock. It clicked, and the door swung open.

Mike lifted Julie to her feet. The retching had left her weak and shaky. He led her into the adjacent cell. A sickening odor filled the air. Julie clung to Mike and kept her eyes away from Omar's body. To reach Saba, they had to carefully step over rivulets of blood streaming from Omar's body.

Saba was a dreadful specter as she worked furiously at the panel with the knife. Her nude body was filthy and smeared with Omar's blood. "There!" she exclaimed with satisfaction as they approached. She banged the panel with her fist, and it fell to the floor with a loud clang.

"Hurry," Saba urged. "We need to replace the panel carefully so it will take them a while to discover it."

"Take this, Saba." Mike stripped off his torn shirt, helped her into it and buttoned it for her. She smiled gratefully.

"Won't they follow us?" Mike asked.

"Yes, but not for a while. When they see what happened to Omar, no one will be anxious to follow us into the dark. I know these people. There will be a great deal of loud debate. Then it will be decided that someone else should decide what to do. There will be more debate as to who that someone should be. Then whoever follows us will insist on bringing an army. We'll be in the computer room by then. And we should be gone by the time they gather their army and work up enough courage to search for us. Leaving Omar that way was not *all* vengeance. Well . . . maybe it was," she admitted, "but it will discourage pursuit and make them *very* cautious and slow them down."

Even with lights, the footing would have been treacherous. In the dark, the power cables snaking along the floor made each step a potential disaster. They fell and stumbled for ten minutes before Mike detected a dull glow in the distance. Saba halted them, breathing heavily. The confinement and abuse had weakened her.

"There, up ahead," Saba gasped. "We turn there."

"How do you know where we are?" Mike asked. They had no choice but to follow her, but it was hard to believe she knew where they were going as they stumbled through the dark.

"There's a small light where another passage joins this one. It bisects the lab. The passages are configured like a four-spoke wheel. This passage runs around the perimeter. The passage up ahead runs through the lab. Another passage bisects the lab at right angles to this one. We have to get to that."

"The computer requires a lot of power," Saba told them when they reached the dimly lighted intersection. "It and its peripherals are located along this passage, where the main power cable is laid. We can tell when we reach the computer room. A big switch box blocks most of the passage. It switches between power sources when there's an emergency. There's a removable panel in the wall just beside it that provides quick access to the switch box in case of an emergency or attack. It can be removed without tools from either side. If we hurry, we can get in, make our copies and get back into the tunnel before our friends get around to searching this far from the cell block. I know how to get to the surface from here. Then we can transmit your data and call for pickup. They *will* pick us up?" she asked apprehensively.

"Yes," Mike lied. He had to make her believe that they had a means to escape, or she might abandon them. He tensed for Julie's reaction. She said nothing.

"Mike, Julie, you'll have to help me," Saba said when they reached the access panel. "This mustn't fall and make noise." They unscrewed the wing nuts and carefully removed the panel. Mike worried about the clank it made when it touched the floor.

Saba poked her head through the opening. After a moment, she pulled back into the passageway. "We're lucky," she informed them. "There's only the guard. I'll take care of him." Before Mike could react, Saba slipped through the opening and disappeared.

Julie squeezed Mike's arm, questioning. "We'll wait," he whispered against her ear. "She's good at what she does."

Julie shivered. Saba was a sleek, beautiful monster. It frightened Julie just to be near her.

There was a short scream in the room. Then silence. A few moments later Saba returned. "Hurry," she urged. Mike and Julie climbed into the room. "Here," Saba said to Mike, handing him his shirt. "I have one now. Fits better."

Saba and Julie went directly to the computer console.

Mike searched out the locker containing their equipment. The packs hadn't been disturbed. Even their weapons had been left in the locker.

With Saba's knowledge, the copying went swiftly. When it was finished, Julie heaved a sigh and leaned back in her chair as the little digital recorder soaked up the stream of bits from the computer. "We have the data, Mike," she said. "Now we need to get out of here and transmit it." It was impossible to transmit through the concrete and sand that covered the room. The transmitter had to be taken to the surface.

They followed Saba back into the passageway and helped her secure the access door.

Fifty minutes later they were climbing a ladder up through a round passage, which was barely large enough for them and their packs. Mike's wound had progressed from pain to agony. He felt too weak to climb a ladder carrying the heavy pack, but he forced himself up.

At the top Mike sprawled off the ladder into a small room onto his stomach. He had trouble dragging enough air into his lungs. He felt as sick and weak as he ever had in his life.

Julie sat down beside him and kneaded his back with her hand.

"Will he make it?" Saba asked, worried.

"Yes," Julie answered. "Just give him a few minutes."

"We don't have many minutes," Saba responded harshly.

It took five minutes for Mike to breathe enough strength back into his body to go on. He sat up. "Let's go," he said. Agony burned through him as he forced himself to his feet. If he had to climb another ladder, he knew he'd never make it. He was almost overcome with relief when Saba said, "This way. There's an unguarded maintenance elevator just through that door."

   The elevator brought them quickly to the surface. The door slid open, and Mike stepped out into the bright afternoon sun. He searched the simmering sand, ready to fire the little Uzi. Saba, armed with the dead guard's M-4, stepped out beside him.

   "Is this patrolled?" he asked.

   "Rarely. There's always the fear that satellites or surveillance aircraft will detect anyone out here, even at night. No one knows what the satellites can see, so it's assumed they can see everything. And there's no ground threat. Any Bedouins living near here were slaughtered long ago."

   Julie joined them.

   "Julie, we can set up the equipment here," Mike said.

   "Will we be able to talk to your people?" Saba asked as she watched them unpack the equipment.

   "No," Mike answered. "We can only transmit digital data, not receive."

   Mike pulled the four flat panels of the array antenna from their cases. He joined them by precision tongues and grooves machined into their frames. They formed an electronically steered active array two feet square. He plugged a small black box into the back of the array. The box contained the equivalent of a small computer. It controlled the hundreds of tiny millimeterwave-integrated-circuit transmitters that drove the radiating elements of the array. It phased the transmitter signals to focus the antenna beam and point it at a MILSTAR satellite. It contained a GPS receiver that provided the precise position data needed to accurately point the beam.

   The apparatus was designed for one-time use. To reduce weight, no cooling was provided, and the circuitry would incinerate itself after a few minutes use.

   Mike snapped together a tripod, placed the assembly on it and bolted it into place. He cabled the digital recorder to the computer-antenna assembly. He pulled a hot-gas generator from his pack and attached its cables. The power unit's turbines were driven by gas from burning solid rocket fuel. Small amounts of the fuel produced enormous volumes of high-pressure gas to spin the turbine blades. The beer-can-sized generator could produce over a hundred kilowatts of power, but only for a few seconds.

When the transmit button was pushed, a ten-second burst of data would flash up to the satellite. The generator would run for another twenty seconds, melting the circuitry and itself into useless globs of plastic and metal.

The computer box blinked a green light. Mike's finger hovered over a red button. He said a little prayer and pushed it.

The hot-gas generator screamed to life. The sound startled Mike. He hadn't expected so much noise. If there were anyone nearby . . .

The generator's scream stopped as suddenly as it had begun. The smell of hot metal and burnt plastic filled the air.

Everything seemed to drain out of Mike. The impossible mission had been completed. It didn't seem worth it to move anymore. His side hurt, and he felt feverish. He was sure he was developing an infection. The Tomahawks were probably being launched now. Sixty minutes and they would arrive. If there had been a decision to use nukes, they would shortly be vaporized. If not, they would be blasted to bits. Mike doubted that in either case there would be enough left of them for even a closed-casket burial.

Chapter Twenty-four

Mike felt like just dropping onto the sand and watching the fireworks until his lights went out. It didn't seem worth it to go through the agony of a futile escape attempt. How far could they get in sixty minutes?

Julie's arm slipped around him and changed his mind. Saving her was worth any effort, and he owed her the chance for survival, no matter how small that chance was.

"Mike, will they launch the missiles now?" Julie asked fearfully.

"Yes."

"What are we going to do? Can we get far enough away?"

"Probably not."

She was silent. She laid her head against his shoulder. She was trembling.

Saba got slowly to her feet and stared at him. "You lied to me, didn't you?" Mike felt cold. "There will be no rescue."

"Saba . . . I'm sorry, but—"

"But you had to," she finished for him. "I knew you were lying. This was something I wanted to do. It was the only way I could destroy Aziz and his gang of traitors. You can tell me now—how will we die?"

"Missiles. They were launched when they received our data."

Saba turned and started into the desert. "Where are you going, Saba?" Mike called.

"I thought I would take a walk . . . leave you two some time alone together . . . before the missiles come," she said without stopping. "I'd like to be alone, too."

"It's not over yet, Saba," Mike called.

She stopped. "It *is* over," she insisted, without turning around. "We had a dream—as your Martin Luther King said. But it turned into a nightmare, and now it's dead."

Saba started away again. "I'm tired of this life. I just want some peace before your missiles come. I can't remember ever having any peace."

"Saba, remember what you told us back there in that cell—as long as you live there is hope."

She stopped again.

"If we can make it back to the hangar in less than an hour, we might get away."

"In an aircraft?"

"Yes."

"We'd never make it back through the complex. They will have blocked everything by now."

"How about on the surface? Can we walk?"

"We could. It's five miles."

"If we hustle we can just make that in an hour."

"But how will we get in and past the guards?"

"The same way we did before." Mike rummaged through his pack until he found the key-card and its box. He held it up. "This will get us in through an unguarded entrance. We got in with this.''

"But the aircraft are single-seat," she argued.

"There is one two-seat trainer. Three of us can squeeze in. All we have to do is get about twenty miles away. That's ten minutes or so at one hundred fifty knots. You sit on Julie's lap and we can fly with the canopy cracked open at that speed. Which way?''

Saba stared at him for a moment, then turned and jogged off at a pace Mike wasn't sure he and Julie would be able to keep up for five miles.

The television monitors in the hidden room showed five guards. The one sleeping at the desk facing the tunnel presented a problem. If he woke up, he'd alert the others, but there was no way around him.

The other guards were gathered, laughing and talking, near the front of the hangar. If Mike, Julie and Saba could get by the sleeping guard without raising alarm, the others could be surprised and mowed down before they could react.

Mike led the women to the tunnel door. He pushed the open button and got a firm grip on his Uzi. The door slid open with maddening slowness. The two women followed him into the tunnel. Mike was sure the crunch of their feet on the crushed rock would wake the guard.

They pressed against the side of the tunnel, ready to fire. They waited, breaths held, but there was only the faint sound of conversation from the hangar. Mike nodded, and they slipped along the tunnel wall.

They reached the loading dock and crouched in front of it. Mike peered cautiously over the top. The guard was still sleeping soundly, his automatic weapon cradled in his arms. Saba flowed onto the dock like a swift shadow, and was on the guard before Mike had time to take a breath.

Saba's knife severed his windpipe and then his jugular. She hugged him like a lover to silence him through his death throes.

Mike climbed onto the dock, pulling Julie after him.

Saba released the guard and eased him facedown on the desk. Fresh blood soaked the front of her shirt. She beckoned Mike and Julie forward. They slipped between the aircraft toward the murmur of voices.

The guards still stood laughing and talking, carelessly holding their weapons. They weren't expecting trouble. It would be the most cold-blooded thing Mike had ever done.

Saba raised her M-4. Sick inside, Mike aimed his Uzi. He told himself that these men would shortly be dead anyway.

Julie stood still and wide-eyed. She couldn't bring herself to murder the men in cold blood.

The raucous sound of an alarm filled the hangar.

Saba fired.

Mike fired.

One man crashed to the floor.

A wounded guard staggered and fired back reflexively.

A hail of slugs tore over them and ripped into an SU-24 behind them.

Saba's weapon emptied.

Another guard jerked backwards and fell to the floor before Mike's magazine was exhausted.

An unscathed guard raced for the rail tunnel.

Saba snatched Julie's Uzi from her hands, and fired after the fleeing guard. He sprawled on his face. He lay on the floor, jerking. Saba took careful aim and loosed a burst that turned his head to bloody mush.

Julie would have thrown up if there had been anything left in her stomach. She swayed dizzily.

What's that alarm?'' Mike asked urgently.

"A plane has landed," Saba answered apprehensively. "It's a signal to send the elevator up. It almost has to be Aziz. He probably left Tripoli the moment he heard they'd captured you.''

''What's the procedure?''

''They take up a small tractor to maneuver the plane into the elevator. The times I've met him, Aziz has cut his engines and has been out of the aircraft waiting for the tractor. I imagine he does the same thing every time.''

Mike looked at his watch. He estimated that they had less than fifteen minutes until the first Tomahawks hit.

''Saba, Julie, we're going to get that tractor hooked up to that two-seater over there.'' He pointed to the Foxbat-C. ''We'll just have to be ready to take Aziz—if that's who it is—when the elevator opens.''

''That won't work,'' Saba argued. ''Aziz trusts no one. Always has his weapon ready. He'll fire the second he sees us.''

''We'll have to chance it,'' Mike replied grimly.

''There is another way. I'll go back through the hidden entrance and surprise him. He won't be expecting anyone to come after him from the desert.''

''All right. Get going. We'll bring the plane up.''

''Not too soon. Give me time.''

''We only have fifteen minutes,'' Mike reminded her.

Saba sprinted for the tunnel.

Mike ran to the Foxbat-C and clambered up the ladder hanging from the cockpit. He breathed a sigh of relief. The helmets, oxygen masks, harnesses and other flight gear were piled on the seats. The only things missing were g-suits. It meant the plane was kept ready for takeoff and probably had a full load of fuel. Mike tossed the gear down to Julie and followed it. He didn't want to take the time, but donning strange gear in the dark—possibly under fire—would be impossible. Mike struggled into the strange, ill-fitting gear, then helped Julie on with hers.

*   *   *

Colonel Muhammad Aziz looked at his watch and knew something was wrong. It had never taken them this long before. He had a feeling that the trouble was related to the shocking message he'd received from Omar. How could he have captured a U.S. Navy captain and a woman scientist inside the secret installation? Madness! Still, the idiot must have captured someone, and he had convinced Aziz they were Americans.

The instincts that had saved him so many times screamed at Aziz. He decided to use his secret entrance.

As Aziz waited for the elevator, his apprehension grew. The elevator door opened and he faced Saba.

Saba recovered from shock first. She hurled herself at Aziz, digging for her knife. The impact sent them both sprawling into the sand.

Aziz managed to get a grip on the ball of fury and lever her over his head. He rolled away, spun on his buttocks, drew his legs up and met Saba's charge with a staggering blow of his feet. She stumbled backwards, gasping for breath.

Aziz did the unexpected. He got his legs under him, sprang to his feet and dashed into the desert. He startled Saba, and it took her a moment to recover and pursue him. A moment was all Aziz needed to yank the machine pistol from his belt. He whirled and slashed a waist-high burst across Saba's hurtling body.

Saba jerked to a stop. She stood staring at him in astonishment.

Aziz tightened his finger on the trigger, then changed his mind. He approached her cautiously. She clutched her stomach. Blood poured between her fingers. Aziz could see her face clearly now. He wasn't surprised.

"Fatima's bitch niece," he snorted. "You'll be the last of the pack."

It was harder for Saba to stand now. The world was dissolving in a red mist of agony. Aziz took a hand from his weapon and drew a knife from his belt. He grinned cruelly. He inserted the long blade into her belly just above her pubic hair. It was very sharp. It went in easily.

Her sharp scream satisfied him. He listened to her desperate breathing with pleasure. He tightened his grip on the knife handle. He drew the blade up the length of her body with a firm, swift stroke.

Saba's intestines spilled out and looped to her knees. She stared down at them in astonishment, sank to her knees, swayed a moment, then fell forward on her face. A damp fetid smell rose from her corpse.

The burst of gunfire startled Mike and caused him to accelerate the little tractor. Still, it took a maddeningly long time to pull the aircraft out onto the airstrip.

Julie rushed to help him unhook the tractor. They fumbled in the dark, and it took a long time. Everything had taken too long. Mike was sure the first Tomahawks would be bursting on them at any moment. His watch said they were out of time.

Mike urged Julie up the ladder hanging from the cockpit. He shoved her in the rear seat and scrambled into the front.

Mike forced his racing mind to slow and tried to picture the intelligence handbooks he'd studied. Holding the images in his head, he kept trying switches until lights came on. Nothing was in English! He calmed himself. There was French, and he knew a little French.

Mike hunted for a way to start the engines. He felt the Tomahawks—and Aziz—closing in on him.

There was a burst of automatic-weapons fire some-

Robert Payton Moore

where in the distance, and a few nearly spent rounds spanged across a wing.

Desperately Mike guessed and punched some switches. An auxiliary power unit whined. There was another burst, and bullets sprayed across the plane with enough velocity to be deadly.

The engines startled Mike with their roar. He released the brakes and shoved the throttle forward. The plane shuddered and moved. Mike started the canopy down. "Mike! What about Saba!" Julie screamed.

"Dead."

"You don't know that!"

"Yes, I do. That has to be Aziz shooting at us, and he wouldn't be doing that if Saba was alive."

Julie fell silent. There was no use arguing, and she knew that Mike was right. A great sadness crushed her.

Mike tried to remember more about the airstrip as the Foxbat gained speed. Huge rocks blocked most of the runway. Over the roar of the engines he heard something rip into the fuselage just back of the cockpit. Aziz! Close enough to kill them.

Thunder shook the plane.

The first of the Tomahawks.

Mike shoved the throttle forward. The rocks loomed. Damn! Well, at least their deaths would be quick.

Mike saw it. A line through the rocks. But he wasn't lined up on it.

He desperately worked the unfamiliar controls. He'd never turned a plane on the ground at this speed.

He thought he heard a wing tip come off as the Foxbat rushed between the rocks. He yanked the stick back and the twin Tumansky engines kicked the Foxbat into the air.

Aziz had slammed a fresh magazine into his TMP when a shock wave flung him from his feet. The blast filled his head and momentarily robbed him of his

380

senses. He got to his feet and staggered again.

The desert complex was blanketed with a clinging cloud of dust and smoke. Something streaked over his head, and a flash blinded him. The hot shock wave knocked him from his feet again.

Aziz got to his feet and dashed for his aircraft. As he climbed into the cockpit, he saw Mike's Foxbat lance into the air.

Aziz worked frantically to get his aircraft started and rolling down the airstrip. He found the line between the boulders and loosed the full power of the two Tumansky turbojets. The Foxbat sprang forward just as a Tomahawk completed its pop-up and drove its earth-penetrating warhead through the top of the fortified hangar. The shock wave tipped the Foxbat, and Aziz thought he was going to smash into the rocks. He held his breath as somehow the plane got by the rocks and lifted from the runway.

Aziz fought the controls as shock wave after shock wave battered the Foxbat.

Aziz felt drained by the time he finally gained smooth air. He switched on his Fox Fire radar. The radar found the American climbing, probably attempting to escape the missile blasts.

Aziz yanked the Foxbat's nose up and followed. His Foxbat had a speed advantage: It was a single-seat aircraft with upgraded engines. Aziz also had an overwhelming combat advantage. Mike's Foxbat-C was a combat-capable trainer, but it didn't have a radar, and wasn't carrying missiles. Aziz's Foxbat had both.

Foxbat-C

The explosion of the AA-7 Apex under the Foxbat's port wing shocked Mike. He instinctively rolled into a high-g turn. The world grayed. He'd forgotten that he didn't have a g-suit. Mike eased the turn, but continued to roll. He knew he had to maneuver, or they were dead. They would have already been dead except for a malfunctioning missile fuse.

Mike backed off the power as the plane stood on its wing. It lost lift and sliced toward the ground. The Foxbat-E flashed pass. The unorthodox maneuver had surprised Aziz, and he was unable to follow.

The Foxbat-C tumbled earthward. Mike barely clung to consciousness as shifting g-forces crushed him.

Mike fought his way back to control of the aircraft, but he knew Aziz was lining up for another pass. Aziz would be more careful this time. Mike's lack of a g-suit gave Aziz another advantage. Mike had no missiles or radar, and he barely knew how to fly the plane. He knew his only chance was to do the unexpected and look for an opportunity to make a run for it. The two planes had approximately the same speed and altitude performance. Maybe if he could get out of range of the Foxbat-E's missiles, Aziz wouldn't be able to catch him.

As Mike brought the Foxbat around, he saw Aziz coming down on him in a shallow dive, a rapidly growing speck against the yellowish blue of the afternoon sky. Mike pointed his Foxbat at Aziz and shoved on the afterburner. The two aircraft closed at more than 1500 knots.

Mike saw the flash of a missile launch. He counted to ten, then pulled into a turn, rolling his wing up until it pointed at the attacking Foxbat. The incoming radar-guided missile saw a suddenly reduced, wavering radar cross section, which varied rapidly between nearly nothing and hundreds of square feet. The change in direction also presented a crossing target whose bearing changed at an enormous rate. The missile's gain-control circuit went crazy. The missile antenna gimbal banged against its top and froze there. The missile skidded into a turn away from Mike and bored a hole in empty sky.

Mike cut power, extended his flaps and hauled back on the stick until he flirted with gray-out. It was like slamming on brakes.

Mike nudged the Foxbat through a turning stall, and eased the power back on.

Aziz had lost 5000 feet after passing Mike before he could force the Foxbat into a climbing turn.

Mike saw his chance. He slammed on full power, and roared toward the point in the sky through which he knew Aziz had to pass. He was cutting across the arc of Aziz's course.

Mike armed the 30mm guns. Foxbats normally didn't carry guns, but this one had guns installed for training purposes. It was the same gun installed in Fulcrums.

Aziz's Foxbat loomed in the optical sight.

Aziz hadn't expected Mike to attack.

Mike fired.

Aziz tried to maneuver.

Bright tracers followed.

Thirty-millimeter shells chewed their way along the fuselage from cockpit to tail.

The rear of Aziz's Foxbat disintegrated.

The front half of the Foxbat continued its climb for a few moments, hung in the air, then nosed over.

Mike jinked around the debris. He could see the front half of Aziz's MiG trailing smoke as it plunged toward the desert.

"Julie!" Mike called, hoping they had flipped the right switches and plugged in the right connectors for the ICS. The oxygen worked—a good sign. Maybe they were hooked up all right. "Can you hear me?"

"Yes," she croaked. "And don't you dare ask me if I'm all right."

Her response relieved Mike. He hadn't known what

the g-forces might have done to her. "I think we're going to make it, Julie." Mike turned his attention to deciphering the instruments.

Fifty miles south of the Libyan Coast

Mike knew he didn't have enough fuel to make the coast, but he managed to nurse the MiG to within a hazy view of the sea before the engines flamed out. He was flying at 60,000 feet. He nosed into a descent steep enough to maintain airspeed and lift and turned on the radio. He'd maintained radio silence in order to avoid alerting hostile aircraft to his presence. Now he needed help, and he needed to identify himself to avoid being splashed by a U.S. Navy fighter. He wondered who was going to reach him first, the Navy or the Libyans.

"Spring Camp, this is Beaver, do you read?" He repeated the call four times before he was rewarded by an incredulous reply. "Beaver, I read you. Where are you?"

"In a Foxbat at fifty-five thousand and sinking fast. Just ran out of fuel. Like a pickup if you can manage it."

"Beaver, wait one."

Mike was beginning to think he'd lost the link when the battle group commander came on the air. "Is that you, Captain Boen?" the astonished admiral asked.

"Yes, sir."

"What happened to Dr. Barns?"

"She's here with me. We're in a Foxbat-C. Has two seats."

"That's incredible!"

"It *is* incredible. I'll tell you how incredible if we get back aboard. We need some help."

"I'm turning you over to Captain Broger. He'll get you whatever you need."

"Where are you, Beaver?" Broger asked.

"I'm passing through forty thousand. I estimate I'm thirty miles from the coast. There is a highway off to port. I think it's the road between Waha and Marsa el Brega. If I'm lucky, I'll make the beach between Brega and Ras Lanuf."

"Think you can make the water? Play hell getting you loose from a bunch of angry Libyans."

"I don't know. Doesn't look good. This thing glides like a rock. My sink rate is increasing faster than I expected."

"More bad news. A Hawkeye just reported MiGs lifting out of Benghazi."

Mike's heart sank. The MiGs would be on him in minutes.

"It's going to be close," Broger informed him. "Our CAP is on its way. We'll try to cut them off, but some may get by. Anything you can do?"

"Fall out of the sky."

"All right, hang in there. A SAR helo is lifting off right now."

Mike fought discouragement, and searched for ways to stretch his glide. He eased the nose down. The Foxbat accelerated and gained some lift. He nudged the stick until he reached the speed and sink-rate combination he thought would maximize glide distance.

"We're going to have to eject, Julie."

"Eject! Again? I can't live through another ejection," she protested.

Mike didn't know whether *he* could live through another ejection. He'd exhausted his luck long ago. And he didn't know the Russian system. The red handle was obvious, but what did you do first?

"Julie, it's either punch out or go in with the aircraft. It'll come apart when we hit or sink like a rock if we land in the water. We *have* to eject."

"*Crash* Boen, if I live through this I'm never ever setting foot inside an amusement park that has a roller

385

coaster. To think—I used to get a thrill out of the damn things.''

She was a strong lady, Mike thought. Damn, how he loved her! ''Unhook everything, Julie.''

''The intercom?''

''Yes, that, too. Better do it now. This thing won't fly much longer. I'm going to punch us out at the last possible instant. And we may have some company in a minute or two.''

''I heard,'' she replied bitterly.

Mike held his breath as the coast loomed.

Two thousand feet.

Would they make it?

Passing one thousand feet.

The coastline passed beneath them.

People were staring up, openmouthed.

Mike hoped he could get beyond the fishing boats.

The three Fulcrums came down on him firing their guns.

The wings shredded.

The canopy shattered.

Mike punched them out.

Searing heat and a shattering roar followed Mike, and he knew the Foxbat had exploded as he left. He wondered how good the MiG's ejection seat was at a low altitude.

The chute jerked Mike away from his seat. He swung once and hit the water. The breeze floated the chute from over his head, and it tugged at his harness. He fought to release the straps, then got control of himself and took time enough to be deliberate. The chute released and floated away.

Mike went under for a moment, reconnected his brain to his arms and legs and surged back to the surface. He treaded furiously, getting his head out of the water as far as possible. He spotted Julie's parachute.

Silent Doomsday

It had collapsed on top of her. Mike stroked furiously toward her.

The water in front of him exploded and filled his nose and mouth. Fulcrums spitting cannon fire roared over.

Mike strangled on a mouth full of water and went under. He clawed his way back to the surface and coughed water from his windpipe. Still choking, he began his furious stroking again.

Mike reached the edge of Julie's chute and paused to take a deep breath. He coughed. There was still water in his windpipe. He glanced up and saw the three Fulcrums fall into single file for another strafing run. They wouldn't miss this time.

The lead Fulcrum turned into a dirty orange ball. Heat washed over Mike, and it felt as though the sound had ruptured his eardrums. Debris showered the sea around him. The remaining Fulcrums rolled into crushing turns chased by four Tomcats.

Mike inhaled more slowly this time, and plunged under the parachute. She wasn't there! Then he saw her hanging limply from the shrouds twenty feet down.

Mike surged down to her. He got an arm around her and struggled to the surface. She was unconscious and not breathing. No! Not after all this! Mike thought.

He got her high enough out of the water to bend her over his shoulder with her head out of the water. The furious paddling was rapidly sapping his strength. He squeezed her desperately, hoping to expel the water from her lungs. She made a sound. His strength gave out. They went under for a moment.

Mike got Julie's head back out of the water and clamped his lips to hers. He drew out a mouthful of water. He spat it out, clamped his fingers on her nose, pressed his mouth to hers and tried to breathe life into her. He kept at it, having no way of knowing whether her heart was beating.

A shadow enveloped him, and helicopter rotor blades turned the sea surface into a storm. Two crewmen splashed into the water beside Mike and pulled Julie from his arms. A line pulled her up to the helicopter. They got another line around Mike before he knew what was happening and pulled him up, too.

The medics worked furiously on Julie. Mike tried to get to her, but two crewmen wrestled him back. "Captain! Let them work!"

Mike's strength deserted him. He slid to the floor, barely able to breathe. He finally gathered enough strength to crawl across the floor toward Julie. They let him get close enough to see her.

Her face was bluish white. Her chest moved, but it was only because of the respirator. Tears fill Mike's eyes.

They took the respirator away. Julie moaned. Mike struggled to her and gathered her in his arms.

After a moment, a corpsman took a firm grip on his shoulders. "Please, Captain, we need to do some more things for her. And we have to work on you." Mike reluctantly let them take her from him. He became aware of the hot blood streaming from the wound in his side just before the world went black.

Chapter Twenty-five

Crystal City, Virginia

Mike followed Julie through the apartment door and locked it behind them. She stopped in front of him, holding a slim navy-blue case against her chest. It contained the Distinguished Civilian Service Medal the President had awarded her in an Oval Office ceremony. Mike had been awarded a Bronze Star. The dejected slump of Julie's shoulders worried and puzzled Mike. "Julie? Are you—I mean . . ."

She turned, smiling. It was a sad, crooked smile. "I'm all right." She dropped her head. "It's just that I feel . . . let down," she murmured.

Mike drew her into his arms. He understood. It was like the letdown he felt during the first quiet moments after combat. The stress that had stretched him to his limits had let go all at once, and it seemed nothing held him together anymore. He always felt like shit until he got a grip on the normal world again.

Robert Payton Moore

She felt soft and vulnerable against him. It was the first time they had been alone together in weeks. There had been hospitals, doctors, debriefings, family, the press; it seemed the whole world wanted a piece of them and was determined to monopolize their every waking moment.

Julie trembled against him. "They shouldn't have given me this medal," she choked. "I don't deserve it."

"You *do* deserve it. What would have happened to the country if you hadn't done what you did?"

"What *you* did. You and all the others saved the world from what *I* did. It'll be years before the country recovers from what I invented and it will take billions of dollars. And poor Scott, he may never fully recover. And—"

"Stop it, Julie!" Mike took her by the shoulders, held her at arm's length and fought the urge to shake her. "Look at me. Julie!" She reluctantly raised her eyes. "I'm not going to try and convince you not to feel guilty—you're too damn stubborn—but learn to live with it. Don't let guilt consume your life. Don't let it spoil the good times. Today was a good time. Doesn't matter why.

"Tell me something, do you love this beat-up old Navy captain?"

"You know I do." She struggled to reach him, but he held her away.

"Then your penance can be me. Pay for your sins by putting up with me, making me happy."

He released her, and she rushed against him, sending him staggering. She put her arms about him and squeezed him with startling strength. She didn't say anything for a long time, just hugged him desperately. Finally her arms relaxed, but she remained pressed against him.

After forever, she asked, "Mike . . . do the dreams ever go away?"

Her question jolted him. He had bunked with men who regularly woke up screaming in the middle of the night. Bloody nightmares would stalk their sleep for the rest of their lives. She didn't deserve that.

"They'll go away." He hugged her tighter, but he knew no embrace would protect her from the terrible memories.

"Kiss me." Her eyes were wet.

He kissed her for a long time.

"Mike, make love to me."

He did. For a *very* long time.

THE PHALANX DRAGON
TIMOTHY RIZZI

"Rizzi's credible scenario and action-filled pace once again carry the day!" —*Publishers Weekly*

After Revolutionary Guard soldiers salvage a U.S. cruise missile that veered off course during the Gulf War, Iran's intelligence bureau assigns a team of experts to decipher the weapon's state-of-the-art computer chips. But fundamentalist leaders in Tehran plan to use the stolen technology to upgrade their defense systems. With improved military forces, they'll have the power to seize the Persian Gulf and cut off worldwide access to Middle-eastern oil fields.

Sent to stop the Iranians, General Duke James has at his command the best pilots in the world and the best aircraft in the skies: A-6 Intruders, F-16s, MH-53J Pave Lows, EF-111As. But he's up against the most advanced antiaircraft machinery known to man—machinery stamped MADE IN THE USA.

_3885-4 $6.99 US/$8.99 CAN

STRIKE OF THE COBRA
TIMOTHY RIZZI

"Heart-in-mouth, max G-force, stunningly realistic air action!"
—*Kirkus Reviews*

THE COBRA TEAM: F-117 Stealth Fighters, F-15E Strike Eagles, F-16C Wild Wealsels, A-10 Warthogs—all built from advanced technology; all capable of instant deployment; all prepared for spontaneous destruction.

THE SPACE SHUTTLE: *Atlantis*—carrying a Russian satellite equipped with nuclear warheads—makes an emergency landing right in the middle of a Palestinian terrorist compound. Soon everyone from the Israelis to the Libyans is after the downed ship.

THE STRIKE: The Cobra Team must mobilize every high-tech resource at its disposal before the *Atlantis* and its deadly cargo fall into enemy hands bent on global annihilation.

_3630-4 $5.99 US/$6.99 CAN

RED SKIES

KARL LARGENT

"A writer to watch!" —*Publishers Weekly*

The cutting-edge Russian SU-39-Covert stealth bomber, with fighter capabilities years beyond anything the U.S. can produce, has vanished while on a test run over the Gobi Desert. But it is no accident—the super weapon was plucked from the skies by Russian military leaders with their own private agenda—global power.

Half a world away, a dissident faction of the Chinese Red Army engineers the brutal abduction of a top scientist visiting Washington from under the noses of his U.S. guardians. And with him goes the secrets of his most recent triumph—the development of the SU-39.

Commander T.C. Bogner has his orders: Retrieve the fighter and its designer within seventy-two hours, or the die will be cast for a high-tech war, the likes of which the world has never known.

_4117-0 $6.99 US/$7.99 CAN

LADY OF ICE AND FIRE
COLIN ALEXANDER

Colin Alexander writes "a lean and solid thriller!"
—*Publishers Weekly*

With international detente fast becoming the status quo, a whole new field of spying opens up: industrial espionage. And even though tensions are easing between the East and the West, the same Cold war rules and stakes still apply: world domination at any cost, both in dollars and deaths. Well aware of the new predators, George Jeffers fears that his biotech studies may be sought after by foreign agents. Then his partner disappears with the results of their experiments, and the eminent scientist finds himself the target in a game of deadly intrigue. Jeffers then races against time to prevent the unleashing of a secret that could shake the world to its very foundations.

__4072-7 $5.50 US/$6.50 CAN

WAR BREAKER
JIM DeFELICE

"A book that grabs you hard and won't let go!"
—Den Ing, Bestselling Author of
The Ransom of Black Stealth One

Two nations always on the verge of deadly conflict, Pakistan and India are heading toward a bloody war. And when the fighting begins, Russia and China are certain to enter the battle on opposite sides.

The Pakistanis have a secret weapon courtesy of the CIA: upgraded and modified B-50s. Armed with nuclear warheads, the planes can be launched as war breakers to stem the tide of an otherwise unstoppable invasion.

The CIA has to get the B-50s back. But the only man who can pull off the mission is Michael O'Connell—an embittered operative who was kicked out of the agency for knowing too much about the unsanctioned delivery of the bombers. And if O'Connell fails, nobody can save the world from utter annihilation.

_4043-3 $6.99 US/$7.99 CAN